I0690874

END GAME

Hat Trick Book Three

Samantha Wayland

End Game

Copyright © 2014 Samantha Wayland

Published by Loch Awe Press
P.O. Box 5481
Wayland, MA 01778

ISBN 9781940839059

Edited by Meghan Conrad
Cover Art by Caitlin Fry

Also by Samantha Wayland

Destiny Calls
With Grace
Hat Trick Book One: Fair Play
Hat Trick Book Two: Two Man Advantage

Dedication

For Meghan. You get all the metaphorical cookies.

Acknowledgements

As always, I must thank my beloved husband, who is still putting up with me after all these years. I'm not sure how he does it some days.

Many thanks also to Victoria Morgan, Penny Watson, Bobbi Ruggiero and Stephanie Kay for their support and friendship. Thanks to Dalton Diaz for always being my rock. And to Serena Bell, who gets credit for talking me down from the ledge on this one.

And to Kari, who I should have acknowledged in the first two books in the series as well. She is not only the person who introduced me to the genre, but a good friend and remarkable beta reader who never misses *anything*.

Chapter One

Savannah threw the door open, the bang of it ricocheting off the wall lost to her whoop of joy as she threw herself into Garrick's arms and he sealed her lips with his. They were probably putting on one hell of a show for the neighbors, but Garrick didn't give a shit.

He kissed her long and hard, their tongues warring. Her back hit the wall and she squeaked as their bodies slammed together.

He pulled back and stared into big, smoky green eyes, his heart galloping, and smiled.

"God, I missed you."

She grinned, looking around the hall before glancing over her shoulder into their apartment.

"Would you like to come in?"

Would he ever.

He staggered through the door. Not because of the woman in his arms or the heavy bag on his shoulder, but because his knees were weak with relief.

It had been two long months since they'd last seen each other, and so much had happened since. Hell, they'd been apart longer than they'd been together. He'd fallen for her so hard, so completely, that their relatively short time in Moncton had been more than enough for him to know that he wanted to spend the rest of his life with her.

Holding her in his arms now, he was more certain than ever.

"I love you."

A slow smile spread across her face. "I love you, too."

He sighed and buried his face in her hair. "I'm so fucking glad." He'd been nervous on his flight from Moncton. Practically sweating by the time he got in his taxi at Logan

Airport. So much could have changed. So much *had* changed.

But not this.

She stoked his back as he carried her down the hall and into the kitchen. Depositing her on the counter, he looked around curiously. He felt like he knew this place already after seeing the pictures and taking a Skype tour with her, but it was amazing to see it in person at last.

In a few more months—when he could finally get the hell out of Moncton—this would be his home. They'd always have the farmhouse up north, but as long as Savannah was the athletic trainer for the Bruins, he'd find a way to do as much of his work as possible from Boston.

There was also the small matter that his boyfriend, Rhian, also lived here in Boston. And played for the Bruins.

"Do you like it?" Savannah asked, jerking him back the present.

Sunlight flooded the open rooms, bright on the scarred wood floors and exposed brick wall in the living room. The bay windows, high ceilings and skylights made the space a unique mix of old meets new. The chandelier in the dining room hung from a velvet rope, the streak of crimson startling, the classic fixture more striking because of its modernized surroundings.

"I love it. It's beautiful."

She stared at him, not the room. "Yeah, it is."

Her half-lidded gaze set him on fire. Sometimes he was overwhelmed by his extraordinary good fortune in finding her—and that she'd stayed with him in spite of the curveballs thrown their way.

Savannah cocked her head. "You okay?"

He grasped her hips and pulled her to the edge of the counter, his heart thumping as she wound her arms around his neck and smiled up at him.

"Yeah. I was just thinking how fucking lucky I am to have you."

"That you are," she said. "And it's entirely mutual."

10

God, he hoped that was true. He hoped like hell he wasn't fucking up everything by discovering he could love two people at once. "I'm sorry it's been so long. That I couldn't come see you sooner."

She smiled and arched an eyebrow. "I can think of a few ways you can make it up to me."

A slow smile spread across Garrick's gorgeous face, his amber eyes heating to warm chocolate. Savannah felt a familiar and gratifying roll of her heart.

"I really missed you," she said, capturing his lips, lost for a moment in his taste. His scent.

He dragged his mouth over her cheek, tilting her head back with his. She gleefully relinquished control as he nibbled under her jaw, teasing her ear with tongue and lips and whispering his love between each suck and bite.

Her heart swelled with each word. This was real. It was *the same.*

His erection, full and thick, dug into the juncture of her thighs and she squirmed against it. It was so goddamn good to be this close to him again.

He hitched her off the counter and she twined her legs around his waist.

"Bedroom. Now," she demanded.

He stalked through the apartment, unerringly navigating to their bedroom. She landed on the bed with a bounce and immediately began to tear off her clothes.

He stopped her with his hands. "Wait. I want to do it."

Oh yes. Yes yes yes.

She held her arms out to the sides and smiled, loving the answering quirk of his lips. She was his to do with as he pleased. And he knew it. This was the Garrick she remembered. The man she'd fallen in love with in Moncton. He was irresistible, then and now.

His dark gaze traced over her with something like awe and

she enjoyed the hell out of it. He *was* damn lucky. But no more so than she.

Every worry and torment she'd suffered over the past two months seemed insignificant now that he was here.

He stripped out of his clothes and she feasted her eyes on his skin. His shoulders, chest and pecs flexed and stretched while he rid himself of his shirt. His lean hips and long, thick thighs looked strong as he stepped out of his jeans. Always a trainer at heart, she spared his right hip an extra glance and saw no sign of pain. Though honestly, it wouldn't have made a damn bit of difference if she had. Nothing would stop her from having him above her, around her, *in* her.

He was more than able-bodied at that moment, as far as she was concerned. At six and a half feet tall, he towered above her. Their ten-foot ceilings looked not nearly as grand for the first time since she'd moved in.

He fit perfectly in their space. He belonged here. With her.

His rigid cock pointed away from his body as if reaching out to her. She knew where *that* would fit in perfectly, too. Just where *it* belonged.

He pushed her back onto the mattress and tucked her hands to her sides, beginning the slow, torturous process of removing her clothes. Anyone else might have done it quickly. But not Garrick. He took his time, stopping to worship each inch of skin as it was revealed. He'd done this before, and the feel of his lips, the tickle of cold air when he moved on to the next spot, made her crazy in all good ways. She tried not to squirm, her heart pounding as he relentlessly ratcheted her anticipation up to near painful levels.

She cherished each brush of his stubbled cheek on her belly, the slow drag of the velvet tip of his nose along her hip and over her collarbone.

She'd felt spoiled when he'd done this in the past. But not today. Today it was the affirmation she needed, appeasing the doubts that had plucked at her heart.

She *had* needed to come to Boston for her dream job.

She *did* want him to take a lover and tell her all about it.

He *could* love her and Rhian at the same time.

He coaxed the last of the tension from her body, and she moved wherever his insistent, infuriatingly slow hands asked her to. She lifted her hips and legs, arched her back, letting him remove the last of the barriers between them.

He peeled her bra away and captured one nipple with his lips, his crow's feet fanning out from the corners of his eyes as he smiled up at her. Then he seized the peak between his teeth.

The delicate pinch sent a bolt of lightning straight through her. Her clit throbbed. He knew just what she needed. Read her like a book. She writhed on the bed, rubbing her legs against his as he rolled above her, supporting his weight on his elbows and bringing their lower bodies into full, delicious contact.

"*Please*, Garrick."

She ran her hands up over his strong arms, then down his chest, his skin warm and firm. Her thumb caught on one cinnamon nipple and rubbed until it pebbled, while her fingers cupped to tickle the underside of his pec. The catch of his breath against her neck was gratifying.

"Please what?" he teased.

She could feel his smile against the sensitive patch of skin beneath her ear.

She'd missed this most of all. It had been a revelation to learn she could have laughter and friendship and sex, all rolled into one wild ride. Nothing to fear. No request too crazy, no shame to be found anywhere. The freedom that came with Garrick's love was heady. Liberating.

Still, she tried to look suitably stern when he raised his head to look down at her. "You're trouble, you know that?"

He winked. "The best kind."

She grinned. No arguments there.

She wrapped her legs around the familiar warmth and breadth of his ribs, and her groan tangled with his as he pressed her into the mattress, forcing her thighs wide. The full lengths of their bodies fitted together, at last, settling into the dips and curves as if made for one another.

She'd had no idea how much she'd needed this.

He shifted until his cock nestled into her slick, swollen folds. It was hard to tell who wriggled harder, pressed closer. She couldn't control the twitch of her hips, desperate to feel him against her. In her. The drag of his heavy shaft along her clit made her whimper.

He stilled her with a hand, and then with one long, slow thrust, penetrated her to the hilt.

"Garrick!"

The stretch was un-fucking-believably good. Intense pleasure rushed from her toes to her fingertips, lighting her up. She'd gone so long without this—without being *filled*. He was a big guy, tall, broad, and blessedly, blessedly proportional. Perfect.

His whispered prayer barely reached her ear. "*Oh, thank god.*"

He surged deeper and his name tore from her again. His pelvic bone ground against her clit and she panted against his neck, already, and he hadn't even begun. Not really. She knew what it would become, how thoroughly he could and would fuck her, and the idea alone almost sent her spiraling into her first orgasm.

She needed him to *move*.

She wanted to beg, but was captivated by the picture he made above her. His eyes closed, he held himself perfectly still. She brushed her fingers through his hair, the other hand cupping his cheek.

"Are you okay?"

His little smile sent a rush of happiness through her. He opened his eyes, so close to her that she could see the few striations of amber left in his dark, hungry gaze. Somehow, the stare felt more intimate than his thick cock lodged deep in her body.

"You're kidding, right?" he asked, his smile growing.

She touched his face gently wither fingertips. "You just looked lost for a moment."

"Not lost." he said and kissed her gently. "Finally home."

Garrick captured Savannah's mouth in a long, drugging kiss, joyfully reacquainting himself with her scent, her texture. Spice and silk. Sex and virtue.

He'd nearly lost his shit when he'd finally entered the sweet refuge of her body.

Their lips parted on a gasp. She squirmed against him, begging him to move, but he couldn't look away from the love and certainty in her gaze.

He could have stayed like this forever.

Savannah, though, definitely had other ideas. Long fingers cupped his ass and pulled him in tight. His cock lodged farther into her heat and in a flash, he lost the battle to hold still.

The next kiss was endless, through gasps and moans, bites and licks. His focus fractured, giving over to their need and the clamor of arousal. Urgency rode him hard, bowing his spine and droving his hips faster. Harder. The sound of their bodies crashing together hardly audible above the constant groans and gasps escaping past tangled tongues and questing lips.

He'd planned to woo her with soft words. To make gentle love to her. But she didn't seem to need it. Or want it. The shouts rattling his eardrums and the fingernails piercing his back were evidence enough she was perfectly happy without it. Ecstatic, even.

He wanted to give her that. Ecstasy. The total loss of control. The feeling of coming unglued in someone else's arms and knowing you are safe. Cherished. It was always missing from phone sex, Skype sex, any kind of sex they'd managed in the past months. But here, now, anything was possible. That was her greatest gift to him. She made him believe in infinite possibilities.

He shifted and found the perfect angle. She keened his name and pressed her face to his cheek. Her fingers fisted in his hair. His blood throbbed in his ears.

He gasped words he could barely understand into her ear. *Love. Thank you. So fucking hot.* Maybe not poetry for wooing, but all he had left to him was the delirious truth.

The ferociously swollen head of his cock rubbed hard, time and again, along her clinging walls. She arched against him, bellowing her pleasure. Her wide green eyes mesmerizing as her body clamped down on his aching shaft like a vise.

There. The ungluing. The brutal honesty and trust. The love.

So fucking beautiful.

He ground against her, shuddering with each ripple along his cock. From one second to the next, the spooling blaze of heat and electricity exploded outward and he was flung into the storm of their climax. Senseless with the release. Absolute fucking relief.

It took a while for him to return to earth, but when he did, the tension left him in a rush. He fell sideways on the bed, holding her close so that they remained connected.

She stared at him with heavy eyes, pink cheeks, and the sexiest goddamn smile he'd ever seen.

He started to laugh, her chuckle joining his as they clung to each other, breathless.

Chapter Two

Savannah lay sprawled across the bed, Garrick's damp face stuck to her stomach, his arms wrapped around her as they tried to catch their breath. He'd walked through the door three hours ago and hadn't let up since. If she didn't know him better, she'd search his bags for little blue pills. The man was relentless.

Not that she was complaining. Hell no, she was not.

She'd missed him for countless reasons, but somehow her brain had done her the favor of forgetting how she adored the aching dots of fingertip bruises on her hips, or the heat of beard burn on her chest. She wasn't into pain with her sex—she wasn't into pain with her anything, thank you—but some tender spots and deep aches she cherished.

Eventually he peeled himself away from her belly to stumble into the bathroom, rubbing his fingers through his hair. It hadn't been cut in a while, maybe since she'd left Moncton. The dark circles under his eyes hadn't escaped her notice either.

She frowned. He was working himself into the ground. As a newly minted hockey team owner, he was determined to bring the Moncton Ice Cats to the top of the league. She believed he could do it, too, but she was still going to give him hell for taking better care of his players, the stadium, and his team, than he did of himself.

As if to prove her point, he returned with a warm washcloth and gently cleaned her skin of the latest evidence of their lovemaking. The soothing strokes had her eyelids drooping.

He tossed the cloth into the bathroom sink while she

scooted to the top of the bed and yanked the bedding back onto the mattress from the floor. As soon as he climbed in beside her, they settled into their customary positions, his body spooning hers from behind. She soaked in his warmth, happily beginning to descend into a post-coital coma.

She might have fallen asleep if it hadn't been for his arms wrapped around her. He held her as he always did—an arm over her hip, hand on her belly—but when the strength of his hold should have gone lax, he held her to his chest so tightly she couldn't draw a deep breath.

She opened her eyes and stared at the bedside table. Five o'clock.

Dreams of a late afternoon nap fled.

She swore to herself she would hold her tongue until she could wrestle her annoyance into submission. She'd known this would happen. Hell, she'd been the genius who'd set the schedule for this weekend.

The words "don't go" stuck in her throat so badly she wanted to gag.

She closed her eyes so she couldn't watch the minutes slip away, and waited for Garrick to leave her to go to Rhian.

Garrick stared at the alarm clock. He was due at Rhian's at six o'clock.

Fuck.

Not that he didn't want to go. He did. He was as desperate to see Rhian as he had been to see Savannah. But he didn't want to climb out of this bed. Leave Savannah.

He considered calling Rhian to delay, but immediately discarded the idea. Rhian would take it as confirmation of everything he believed about himself, his relationship with Garrick, and their prospects for longevity. And realistically, it wasn't going to be any easier to walk out of Rhian's apartment tomorrow morning to come see Savannah. Or leave again from here.

Garrick bit back a groan. He was a complete fucking idiot.

Seeking comfort he knew he had no right to ask for, he buried his face in Savannah's hair and squeezed her until she squeaked.

"Sorry," he mumbled, loosening his hold.

She sighed, then rolled over to face him. "You have to go."

It was a simple statement, made without a whiff of sarcasm or anger. He didn't think he could have managed it if the situation was reversed.

His guts clenched. What did it say about him that he asked it of her?

"I'm sorry," he said.

"Are you?" She sounded curious.

He understood that if he was having regrets, she needed to know. Her ability to talk to him, to listen, was the only reason any of this was possible. He was perfectly aware that almost anyone else would have dumped his ass.

"I'm sorry that it upsets you. I'm sorry that it upsets *me*. But I'm not sorry I have Rhian."

They'd sworn they wouldn't lie. About anything. That sure as shit didn't make it any less awkward to talk about Rhian while they lay in bed naked. In fact, *awkward* felt like a really nice word for whatever the fuck this was.

Savannah nodded. "You better get going, then."

"Sav—"

"No, Garrick. This is what we knew would happen. What we agreed to."

"Yeah, but I didn't think it would be..." He didn't know how to finish that sentence. He hadn't thought at all. *Fucking idiot.*

"I did," she admitted with a shrug. She ran her fingers over his cheek. "You still love him, right?"

"Yes." Any hesitation would have been a lie.

"Then go. I'll see you tomorrow morning for breakfast while Rhian has practice."

Savannah had proposed the weekend's schedule, since she knew when Rhian had to be where and could make her schedule more flexible. Garrick hadn't questioned it, nor had Rhian. They weren't stupid enough to miss the fact Savannah was being extraordinarily generous.

Guilt burned a hole in Garrick's stomach. It was agony to crawl out from the covers and pull on his clothes. She lay in their huge, new, freshly christened bed, watching him, smiling when he missed his pant leg and almost fell over into a heap on the floor.

Shit, on top of everything else, he was so fucking tired.

"Try to get some sleep tonight." She always saw everything.

"I will. I promise. A solid eight hours."

She smirked. "Yeah, *right.*"

He smiled and kissed her hard, once, thanking god that she could make a joke at a time like this. He also started to contemplate all the things he would do with Rhian that night that wouldn't involve sleep. A shiver worked its way over his entire body.

Her eyes lost their focus and he guessed she was thinking about the same thing. Nothing turned on Savannah more than his detailed descriptions of being with men. She had her share of other little kinks, but this, above all others, hit her sweet spot. He didn't know why. He didn't care.

He pressed his lips to hers again. "We'll be good," he promised in a husky voice.

Her cheeks warmed to pink before she smiled wryly. "I love you," she murmured. "Now go."

"I love you, too."

Miraculously, he left the apartment with a smile on his face.

Savannah lay in the bed, the apartment quiet around her.

For a few blissful hours, the place had felt full of Garrick.

Like it was finally the home she'd been piecing together for them.

Now he was gone and it was too still. Too silent.

She flopped onto her back and stared at the ceiling.

Was she deluding herself about all of this and secretly harboring deep-seated rage about Garrick being in love with someone else in addition to herself?

She kept coming back to this question. And the answer was always no.

She rooted around in her heart and head, like she might uncover that anger hidden in some back cupboard of her mind. She still came up empty.

So why couldn't she stop asking herself the question?

She was desperate to talk to someone about it. But who could she tell? No way in hell she could go to anyone in her family. If she told one of her six brothers, they'd tell the other five in a red-hot minute, the gossiping hags, and then they'd collectively freak out and default to over-protective Neanderthal behavior. Not helpful.

Her mom and dad were great, and she could usually tell them anything, but they were still her *parents*. They understandably didn't need or want to know the details of any of their children's sex lives.

The safest option was her dear friend and college roommate, Grace. Unfortunately, they were in the midst of an epic game of phone tag.

She grabbed her phone off the bedside table and dialed. Maybe she'd get lucky this time.

"Hello?"

"Hi, Gracie, it's Savannah. Is now a good time?"

"I teach an extension class in about five minutes, but I'm all yours until then."

Savannah could hear the echo of student's voices in the background and sighed. Not enough time to get into an in-depth conversation about her love life.

Still, maybe they could squeeze in a sanity check. "Can I ask you something totally out of right field?"

"Sure."

She knew she risked sending Grace into a death spiral of questions that couldn't be answered in the next three minutes, but she had to ask. "Do you think someone can be in love with two people at once?"

"Yes."

Savannah blinked at Grace's immediate and unequivocal affirmation. "Wow. You sound really sure."

"I am." Someone called Grace's name in the background. "Shit. Let's have dinner. Soon. Like, immediately."

"Yes."

They quickly compared schedules, but weren't able find a time that would work for the remaining weeks of the season, thanks to the Bruin's travel schedule. They settled on a date to meet soon after.

Until then, Savannah was on her own. Still not mad. Still really fucking confused.

She'd spent a lot of the last month wondering if, rather than force Garrick to admit he was in love with Rhian, she should have put the kibosh on it. Ended it before the idea was fully formed in Garrick's head, before he could tell Rhian. Before Rhian could say it back.

Instead she'd encouraged Garrick to be honest. To be generous. She'd listened to what little he'd learned of Rhian's childhood, heard the emotion in his voice. Her own heart had ached for a little boy in the foster care system, without a family. Without love.

She'd also listened to Garrick describe, in exacting, delicious detail, everything he and Rhian had done. She had a voyeuristic streak a mile wide. And that, coupled with the belief that she and Garrick could be happy together, forever, without monogamy being an absolute requirement, meant she had more or less brought this on herself.

She was, very likely, a fool. But she'd started them down this crazy path based on her instincts, and she was going to stick to them.

Garrick and Rhian were in love.

She and Garrick were in love.

Somewhere in all that good, they'd have to tackle the crap that came with it and find a path forward.

Chapter Three

Rhian sat in his tiny apartment at the extended-stay hotel and stared at the television, completely oblivious to what was on the screen.

Garrick's flight had landed—Rhian was an idiot and hadn't been able to resist checking—but he hadn't yet gotten word that Garrick wasn't coming tonight. Rhian swore to himself he wouldn't be mad when he did. He didn't pretend he wouldn't be crushingly disappointed—his denial only went so far—but he was trying to be realistic. It didn't make sense for Garrick to come to him. He'd gone to Savannah first. How the hell could he leave her and come here?

Rhian had played along for the month this weekend's plans had been in the works. It wasn't like he was going to argue with Savannah about it. She'd been incredibly fair. Painfully so.

She and Garrick were perfect for one another. Beautiful, smart, successful, and in love. Both wanted a family, a cozy farmhouse, and probably a white picket fence to wrap it all up.

Rhian would concede he, too, was successful in his career, particularly now that he'd made it to the NHL. But the rest? He wouldn't even know where to begin.

Just thinking about it made his stomach churn. Which was why, in spite of his genuine, sometimes terrifying, always overwhelming love for Garrick, he would accept an offer from whatever team asked and get the hell out of Boston as soon as his short-term contract with the Bruins was done.

God help him if the B's kept him. He'd have to find the guts to end things regardless.

Because really, what the hell would Garrick *do* with him if he didn't walk away? Would he be the secret lover Garrick got to sneak away with here and there? The guy who got to suck Garrick's cock while Savannah was home with the kids?

Right. Never going to happen.

Even if Savannah was okay with it, Rhian wasn't. He suspected Garrick wouldn't be either in the long run. It was bad enough to be faced with Savannah every day at work now. What would it be like in a year? Or once Savannah and Garrick were married? Had kids? Jesus, it would be *hell.*

He heard a sound out in the hallway and cursed the way his heart leaped. His need for Garrick haunted him. He couldn't do anything without thinking of the damn man. Rhian had never been in love before. Had never guessed it was so goddamn consuming. If he'd had the slightest clue what was happening when he'd gone and done the unimaginable and fallen in love, he'd have run in the other direction from the start.

If not to protect his own heart, then to spare Garrick the foolishness of loving someone like him.

Garrick stood outside the door to Rhian's apartment and collected his thoughts. The stench of over-shampooed carpets and disinfectant suited the drab décor and singed the inside of his nose. He couldn't imagine a living space more removed from the welcoming warmth of Savannah's apartment.

Their apartment.

He'd offered Rhian the name of the real estate agent who had helped them, but Rhian wasn't interested. He'd only been called up to Boston to cover some injuries, and was convinced the Bruins would ditch him at the end of this season.

Garrick had seen every game Rhian had played for the B's—even recorded them so he could watch them more than once—and he had little doubt the Bruins would keep Rhian.

But then, Rhian didn't believe anyone would ever keep him, did he?

Sighing, Garrick knocked on the door.

And waited.

He was about to knock again, the devastating thought that

Rhian had blown him off just beginning to circulate in his brain, when the door swung open.

Garrick's heart broke a little when he saw the ill-concealed surprise on Rhian's face.

He thought I wouldn't show.

Suddenly furious, Garrick shoved his way into the room, slammed the door, and threw his bag to the floor. He cupped Rhian's face in his hands and pinned him to the wall.

Rhian stared at him, his beautiful, dark blue eyes wide. It hit Garrick hard, just how much he'd missed him.

"I love you," Garrick said, trying to chase the haunted look from Rhian's eyes. Trying to make him believe the words were true.

Rhian didn't say anything. He didn't need to. Almost as obvious as Rhian's love was his fear. Garrick hated that it frightened Rhian, that *he* frightened Rhian, but he wouldn't deny how he felt.

"I love you, too," Rhian said at last, his voice rusty.

Garrick kissed him gently, pouring every ounce of his love and gratitude into the simple press of lips. His cock twitched in his jeans, demanding he do more than this almost chaste, lingering peck. He didn't.

He waited until Rhian's hands slid around his waist and held on.

Garrick stepped away.

"Go to the bedroom, strip, and lie down on the bed."

Rhian blinked but didn't move otherwise. Garrick questioned the wisdom of his hastily developed strategy but held firm, not touching Rhian in any way.

At last, Rhian turned and went through the door to his bedroom. Garrick followed.

If Garrick had had any doubts, they were obliterated when Rhian shed his clothes and lay face down on the bed, legs and arm spread. He hadn't told Rhian how to position himself, but he wasn't the least bit surprised by Rhian's choice.

Garrick stripped, rooted around in his luggage, and tossed supplies on the bed by Rhian's hip. Rhian didn't move, not even when the bottle of lube bounced off his thigh. The long line of his back was rigid as he waited for Garrick, his tense glutes carving angles into the soft curves of his perfect ass. He was fitter, even more ripped now than when Garrick had last seen him. He was also wound up tighter than a spring.

As always, the vulnerability and need he saw in Rhian, that only he was allowed to see, called to him. The compulsion to touch him, comfort him, was a physical thing—a low ache in Garrick's gut that wouldn't go away.

He climbed on the bed and ran his hands over Rhian's soft skin, letting Rhian know he was there before he lay down on top of him. He did not spare Rhian an ounce of his full weight as he bore him down into the bed.

Once their arms and legs were aligned, no part of Rhian uncovered, Garrick let out a deep breath. He buried his face against Rhian's silky blond curls and threaded their fingers together.

Rhian's eyes fluttered closed, then with a shuddering exhale, he melted into the mattress. Garrick didn't worry that he was squeezing the breath out of his lover. They'd done this before.

This was the only time, the only way, Rhian seemed to find true peace. To release the constant simmering tension beneath his calm façade and relax fully.

Garrick closed his eyes and savored the smell of Rhian's shampoo and the brush of stubble when their cheeks slid together. Rhian's long, rhythmic breaths soothed Garrick. He was learning to capture his own kind of tranquility in these moments. To ease his own mind.

He'd been so damned tired, running on fumes by the time he'd boarded the plane that morning. But now he didn't need to sleep. Instead, he let Rhian's warmth, his trust and love, recharge him.

After being with Savannah, and now holding Rhian, Garrick

felt whole again.

Chapter Four

Rhian's head was a quiet place for the first time in weeks.

He let go of his concerns about his place on the team, the apprehension that had steadily risen since the day he'd arrived. Was he playing hard enough? Did he have what it took? He'd made himself a little crazy, but it drove him to play better. Work harder. It had gotten him to the NHL.

Right now, though, it didn't matter at all.

Even on the most stressful days, no worry about his career compared to the gut wrenching anxiety of knowing he didn't have a place in Garrick's life. It gnawed at him, scraping him to the bone. He spent hours every day at the gym, going miles on the treadmill, stretching, lifting. Any distraction so he wouldn't think about it, knowing he would never be able to run fast or far enough to escape it.

But now, lying beneath Garrick, he let himself forget.

He thought he should be embarrassed that not only did he have some weird need to have his boyfriend lie on top of him, but his boyfriend was more than aware of that need. Fortunately, if the firm grip on his hands and completely relaxed body draped over him was any indication, Garrick didn't mind accommodating his bizarre issues.

Rhian would sigh, but he didn't want to draw so deep a breath. Or let it out. The calm, steady pull and release of his lungs was too good to disturb. That Garrick's breath matched his perfectly made it almost hypnotic. He was warm, in spite of the cool air leaking through the cheap aluminum windows. At home, in spite of the butt-ugly polyester bedspread beneath his cheek and the cheesy art on the walls.

But then, home wasn't a place. It was the two hundred and

29

thirty some-odd pounds of man plastered to his back, patiently smashing him to the bed the way he desperately needed.

He wanted to lie like this for hours, but the press of Garrick's semi-erect cock against Rhian's thigh teased the edges of his awareness. His own cock stirred. He wriggled to make room for it against the bed and ended up with Garrick's junk wedged against his ass.

The semi-erection went full blown along the curve of his butt. Rhian smiled.

Their breathing fell out of sync, but Rhian didn't mind. He squirmed. Garrick drove his rigid shaft into the valley of Rhian's ass and against about one million happy nerve-endings.

Garrick's lips traced his cheek. Rhian's smile grew but he didn't open his eyes, curious what Garrick would do next. Rhian's pulse throbbed, his body flushing against Garrick's heat. He'd gone from totally relaxed to fucking desperate in the blink of an eye.

He hated to shake off the lassitude that had been seeping into his bones, but he *had* to grind his ass against Garrick's cock. He begged shamelessly with his body, his eyes shut tight as arousal lit him up and he searched for some relief.

God, he'd missed this. He'd missed Garrick. Every goddamn minute of every goddamn day.

At any other moment, it frightened him. Right now, with Garrick on top of him and that huge cock digging against his skin, he didn't care. It wasn't like he could change it, and lying to himself wasn't working for shit.

He loved this man. Craved his touch, his softly murmured sounds of approval as they rubbed against one another. Garrick's fingers released his and he grabbed fistfuls of the bedding instead, using the leverage to surge harder against Garrick.

Garrick's knees slid between his, landed on the mattress and spread Rhian's legs. Cool air wrapped around his balls and teased his shaft when ground up against Garrick again.

Garrick chuckled, then knelt between Rhian's wide-open

thighs and placed a hand on the small of his back. Rhian immediately settled on the bed, cheerfully exposed, trusting, in spite of his vulnerable position.

"You look so fucking hot like this," Garrick muttered.

Rhian felt fucking hot. The thought made him grin. He lifted onto his elbows, dug his knees into the mattress, and tipped his ass into the air in clear invitation before glancing back at Garrick.

Garrick's dark gaze tickled down the deep arch of his spine. Garrick's skin glowed in the frail light of the bedside lamp and Rhian's eyes trailed over every inch he could see, the shadow of hip bones and swell of biceps almost as appealing as the thick shaft and red, velvet head of Garrick's cock. *Almost.*

Garrick dropped over his back, catching himself on one arm and shoving that beloved cock up against Rhian's up-tilted ass. He captured Rhian's lips in a kiss designed to blow off the top of his head. Their tongues warred. Rhian strained his neck to press his mouth to Garrick's fully, to feast as Garrick devoured him.

He groaned when Garrick pulled away. He hadn't had enough of Garrick's taste. His demanding kiss. He wriggled against Garrick's cock, still jammed against his butt, until a dribble of freezing cold lube slid down the crack of his ass. He gasped, frozen in place.

Holy shit, that was *cold.* Garrick clearly hadn't realized how frigid the stuff was either until it trickled over his cock.

"Yikes." Garrick hissed and yanked all that heat and hardness away.

Damn it.

Rhian jumped when Garrick trailed a finger down his ass, warming the liquid along Rhian's sensitive skin. The tip of one finger rubbing over his anus, circling time and again.

Rhian dropped his head, chin to his chest, and sucked air into his lungs. His head spun. He was fast losing command of his wits.

31

He was ready, hardly surprised when Garrick eased his thick finger into his body, meeting zero resistance. He shoved himself back and groaned.

More. He needed more.

A second finger slipped in next to the first and pumped deep. Fingertips brushed his prostate and he grunted at the rush of pleasure, jerking against Garrick's hand. Another rush.

"How's that?" Garrick's rough voice tickled over Rhian's skin. Fingers spread and tugged against muscles that gave willingly to Garrick's demands.

Rhian tried to say "unbelievable". Judging by Garrick's rich chuckle, he didn't quite achieve articulation.

The third finger dragged a long, embarrassingly loud groan from his chest. His arms gave out and his chest hit the mattress. Every push of Garrick's hand stretched him wide, thick knuckles bumping past tight muscles, fingertips grazing his prostrate.

Garrick's other hand rubbed along his back, soothing him.

God, Rhian wanted Garrick to fuck the bejesus out of him, but Garrick didn't rush. He rarely did. He knew how much Rhian enjoyed just this and as usual, he patiently coaxed as many reactions, as much emotion out of Rhian as he could.

Gentle, generous. An exceptional lover. Add the fact that Rhian loved him with a strength and ferocity that often left him breathless, and his balls drew up tight to his body, his arched back bowing to the point of pain.

Rhian wished he had words to tell Garrick how good it felt, never mind sufficient vocabulary to say the things in his heart, the sentiments he could barely put a name to, let alone speak.

The slow drag of Garrick's fingers from his body left him bereft, his mouth hanging open as he gulped in air. Cool lube flooded his ass as anticipation shook his limbs and stole his breath. Foil tore.

Rhian took satisfaction in how Garrick's hands trembled against his hips before grabbing hold. Any other time, his intimate knowledge of the sheer length and breadth of Garrick's cock might have made him clench. Tonight, now, he knew that no other man would ever make him feel *this*. Could bring him to this point, hanging over the precipice, desperate for more. For all of it.

The thick head of Garrick's cock popped past the tight ring of muscles and Rhian hummed with pleasure. *Perfect.* Garrick's fingers dug into his skin, anchoring them as he powered forward. He filled Rhian slowly, relentlessly, and whispered his dark words into Rhian's ear as he stretched him to the limit.

"Did you miss me?"

Rhian felt blown wide open, every nerve on high alert.

He opened his mouth, tried to communicate the rush of bliss and dark, unfettered desire, but failed utterly except for the escape of one little sound. Too guttural to be a whimper, too damn squeaky to be a manly grunt.

He hated it when he made that stupid noise.

Garrick thrust forward, hard, and it ripped from his throat again.

Garrick loved that sound. Eliciting whimpers from a big, tough guy like Rhian was hot, but sometimes Rhian made a noise so honest, so outside his control, it sent chills down Garrick's spine.

Joy and need all jammed into a single, tiny sob.

His heart, already pounding, did a somersault in his chest. Rhian might be surprised every time Garrick showed up, flustered when he told him he loved him, and so fucking uncertain about how that love changed the physical connection between them. But always, in the end, they found themselves here, drowning in the truth.

Garrick draped himself over Rhian's torso, their faces pressed together. He let Rhian take his weight and wrapped an arm across Rhian's chest while he fisted Rhian's cock in his other hand, spreading pre-come over soft skin and throbbing veins. Rhian's ass danced against him, forcing him deeper.

Garrick spread their knees wider. Sank deeper. He ground against the flex of muscles in Rhian's glorious ass and thumped his prostate hard. More come leaked into his fingers, easing the slide of his fist.

Rhian was lost. He shoved himself up onto Garrick's aching cock, head thrown back, eyes screwed shut. Garrick's hips worked in tight circles, stretching Rhian wide.

Rhian would feel it for days. Garrick wanted to leave that reminder. He hoped that for the time it took Rhian's body to recover from Garrick's lovemaking, he would continue to believe.

Garrick buried his lips against Rhian's ear. "I love you."

Rhian's eyes popped open.

Garrick could hide nothing from Rhian, and at moments like these, Rhian had no secrets from him. In the morning, when he left to go to Savannah, the uncertainty would return, but right now, there was no doubt. There was only this, and this was pure. Simple. It was uncomplicated, unadulterated love.

He took the kiss he needed, thanking god he was a few inches taller than Rhian. He could keep up a steady, relentless plunge and retreat without having to pull his mouth away.

Too soon, the powerful and electrifying sensations firing through his body and frying his nervous system stole his coordination.

His hips thrust faster, harder, and Rhian surged up to meet him, his extraordinary strength nearly lifting Garrick's knees from the bed. Garrick's fist pumped Rhian's shaft mercilessly.

Rhian was never more striking than like this. No hesitation, no insecurity. He was completely in the moment.

"Beautiful. God, you're beautiful," Garrick moaned. "I love you so fucking much."

Rhian's mouth dropped open as he plunged into orgasm. He arched beneath Garrick, his racking shudders shaking them both as Rhian threw his head back and roared.

He'd barely crested, the last blast of warmth filling Garrick's palm, when Rhian sucked in a desperate breath and pressed his lips to Garrick's ear.

"I love you, too," he panted. "God help me, I love you so much."

Joy swamped Garrick as he ground into Rhian's tight, clenching heat and he fell over the edge. He clung to Rhian, to his words, and willfully ignored the ill-concealed agony in Rhian's shaking voice.

Chapter Five

Two weeks later, Garrick sat in his office at the arena and stared at his Skype screen, willing Rhian to answer his call. Garrick had a ton of work to get through that day, but he couldn't focus on any of it.

A monster headache beat like a bass drum against his skull.

Rhian didn't answer.

Garrick took more ibuprofen and tried again.

Goddamn, he was tired and cranky. What had begun two days ago as an inconvenience, something easily explained by changing schedules and bad timing, was fast becoming cause for full-blown panic.

For the first week he'd been back in New Brunswick after his whirlwind and *way* too short visit to Boston, he and Rhian had resumed their regular Skype and phone calls. The first few had been fantastic. Rhian had smiled and laughed, without the hesitation Garrick had previously blamed on the technology.

Garrick had foolishly hoped he'd finally broken through to the stubborn man and convinced him that their relationship was for real.

By his second week back in New Brunswick, the doubt had returned. Dropped eyes, half smiles, no laughs. On their last call, there hadn't been so much as a chuckle, and Rhian had hung up quickly, claiming he wasn't feeling well.

Now Rhian wasn't answering his calls or returning his voicemails. Nothing. Total radio silence. Garrick was ready to get on a goddamn plane. To hell with the Ice Cats and the endless meetings to prepare for the draft and the construction on the arena. He needed to know everything was okay in Boston.

Fuck that, everything *wasn't* okay in Boston. What he needed to know was *why*.

Of course, there was someone he could ask for help, but the idea of asking Savannah to check up on Rhian made him ill. Not only was it way above and beyond what she should ever have to do, but the last thing he wanted was to give the impression that his issues with Rhian would spill over onto her.

Fuck. This just kept getting more complicated.

He hit END.

Tilting his chair back, he ran his hands over his face and tried to shake the anger. There was no fucking way to kill his anxiety.

He'd call Rhian's cell and leave yet another voicemail, and he'd do it without sounding pissed off. At this point, he didn't want to do anything that might scare Rhian off. Anymore than he was *already* scared off.

An incoming Skype call chimed and he sat up fast, hitting the ANSWER button before he registered it was Savannah, not Rhian. Now he *really* needed to pull his shit together.

He slapped on a smile. "Hey there, beautiful!"

Savannah cocked her head. "You okay?" She never missed *anything*.

"Oh yeah, I'm fine. Just busy."

Her expression made it clear she didn't believe him, but she let it go. They chatted about nothing in particular for a while. It took Garrick far too long to stop obsessing about his own shit and realize Savannah was working her way up to something.

A band of tension squeezed his chest. They'd spoken last night, barely twelve hours ago, but a lot could happen.

Jesus Christ, he hated being this far away from her.

"Garrick, can I ask you something?"

He braced himself. "Yeah, sure. What's up?"

"I know this is kind of weird, and really not my place, but I was wondering if there is anything going on with Rhian."

Dread settled like a lead weight in his gut. He kept his tone neutral. "I don't know."

It was the truth as far as it went. He had no fucking idea what was going on. It wasn't Savannah's fault or problem that he wanted to wail those words at the ceiling.

Savannah cocked her head and studied him. "You guys okay?"

Garrick sighed. "I don't know."

He didn't elaborate. Maybe he should tell her about Rhian's disappearance. Probably not. It was impossible to figure out the right level of communication. Over-sharing seemed as deadly a minefield as not telling her anything.

"Oh boy," Savannah said with a sigh. "Look, it's not any of my business, but something isn't right with him."

Garrick's guts twisted into knots. "What do you mean?"

"He's playing well, as I'm sure you've seen. But he's quiet. Really quiet. Quiet for Rhian, even. And he's actively avoiding me, which I kind of understand, but until this week, he still came to see me for game prep and training stuff. He went out on the ice last night without getting any of his wraps, Garrick. And aside from that being stupid and a huge risk, if the coaching staff found out he'd been so careless, they'd freak."

"Shit, do you have to tell them?"

She gave him the exasperated look that question deserved. It was hardly the issue. "I'm supposed to, but I won't. I can only cover him for so long, though. If he gets hurt..."

She'd be in trouble, too. *Fuck.*

"This isn't like him," he said lamely, stating the obvious.

"No, it isn't," she agreed. "Has he said anything to you? Why freak out about me now?"

Garrick swallowed hard. "I don't think it's you. It's me. He hasn't spoken to me in days. I think he's trying to end it."

Savannah's jaw dropped. *"What?"*

"I think I'm being dumped," he whispered. He was losing control of his voice. His face. He pinched his leg beneath the desk. He was absolutely *not* allowed to cry all over Savannah about his boyfriend.

But god, he wanted to talk to her. She understood how people worked so much better than he did.

"Did you two fight about something?"

He put his forehead on his desk and wrapped his hands around his aching skull.

"No," he admitted to the stack of paperwork under his face.

"Has he said anything to you? Sent you an email?"

"Nothing." He spoke in a monotone. "Not a word."

"Oh, baby, this is killing you, isn't it?"

It *was* killing him. And not just Rhian's disappearance. Being so far from Boston, the mountain of work he was shoveling through every day, trying to get on top of the pile so he could get the hell out of Moncton sooner.

He nodded against the desk. He wanted to close his eyes and sleep right there, not waking up until all this shit was over.

"Garrick, honey? Look at me."

Great, now he was stressing her out. He lifted his head and saw her face, close to the camera, as if she could lean in and lessen the five hundred miles that separated them.

"Yeah, I'm okay," he said. They both knew he was lying. It wasn't like Skype hid the bags under his eyes, or the red streaking through them. "Just really tired and worried sick."

"I'm sorry. How can I help?"

He refused to ask her to find Rhian and kick his ass. "Maybe pick me up from the airport?"

Her eyes widened. "I can't. *You* can't."

He grimaced. "I can get a flight today."

"Garrick, we leave in a couple hours for our last road trip.

39

We're on the road for the rest of the season."

"I'll meet you in Tampa, then."

Savannah sat back. "And miss all your meetings? Don't you break ground this week?"

Yes. He hadn't forgotten. It just didn't matter so much.

"Garrick, let's be realistic. We've got less than a week left in the season, and you have to stay up north. I'll find Rhian and figure out what's going on. Tell him to call you."

"I can't ask you to do that."

"You're not. I'm offering. I'm not going to play matchmaker, but as his trainer, I have the right to read him the riot act for last night. And for today, since it's the first time since he arrived in Boston that I haven't seen him at the gym."

Garrick's guts now had so many knots, they might be knitting a sweater. "Will you...do you mind telling me..." He couldn't bring himself to ask.

"I'll tell you everything. I promise."

"Thank you. Thank you so much. I'm sorry about this. I didn't mean..." He stopped before he fell into a full-on babble. She didn't need him falling any further to pieces than he already was. "I love you. I can't tell you what this means. It's just...you're fucking amazing, you know that?"

She smiled. "I love you, too. Try not to worry. We'll figure this out."

He nodded, promised to get some rest and she said goodbye, leaving him alone again. Far away from everyone who mattered.

We'll figure this out.

His head throbbed and he rubbed his fingers against the tension in his temples. He'd actually believed this couldn't get any more complicated. When would he learn?

Savannah smiled sweetly at Craig Willette, the team enforcer, while she tried to stem the bleeding from his hairline.

40

For a guy who made his living getting hit in the head, he was a remarkably sensitive and intelligent man.

Too bad every word coming out his mouth tonight was making her want to spit nails.

"Then Savage hit that guy so hard, I thought for sure he'd go down. Did you see that? Man, my teeth hurt just watching it. I didn't know Rhian had it in him. He's living up to his last name."

Savannah grunted. An undignified response, but the best she could manage.

"Aren't you friends with him from up north somewhere? I thought you two came from the same team or something."

"Yes, we were both with the Moncton Ice Cats before coming to Boston," she said calmly through her gritted teeth.

"Cool. He's a good guy. Hell of a fighter. Hope to see him again next year."

It was good news that Rhian, who she had brought to the attention of the Bruin's scouts, was winning over teammates and management alike. For that reason, if no other, she kept a smile plastered on her face and shut up.

No one else needed to know she was going to hunt him down and rip him a new one as soon as she had a chance.

Craig kept chatting away, as if the blood pouring down his face and into his eye was of little consequence, and Savannah kept working, her jaw locked and her smile in place. A few minutes ago, she'd sent Rhian back to the team doctor, not liking the way his eyes responded to her flashlight or that his jaw didn't seem to be working properly. The other guy was in worse shape, but he'd landed some solid punches to Rhian's lovely face before the officials had jumped in.

In over a year of watching Rhian play professional hockey, she'd never seen him start a fight like that. What the fuck was the matter with him?

She still had no idea, and neither did Garrick. She'd seen Rhian a few times since her call with Garrick last week. The

41

first time she cornered him, he'd barely listened to her lecture about his responsibility to the team and himself. She'd made her points, but before she could bring up the personal shit, Rhian had called out to several of his teammates, garnering them an audience and effectively shutting her down.

Through all of it, he hadn't made eye contact with her once. She'd sworn in a furious whisper, as the others approached, that if he went out on the ice again without seeing her, she'd blow the whistle. That part, at least, he must have heard. He'd dutifully shown up at the required times and places, always with at least two other players with him.

The rest of the time, he was a fucking ghost. She'd looked for him on the flight, the bus to the hotel, even knocked on his hotel room door—at huge personal risk, as that would be viewed as pretty fucking inappropriate in the eyes of management. The jerk hadn't answered, leaving her out in the hallway, banging on his door like a stood-up date.

If anyone from the team had seen her, she might have kicked the damn door down and beat him over the head with it. She wasn't usually given to violence, but for Rhian, she was willing to make an exception.

And as if being ignored, avoided and dismissed weren't bad enough, her calls with Garrick were the absolute worst. Each time she had nothing to report, Garrick got more distraught. And she got more steamed.

She'd gone *way* the hell out on a fucking limb and not just accepted, but actually *supported* her boyfriend having a boyfriend, and the stupid fucker was throwing it all away without so much as a goodbye, let alone an explanation?

Well, *fuck him*. She and Garrick deserved answers. If she had to spend her entire post-season week off running Rhian to ground, she'd damn well do it.

Too late, she realized Craig had stopped speaking and was staring up at her as she applied a butterfly bandage to his head with rather more force than necessary.

"Sorry," she muttered, gentling her hands and wiping his

face clean to see if she'd missed anything. His eye was going to blacken, but that was nothing new.

"Don't worry about it," Craig said kindly. "You okay?"

"Oh, yeah, I'm fine," she lied.

This season couldn't be over soon enough. Two days. She'd hoped the B's would make it into the post-season, but given the extraordinary number of injuries they'd suffered in the first half of the season, it wasn't a surprise they weren't a part of the play-offs this year. And secretly, she was relieved. She had a busy summer ahead, with her first full season with the Bruins to plan.

The last thing she should be doing was chasing her boyfriend's erstwhile lover around the city of Boston. But she would.

For Garrick.

And because her pride damn well demanded it.

Chapter Six

Rhian sat on the hard couch in his cold apartment and stared at the truly hideous seascape painting on the wall. He'd been here a couple months now and it still struck him as the worst painting he'd ever seen. But then, why should he care?

This wasn't home. Such a place didn't exist.

He ran a finger over the rough, vaguely plastic, industrial-strength upholstery beneath him. The indestructible carpet was cool and unwelcoming against his bare feet. He hadn't bothered to turn on the heater, though its persistent rattle normally blocked out some of the sounds from the rooms around his.

No amount of air circulation would rid his apartment of the smells. Cleaning agents barely disguised the stench of mold most days, but today all he could smell was an endless, delicious waft of curry emanating from the apartment across the hall. It smelled fantastic.

His stomach agreed, protesting loudly.

He ignored it. Couldn't eat. He'd tried to choke down breakfast before going to the arena and playing the last game of the season, probably his last game ever for the Boston Bruins. It hadn't gone well.

He frowned at his cell phone on the coffee table. He should probably turn it on in case Sergio called with news. His agent was talking to the B's about keeping Rhian on, while reaching out to others teams about picking him up. Rhian didn't care where he landed. It didn't matter.

It had, for a while. For the week after Garrick's visit, he'd believed there might be a reason to want to stay in one place. In Boston. But he'd let that go. And he wasn't going to give anyone a chance to change his mind.

It would be so easy to change his damn mind.

His laptop sat on the bar separating the tiny kitchenette from the rest of the room, shut off for days. He couldn't stand the chime of another incoming Skype call any more than he could tolerate seeing Garrick's number on his caller ID.

He wasn't trying to punish Garrick. But he refused to drag Garrick through the shit his life consistently fell into. He was toxic. He couldn't bear to put that stain on Garrick, too.

Rhian had no home. No team. No idea where he'd be next month. Next week. He had nothing to offer anyone and wouldn't sponge off the happiness and generosity of others, no matter how genuinely they seemed to offer. He'd been here before and learned. Survived. He had focused on the game, his career, and attained the kind of financial and personal security he'd craved his entire life. Finally.

What he hadn't realized was that to make it work, he needed something he'd always taken for granted.

His health.

He blinked hard, trying to push them back, but the tears fell anyway. He didn't bother to brush them away. He could recall, quite vividly, the last time he'd cried, over a decade ago. His foster "father" at the time hadn't believed that was appropriate behavior for a teenage boy. Rhian hadn't made the mistake again.

This was different than those pitiful tears over some middle school slight. It felt like a truck was parked on his chest and he fought to breathe through it, his chest heaving to release the sobs he fought like hell to contain.

He wasn't going to lose his shit.

Maybe if he kept telling himself that, he could make it true.

He cursed Garrick for changing him, thought he knew that wasn't fair. He'd always been weak this way, incapable of shutting off his emotions. He should have known being with someone like Garrick, who made him feel and want so damn much, was a huge mistake.

Now he wasn't just alone. He was *lonely*.

The tears came faster.

He wanted to rage, to punch the wall and howl his frustrations, but a strong self-preservation instinct held him in check. A certain Miami forward had already done enough damage, and Mother Nature seemed determined to do the rest.

He flinched when someone pounded on his door.

Whoever it was meant business. They didn't bother to knock, skipping directly to a slamming fist.

What if it was Garrick?

His heart lurched and he muffled his racking breaths, holding on to the couch like an anchor in rough seas.

It couldn't be Garrick. He was in New Brunswick.

"Rhian Savage, open this goddamn door before I kick it in!"

His mouth fell open and for the first time in hours, grief took a backseat to another emotion. Shock.

"Rhian! I mean it! Let me in, goddamn it!"

The door knob jiggled. Then it sounded like Savannah Morrison was, indeed, kicking the door.

Rhian stood.

"Lady, you need to leave." Rhian recognized the hotel manager's distinct three-pack-a-day voice and hoped that Savannah would give up.

"I'm not leaving until I see Rhian." She struck his door again, making it shudder. Had she hurled her entire body against it?

"I'm calling the cops!" the manager bellowed.

This didn't slow Savannah's assault on his door in the slightest.

Rhian waivered.

He imagined Savannah explaining her behavior to the cops. The Bruins. *Crap.* She'd worked as hard as Rhian had to get where she was—the only female athletic trainer in the NHL.

Rhian yanked his door open.

Savannah stood directly in front of him, fist raised, her face twisted in a furious scowl. Funny how that didn't make her any less beautiful.

"What the hell are you doing?" Rhian asked.

Savannah's jaw dropped and too late it occurred to Rhian he must look like hell. Covered in bruises, his eyes scratchy and swollen, cheeks wet.

Way to make a spectacle of yourself, Savage.

With an apologetic smile for the manager and his neighbors, he hauled Savannah into his room and slammed the door behind her.

"Are you out of your damn mind?" he snapped.

She stood her ground, her nose just inches from his. "You have the nerve to ask *me* that question?"

She planted her hands on her hips and he noticed she still wore her game clothes. Her tight ponytail and black yoga pants were a futile attempt to disguise her long legs and innate beauty. *Total fail, Savannah, I still see you.*

He dragged his eyes back to her fierce green gaze. "I'm not the one beating down doors. What the hell do you want?" He hated how high his voice had become, betraying his emotions. Now, of all times, he needed to be a goddamn hard-ass.

She'd obviously come to deliver an epic tongue lashing and Rhian prepared to forcefully eject her from his apartment. Her eyes searched his face and the blaze of fury faded.

He felt as if she looked right through him. Saw it all.

"Good god, Rhian, what the fuck have you done to yourself?"

Rhian's shoulders sagged. Savannah grabbed his arm before he could storm away or shove her back out into the hallway.

She'd made it through the door on a full head of steam and a mountain of outrage, intending to beat the truth out of him. Now, instead of the asshole she'd put up with for the past few weeks, she was faced with this quiet mess. It dug at her heart.

Goddamn it. She could never stay mad when men cried. Six goddamn brothers and any one of them could reduce her to a puddle of goo with a single tear.

A hint of ire resurged. She was going to have to revise her beat-it-out-of-him strategy, damn it. She didn't want to let go of the towering and entirely righteous anger that had fueled her trip across the city and delivered her to his door. For Christ's sake, this guy was breaking her boyfriend's damn heart. Why should she be nice?

Because I'm a sucker, that's why. Tear tracks stained his cheeks, his not-already-blackened eye red and puffy. Some evil part of her took comfort that even someone as gorgeous as Rhian Savage looked like shit when he cried.

The question remained, though, why was he crying? Something told her this wasn't about a break-up that he'd instigated in the first place.

"What's going on, Rhian?"

His jaw worked side to side and he focused on something over her shoulder. "Please go."

"No."

"You don't want to deal with this. With me."

He was right. She almost nodded, but stopped herself. There was something about the way he said *with me.*

"I'm not leaving. Not until you tell me what's going on. And, while you're at it, you can explain why you've hurt Garrick."

He swallowed hard and screwed his eyes shut. A tear squeezed out of the corner of one eye and she fought the urge to wipe it away. Not her job. It killed her to watch it track down his cheek. She wanted to screech at him to tell her the truth so she could fix it. And leave.

She took some deep breaths.

"Look at me," she demanded.

He did, his dark blue eyes swimming. Her heart lurched, and empathy kicked into overdrive.

Sucker.

He waivered on his feet and she caught his arm.

"Come on, you idiot. Let's sit down."

He grunted at the insult, but let her tow him to his couch.

She took in the room for the first time and grimaced. Freezing, dark, and butt-ugly. What a lovely combination.

She dropped her bag on the floor and nudged him onto the couch. "Sit. Stay."

One brow popped up at her imperious tone, but he did as she asked. Had it been one of her brothers, they would have panted like a dog and offered her a paw.

At least Rhian didn't look like he was going to cry anymore.

She turned on a lamp, dialed up the heat, and sat on the coffee table in front of him, her knees tucked between his. He was a damn mess. His blond curls stuck up in all directions. Face blotchy. Silent, sullen. Depressed.

A little of the anger seeped back in.

How in the name of all that is holy has it become my job to fix this shit?

Then she pictured Garrick's face each time he'd admitted he hadn't heard a word.

Fucked up as it was, they both needed to know if this thing with Rhian was over and this jerk was going to break Garrick's heart.

The growing silence was interrupted by a loud and fairly rude noise from Rhian's stomach.

She gave him an exasperated look. "When was the last time you ate?"

He shrugged. "Not hungry."

Of course not. She rolled her eyes.

She had no desire to stay here any longer than necessary, but it was late and he hadn't told her jack shit yet, so it wasn't like she was going anywhere.

"Well, I am," she said. "I haven't eaten since before the

game. Do you have any food?"

He shook his head.

Comfort food was clearly in order. If he didn't need it, *she did*. "Chinese okay?"

"Uh, sure."

She frowned. "You going to shake yourself out of your funk long enough to pick something, or should I guess?"

"Steamed chicken and vegetables, please."

She smirked. "And men complain about women ordering salads."

His brows drew down and he looked completely confused.

She almost laughed. *Duh, Savannah, he's gay. He doesn't take girls on dates.* "It's the end of the season. Why don't you splurge a little?"

The ghost of a smile passed over his lips. "Only if you promise not to tell my trainer. She's a real hard ass."

She smiled a genuine smile. It hardly hurt at all. "I promise your hard-ass trainer won't give you any shit about this."

He shrugged. "Okay, I'll have egg rolls, General Tso's chicken, pork fried rice and extra fortune cookies, please."

She chuckled. "Coming right up."

Once he listed all his favorite Chinese food dishes, Rhian felt like eating for the first time all day, despite knowing he'd feel like dog crap if he ate it all.

He watched Savannah wander around his tiny apartment while she ordered them dinner. Bizarre didn't begin to describe it. He considered trying to boot her out, but had no illusions that she would go willingly. He didn't need or want another scene in the hallway.

So what the hell was he supposed to do with her?

She wanted explanations he wasn't interested in giving. Maybe she and Garrick should have taken the hint about that when he'd been ignoring them.

Savannah tossed her cell phone on the counter, opened the fridge and bent to check its contents.

Geez, make yourself right at home.

She stood and reached for the freezer door.

Rhian nearly shot out of his seat. There was no way in hell she could miss the butt plug Garrick had left in there. That and a pint of Ben & Jerry's were the sum total of the freezer's contents.

Holy hell, this was awkward. Never in his life had there been something *more* awkward than this. He had the hysterical urge to laugh.

Man, this was *ridiculous.*

Savannah shut the freezer door and returned to the living room with two bottled waters and two beers. She sat on the coffee table and gave him a considering look.

The desire to laugh fled. He slumped back into the couch.

She pointed at him. "You have until the food arrives to explain what the hell is going on, then we're going to eat. After that, we'll see. Got it?"

Still picturing the toy in the freezer, he nodded. Mute.

Dinner with Savannah. Right.

"Great." She nodded, the logistics settled. Then she cocked her head. "Does it feel good? Frozen?"

Rhian was sure he hadn't turned this particular shade of red since leaving puberty happily behind. "*Jesus.*"

"Is that a good Jesus or a bad Jesus?" she asked in a throaty, suggestive voice.

"Guh—"

Chapter Seven

Savannah doubled over and howled with laughter at Rhian's inarticulate gurgle. His face burned. What the fuck was he supposed to say?

"Okay, sorry. *Sorry!*" She warded off any response from him with flapping hands. "I'm just teasing. I couldn't resist. I mean, you have to admit, this is all kind of..." Her hands waved around again, as if trying pluck the right word from the air.

"Fucking bizarre?" he offered.

Her hands dropped into her lap. "I was going to go with surreal."

Rhian huffed out a laugh. "Yeah."

She opened the bottles of beer, handed him one, took a sip of hers and waited quietly, gaze direct, not giving him an inch. *Damn.* He liked it better when she was screaming and shouting.

He swallowed hard. "I found a lump. A couple weeks ago."

He said the words too fast, the confessional equivalent of ripping off the Band-Aid.

She paused with the bottle halfway to her lips, then gently placed it on the table.

"Where?"

"In my...my testicle." The stutter wasn't because he was embarrassed. He was petrified. Somehow saying the words out loud to the very efficient nurse on the phone hadn't been this scary. "I have an appointment in a few days to see a doctor to have it looked at."

"Where?"

"The right."

Savannah paused and cocked her head in confusion. Then she chuckled. "No, not where...okay, good to know. Thanks." She shook her head, smiling wryly. "Where's the appointment?"

He turned that awful shade of red again. "Dr. Kantov at Dana Farber."

Savannah nodded. "You can't do better for cancer care."

Bright lights burst to life before his eyes and he swayed in his seat.

"Whoa!" Savannah lunged forward and grabbed his arms.

"I don't know if it's cancer," he choked out.

"What?"

"I haven't been tested yet. Maybe it's nothing."

Savannah sat back, watching him. That see-right-through-you stare again. Why on earth had he told her?

"It's okay to be scared."

Rhian nodded. There was no denying he was terrified. It didn't mean he wanted to admit it. Or discuss it. God, she was just like Garrick. She was going to want to *talk about it.*

"I don't talk about my feelings."

She blinked, eyebrows lifting.

He sighed. "Ever."

It brought back painful memories of sitting in the state-funded shrink's office in Chicago, the stranger behind the desk searching for a reason to pull him out of his foster family and place him in a group home. To move him again. The family hadn't liked him—an entirely mutual feeling—but they'd coped by sending him to the rink to play hockey every minute he wasn't in school or asleep.

He was startled from that memory when Savannah snorted with laughter and dropped her forehead into her palm.

"God help me, only Garrick."

"What does that mean?"

"Nothing. Forget I said it." She waved a dismissive hand

and sat up. "The only thing that matters is that he's in love with you."

Rhian's heart squeezed painfully in his chest. "Don't say that!"

"What?"

How could she be so nonchalant about it? "It's not true. It's not—"

"Rhian," she snapped, and he flinched. Her glare held him in place when he wanted to run from the room. "Garrick *loves* you."

He stared at her, mute.

She sighed and pierced him with her see-everything gaze again. "Look, I know it's weird to hear it from me. But I also know it's goddamn true. You think I'd be putting up with this crap if it wasn't serious?"

"You shouldn't..."

"Shouldn't what? Accept it? Well, I do. Like it? I can't pretend it was Plan A. Or Z. I'm not thrilled about it, okay? But that doesn't make it a lie."

"You should hate me."

"Hate you?" Savannah asked, bewildered. "Is that what you think?"

He nodded slowly.

"Christ," she muttered, pushing the loose strands of her hair off her face. At some point she'd slid to the edge of the table, her knees pressed against his inner thighs. It was the only warm spot on his body.

"I don't hate you, Rhian."

Yeah, right.

She took his hand and pulled it into her lap. He usually didn't like to be touched—except by Garrick—but she had him pinned beneath her stare and against her legs. Not that these things explained why he clung to her fingers like a drowning man.

"Listen to me," Savannah said quietly. "I don't hate you. And I'm not mad. Not really. Yes, it isn't ideal, but that's hardly the most important thing right now, is it?"

He looked down at their joined fingers, overwhelmed by her kindness.

"Is there someone in Boston who can help you through this? Someone to go to the appointment with you?" she asked.

He shook his head. There had never been anyone else, anywhere, who would help him through this. He could do this alone. Didn't need anyone. Had proven that time and again in his twenty-four years.

He was saved from saying something foolish, like *please don't leave me*, by a knock on the door.

Savannah set out their dinner on the breakfast bar while Rhian sat on the couch and stared into space. She had to keep busy, give the appearance she was just getting things done. In reality, she was one deep breath from locking herself in the bathroom and bawling her eyes out.

She'd left the arena ready to rip Rhian a new asshole. It should have been easy, quick, and relatively painless, for her anyway. Instead, he'd confessed anyone's deepest fear. She'd felt like someone had punched her in the chest when his voice cracked over the word "cancer".

There was something about this guy. A hidden vulnerability beneath the thick skin. She wanted to wring his neck one moment, then climb on his lap and hug the stuffing out of him the next. What the fuck was that?

Dangerous stuff. No wonder Garrick had fallen on his face for the man.

At least now she knew why he'd been quiet for the past couple weeks, and maybe why he'd started that damn fight at the game last night.

But why cut Garrick off?

A very small, petty voice in her head suggested she ought

to leave and let Rhian keep hiding. End the confusion and frustration. Keep Garrick all to herself.

She pictured Garrick's anguished expression again. Imagined what his reaction would be to learning Rhian had found that damn lump.

She squashed the nasty internal voice and got down to business.

"Come eat," she ordered, pointing at Rhian's plate on the other side of the bar. She chose to eat standing in the kitchen, the cabinets between them. A pitiful shield at best.

Rhian slid onto a stool. "You're really bossy, you know that?"

"Six brothers," she said between bites. "You have no idea how bad I can get."

A ghost of a smile hovered on his lips. She stuffed another heap of pork lo mien into her mouth. No amount of separation-by-cabinet would be sufficient defense from Rhian Savage.

The image of Rhian bent over the counter, his ass jammed full of frozen butt plug, popped into her head. Again.

Thanks a lot, Garrick. There wasn't a doubt in her mind he was responsible for the nice—rather large—surprise in the freezer. He'd mentioned wanting to try it with her. He apparently already had, or was about to, with Rhian.

She stopped chewing, her mouth full of food, and waited for the bitter sting of jealousy.

Nope.

The only thing different was now she knew what she'd be thinking about when she next brought herself to orgasm.

She really was wired differently, and there was nothing wrong with that. On top of everything else he'd given her, Garrick had taught her not to be ashamed of what she liked, and to ask for what she wanted.

Maybe he was teaching Rhian the same.

She took a sip of beer to hide her smirk. She'd teased him about the plug and he'd turned such a dark red, she'd worried he was going to stroke out.

They ate in silence. He sat on the edge of his stool and shot her increasingly frequent looks. She didn't respond, but watched to see he ate most of his food.

He could joke about his diet, but with a body like that, and a gym habit like his, he needed to take in a hell of a lot of fuel. If he was facing a major illness, he needed to maintain his current strength and fitness.

The lecture hovered on the tip of her tongue but she swallowed it back. No point going down that road until they knew there was something to it. Not all lumps were cancer, right?

She had no idea what the hell else it could be, but hoped there existed other possibilities. She made a mental note to call her brother Murdoch. As a doctor, he could give her a crash course on all of the potential outcomes.

Rhian cracked open his fortune cookie and smiled.

"What does it say?" she asked.

"Once you find a problem, take hold of it with both hands."

"Might make walking around a bit of a challenge for you."

Rhian laughed, a real, full-bodied sound that ended abruptly. "Wait, did you just make a joke about the lump in my junk?"

She shrugged. "Did you just laugh at it?"

He blinked, a smile still hovering on his face. He was too handsome by far, his laugh entirely too engaging.

Savannah pushed her plate away. Might as well get this over with.

"Why'd you do it, Rhian?"

The smile disappeared. "What?"

"Why'd you cut Garrick off?" The temper she'd banked started to simmer again.

Face pale, he stared down at his empty plate. "You know why."

"I have no idea. Honestly. It seems to me you've never needed him more."

He shook his head. "Have you seen how stressed out he is? He's got too much going on already. I didn't want to drag him into my shit."

"Drag him into your shit?" she repeated, wondering if she'd heard him wrong.

"Yeah. He's better off without having to deal with me being sick."

She glared at him until he looked up at her. His imploring gaze, silently pleading for her to understand, sent her over the edge.

"You. Fucking. *Asshole.*"

Rhian jumped to his feet.

She hoped he tried to run. She'd love an excuse to tackle his stupid ass to the floor. He held his ground, though, when she came around the counter and got in his face.

"You think that's how this works? That you get to tell that man you love him and then walk away without so much as a word? That you get to decide what's best for him?"

"But what if—"

She wouldn't even let him finish the thought. "You know what? Fuck you. That man loves you with all his damn heart. Don't you get it? He didn't just throw those words out because he thought it might be true or because you needed to hear them. God knows, they haven't been convenient for any of us. He said them because they're true. And they mean something. Something that you, apparently, don't even fucking understand."

She stopped to catch her breath. She shook with the desire to holler more, possibly cry and certainly smack Rhian upside the head. She'd been willing to share Garrick with *this* piece of shit?

"You're right." He said it so quietly, she almost didn't hear him.

"What?"

"You're right. I don't understand. I'm not sure what it means."

He looked so damn lost, she bit back the scathing retort on the tip of her tongue.

"I thought you loved him."

He swallowed. "I do. I think."

"You think?"

Rhian stared at his feet, his face flushed, eyes blinking fast. "You're right. I should know. And he should be with someone who understands these things." He looked at her and she steeled herself against the sheen of moisture in his eyes. "He already has someone who understands. He's better off without me."

She cast around in her head for a good argument, something to stop him from giving it all away, giving her what she wanted. This was all wrong.

His smile was sad. "Weird as it is, I feel better knowing he has you. You'll help him. Make him happy."

Savannah's stomach twisted. Her arguments honed down to a few simple truths. "You make him happy, too. He loves you." She could never have tolerated sharing him otherwise.

Rhian shook his head, retrieved her bag and handed it to her. She took it automatically, standing there stunned while he walk over and opened his door.

"I'd like you to go now."

Rhian stood in his front door, staring at the wall over Savannah's shoulder, and waited.

"What do you mean you don't understand?" she asked.

He sighed. "Just what you said. I don't know what it means when Garrick says he loves me." He hated having to explain this, particularly to her, but she deserved an honest answer. "No one has ever said it before, okay? How the hell would I know   what   it   means?"

Chapter Eight

Rhian watched, dismayed, as Savannah stomped into the living room and plunked down on the coffee table.

"Come here." She pointed at his spot on the couch in front of her.

He trudged across the room and sat. They settled with her knees between his again. Savannah put her hands in her lap, not trying to take hold of him. He kept his hands tucked under his thighs, just in case.

"What would you do if Garrick called and said he had cancer?"

A bolt of pure terror shot through him. "Don't *ever* say that!"

She nodded as if he'd answered something for her. "Tell me."

"I don't know," he said, trying to calm his racing heart. "I'd go to Moncton. To help him. Hear what was going on. I'd want..."

He stopped. He'd already said more than enough to make her point.

"What?" she prompted. When he shook his head, she put a hand on his knee and squeezed. "Say it."

"I'd want to hold him," he confessed quietly.

Her grip on his knee gentled but she didn't let go. "And how would you feel if he told you he wouldn't allow it? That you had to stay away, and he wasn't going to tell you what was going on."

His throat tightened. "Pissed."

"Because it would be so fucking..."

"Unfair," he whispered in utter defeat.

That was what he'd been. Unfair.

"Rhian Savage, you know exactly what love means. You just have to accept it's a two way street."

He blinked furiously, fighting the sting in his eyes.

"Do you love Garrick?" she asked again.

"Yes."

"Does he make you happy?"

He almost smiled. "When he's not scaring the shit out of me."

"Oh, honey," she said, taking both his hands. He didn't remember putting them next to hers on his thighs. "He scares the hell out of me, too. All the time. His love is so *big*. And he's so damn..."

"Fearless?"

She laughed. "Yes, he's fearless, isn't he? Though, to be honest, I think we scare the shit out of him, too. Particularly this whole"—she gestured between them—"loving two people thing. I think he worries about that, about us, all the time."

Rhian nodded. It was true. Didn't make it less weird to be talking about it with her, though.

She squeezed his hands. "You need to get used to it, too."

"What? That he loves you too?"

"Yes."

He frowned, confused. "I am. I mean, I knew about you from the beginning. You know that."

"Then what—"

"It's just weird to be here. With you," he said. "No, wait. I take that back. It's weird that it's not...weirder. By all rights, you should..." Her black look stopped him from saying *hate me*. "You should be annoyed by me, how's that? But you seem remarkably..."

"Cool?"

He smiled. "Yes."

"Awesome?"

"Uh-huh."

"The nicest and most incredible girlfriend *ever*?"

"Don't push it."

She laughed and his heart skipped a beat. He suddenly remembered asking her out, not so very long ago, and it wasn't hard to recall why. Her jade green eyes danced, mesmerizing him.

She reached for her bag and fished out an iPad. "Okay, then. Let's call Garrick."

Rhian froze. *Oh shit.*

Garrick lay in bed, his hand splayed atop the iPad at his hip, silently praying it would chime. His phone was in his other hand, same deal.

He'd been like this for over an hour, desperate to hear from Savannah. Or Rhian, though he wasn't holding out a lot of hope for that. All he knew was that Savannah was *tackling the issue once and for all*, per her cryptic text message. He had no idea what the hell that meant, but he trusted her.

When his iPad chimed, he bolted upright, propped himself against the headboard, and answered Savannah's hail.

"Hey, baby." He forced a smile.

His lungs locked up when Rhian appeared on the screen. He looked terrible, ravaged, but Garrick had never seen a more welcome sight.

"*Rhian.*"

Rhian stared at him, as seemingly shocked as Garrick to be on the call.

"Are you okay?"

"Yes," Rhian said quietly. He paused. "No."

Garrick gripped his iPad so tightly, he worried it might crack. "What's wrong?"

Rhian still didn't answer.

"Rhian, please, talk to me. What's going on?"

The screen shifted as Savannah sat down next to Rhian. He watched her pry one of Rhian's hands off the iPad and lace it with hers. She looked sad. Rhian looked terrified.

Garrick's fear went through the roof.

"Please, god, tell me. What the fuck is going on? What happened?"

Savannah pursed her lips, shushing him silently, and he subsided. The next two minutes were some of the longest of his life, but he waited patiently for Rhian to say something.

"I have a lump. In my testicle."

Garrick could barely breathe. He couldn't tear his eyes from Rhian.

Rhian continued in a dull monotone, describing the details of his discovery, his appointment that week, how little he actually knew at this point.

Tears rolled down Garrick's face. He saw Savannah was in the same condition, her eyes pinned to the screen. Rhian was dry-eyed, his gaze as hollow as his voice.

Garrick wanted to jump from his bed and drive to the Moncton Airport without hanging up. He wanted to beg, borrow or steal his way onto the next flight to anywhere that would connect him to Boston. Maybe he should drive? It was only eight hours. It might be faster.

But goddamn it, he couldn't do *any* of those things. He had a meeting at seven o'clock tomorrow morning and he had to be there. Rupert Smythe, the Ice Cats' manager, was in Montreal searching for his missing 4-year-old brother. Rupert was becoming understandably frantic. Garrick couldn't ask him to wait on that.

Not to mention, Garrick realized with stomach-plunging dread, he had no idea what the status of his relationship with Rhian was right now. He hadn't heard from the man in weeks. Maybe this was just a courtesy call.

Rhian had stopped speaking. In spite of the fear radiating from him, or maybe because of it, Garrick had to ask.

"Where'd you go, Rhian? What happened to you? To us?"

Rhian flinched.

Savannah slid from the couch. "I'll be back in just a minute," she said quietly.

Garrick was so fucking grateful that she understood. It was hard to imagine how he could ever thank her sufficiently. It had to be brutal for her to deal with this shit, let alone graciously.

Garrick heard the sound of a door closing over the line.

Rhian stared at something off camera.

"Rhian?"

He frowned and looked back at the screen. "Yeah. Sorry. Just worried about Savannah."

"That makes two of us," Garrick said. "Do you need to go?"

"What? No. She's okay. I was just thinking about how hard this must be for her."

Garrick sighed. "Me, too."

Rhian worried his lower lip with his teeth. Garrick waited.

Rhian opened his mouth a few times before finally spitting out, "I love you, and I screwed up. Big time. I'm sorry."

Garrick closed his eyes as the hundred-pound lead weight was lifted from his chest. "Say the first part again and it'll go a long way toward making me feel better."

"I love you."

Garrick smiled. That was the first time Rhian had ever said it without *any* hesitation. "I love you, too."

"I'm glad," Rhian said in a raspy voice.

Garrick's eyes popped open.

Rhian was holding it together, but it looked like it was by a thread.

"Why, Rhian? Why did you leave me?"

"Because I'm an idiot. Because I thought it would be easier for you if I went away and didn't drag you along if I get sick."

"You're *not* going to get sick."

Rhian smiled a little. "Okay."

"And if, god forbid, you do have to get treated or whatever, I'm going to be there the whole way. I'll get the hell out of Moncton as soon as I can, I promise."

"Stay and finish what you need to, Garrick. I'm okay. For now it's just appointments, tests, and waiting."

It sounded like hell on earth, especially the waiting part.

"You won't disappear again, will you?" Garrick hated the fear in his voice almost as much as the way it made Rhian cringe.

"No, I won't."

"Why the hell did you think you could spare me this? Even if you dumped my ass, I would be worried sick. I love you, Rhi. What part of that is hard to understand?"

"It's not hard to understand. Not anymore." Rhian smiled. "But yell if you need to. Savannah already tore up one side of me and down the other."

"She did?"

"Yeah, she did."

Garrick smiled. "That's my girl."

"I can see how you two get along so well. She's just like you."

"Really? I think we're totally different most of the time."

Rhian laughed.

Garrick could guess some of the ways Rhian would see them as alike. Probably their shared propensity to talk about scary shit, like *feelings*, had come up.

Garrick grinned. "God, I've missed you."

"I miss you, too." Rhian's eyes filled.

Garrick almost lost his supper. "I'm sorry I'm not there. You shouldn't do this alone."

Savannah dropped onto the couch next to Rhian. "He won't. I'm going with him to his appointment," Savannah told Garrick.

Rhian looked at her like she was insane. "But—"

"And he's going to get over it," she stated firmly, still without sparing so much as a glance in Rhian's direction.

Rhian turned pleading eyes to Garrick. "She's awfully fucking bossy, isn't she?"

Garrick chuckled. "Accept it. It will hurt less."

Savannah smiled. "Well, we have an early start tomorrow, and it's getting late."

Rhian's mouth fell open then snapped closed, repeatedly, until he managed to say, "But, I don't have any plans tomorrow."

"You do now. We're going for a run."

"A what? We are?"

"Yep. And we're going to eat at least three healthy meals. Maybe get a little sun and fresh air. Got to keep you healthy in all ways, my friend."

Rhian stared at Savannah, agape. Garrick laughed. The poor man had no idea what was about to happen to him.

Savannah wasn't just picking up the pieces. She was going to glue the damn things back together.

"I love you, Savannah," Garrick said. He only wished he had the words to tell her how much. How grateful he was.

Savannah smiled. "I love you, too. Goodnight."

Savannah tilted the iPad toward Rhian.

"I love you, too, Rhian. Very much. Please don't forget that again, okay?"

Rhian swallowed and cast a sidelong glance at Savannah. "I love you, too," he croaked.

Garrick couldn't decide if the two of them together was the best or worst thing that could happen at this point. Hell yes, it was weird. But after two weeks of hell, he finally felt whole again.

Chapter Nine

Savannah tossed her iPad on the couch and stood. Time for bed.

"Come on." She held her hand out to Rhian.

He took it reluctantly and let himself be led to the bedroom.

"Okay, so here's how it's going to work. No more starving yourself and you're going to drink plenty of water. And if you haven't been getting enough sleep—which by the look of you, you haven't—that ends now, too."

"Oh really?"

She smiled sweetly. "Yes, *really*. Now strip."

She almost burst out laughing at the scandalized look on Rhian's face.

"Buh...wha...why are you doing this?"

"Getting you naked? Because I happen to know that's how you sleep."

Rhian turned a fairly adorable shade of pink. It was probably indelicate to remind him that Garrick had told her everything. Rhian had known going into his relationship with Garrick that this had been the deal, just as he knew it wasn't the deal any longer.

She decided to let him off the hook. "Or do you mean, why am I helping?"

He made a face. "If that's what you want to call this, yes."

"Because I love Garrick and I never want to see him hurt. You getting ill and not taking care of yourself would hurt him." She thought about leaving it there, but figured she should be honest. "And because I like you, Rhian, and no one, not even the man who gets to spend quality time with the man I want to horde all to myself, should go through this kind of shit alone."

"Well, that's honest."

"It is. You know that's how I roll. I haven't changed since we were friends in Moncton. It's just weirder now, that's all."

"You can say that again."

"It's just weirder now, that's all," she repeated, deadpan. "And while I'm saying shit for a second time—*strip*."

His eyes widened comically. This man got naked in a room full of other men on a daily basis, but one woman—who swore to herself she wasn't going to stare—was freaking him out?

"Relax," she scolded with a chuckle. "It's not like I haven't seen most of it before. As your trainer, I had the opportunity to inspect almost every inch of that fabulous body on a regular basis. Also, we both know you don't swing my way, so really, there's nothing to worry about."

"But I—"

"Mind if I use the bathroom before I go?"

The change of subject threw him for a second. "No, not at all. It's through there." He pointed at the door off the bedroom.

"Thanks." She smiled. "Get ready for bed while I'm in there, okay? I'm not leaving until I know you're tucked in."

He looked like he considered arguing, but remained silent.

Smart boy. He was getting the hang of it already.

The sound of the bathroom door locking threw Rhian into motion. He found his only pair of pajama bottoms—usually reserved for answering the door when he would otherwise be naked—and stripped out of his clothes.

He dove into bed, yanked up the covers, and settled against the mountain of pillows.

Then he laughed at himself. He'd had *zero* intention of going to bed so early, but had just been very effectively railroaded. It was just what Garrick would have done.

Ha. Garrick thought he and Savannah were so different. They were *exactly the same.*

He tried not to look nervous when she came to the side of the bed and sat by his hip. On the weirdness scale for tonight, Savannah tucking him in ranked almost as high as her teasing him about sex toys.

"You doing okay?"

He shrugged. "I'm fine. I don't feel sick or anything."

She took his hand. "I mean after talking to Garrick. I know it's hard to be away from him. And to be stuck with me."

"I'm not stuck with you."

She searched his face, uncertain.

"I mean, I don't feel *stuck* with you," he explained. "Mostly I'm just relieved to have told Garrick everything."

She smiled. "Good."

"You know, it would be perfectly human of you to be a little disappointed over how things turned out tonight."

"Yeah, maybe. But when you were throwing me out and I knew you'd screw things up with Garrick permanently, it didn't feel like winning. I'm glad things worked out the way they did."

He must have looked as dubious as he felt.

"Okay, even if it is a pain in the ass."

He laughed. "Always honest, right?"

She smiled. "Yup."

He smiled back, distracted by the bright green of her eyes, the hint of pink on her cheeks. "Thank you, Savannah."

"You'll take that back when you figure out you've only just begun to experience my bossy side," she joked. She leaned in and kissed his cheek. "Sweet dreams."

"Goodnight," he said, his voice lower than intended.

She patted his arm, helped herself to his key card and both TV remotes and left.

Witch.

Savannah inserted the key card into Rhian's door at six o'clock the next morning, wondering if he'd asked the hotel to change it. She smiled when the light flashed green, delighted to find the apartment still dark and Rhian passed out in the bedroom.

She'd woken this morning to a text from Garrick.

Thank you thank you thank you.

She'd sent him a *good morning* reply, purposely not writing *you're welcome*. Not because she was pissed, or because he wasn't in fact welcome, but because it implied she was doing it for him.

She'd like to pretend she was such an awesome, generous girlfriend that she was doing this for Garrick. But it would be a load of crap. She wasn't that altruistic. If that was all there was to it, she'd be gone.

Rhian shouldn't have to go through this alone. Seeing the doctor, getting whatever tests were ordered, waiting for the results—it was going to be an ordeal. He would need someone, even if he didn't believe that now. Someone to ask questions that he was too stressed to ask. Someone to advocate on his behalf. She could do that for him.

He needed a friend. And regardless of their situation with Garrick, she still thought of herself as Rhian's friend. At least as far as cancer was concerned.

Settling on the couch, she took out her phone and poked around online. She wanted Rhian to get as much sleep as possible.

A half hour later, the bedroom door opened and Rhian stepped out.

"Good morning" she said, laughing when he jerked back, sloshing water from his bottle down his bare chest.

"Jesus Christ. You scared me half to death."

She sat up. "Sorry."

He came closer and she told herself she wasn't

disappointed he was wearing pants. His hair stood on end and his eyes were puffy with sleep. In spite of all that, he looked pretty damn good.

She refused to let her eyes dwell on the drops of water still coursing down his exceedingly toned chest and abs.

Leaping to her feet, she smiled. "You about ready to go? I was thinking we could run out to Harvard and back."

His blank stare made her wonder if he'd forgotten about their run. Maybe he wasn't a morning person.

He scratched his head. "We're going to run on the street?"

"Just until we get to the river, then we'll run the Esplanade and along the banks. Trust me. You'll like this route."

He shrugged. "Okay. Give me five minutes."

Rhian stood behind his bedroom door and tried to rein in his wayward imagination. His morning wood had barely subsided—*thank god*—when he'd staggered out of his room. Now it was back for an encore.

He'd never had a thing for loose T-shirts over sports bras and running shorts before today. Savannah filled them out better than anyone else he'd ever seen. He'd practically drooled over her long, bare legs stretched out on his couch.

He shook his head to pry the image loose from his brain. It was either that or figure out how the hell to run with a hard-on.

Yanking off his pajama bottoms, he gave his dick a thump to try to get it to behave and quickly got dressed. Usually he went without underwear, but not when he ran and definitely not today. Today, a tight jock-strap was definitely in order.

He briefly considered reinforcing it with duct tape.

Almost two hours and more than ten miles later, Rhian ran up the stairs to his apartment right behind Savannah. He'd conquered his rising physical interest quite easily once he determined that Savannah ran like the fucking wind. He hadn't had trouble keeping up, but he'd been focused on putting one foot in front of the other and not on how great her ass looked when he was running behind her.

Well, okay, mostly not focused on that, anyway.

Stopping inside his door, he was pleased to see she was as winded as he was. Her legs were shorter—though not by much—but he was carrying around a lot more muscle. His lips twitched when she grabbed his wrist to check his pulse.

Always a trainer at heart.

"How am I doing? You going to have to whip me into shape?"

She staggered into the living room and leaned against the kitchen counter to stretch out her legs. "Yeah, Savage. I'm super worried about your fitness levels. I mean, wow, somewhere on that body is at least one ounce of fat. Though where, I don't know."

He grinned at her compliment, biting back the suggestion she conduct a thorough search. Jesus, was he about to flirt with Garrick's girlfriend?

Then she pulled off her T-shirt and used it to wipe her face.

Rhian's mouth fell open.

Holy. Shit.

Apparently there wasn't the need for a lick of modesty when it was just her with the supposedly gay guy.

This was bad. A sports bra shouldn't have been sexy. The shadow of nipple beyond white cotton, and the hint of swelling flesh above, shouldn't have been nearly so enticing. Her flat, well-defined stomach definitely shouldn't make him want to press his face there.

God help him, his problem from earlier arose once more. With a vengeance.

Savannah wandered past him, oblivious to his slack-jawed daze, and went into the kitchen. "I'll see what I can make us for breakfast."

He remembered the butt plug in the freezer. "How about we go out? My treat. I don't have anything in the house that will feed us both after a run like that."

She smiled then looked down at her bare torso. "Okay, but it can't be fancy unless you want to swing by my place first."

"There's a decent diner around the corner." He gestured, as if she could see it through his closed blinds. "I'll go shower and you can borrow one of my shirts. Top drawer, bottom of the stack. There should be some smaller ones that don't fit across my shoulders well right now.

Her eyes dropped to his chest, and he froze, the proverbial deer in headlights.

He had shucked his shirt and tucked it into the back of his waistband around mile three of their run. Now heat spread along his bare skin wherever her eyes traced across it.

If she glanced lower, he was screwed. He spun for the bedroom. "I'm going to hit the shower."

He didn't wait for a response. Hell, he was stripped down and under the spray before it had a chance to warm up. He hoped the frigid water would help.

It didn't.

Maybe he was delirious from the early run and weeks of sleep deprivation. It was just a woman in a sports bra, for god's sake. It wasn't a big deal. He'd seen a lot more of a woman's bare skin than that in the past.

He focused on that as he wrapped his hand around his cock and propped one shoulder against the tile wall. Eyes closed, he shuddered at the squeeze of his palm and still-cold water.

It didn't take long. His hand flew over his dick, his fingers plucking at the sensitive head on the first few passes, then giving up for a strong, steady pump. He pictured Garrick's cock down his throat, big hands fisting in his hair. He loved to watch Garrick's face when he took him all the way down, how his eyes widened, his nostrils flared. The hot pink splotches on his cheeks.

Only this time, it was Savannah who watched him swallow around Garrick's heavy shaft, Savannah's hands that traced

Garrick's hard belly in front of his eyes, Savannah who groaned his name as he trembled and came in hard bursts.

Chapter Ten

Savannah sat across from Rhian in the diner and watched him dig into his second plate of eggs. Her suspicions about how much it would take to feed a man his size and fitness level had been confirmed over the past few days. Rhian scarfed food like an eighteen-year-old boy.

She cringed. He *wasn't* all that far from eighteen—only twenty-four. Not that she was much older at twenty-eight, but Garrick had a good ten years on Rhian and was long past being able to eat a pound of bacon just because he'd run ten miles that morning.

She suppressed the urge to text Garrick to tease him about that, about Rhian. She'd decided it was poor etiquette to send notes to her boyfriend about *his* boyfriend. Especially when he was sitting right there.

She couldn't tease Rhian about Garrick either. If she brought Garrick up, Rhian switched to mumbled half-answers. And forget talking, joking, or even *hinting* about anything to do with sex. Even if she left Garrick entirely out of it, Rhian turned bright red and changed the subject.

There was something vastly amusing about the idea of Garrick falling in love with a prude.

Rhian was captivated by something out the window, so he didn't see her grin. She imagined Garrick trying to talk a blushing Rhian into doing naughty things. She almost snorted with laughter. It couldn't be true—if for no other reason than a prude would never keep a sex toy in his freezer—but the image was irresistible.

She noticed the expression on Rhian's face and her amusement fled.

"What's wrong?"

Rhian spoke softly, though no one sat near enough to hear them. "Do you see the girl across the street? The one in the purple coat. *Shit*, she saw me looking. "

Savannah spun in time to see a flash of purple disappear around the corner. "Damn. I missed her."

"I know I've seen her before."

"Maybe she lives around here."

"Maybe. But I think I've seen her at after-game stuff a couple times, and at a practice up in Wilmington."

"An overzealous fan?"

He cringed. "God, I hope not. I don't need another puck bunny drawing a bead on me."

Savannah knew he was thinking about Deena, the unfortunate Ice Cats fan who'd created a mountain of trouble for Rhian and Garrick earlier in the season. "No, you don't."

"She looked young," he said, still staring at the point where the girl had disappeared. "Too young to be stalking hockey players."

"I'm not sure there are age limits on that, but let's hope she's just a neighbor or a run-of-the-mill fan. Next time you see her, point her out to me. I'll tell you if I've seen her at the stuff I've attended."

She touched his hand, pulling his attention back inside the diner.

He sighed, his shoulders easing down. "Okay, thanks. I'm sure it's nothing."

"Let's not assume anything. We both know how quickly a broken mind can fixate on someone."

Rhian grimaced. "Yeah, I guess we do."

She rubbed her hand over his while he frowned down at his breakfast. He had far bigger concerns to focus on. His appointment at Dana-Farber was just two days away.

Rhian tried to listen to the doctor talk about next steps. All he heard were words like *biopsy, likely to be treatable* and *chemotherapy.* He nodded when he guessed it was appropriate and agreed to the next available appointment time.

He stood and shook the doctor's hand, assuring him that someone was waiting for him and that he wasn't going to be alone for the rest of the day. He was surprised they cared.

He would have lied, well used to maneuvering past these sorts of questions, but for once he didn't have to. He had Savannah.

He felt better for all the sleep, food and exercise she'd forced on him for the past three days. By the end of the second day, he'd even stopped resisting. These were the right things to do. And he wouldn't have done any of them if she hadn't inserted herself into his life.

He was so damn grateful to see her jumping up from her chair in the waiting room, it seemed perfectly natural to catch her in his arms and pull her in tight.

She was pressed the full length of his body, his face buried in her soft hair, her arms clutching his waist, before it crossed his mind that this was probably inappropriate.

He didn't give a crap.

She rubbed her hands up and down his back before stepping back. "You ready to go, or do you need to do something before we head out?"

He appreciated that she focused on the practicalities. They all seemed too slippery for him to grasp right now. "No, I'm all set. I have a biopsy on Thursday."

She blinked and mouthed the word biopsy, silently processing that as she led them to the elevators. "Thursday, as in the day after tomorrow?"

"Yes."

She nodded. "Okay. I don't think Garrick will be able to get here that soon."

Rhian realized he was holding her hand. He didn't let go.

"They said it's a pretty quick out-patient procedure. I don't have to spend the night or anything."

"I'll be here the whole time."

He watched the numbers on the elevator as it rose to retrieve them. "Thanks."

She squeezed his fingers and left it at that. Thank god. In the past five minutes alone he'd swung from numb, to the razor's edge of hysteria, and back again. He wanted to cry. Or hit something. He couldn't remember ever feeling so powerless. Not since...

Well, not since a very long time ago. That was the last thing he should be thinking about.

The ding of the elevator doors opening yanked him back to the present and he focused on putting his feet in the right places so he didn't fall on his face. He wanted to hug Savannah again, but squashed the idea. The last thing they needed was for him to act completely out of character. He wasn't sure who it would freak out more.

Probably him.

They had the elevator to themselves, only the Muzak to fill the silence until Savannah asked, "Is there anything else I need to know?"

He shrugged, trying to think back. "They're not going to make an incision. They think they can take a good sample with just a needle." He shuddered. "And if it's cancer, it's very likely treatable, though they might remove the testicle as a first step."

He failed to keep his voice even at the end. Savannah gripped his hand tighter.

"When will they know?"

"They said they'd call in a week or two, depending on the results and if they have to retest anything."

"Okay, that's not too bad."

The weeks stretched out before him like the ninth circle of hell, but yeah, *not too bad*.

"Do you need to do anything in the meantime?" she asked.

"Nope."

She smiled brightly. "Great. Let's go out. Get some lunch and just goof off."

He'd been planning to sit in his apartment and stare at the wall. He liked her idea better.

Not to mention he'd bet his more-precious-than-ever left nut she wouldn't let him sit at home alone anyway.

"Sure, what do you have in mind?"

A few hours later, Rhian sat in the back of the cab, his arm pressed to Savannah's, his knees spread as wide as the limited space and his jeans would allow. He tried to control himself, but he just couldn't stop laughing.

"I can't believe I let you talk me into that." He planted his fists on the seat so they wouldn't grab his junk.

Savannah laughed at him. "Don't be a baby. You'll survive."

"I'm sure I will. I can't say the same for my dignity."

Savannah smirked and glanced at his crotch meaningfully. "I promise you, when Garrick sees you waxed clean, your pride will be restored."

Rhian's laughter choked off, his mind zinging to what Garrick's reaction might be. *Yowza.*

Savannah smirked and he wiped whatever his expression was off his face. Thank god for the privacy glass separating them from their driver. This was not a conversation he would want repeated. "You may have a point. I'm sure he'll be equally pleased to see whatever you've done to yourself."

She waved a dismissive hand. "Nothing he hasn't seen before. I've been down to a landing strip since long before he and I met."

Rhian was almost afraid to ask. "A landing strip?"

She grinned. "Use your imagination. I'm sure you can figure it out."

He did. He could. He shook his head to try to get that image out of his head. *Holy crap.*

"Wait! You have hair still? That's not fair. You told that crazy woman to take everything off of me. She removed hair in places I didn't know it existed."

Savannah snorted. "You and your doctors will thank me. I figured they would shave you for the biopsy. This way, they have a clean surface to work with and you won't get the itchies while you're healing."

"The itchies?"

"Yeah, you know? Crotch crickets? Dude, haven't you ever shaved down there before?" At his blank stare, she turned to stare at him. "Really?"

"What? Why would I? The only places I shave are my face and where I need to stick sports tape."

She looked at him like he was the eighth wonder of the world. "You've never manscaped? Never once?"

"Did you just say *manscaped*?"

She rolled her eyes. "Well, welcome to the big boys' club, Savage. I bet now that you've done it, you'll never go back."

"To the crazy lady with the hot wax and an intimate knowledge of my undercarriage? You're right, I'm not going back."

She grinned. "I meant you'll never go back to letting it grow out."

Rhian opened his mouth to argue, but the words stalled in his brain. He shifted against the seat.

Truth was, it felt kind of freaky. In a *good* way.

She smirked, her eyes sparking with laughter as she studied his face. He had no doubt she knew exactly what he was thinking. The idea of Savannah also feeling the strange tickle between her ass cheeks sent heat rushing through his veins.

He needed to think about something else. Now.

He thought about his appointment that morning. That

worked.

He still smiled, though, watching the city fly by as they were taken to the next destination on Savannah's goofing-off list. The taxi took a corner at thirty miles per hour and the unfamiliar rub of fabric against freshly exposed skin shivered through him.

She'd pledged to take his mind things.

And she'd sure as hell succeeded.

Chapter Eleven

Savannah wandered around the open cart and stall vendors, one eye on Rhian farther along the North Canopy of Quincy Market. She hadn't had time to visit here or Faneuil Hall since she'd returned to Boston. The popular attraction was packed with tourists, but still rang with the familiar accent of the locals as well.

They'd stopped by Rhian's apartment long enough for him to call Garrick. Then they'd come to have lunch in the main hall, packed cheek to jowl with everyone else in the undersized rotunda seating area. Rhian had never seen the sights in Boston before, so she'd gone for the full experience.

Catching up to him, she heard him ask the cashier to repeat what he'd just said.

Savannah burst out laughing when Rhian leaned in to listen carefully, obviously not understanding a word.

"He said you'd have more luck at the Globe Corner Bookstore."

"No he didn't."

"I did," the cashier assured him with a big laugh.

Rhian smiled sheepishly and nodded his thanks before turning away and whispering furiously into Savannah's ear. "He didn't say that. He said *tryda kahna bukstah*. That's not English."

She laughed as she threaded her arm through Rhian's, steering them out into the cool spring air. It was late afternoon and time to stop for a beer. If they were going to do the full-on Boston experience, they had to make their way to the replica Cheers tavern at the other end of the market.

They strolled around to the South Canopy, where she dragged him to look at the outdoor kiosks, releasing his arm when he wandered to a different vendor while she sorted through a pile of lovely scarves, trying to choose only one. She jumped when he slid an arm around her waist from behind and spoke directly into her ear.

"Don't turn around, but that girl is here. I think she followed us from my place."

He was a warm, living wall at her back. His scent teased her nose.

She turned her face to his, as if canoodling rather than doing a pathetic job at amateur spying. "Where?"

"To the right, a couple kiosks down. She's watching us in the reflection of the Victoria's Secret window."

She nodded but didn't look. She had to bite off a whimper when he stepped aside and peeled all that warmth away from her back.

Geez, she needed Garrick to visit soon. Her hormones were out of control.

Shuffling through the stack of scarves, she waited for Rhian to ease to the left, leaving her a clear view of his stalker.

Savannah's eyes nearly bugged out of her head. "*Holy shit, she looks just like you!*"

Either her voice carried to the girl or she realized she'd been spotted, but she took off like a shot down the marketplace, disappearing into the crowd.

Cursing her stupidity, Savannah turned to Rhian. He staggered backward, pale as a ghost.

She caught his arm before he fell over. "Whoa, hey, are you okay?"

He shook his head.

She dragged him to the restaurant and plunked him down at the nearest table, not bothering to score Norm and Cliffy's spots at the bar, as was tradition. Rhian would probably fall right off a barstool at this point.

The waiter appeared and Savannah ordered for both of them. Rhian sat mute, pale-faced and unmoving.

She put a hand on his arm. "Are you okay?"

"You said...You said she looked like me. What if..."

Something clicked in Savannah's head. "Easy there. She's *way* too old to be yours, if that's what you're thinking. She looked like she was eighteen. Maybe less. So unless you were a *very* precocious six-year-old, I think you're safe enough."

He nodded, not as reassured as she'd hoped by her math.

"Could she be a cousin or something?"

Rhian shrugged and stared out the window at the passing crowds.

Savannah cringed at her insensitivity. God, she was an idiot.

"I'm sorry, Rhian. That was a stupid thing to say."

"It's okay."

"No, it's not. Maybe I shouldn't know, but I do. And I know you don't like to talk about it."

"Garrick told you."

It wasn't a question, but she answered it anyway. "Yeah. But I swear that's all he told me. No details. Just...just that you were in foster care and you don't have a family."

Rhian smiled wryly. "Actually, Garrick told you everything he knows. That's all I've ever told him. More than I've told anyone since I got out of the system."

"Oh," she said softly, kicking herself.

"Savannah, it's cool." He put his hand over hers. "I trust you."

The words hung in the air between them. Savannah blinked, clearly startled by his earnest declaration. She couldn't be nearly as shocked as he was.

"Thank you," she said.

He probably ought to thank *her*, but he didn't say anything, pulling his hand back while the waiter put down their drinks.

Maybe he was having some sort of post-traumatic-doctor-visit moment. Or maybe now that Garrick had pried the lid off Rhian's emotional lock box, he couldn't control it anymore, giving away sacred things like trust willy-nilly.

No, that was bullshit. She'd earned his trust. As difficult as it was to navigate their love for Garrick, it didn't change the fact she'd been a good friend to him today, for the past three days, and back in Moncton. After all, she'd been the one to tell Garrick it was okay to love him. How the hell could he not trust her after doing something like that?

"I do have a family. Somewhere."

She looked at him, intrigued. And alarmed.

It would have been funny if he wasn't choking on what he was going to say next. He'd never told anyone this. He wasn't sure why telling Savannah in the middle of Boston's biggest tourist trap felt like a good idea, but he went with it. He was haunted by the girl's face.

"My mother's last name was Lynch. We lived in Chicago, but she was from Boston, I think."

Savannah nodded. "And your father's last name was Savage?"

"No."

She looked understandably confused. He knew if he deflected, she wouldn't press him on it.

In this way, she *was* different from Garrick, in spite of his assertion that they were so alike. He wouldn't change a thing about Garrick, ever, but there was something soothing about Savannah's quieter strength.

He took a long drink of his beer and made a decision. He prayed it was the right one.

"My mom left me with a neighbor when I was four. Almost five."

She cocked her head. "Okay."

"She didn't come back."

Now she understood. Her face fell, shock etched into every line.

He plowed on. "Mrs. Rosenberg was nice and had babysat for me a few times. I can remember her trying to reassure me that my mom would be back soon, but I think by day four or five, I knew she was lying. That's my earliest memory," he told her, thinking back with a sad smile. "I knew my name, my birthday, a few brief flashes and details that I still carry with me, but the earliest recollection I have of a time and place, an event, was my mother leaving me with old lady Rosenberg."

Savannah laid her hand over his on the table and held on.

He tried, and failed, to smile. "After a week or so, poor Mrs. Rosenberg gave up and called social services. She was so upset." He remembered her distress, seeing it through the eyes of an adult instead of a child. He felt sorry for her now. "I think she hated to give me to the state, but she was in no position to take on a child. Before they came to take me away, she and I sat and talked about what to tell them."

Savannah's brows drew together, the questions on her face, and he tried to answer them as best he could. There was a certain comfort, an insulation from it becoming too intense or emotional, by doing this in a crowded bar. There was also a lot of risk as he struggled to maintain his composure.

"Mom was an addict. Couldn't tell you what, exactly, but she was out of it a lot. I didn't trust her, but I loved her. She was my mom," he said softly, swallowing hard, "and I was just a little kid, you know?"

Savannah nodded and pulled his hand into her lap.

"She wasn't the problem, though. She had a boyfriend. Jimmy. I don't think he was around for long, but I can't say for sure. All I remember is that I was afraid of Jimmy. Really afraid. Maybe my mind has done me the favor of forgetting *how* I knew it, but I knew Jimmy was bad."

Savannah's grip on his hand was almost painful, but it was also reassuring. If nothing else, it kept him grounded in the here and now.

"Mrs. Rosenberg agreed, I guess, because—and I remember this so clearly—she asked me if I wanted to go back to my mom and Jimmy."

He took a big slug of beer. He could still see Mrs. Rosenberg's floral couch. Recall the awful smell of the heavy smoker DSS sent to take him into custody. But nothing was clearer than his answer to that question.

"I said no."

Savannah bit the inside of her lip hard enough to draw blood. By all that was holy, if Rhian could get through telling her this without crying like a baby, she sure as shit wouldn't either.

She eased her stranglehold on his fingers and rubbed her other hand over his to soothe him. Okay, and to soothe herself, too.

She didn't allow herself to dwell on how he knew Jimmy was dangerous. She could only pray he'd had good instincts, and that few or no actual learning experiences had been required.

She didn't say anything, even if the questions practically choked her.

He sat silent, looking far older than his twenty-four years. But then, he'd made a decision at age four that few people would have the courage to make at any age. To have so little innocence left, so young, was heartbreaking.

She bit down harder.

"When DSS showed up, Mrs. Rosenberg pretended she'd never met me before I'd turned up on her doorstep, and I played along. I gave them my first name, but she came up with the spelling. I suspect that if I have a real birth certificate out there somewhere, it's spelled the normal way."

She smiled. "I bet she was a Fleetwood Mac fan."

Rhian cocked his head. "Huh?"

"Rhiannon. Every time I see your name, I think of that

damn song. It's probably why everyone pronounces it wrong when they see it, saying *Rhee-an* instead of *Rye-an.*"

He laughed. "I never thought about it, but you might be right."

He seemed pleased with the idea. She was relieved to see his shoulders come down a little, his posture less rigid.

"Anyway, we agreed that we would pretend not to know my last name, but when I told them that, they kept asking. I can remember thinking they knew I was lying. So I made one up."

"You made it up? Savage? How on earth did you choose that?"

Rhian grimaced and she instantly regretted opening her mouth.

"It's what he called me," he said quietly.

"Who?"

"Jimmy. He called me *the little savage.*" His eyes narrowed on the table, as if searching his memory on its surface. "He'd knock me around and complain about all the noise and mess I made." He blinked and looked back at her. "I just remembered that. That he used to hit me. Lock me in the bedroom."

He fell silent. Savannah didn't move or speak.

"Funny, I remembered how I chose the name but I didn't remember the context until just now." He seemed more curious than upset.

"You all right?" she asked, just to be sure.

"What? Oh yeah, it's okay. I mean, I knew he was bad and I figured it was shit like that. Better than some other stuff he could have done, I suppose. Sexual stuff. I don't remember being aware of that kind of abuse, though, until later. In foster care."

She didn't ask when and why it came up in foster care, even as a smoldering rage ignited in her gut.

"Anyway," he continued, and she told herself to let it go, "I told them my last name was Savage and they believed it. Some poor slob probably spent hours searching for the family of

Rhian Savage when he didn't exist before that day in Mrs. Rosenberg's living room. Tough old bird. She was pretty clever to have schemed up a way to hide me with the state."

Seemed to Savannah, the tough one was the four year old who'd carried out the deception, flawlessly, for twenty years.

"So your original name," she said, careful not to call it his real name, "was Ryan Lynch?"

His lips twisted. "I think so?"

"Do you ever think about looking for them? Your family? Your mother?"

He shook his head. "Never. Truth is, we didn't do that great a job of hiding me. Same first name, same birthday, same city. And it's not like I changed my face. If my mother or her family had wanted to find me, they could have. They didn't."

"For what it's worth, it was entirely their loss."

He smiled, some of the light returning to his beautiful eyes. "Thanks. And for listening."

She laced her fingers with his. "You're welcome. Thank you."

For trusting her. For being her friend. For being possibly the strongest, bravest man she'd ever met.

It was a damn good thing she was already in love with Garrick, and Rhian was gay. It would be entirely too easy to fall in love with this man.

Chapter Twelve

Savannah spent the afternoon of the biopsy pacing the waiting room, texting back and forth with Garrick non-stop. She tried to be patient and failed miserably. It was impossible not to worry.

Not that they'd get answers today, but this step would get them closer.

In the past few days, she'd stopped thinking of Rhian as Garrick's boyfriend. Of course, he was that still, but he was also just Rhian again. Their friendship was no longer defined entirely by their relationships with Garrick.

It was weird, but it might make it...not easy, but *easier* going forward. She'd lost sympathy for Rhian over the past months. Had been well on the way to losing all sense of him as anything but the "other man". Now she remembered who he was. And why she liked him.

His life could have made him hard. Angry. It would have made most people all that *and* bitter. But he was remarkably gentle. Kind. Smart. And as much as she tried, she couldn't pretend she was unaware of him on a physical level. His good looks, his spectacular body. She told herself to think of him as a brother, but somehow that felt *wrong*. Her reaction, particularly when he caught her off-guard with a smile or a touch, both so rare from him, was *not* sisterly.

She sat next to him in the cab as it careened down Huntington Avenue toward the city and held his hand as he fought not to wince against the jarring bumps in the road.

"You okay?"

He nodded a little too quickly. "Yeah. But we might have to walk from your place." He tried to smile, but a particularly

91

deep pothole killed the attempt.

She breathed a sigh of relief when they made it to Charles Street, the traffic and narrow roads in her neighborhood forcing the cabbie to slow down. She rubbed his hand where it rested on her thigh, trying to distract him from the quick turns that shifted them against the seat and each other.

"We're almost there, then we don't have to go anywhere."

He gripped her leg. "I shouldn't go up. I can wait on the street."

He hadn't been to the apartment yet and she regretted that his first time seeing it would be when he was feeling so low. She wondered how Rhian felt about Garrick "officially" living with her and not with him.

Then again, Rhian lived in a hotel. Maybe Garrick was waiting to see where Rhian ended up. Foolishly, it hadn't occurred to her before now that Garrick might *not* make their apartment his primary residence.

But it was supposed to be their home. Could he have two of those?

She looked out the window and stuffed that thought into the back of her mind for another time. Right now, she needed to get Rhian up three flights of stairs before informing him that he was spending the night.

Rhian stared up at the elegant brick and black-shuttered Beacon Hill row house. It was beautiful. He knew without a doubt that inside he would find a warm, welcoming home.

He pointed down the street. "I can walk to my place from here."

Savannah shoved him up the front stairs and through the door, ignoring his protests. He almost smiled at her pushiness, not sure when that had become endearing. Then he saw the mailboxes.

LeBlanc/Morrison

Garrick was going to live here. With her. Where he

belonged. Rhian hadn't needed the sobering reminder.

"Come on." Savannah nudged him farther into the building. "You think you'll be okay for three flights of stairs?"

"Only one way to find out."

He started the climb carefully. It didn't hurt any more than just walking hurt. Not bad, but not that comfortable either. Mostly, he was exhausted. The doctor had warned him that a procedure like this, no matter how minimally invasive, might hit him harder than he expected.

Savannah caught up to him, a hand on his back. "We can stop."

Over his dead body. "I'm fine."

She didn't point out that he was using his grip on the banister to do a lot of the work. Or that he was going at half his usual pace. She just climbed the stairs beside him, silently supportive.

By the time they made it to the third floor, he'd begun to sweat. He felt utterly pathetic. For Christ's sake, he could run up ten times this many stairs on a normal day.

"Let's get you into bed," Savannah said, oh-so-casually.

He wondered if he was hearing things. Maybe he *shouldn't* have climbed all those stairs.

She smiled at him and he became even more suspicious.

He followed her into the apartment and stopped to stare. The kitchen shone with warm wood and dark granite to his right, divided from the living and dining rooms by the suggestion of a hallway where he stood within the open space. To his left, a big couch that looked like heaven—particularly compared to the hard plank at the hotel—faced a big TV, the light streaming in from the bay window and skylights making the wood floors and soft yellow upholstery glow. The dining room was also lit from above, the old chandelier sparkling above a big table.

A home. Just as he'd suspected. He almost marched right back out the door.

"Come on." Savannah grabbed his elbow and towed him down the hall, past the open door to what appeared to be an office, another to a pretty white and blue bathroom, and finally to the door at the end. He knew where it led without being told and suddenly, with all his being, he didn't want to see where Garrick and Savannah curled up together, in the heart of their lovely home.

It wasn't contempt. It was pure, unadulterated envy.

There was no graceful way to stop, short of digging in his heels, and he had enough pride left to prevent him from running, screaming, from the apartment. Before he knew it, he was standing in the middle of their bedroom.

It was, he thought with wonder and bemusement, a nest. The walls were plum-colored, the one window heavily draped in something soft and romantic. The bed was huge, the dark wood fitting against the rich wall color, the warm yellow light from the bedside lamps casting a glow over the piles of pillows and heaping duvet.

Savannah smiled as she looked around at her own creation. "I call it bordello chic."

He chuckled at the apt description.

"I like it," he admitted. In truth, he loved it, which wasn't like him. Home decoration was right up there with soap operas and knitting on the list of things he never thought about.

"Great. Why don't you strip down and hop into bed, and we'll get you settled in for the night."

"Uh...what?"

She breezed past him, as if she hadn't said something completely outrageous. "Go ahead and get into bed. You know I have to go out for a while tonight. I'm sorry about the timing. I want to make sure you're settled in and have everything you need before I go."

"I...I can't stay here," he stammered.

"Why not?" She stopped in the process of folding down the covers and gave him an exasperated look. "I promise I've changed the sheets since Garrick was here. Does that help?"

Great, now he was staring at the bed, picturing Garrick and Savannah in all kinds of compromising positions. "No," he answered honestly.

"Do you want something to wear? I know you've got boxer briefs on for once, and I've seen you in less."

He chose not to address the fact that she knew he didn't normally wear underwear with his street clothes.

"I can stay at my place."

When her hands landed on her hips, he knew he was in trouble.

"Look, I know it's weird, but please get over it. At least for tonight? It's easier for both of us if you stay here. If you're still not comfortable when I get back, I'll take you to your place and we'll crash there."

He didn't remember deciding that she was going to spend the night. Or that he was. When had they decided that they should *ever* spend the night in the same place?

His instinct—okay, maybe it was a compulsion—to keep his distance kicked into overdrive. Way too late, but here it was.

"I'll be fine on my own," he said firmly. "You go ahead, and I'll check in with you later."

She sighed. "No, I'll cancel my plans." She went to her bag and started rooting around its contents.

He slumped, caving like a badly drafted rookie.

"*Fine*," he muttered, "I'll stay here. But I'll be on the couch."

She smiled, confirming he'd just been neatly manipulated.

"Your brothers hate you, don't they?" he groused.

"They adore me," she assured him. "Now, I have to get ready or I'll be late."

He stepped back, unsure what he was supposed to do. He might have gone for the door and the living room couch beyond, but was stymied when Savannah toed off her sneakers and stripped her jeans down to her ankles.

Momma mia.

Her legs were *endless*. Her ass, spectacular.

His cock stirred, then immediately subsided because it *fucking hurt*. He was reminded, forcibly, that he wasn't supposed to do anything of a sexual nature for a couple of days.

She plucked an outfit out of the closet and tossed it on the bed. Oh god, he knew what would come next, knew he should tell her to stop and explain that he wasn't immune, wasn't in fact *gay*, but it was too late.

He tried to play it cool, discretely tucking his hands into his pockets while she hauled her fleece and T-shirt up over her head. He didn't think his dick could surmount the effects of the biopsy, but her midnight blue lace bra, standing out against her smooth, pale skin, might just do the trick. The brush of her dark, silky ponytail across her shoulder drew his eye and he admired the long curve of her neck, the arch of her back, the flare of her hips.

He dragged his eyes back up and stared, fascinated by the dusting of freckles across her collarbone.

Jesus, she was gorgeous.

He gulped when the straps of her bra slid down her arms before she turned her back to him.

Now she turns away? Maybe she feared the sight of her bare breasts would overset his gay sensibilities.

Well, his sensibilities *were* definitely overset. The low-grade sting in his balls was an effective erection-killer, but it wasn't enough to shut off his brain.

She slipped on a soft pink lace and satin bra, then a fuzzy pink sweater with a wide scoop neck over it, the straps peaking out.

Fuck it, he was going to have to run for the bathroom. Another pinch in his nuts forced him to amend that plan. He was going to have to *limp* to the bathroom.

"I'll be right back," she said, and turned for the door before he could make his escape.

The soft sweater hugged her waist, the soft cotton clinging to the peaks of breasts, the hem barely covering the tops of her thighs. She was at least five-ten, and the full length of her bare legs etched themselves in his mind.

She paused in the doorway to look back at him, and he worried he was supposed to have said something in the last two minutes. He had lost access to any higher brain function.

Sure, he was in love with Garrick. But he wasn't *dead*.

He smiled weakly, hoping like hell she hadn't caught him staring, and nodded to tell her it was okay to leave him alone. The minute she was out of sight, he stripped out of his jeans and T-shirt and hurled himself into the bed as quickly as his sore spots would allow. He needed the distance. The shield of the bedding. To shed his snug jeans and let his legs fall open so he could cradle his achy bits for a second.

Of course the mattress was like sitting on a cloud. He caught a hint of a familiar scent.

Savannah.

The antique floorboards in the hallway creaked and he yanked the covers up over his lap.

Savannah stared at Rhian in her bed.

He was settled back against her pillows and she wondered if he, like she, had taken to sleeping on that side because Garrick preferred the other. His bare chest was pale in the light of the bedside lamp, the dark sheets piled at his waist a pleasant contrast. She told herself that was the fascinating part, the colors, and not the hard ridges of his abdomen, the huge shoulders and nervous, constantly moving hands.

He smoothed the sheet repeatedly, hiking the comforter here and there while he made himself at home in her bed. He looked like he belonged there.

She shook her head and backed out of the room. "I'll be right back."

She raided the kitchen, collecting the snacks, water, and critical first aid supply she'd stashed there that morning.

Returning to the bedroom, she brought him all that, plus the TV remote, and piled it on the bedside table. His cell phone was already there next to her favorite picture of Garrick. She thought about offering him a copy, remembering that he didn't have any pictures in his apartment, but held her tongue.

They were officially well into strange territory, barreling toward fucking bizarre and on to hideously awkward. She'd save that offer for another time.

"I'm glad you changed your mind. I think you'll be more comfortable in here," she said. She snagged her skirt from the foot of the bed and tugged it on, working the zipper over her hip.

"Is the bag of frozen peas for what I think it's for?" he asked.

She laughed. "Yes. Shove them in your shorts and you'll feel better."

He eyed the bag dubiously. "I know you're right, but I feel bad about molesting your vegetables."

"Don't worry, I bought those for you. I won't be serving them for dinner next week." She paused, an image forming in her mind. "Though, maybe the next time Garrick is being a pain in the ass, I can feed them to him."

Rhian laughed. "Please let me be here when you do."

Savannah chuckled, ignoring the twinge of sadness. She probably wouldn't be having Rhian over for dinner once Garrick was in Boston. Instead, they'd likely go back to their separate corners.

That sucked.

"I'll be back in a couple hours," she promised. "I have my cell phone and will come right home if you need me."

He smiled. "Stop hovering. I'll be fine on my own."

Perhaps he would be, but she planned to leave him with a babysitter anyway.

Chapter Thirteen

Garrick's Skype chimed right on time and he was ready, sitting in front of the computer, prepared to spend the evening with Rhian.

He smiled when the camera kicked in. Savannah smiled back and sat down on the edge of the bed beside Rhian who was, based on the comforter covering his bare chest, already tucked in for the night.

It took Garrick a few seconds to figure out what was strange about what he was seeing.

Rhian is in our bed.

Wow, why was that so fucking hot? Garrick forced the stray thought aside. It was easy to do when he got a closer look at Rhian's face. He was obviously wiped out.

Savannah was also studying Rhian. Garrick could guess she was thinking about staying in.

"Have fun tonight," he said, pulling her attention back to him.

"You're in charge of keeping an eye on him while I'm gone."

Garrick smirked. "My pleasure."

She arched a brow. "Try to behave." When his grin widened, she snorted. "I think you'll find he's not in the mood for games. I wouldn't be if I'd had a needle in my doodads."

Garrick and Rhian cringed in unison.

"Gee, thanks, Sav," Rhian muttered.

Garrick laughed when Rhian shot him a pleading look. He could no more save him from Savannah than he'd been able to save himself. And in either case, he didn't want to.

"Oh, Rhian," Sav said, as if something had just occurred to her. "I forgot to mention we're headed to Connecticut tomorrow. I hope that's okay."

"Uh, what's in Connecticut?"

"My family."

Garrick studied Rhian's reaction, while Rhian stared at Savannah like she was a madwoman.

"Your family?"

"Yeah, it's our annual end-of-hockey-season gathering. We never get to see each other over the winter, so we make it a point to catch up this time of year, depending on post-season schedules."

Garrick had already had to decline this invitation. He was glad Rhian was going to go instead. Savannah's big, loving family would probably be a revelation for Rhian.

Rhian looked terrified.

"It will be great, Rhian," Garrick said, forestalling Rhian's denial. "You haven't been to the Berkshires before, have you?"

"Uh...no."

"It's beautiful," Savannah said while she checked her watch. "I have to run or I'll be late." She smiled at Garrick, who tried not to laugh at Rhian's mouth still hanging open. "Don't keep him up late, okay? He needs sleep."

Rhian shut his mouth at last. "Thanks, Mom."

She ignored him. "I love you."

"I love you, too," Garrick said. And he did. Sweet baby Jesus, did he ever.

She passed the iPad to Rhian and then bent to kiss his cheek. He not only tolerated it, he tilted his face up to her lips.

Garrick grinned. These two were becoming quite a pair.

He told his dick—again—that there was nothing to get excited about.

Savannah left and Rhian settled back against the pillows. "She's been amazing."

"She is amazing. I'm glad she's there for you."

"I think she's more here for you, but yeah. She's a godsend."

Garrick knew she wasn't doing this for him. She'd been honest with him about that. He didn't say as much to Rhian, though. It was up to Savannah to disclose her reasons, when and if she wished.

Instead, he focused on what he knew would be an issue for Rhian. "Please go to Connecticut with her." He hated the idea of Rhian spending the weekend alone.

Rhian sighed, resigned. "Do I have a choice? I can't imagine what torture she'd come up with if I tried not to."

Garrick chuckled. "You don't want to know. Now, tell me, how are you feeling?"

"Not bad, actually. A little sore. Nothing serious, though."

"Good."

Rhian bit his lip. "Listen, there is something I want to tell you," he began.

Garrick tried not to look nervous. "Yeah?"

"I told Savannah some stuff. Some things I want to tell you..."

Ten minutes later, Garrick sat silent, reeling.

"I'm not sure why I told Savannah first. Or at all."

Garrick did. "She has that effect on me, too. I'd tell her anything. Half the time I figure I might as well, since she can see right through me."

"Well, you *are* the worst liar I've ever met."

"Thanks," Garrick returned dryly. "But it's more than that."

"Yeah, I know. I hope you're not upset. I know I'm a little closed-mouthed sometimes."

Sometimes? "It's okay. Really." And it was.

Savannah and Rhian were a lot alike. They both had this thing Garrick could never quite find the right word for. A quiet strength and dignity that drew him to them both. It was hardly surprising Rhian responded to that and trusted her.

It gave Garrick hope. Rhian needed more people in his life. He had no family. He only had Garrick. And now Savannah.

At least until Garrick came to Boston and fucked it all up again.

So much for hope.

Garrick ran his fingers through his hair and tried to find a more lighthearted subject, only then remembering he had news of his own to share. "Shit! I almost forgot to tell you. The league called today, and the deal is finalized. The Ice Cats are officially ours."

Rhian whooped, congratulating him. It was one more step toward Boston.

The conversation settled into the usual talk of teams, the sport and the day-to-day stuff of their lives. They lingered on the call, neither wanting to hang up.

Rhian was remarkably relaxed, probably from exhaustion, his usual guardedness nowhere to be found. Garrick didn't take advantage, but he treasured what Rhian told him, the easy way he let little things about his day, his *feelings,* slip.

Oddly, he found himself wishing Savannah was there to see it, too.

Savannah stepped into the comforting warmth and buzz of Valentine's. Once her eyes to adjusted to the soft lighting, she found Grace sitting with her boyfriend Philip in an intimate, curved banquette in the back corner.

She kissed Grace hello and slid into the booth across from the couple, smiling at the picture they made curled up together. They appeared right at home, the staff calling them by name when they stopped by to take food and drink orders.

They caught up over drinks and appetizers. She and Grace always had things to tell each other, and Philip was easy to talk to. He radiated a quiet confidence and power that was extremely attractive—not that he needed any help in that department.

Savannah was still trying to work up the courage to broach the subject of Garrick and Rhian when dinner arrived, held aloft by their waiter, trailed by the restaurant's chef-owner, Mark Valentine.

He was reaching for her hand as soon as he arrived at the table. "Savannah! How wonderful to meet you."

Savannah shook his hand, surprised that he seemed to know who she was.

Mark stood by Grace while the food was placed before them, waiting until the waiter moved away before he leaned down and captured Grace's lips in a long kiss. He brushed his hand over her cheek as he lifted his mouth away.

Grace's smile as she stared up at Mark made Savannah's heart skip in her chest. Holy shit, that was *love*.

Her heart stopped altogether when Mark leaned over Grace and treated Philip to the exact same kiss.

And got the exact same smile from Philip when he was done.

Mark stepped away from the table. "I have to go back to the kitchen," he announced, winking at Savannah as if he hadn't just swept her legs out from under her.

She watched him walk away.

Grace smirked. "I was going to find a more subtle way of telling you, but Mark thought I was taking too long."

Philip's chuckle rolled across the table, tugging Savannah's lips up into a smile.

"What do you think?"

How very like Grace to ask a question like that, and with Philip sitting there, no less.

Savannah laughed. "I think it's totally irrelevant what I think. But for what it's worth, I'm happy for you. You should see your face when you look at them. How could I not be happy for you?"

Grace smiled. "Thanks."

"I can't believe you didn't tell me. I'm guessing this isn't new."

"No, it's been a while. I'm sorry I didn't say something sooner. It's not an easy thing to explain to people."

"Try to explain it to me," Savannah urged.

"We're in love. The three of us. In one relationship. And we live together. As a single couple. Sometimes called a triad. Or a thruple, though I loathe that term."

Savannah cocked her head and stared at Grace. "You're right. You're terrible at explaining it."

Philip threw his head back and roared with laughter.

Mark popped out of the kitchen and wove through the tables toward them. "Wow," he said with a big smile for Savannah, "are you responsible for making our serious lawyer cackle like that?"

"I was not cackling," Philip intoned, all serious lawyer again.

Mark rolled his eyes but kept his attention on Savannah. "I guess you took it well."

"I guess I did."

"Thanks. Grace worries. She doesn't believe people can get past anything that's not conventional."

"I get unconventional. My boyfriend is in love with another man," Savannah blurted, surprising everyone, including herself.

Grace and Philip stared at her, blinking. Mark looked at the kitchen door, his eyes narrowing as if doing calculations in his head. He nodded, then he sat next to Savannah, bumping her further into the booth with his hip and shoulder.

"Make yourself at home, Mark," Philip said dryly.

"I do own the place," Mark shot back before turning to Savannah. "I know we just met, but do you want to tell us about it? I've got at least ten minutes before my sous chef comes looking for me with a cleaver."

It was impossible not to like this man. "I don't mind telling you about it, if you don't mind listening to me whine about my problems."

Mark smiled. "So I wasn't imagining the tone of voice when you said your boyfriend has a boyfriend, huh? You're pissed?"

Savannah glanced at Grace and Philip, who had both leaned forward. The audience was daunting, but she'd come to talk about it and had *three* open-minded people to hit up for advice. She'd be an idiot not to take them up on it.

"I'm not pissed," she began, and, in as few words as possible, told them what was going on, including the fact that she was friends with Rhian. Then she laughed. "I came here tonight to ask Grace if she really thought someone could be in love with two people at once."

Three grins appeared around the table.

"Yeah, I can see that it is." She paused, trying to figure out how to articulate her other worry.

"And?" Grace prompted.

"And I guess I want it to work. Garrick having us both in his life. Long term. But I can't figure it out. The logistics *suck*. He's constantly pulled in two directions and one of us is always without him."

"Have you—" Mark didn't finish the thought, folding his lips and looking at Grace with a host of questions in his eyes.

Savannah bumped her shoulder against his. "Just ask me. I hardly think you're going to insult or offend me at this point."

"Have you thought about moving him in with you?"

"Who? Rhian?"

"Yes. Have him move in. The three of you can live together."

Savannah shook her head. "He's gay. He would have no interest in being with me."

"Be that as it may, it doesn't mean you can't live together. It seems like you get along well."

"And what? Garrick would switch beds every other night?"

Mark grimaced. "Okay, it's not a perfect plan, but at least he'd be home. You'd live with him all the time, not just some of it." The last statement ended up sounding more like a question as Mark's confidence in his plan started to fail. "Yeah, you're right. The logistics *do* suck."

Savannah snorted.

"Are you sure he's gay?" Mark asked hopefully.

"Pretty sure. And, to be honest, I'm not convinced everyone can love two people. I mean, clearly you three can, but maybe Rhian and I can't. I figure for Garrick, at least, it's partly that Rhian and I offer him two different things. Physically, at least."

Three blank stares met hers and she worried she'd offended them. Philip leaned over the table and put a hand over hers. "For what it's worth, that's not how it ends up working."

"Really?"

"Really. The variety in body parts can be..." he paused to glance at Mark with a little smile, "...a joy, but ultimately, what makes my heart beat harder, what really gets me, is Mark. The equipment is just a nice bonus."

The smoldering look Mark sent Philip took Savannah's breath away. Then Mark's eyes narrowed. "I'm going to remind you about that *nice bonus* crap later, so you know."

Philip sat back and cut into his steak, obviously unconcerned. "I look forward to it."

Mark grinned, his cheeks turning pink. Grace and Savannah laughed.

Savannah climbed the stairs to her apartment with a whole heck of a lot less speed and enthusiasm than usual. She was glad to be home, but her trip to Valentine's had given her a lot to think about.

She opened her front door and knew Rhian was asleep. The apartment was silent, the bedroom dark. She moved quietly through the rest of the rooms, shutting off lights, then ducked into the bedroom.

Rhian was curled up on her side of the bed. She'd expected

him to be beautiful when asleep. She was shocked at how damn young he looked.

She hadn't realized how tightly he carried himself, how much tension pulled at his face when he was awake. She barely checked the urge to run the back of her hand over his cheek.

Turning away, she threw off her clothes and searched her dresser for something to wear to bed. Rhian wasn't the only one who preferred to sleep naked. She eventually found an old camisole and a pair of loose cotton shorts, dragging them on before crawling onto the bed and staring down at the man hogging her pillows.

He didn't move, not even a flicker of an eyelid.

She wanted to sleep like that. Right now. And it wasn't going to happen on the couch.

She slipped under the covers and lay on her back. It was weird to be on this side of the bed. She could have slept here for the past months, but she'd always known where Garrick would end up.

She wished now that she hadn't washed Garrick's pillowcase after his visit. She would have liked a hint of him to help calm her jumbled thoughts.

She looked at Rhian. He was as caught up in this frustrating and confusing situation as she was. Impacted in all the same ways. That affinity was increasingly hard to ignore.

Rolling toward him, she took comfort from his solid presence, the soothing sound of his deep, even breathing. She snuggled into the bed and allowed herself the pleasure of inhaling his scent.

Her mind quieted and she slept.

Chapter Fourteen

Rhian woke with Savannah plastered to his back and one of the most agonizing erections of his life.

Savannah was curled around him exactly like Garrick loved to do. She wasn't nearly as tall or large as Garrick—or Rhian, for that matter—so instead of enveloping him, she burrowed into his back. Her lips were pressed to the nape of his neck, her knees tucked under his thighs, and her delicate hand tickled the fine hairs on his belly.

His dick was doing its level best to stretch up and nestle into her palm.

The good news was he was hard and it only hurt a bit more than the normal raging-morning-wood discomfort. The bad news was that if he shifted so much as an inch, if Savannah's hand wriggled south at all, she'd probably start dreaming she was driving a stick shift.

And if she woke up? Well, she might be disabused of the notion that he was gay.

There was only one way out of this—all or nothing. With a prayer that she would wake too slowly to notice the steel bar in his shorts, Rhian rolled out of bed, onto his feet, and out the bedroom door before Savannah mumbled, "good morning."

"Good morning," he called back as he shut the bathroom door. Leaning his head against the doorjamb, he let the cool air against his skin do its job.

I have to tell her I'm bi. Today.

He was in the shower for a good four minutes before he turned on the hot tap.

Three hours later, Rhian watched the Berkshire mountains slide past the car window. How the hell had he ended up here? The scenery was amazing. The bright greens of the forest, the quaint little shops and inns as they drove south from Massachusetts into the Northwest corner of Connecticut. Rhian thought he ought to be glad for the chance to see a place like this.

It turned out, though, he was something of a city slicker. Hockey had taken him to a lot of backwater towns, but there'd been a bus, a team, coaches, arenas and a hotel. As Savannah's car rolled over hills and around the crazy turns—did these people have something against driving in a straight line?—Rhian felt like he'd never been so far off the map.

It wasn't strictly about the geography either. He was about to meet the Morrison family. Six brothers, one sister, one mom, one dad. The list of her brothers' accomplishments was long and daunting. Two NHL players, one of whom was an Olympic silver medalist, a doctor, a sculptor, a PhD philosophy professor, and a college student. Other than the two NHL players, he didn't have a damn thing in common with a single member of this jumbo-sized Morrison clan. Unless, of course, he counted the fact he and Savannah shared a boyfriend. That was sure to endear him to everyone.

He wedged his elbow against the car door and dropped his forehead into his hand. He was in way over his head, and there was no going back. He'd never find a bus station, let alone an airport, out here in the boonies. He was officially Savannah's captive.

"You'll be fine," she said again, casting him a worried look. He wished she'd keep her eyes on the road.

"Uh huh," he returned, not believing a word of it.

"Everyone is really nice. You'll see."

He tried to smile. His strategy would be the same one he'd employed in foster care. Be extremely polite and stay out the way of the people who belonged there. "Is anyone else bringing a friend?"

"Uh..." Savannah bit her lip. "No. We don't usually bring anyone home for this unless they're, you know, actually or all-but married to one of us."

Rhian bit back a sigh. She'd been planning to bring Garrick. "How many of your brothers are married?"

"Just one. Kieran. He and Chance got hitched a couple years ago, but Chance started coming round a few years before that."

"You have a sister-in-law named Chance?"

Savannah pulled up to a stop sign and gave him an arch stare. "I have a brother-in-law named Chance, you dork. Kieran is gay."

"Oh. Sorry. That was a stupid assumption."

"Sure was, especially coming from you," she admonished.

Rhian almost blurted out that he wasn't gay, desperate to confess the truth before the hole he was digging got any deeper, but he didn't want it to sound like he was making an excuse for saying something idiotic. He shouldn't have assumed Kieran was straight, regardless of whether or not he himself was gay.

He was still trying to figure out when exactly he *was* going to set Savannah straight when she drove past a beautiful village with a huge inn and a handful of shops, then put on her blinker and turned down an even windier, narrower street.

A half mile later, they parked behind a line of cars in a long driveway.

"We're here!" Savannah declared needlessly.

He stared at the white picket fence. *Figures.*

Dragging his ass from the car, he followed her up the path to the wide front porch. She hadn't even knocked before the door was thrown open and an attractive older couple rushed out.

"Mom! Dad!"

Savannah hugged her mother and her father embraced them both.

Rhian's legs twitched with the desire to run down the driveway and to the street. There had to be a bus station somewhere.

110

Savannah's mom pulled away and they all turned to him. Rhian plastered a smile on his face.

"Mom, Dad, this is my friend, Rhian Savage."

Mr. Morrison thrust out his hand. "Hello. Welcome to our home."

Rhian shook Mr. Morrison's hand, surprised by the sheer force of the older man's grip. Not rude, but unexpected for a man his age. Mr. Morrison radiated good health and kindness.

"You did great this season, son. It's a pleasure to meet you. The B's were embarrassing us until you came along."

Rhian blinked at the hint of a Scottish accent and Mr. Morrison's enormous smile. "Thank you, sir."

"Call me Bruce. This is my wife, Mary," he said, putting a hand on her back.

She smiled, and Rhian was looking at a silver-haired version of Savannah. "Ma'am. It's a pleasure to meet you. Thank you for having me to your home."

"Oh, good lord," Mary said with a delighted laugh. "Don't call me ma'am. It's Mary. Or Mom. You have to be the politest young man we've had here in a long time. And I *am* counting my own children in that." The last sentence was called over her shoulder to anyone listening through the door.

Rhian smiled. How could he not? She was as sassy and beautiful as her daughter. "Thank you, Mary."

"Oh, you are just *adorable*. It's so nice to meet you." She had him in a hug before he knew what hit him.

Rhian blinked, taken aback. God help him, the Morrisons were like Garrick and Savannah. She'd suggested he could call her *Mom*, for God's sake. He might as well have been vacationing on Mars.

Savannah put a hand on his arm. "Uh, Mom ..."

Rhian heard Savannah's concern and for reasons he wasn't going to spend a lot of time dwelling on, he embraced the beautiful woman in his arms. Mary's hold tightened, her hand rubbing between his shoulder blades as if she sensed he needed comfort.

Which he didn't.

She stepped back and smiled up at him, her green gaze warm, her hands lingering on his shoulders. She had the same clear-eyed look as Savannah.

But while Savannah saw more than she should, Rhian was certain her mother saw every damn thing.

Savannah sat with her mom at the old, scarred kitchen table, tucked in a corner with their plates and mugs of tea. It was always a comfort to retreat to this house, this room in particular. Savannah had grown up here. At this table. She wished she'd had more time to come home since. She always felt at peace here. Safe.

Not that the house was peaceful right now. The air rang with howls of victory and defeat from the family room, where the guys were watching the playoffs. Savannah fought the urge to get up and check on Rhian.

Rhian was a professional hockey player. He'd watched big games from the bench. Even her family couldn't replicate that kind of noise.

She smiled into her tea when her mom popped up and peeked through the door.

Her mother smiled reassuringly when she came back. "He's fine."

"I know."

"You do? Because I was beginning to worry that he was going to spend the entire weekend doing that deer-caught-in-the-headlights thing."

Savannah laughed, the sound drowned out by Callum's roar of displeasure.

"Goddamn it, Evanson, you always screw that up!"

Callum would know. They'd been on the US Team together.

Her mother rolled her eyes. "You'd think he'd stop being

surprised."

"He likes being surprised. It gives him something to shout about, since he's not in the playoffs."

Callum was a goalie for the Colorado Avalanche. At thirty-four, he was a veteran of the league. He was also, along with their brother Duncan, and Garrick, one of the partner-owners of the Ice Cats.

Savannah hoped Callum would focus on his new role. Enjoy it. The entire family did. They all wondered when he would give up the NHL and start having a *life*. He claimed he wouldn't retire while he was still playing at the top of the league.

She smiled at her mother when Rhian's voice joined the barrage. "Rhian will be okay. It's just going to take him a while to get used to us, I think."

Her mother cocked her head. "So he'll be back? I thought you and Garrick were serious."

"What? We are. No...oh, no. Rhian and I are just friends."

"Okay..." Her mother paused. "And not that he's not welcome, but how did he end up with us for the weekend?"

Savannah glanced at the doorway to make sure no one was listening before speaking softly to her mom. "Rhian found a lump, and he's waiting for the results. The biopsy was yesterday. I couldn't bring myself to leave him alone in Boston for the weekend."

"Of course you couldn't," her mom agreed, casting a long, worried glance at the family room door. "Does he have family? Do they know?"

Savannah shook her head. "No, he has no one."

"At all?"

"Mom, the story would break your heart." It sure as hell had put a dent in hers.

Her mom laid her hand over Savannah's on the table. "Well, that explains why you're so tender with him. I've never seen you so attuned to someone."

Savannah sat back. Was that true?

"Are you sure Garrick doesn't mind?" her mom asked carefully.

Savannah laughed. She could barely imagine what her mother would say if she knew the whole story.

"No, Mom. Garrick is cool. And, for what it's worth, Rhian is gay." She wouldn't normally air other people's business, but she didn't want her mother sticking Rhian in one of the boys' rooms, either. She wanted to keep him close.

She pictured him sleeping in one of her matching white canopy twin beds and grinned. The decor wasn't as pink and frilly as it had once been, but he would definitely stand out in her girly room.

Her mom cocked her head. "He's gay? Really?"

"Why are you surprised?" Her parents didn't have any issue with anyone being gay. Ever. They had two gay sons—three if you counted Chance, who they all thought of as one of their own—and hadn't batted an eye over it. In fact, it drove them crazy that one of their sons insisted on living at the very back of his closely guarded closet.

"No reason," her mother said with a shrug. "I just got a different impression."

"You did? How?"

"Oh, I don't know. He just looks at you like...well, nevermind." Her mother waved it away. "The important thing is that he's here, and we'll help you take care of him."

"Thanks." She squeezed her mom's hand and pretended not to notice her continued close scrutiny. A tactical retreat was definitely in order. She stood. "I'm going to go watch the game with the guys."

Her mother's eyebrows rose higher and she opened her mouth.

Savannah fled the kitchen before her mother could say another word.

Chapter Fifteen

Rhian watched, wide-eyed, as mountains of breakfast food disappeared before his very eyes. Somehow eleven people— most of whom were tall, broad-shouldered men— enjoyed a lively meal around a kitchen table designed to seat eight.

He was smashed between two of the Morrison brothers, having finally convinced Savannah that she didn't have to hover like a mother hen. She was probably worried about his reaction to the fact that everything the Morrisons did together was loud and rambunctious. It *was* a little overwhelming, and he'd been quieter than usual since arriving while he tried to acclimate to the insanity.

A piece of wheat toast flew past his nose and beaned Angus in the side of the head.

Rhian gave up. He would never get used to this. But he did, surprisingly, enjoy it. The Morrisons were pretty hard to resist.

Callum sat on his right, powering through a pile of scrambled eggs and bacon. It was weird to witness his long-time hero doing something so utterly mundane. Rhian had been dangerously close to having a giddy fan-boy moment of stupidity when Callum introduced himself. He was still shocked that Callum knew who he was, had watched him play. Had sat with him while they ate dinner and talked like they were friends. They *were* friends, or fast on the way to becoming so.

Rhian was absurdly grateful to Garrick for showing him he could have friendships. A year ago he would have kept his distance. For a lot of reasons, he still should, but Callum Fucking Morrison was asking about his career. Giving him advice. Teasing him about the fight he'd started. How the hell could he refuse that?

On his other side sat Lachlan, the brother who appeared to be Callum's opposite. Where Callum was loud and brash, bordering on antagonistic, Lachlan was quiet and affable. He still argued and bantered—he was a Morrison, after all—but sometimes he stood back and watched the melee with an affectionate smile.

Rhian had caught Lachlan studying him a couple times, a thoughtful expression on his face—particularly when Savannah was nearby. That made Rhian nervous, but whenever he spoke with Lachlan, he felt at ease, as if he'd known the man for years, not hours. It was disarming. He'd never met anyone as smart or educated as Lachlan. It should have made him hard to talk to, but the opposite was true.

Squashed between these two men, Rhian focused on being polite and not eating as if someone was about to steal the food off his plate. This wasn't like the foster houses, where there had been only so much to go around and often it hadn't been enough for the athletic kid who skated every second he could. This morning there was sufficient food on the table to feed an army, and he had little doubt that if they ran out, Mary, Chance, and Angus—the team responsible for this morning's feast— would simply make more.

He glanced around the table and caught more than one brother eying him speculatively. He smiled at each of them and went back to his breakfast. The looks had started last night when he'd gone to sleep in Savannah's room. Rhian couldn't imagine what they thought would happen on one of those silly princess beds, but it sure as hell hadn't been more than sleeping.

No one would ever know that he'd dreamed of doing all kinds of freaky things beneath eyelet-lace canopies.

It had made for a long night, and he was tired, but he still was in much better condition than he'd been yesterday or the day before. The effects of the biopsy were definitely wearing off.

Which was good. He needed his strength. Because God help him, if Savannah paraded around in her underpants in front of him one more time, he was going to have heart failure.

Smiling around his bite of toast, he caught Savannah's

curious gaze and winked. Callum shifted, leaning into him, glaring at Rhian with narrow eyes and more than a hint of warning.

Savannah rolled her eyes and Rhian smirked. These guys didn't mess around. It was a miracle Savannah dated at all, let alone had the guts to bring a man home. And Rhian was just a friend. Garrick, as the boyfriend, was going to be put through the wringer.

The idea made Rhian downright gleeful.

Maybe if he was feeling generous someday, he'd warn Garrick to reserve a room at the inn down the street. Kieran and Chance had stayed there last night, forsaking the bunk beds in Kieran and Duncan's old room. The rest of the brothers had mocked them for bailing out, but Chance was unapologetic. He'd told them, in no uncertain terms, that he was too old to crawl into a top bunk and his husband's shoulders were too damn broad to share a twin bed.

None of the brothers seemed the least bit bothered by Kieran being gay or Chance joking about their sleeping arrangements. Indeed, their suggestions for workable sleeping positions had been nothing short of graphic—and often physically impossible. It was a good thing neither parent had been in the room at the time. Mary and Bruce spent lot of time and energy affectionately reminding this rowdy crew to behave themselves.

He scraped every trace of food from his plate with his last corner of toast.

Mary smiled at him. "Would you like more?"

"Yes, please. This is all wonderful. The eggs are terrific."

"*Oh, here she goes,*" groaned someone down the table.

"What a nice boy you are, Rhian Savage." Mary jumped from her seat and shot dirty looks at her children. "Did you hear that, kids? He complemented my cooking. He was polite and charming. Can you *imagine?*"

Seven pairs of eyes rolled.

Angus muttered, loudly, "I made the damn eggs. She made the *toast*."

Rhian's lips twitched.

"I'll tell you what, Bruce." Mary raised her voice above the growing commentary. "I'd like to snap this one right up and keep him for myself. You're lucky he plays for the other team."

Kieran sat up and beamed at Rhian. "Go team!"

Rhian gurgled around his orange juice.

"Mom!" Savannah shot Rhian a horrified look. "Oh my god, I'm so sorry."

Everyone stared at him with varying degrees of surprise and amusement. Rhian's face heated.

He'd been outed, which was bad, really bad, but now he was also effectively lying to the entire family.

Shit. Shit. Shit.

"Ummm...not really."

Savannah blinked. "What?"

"Well, yes..." He hesitated, not sure how to say this in front of her *mother*. "For that team. But also...you know, for the other." He pointed vaguely as if the teams in question were sitting on either side of him, his face hotter with every word.

Mary's hand patted his shoulder. "You mean you're bi, dear."

Kieran's shoulders convulsed and milk shot out his nose.

Duncan dropped his fork onto his plate with a clatter. *"Ma!"*

"What?" Mary asked innocently. "That's what it's called."

Rhian was now, without a doubt, beet-fucking-red.

Not that anyone would notice. Most of the brothers had their heads in their hands or down on the table, having dissolved into hysterics. Kieran coughed, repeatedly, trying to clear his sinus cavity while his husband pounded on his back and roared with laughter.

Savannah's father slammed his fist on the table so hard

their dishes jumped. "Enough! You're embarrassing our guest." Rhian could tell he was trying to look stern, but it was obvious how hard he fought not to laugh.

Rhian tried to smile gratefully, but it ended up more like a wince and a grimace. Swallowing, he smiled weakly at Savannah. "I'm sorry. I didn't realize you thought that until...well, until recently. I thought you knew. I mean, hell, I asked you out once, or did you forget?"

She didn't look as pissed off. That had to be some kind of miracle.

"Of course I remember, but when I heard about you and Gahhhh..." She barely stopped herself in time. She swallowed. "When I found out you were gay, I figured you were just looking for me to be your beard."

Rhian shook his head. "I'll ask you all to keep this to yourselves," he said, raising his voice enough to be heard over the lingering chuckles. Everyone nodded immediately. "But it's cool. I wouldn't fabricate some elaborate lie just to fool people."

In the span of one breath, everyone went dead silent.

Savannah's eyes bulged, and Rhian was pretty sure she mouthed *oh shit.* Her gaze flickered between him and Callum. As did everyone else's. Rhian's stomach plummeted to his feet.

What have I done?

Thirty seconds too late, he pictured countless photographs of Callum and celebrity model Michaela Price. They'd been dating for years, and the media speculated constantly on when they would marry.

But she wasn't here. And Callum hadn't mentioned her once.

Rhian tried to stand. Lachlan's hand clamped on his arm and kept him where he was.

God, he was an idiot. Why didn't he keep his mouth *shut*? He didn't know how to be with these people. Now he'd insulted one of them. A man he'd admired for years and whose kindness he'd cherished.

Fuck. Fuck. Fuck. Why wouldn't Lachlan let him leave?

The excruciating silence stretched.

Savannah bit her lip and looked at him with such pity, he wished the floor would open up and swallow him whole. Then she narrowed her eyes. "I cannot *believe* you let me walk around in my underwear in front of you!"

As distractions went, she'd picked a winner. The room exploded, half the men leaping to their feet, everyone shouting their outrage. Brothers, father, brother-in-law all skewered him with death-ray glares.

Rhian had never in his life been so fucking happy to be thrown to the wolves.

He just wished Callum would do something other than sit in his chair, silent.

Rhian laughed when Bruce leaped to his defense only when someone threatened parts of Rhian's body Bruce considered necessary to play hockey. The list of sacred parts was a lot shorter than Rhian liked. There was one in particular that seemed to be under constant threat that he'd really like to keep.

God help the man who ever truly hurt Savannah. Her family would squash that son of a bitch like a bug.

With my help.

But then again, Savannah could take care of herself. She grinned at him, one eyebrow lifted, while her brothers devolved into ever-more creative insults and threats.

Rhian would apologize to her again, in private. In the meantime, she'd had her revenge.

He smiled at her. She winked back.

His stupid heart did a flip.

Chapter Sixteen

After helping clear up breakfast, Savannah and Rhian took a short jog around town. Savannah had needed to get out of the house, particularly after that breakfast. She kept their route to three miles in deference to his healing body. He swore he no longer felt any effects, but she wasn't taking any chances.

As they ran out of the village and into a quieter neighborhood, he apologized for misleading her about his sexuality. She was glad he couldn't see her face. She didn't need him to know how much turmoil his revelation had caused her. She assured him she wasn't angry and did some apologizing of her own. No one in the family talked about Callum's choices, or of his sexuality, by Callum's request. She wished now she'd broken that rule.

They returned to the house and Rhian jumped in the shower. She paced her room, straightening things that didn't need straightening, and waited for her turn in the bathroom. She'd just brushed out her hair when Rhian appeared in her mirror, a towel slung low across his hips.

She tried not to stare at all that bare, damp skin. Really. But then she caught him peeking beneath the knotted cotton at his waist.

She smiled uncertainly. "Everything okay under there?"

Red spots appeared on his cheeks. "Um, yeah. Just a rather disconcerting bruise."

She considered asking if he wanted her to take a look. *Bad idea, Savannah.* Not because she didn't want to. Nooo, that wasn't the issue at all.

"Do you want to call the doctor?" she asked.

"No. I'm okay. They told me it would happen. It's just..."

"Weird?"

One side of his mouth curled up. "Yeah."

Nodding, she spared him any further embarrassment and ducked into the bathroom.

Standing under the cool spray, she closed her eyes and tried to still her mind. Instead, her traitorous brain conjured the image of Rhian standing in her girly room wearing only a towel. It was amazing the cold water didn't sizzle when it hit her skin.

What was the matter with her? She'd seen him in less on her table in the trainer's office. She examined barely dressed men all the damn time. It was her damn job.

But this was Rhian.

And he was bi.

Which, she scolded herself soundly, *changes nothing.*

She lingered in the shower, trying to get her head screwed on straight. Rhian would be all right with her family for a while without her. It was hard not to hover when he could look so lost in all the noise and activity.

Then she recalled the fiasco at breakfast this morning. She shut off the shower, bolted for her room, and threw on some clothes.

She found Rhian in the corner of the kitchen with Callum and Duncan. She used the excuse of helping her mom put away groceries and get things organized for lunch so she could listen to her brothers give Rhian a frank run down of how it really worked in the NHL. They didn't spare him anything, telling him everything they'd wished someone had told them. She worried they'd scare him with tales of politics and crazy fans, but he sat and listened carefully. Always so serious when it came to hockey.

Eventually, Duncan wandered off and Rhian and Callum were left alone. She was prepared to plunk her butt down and make sure her stubborn and often abrasive brother didn't make Rhian feel any worse than he already did. Rhian shook his head gently when she caught his eye. She hesitated, then turned away to give them privacy. She barely overheard Rhian's murmured apology. Callum's admission that the problem was his, not Rhian's, broke her heart.

Rhian's sincere offer to help Callum any way he could, without a hint of judgment or criticism, made her want to kiss him.

Which changes nothing.

She threw herself into organizing the pantry. Her mother came into the kitchen and watched her, eyebrows raised. Savannah ignored her. She could organize the damn pantry if she wanted to.

Callum excused himself and Kieran and Chance wandered in a few minutes later. They sat with Rhian and offered to help him find a place to live in Boston when he got his contract from the Bruins. She loved their confidence that Rhian would be staying and was grateful for their suggestions, even if the idea of Rhian getting his own apartment irked her. She wanted to blame the potentially shitty logistics for her annoyance, but then she pictured Grace's happy smile the other night.

Which changes nothing!

She started cleaning the oven. Her mother leaned one hip against the counter, folded her arms across her chest and stared at her like she had two heads.

Next up was Murdoch—Doc to everyone but their mother. He slapped a hand on Rhian's back and asked if he wanted to talk in their father's office.

Rhian looked at her. "Do you want to come with us?"

It didn't matter if she did or didn't. He obviously wanted her to, and that made her happy, for some damn reason.

Leaving the oven cleaner than it had been in twenty years, Savannah peeled off her rubber gloves and held out a hand to Rhian. He took it and she led the way down the hall.

Rhian took the big chair her father liked to read in and she perched on the arm, holding Rhian's hand while Doc answered every single question Rhian had about testicular lumps and cancers. Savannah learned all she could, only leaving when her father called her name. A few minutes later, Doc slipped out of the office without Rhian and she went to check on him.

Her heart hurt at his feeble attempt at a smile.

"You okay?"

He rubbed a hand over his face and shook his head. She hesitated, not sure what he needed, then went with her gut and climbed onto his lap, curling her arms around his neck. He went rigid for all of three seconds, then wrapped his arms around her and buried his face against her neck.

They stayed like that for a very long time. They didn't talk. There was nothing that needed to be said. Or done, other than to hold him. Her mind settled and, for the first time since breakfast, she could *think*. Garrick was a lot of things, all of them wonderful because they made him who he was, but he didn't often sit still. She smiled fondly thinking of him. Hoped Rhian could take similar comfort from knowing he was out there with all that crazy love.

Rhian was a different man than Garrick, but in a good way. She discovered she liked to be held like this. Liked holding him. In Rhian's solid presence, there was a peaceful calm to be found. Her brain wasn't bouncing between countless anxieties. She could focus.

She kissed the top of his head and his arms squeezed harder.

Changes. Nothing.

By the time they emerged from the office, Rhian was pale but steady. She almost suggested he take a nap, but her mother swooped in and commandeered him into helping her make lunch. His protestations that he didn't know how to cook were brushed aside. Before he knew what hit him, he was chopping the ingredients for potato salad, rallying under her mom's attention.

Ryan appeared quite taken with her mom, his usual reserve replaced by a quick smile. It tickled Savannah even as it made her sad. He should have had a mom like hers.

They ate lunch and Savannah helped her mother clean up while everyone else, including Rhian, wandered off to do various chores or goof off. When finished, she went to stand in the doorway to the family room and watch her brothers play Wii. They were boxing and, as usual, getting rowdier by the second. All hockey-themed games had been banished from the house years ago, after Angus had to get twelve stitches in his forehead.

As if on cue—Angus was never one to miss a Wii match—her baby brother came in from the front porch with Rhian in his wake. Angus had been half-joking during lunch when he'd asked if anyone wanted to help him chop firewood. Rhian had surprised everyone by saying yes.

He'd apparently never done it before, so he agreed to help if Angus taught him how. Based on their grins, the lesson had been a success.

Rhian touched the small of her back on their way past her into the family room. She smiled to cover up her shiver.

Angus asked to play the Wii winner and a debate sprang up between him and Kieran, who had been waiting. Rhian went to the couch and sat next to Lachlan, watching the escalating argument warily. He was getting used to them, Savannah thought with a smile, but he wasn't there yet.

Lachlan distracted Rhian from the idiots bickering in the middle of the room, until Kieran's loud shout bounced off the walls. In the span of two seconds, heated debate devolved into a wrestling match on the floor, centered around Angus and Kieran's battle for one of the four remotes, with the other four players all refusing to relinquish.

Savannah laughed at their typical antics. Until she saw Rhian. He recoiled, his eyes wide as he stared at the chaos at his feet. He was sheet-white.

Lachlan put a hand on Rhian's shoulder. "It's okay, they're just messing around."

Rhian didn't respond, just continued to stare in horror.

Lachlan stood and waded into the knot of flailing arms and legs. With a few yanks and some quiet whispers, her idiot brothers—and one idiot brother-in-law—stopped horsing around and returned to the game peacefully. Savannah smirked at her dad. He hadn't even put down his newspaper when the fight had rolled right over his feet.

Lachlan returned to the couch and Rhian, who still looked horrified. And confused.

How did he not know that boys wrestled for their video game remotes? Fought for fun? Even she, who was generally exempt from the roughhousing, jumped in sometimes. Left a few bruises, too.

But then, Rhian had no idea what it was like to have a family. To have brothers who played rough and wrestled for the pure joy of it. He had never even mentioned a close friend, let alone someone close enough to tussle with him over something stupid and still fight to the death to protect his back.

He had no one.

And now he'd found this goddamn lump. Alone, living in a new city, with no contract to tell him where he was going next. She'd cluelessly wondered why he didn't put down roots. She doubted he knew how. And why would he? He was in complete and utter limbo.

How had she never realized how lonely he must be?

She wished like hell he'd told her, but it wasn't his style. She'd watched him play hockey, and now she understood that was precisely how he lived his life. He didn't complain, he worked harder. He didn't blame others, he improved himself. He didn't talk about his feelings, he just kept moving forward.

A knot of something tight and hot lodged in her chest.

She'd blithely forced him into a situation with which he had no experience, into the heart of her family. And they'd already circled the wagons to offer him their support, their protection. She could not, for one moment, regret bringing him here, but she hated that she'd been so *blind*.

Crossing to the couch, she curled up next to Rhian and laced her fingers through his. He sent her a quick smile.

Lachlan's eyes dropped to their clasped hands but she

didn't let go. She wanted Rhian's thumb to keep rubbing over hers. It gave her strength. Hope. And she needed it, because god help her, she was falling in love with Rhian Savage.

And that changes...everything.

Chapter Seventeen

As usual, the Morrison kitchen was in chaos. Rhian tried to find a space as the entire family pulled on hats and gloves and shrugged into their jackets. Everyone, including Rhian, had already changed into their hockey pants and socks. Bags full of pads and skates were piled high on the floor. Sticks leaned against the walls and doors. It was like an undersized locker room holding an oversized team.

Rhian anchored himself against a wall, unsure of what he was supposed to do. It was times like these that he wanted to drag Savannah back into her father's office and haul her onto his lap. He hadn't felt that kind of peace since the last time Garrick had laid down on top of him.

He honestly didn't know what to do with that realization, so he focused on the insanity that was the Morrison family instead.

He'd brought his hockey gear from Boston, per Savannah's instructions. He'd wondered why they were lugging it across the state, but he was so used to lugging it *everywhere* that he hadn't questioned it.

It wasn't until dinner tonight that they'd all begun talking about the hockey game, the energy building as they recounted past victories and defeats. It seemed they *all* played. Together.

He blinked when Mary came into the room wearing ref's stripes, her skates over her shoulder.

Savannah leaned against the wall next to him and fixed a twisted sock, then retied her hockey pants like she'd done it a thousand times before. Rhian's heart clenched in his chest. Holy shit, she was fucking adorable.

His surprise must have shown because Callum cuffed him on the shoulder, laughing. "She's been playing longer than you, my friend. Watch out for her."

She grinned.

"You have?" Rhian said.

Everyone turned to look at them.

Savannah's cheeks warmed to pink. "Yeah, I play."

"Someone write this date down!" Kieran hooted with laughter. "*Savannah* is being modest."

Chance threw an arm around his husband's shoulders. "One of our first dates was to watch her lead Harvard to the Women's Division One championship. Captain and MVP, if memory serves."

Savannah smiled at her brother-in-law. "Your memory does serve. I remember meeting you and thinking I'd have to beat my teammates off with my stick to get the two of you out of the arena in one piece."

Chance grinned, totally unabashed.

"Wow," Rhian murmured. "Look who has secrets."

Savannah's eyes lit with amusement. "I don't advertise it to the team because I don't care to hear their opinions on women's hockey. I've heard enough of that crap to last me a lifetime." There was a hint of warning in her voice, and it wasn't just for him, judging by the hairy eyeball she cast around the room.

Rhian grinned. "You mean, like how it's not a real sport because you actually have to skate and shoot and not rely on violence to get it done?"

She'd opened her mouth to tell him to shut up, he was sure, but ended up smiling at him. "Exactly."

Rhian bumped his shoulder against hers, trying to wrap his head around the curl of pleasure in his gut her smile brought. He was distracted from his growing alarm when she threw two jerseys into her bag. Looking around, he saw everyone had two jerseys, either in hand or in their bags. One green, one white.

Savannah's mom came to them, holding out a pair of jerseys. At his hesitation, she smiled encouragingly. "You don't have to play."

And miss a chance to play with Callum and Duncan

Morrison? Not to mention Savannah? Not a chance.

"I want to," he assured her.

"Great. Here." She handed him the jerseys. "I hope you don't mind."

He had no idea why he would. He held one up and saw the emblem on the front appeared to be some kind of belt fashioned into a circle, with waves and a castle and a hand holding a dagger, of all things, in the middle. Rhian had no idea what the hell he was looking at, but at the top arch it read MORRISON.

They had their own team jerseys.

"That's the Morrison crest. It's a Scottish thing," Savannah explained with a fond smile at her father.

Rhian flipped the jersey over and saw the name across the back.

LeBlanc.

The blast of jealousy would have staggered him had he not been holding up the wall. The Morrisons had never met Garrick but they accepted him as one of their own because it was what Savannah wanted.

When had that become something Rhian wanted, too?

Determined to ignore that terrible thought, he turned to Savannah. "What's with the two jerseys?"

"We play each other, usually four on four, though dad's all excited because with you here, we can try five on five. Anyway, you have home and away jerseys depending on what team you get picked for."

That made sense. "Which team needs a defenseman?"

She grinned mischievously. "My dad thinks if you play the same position for too long, you lose your edge and appreciation for the whole team."

Rhian had no idea why this was relevant. "Okay."

"So, we pick teams from a hat. Home or away. Then we pick positions."

Rhian blinked, certain he'd heard her wrong. "What?"

"We pick positions. You can end up anywhere. Including goalie."

Rhian's mouth dropped open. "I haven't tended a goal since I was ten!"

Several of her brothers laughed.

"Welcome to the Morrison hockey tradition," Savannah said brightly, bumping their shoulders again before heading out the back door.

Rhian followed the long line of Morrisons as they tromped along a path through the woods, equipment bags in tow. He was stunned when they popped out into the parking lot of a large arena.

"Where are we?" he asked no one in particular.

Savannah's mom came to walk beside him. "Berkshire Academy."

Rhian didn't know shit about private schools, but even he'd heard of this one.

"Bruce is the athletic director and hockey coach here. One of the perks of the job is he can use the ice when it's available, like tonight."

"That's fantastic."

"Yes, it is."

She threaded her hand around his elbow and they walked together into the arena. He liked having her on his arm. He liked her. Did her boys have any idea how fucking lucky they were to have a mom like this? She loved her kids. All of them. Equally and without condition.

What would that be like?

They gathered in a locker room and drew teams. Rhian ended up in a forward position on the green team. He took a moment to thank the stars he hadn't picked goalie.

He pulled Garrick's jersey over his pads. It was too long, but it fit. Barely. He'd be sure to give Garrick shit about how tight it was in the shoulders.

As each player left the locker room, they kissed Mary's cheek, including Chance. *What the hell*, Rhian thought, before he did it too.

She patted his cheek and grinned. "Such a nice boy."

He grinned back.

Stepping onto the rink, he went automatically into his usual pre-game routine, starting with stretching out on the ice next to Savannah. It was hard not to notice just how flexible she was. *Wow*. Her dad dumped a bag of pucks and they took shots at the goals, warming up their goalies and their arms, just like any night at the Boston Garden or any other hockey arena in the world. The familiarity was soothing. Rhian was at his calmest right before a game.

Tonight, the best part was watching Savannah skate. She floated on the ice, in total command of her body, shifting forward and back effortlessly, speeding into the corners with confidence about her position and timing, never crashing into anything or anyone unless she wanted to. She was fantastic.

And why the hell was that so fucking sexy?

He tore his eyes away from Savannah and looked around. There was a shitload of talent on the ice. This wasn't going to be some easy pick-up game. His first face-off was against Callum, of all people. Mary skated up to begin the game, puck in hand, and Rhian dropped into his game brain.

From there, it was pure heaven. There was no checking. No threat of a fight. And no second or third line to back them up. But there was something he hadn't heard on the ice in a damn long time. *Laughter*. Better yet, it came with genuine friendship. An arm slung around his shoulders. A stern lecture from the referee for "accidentally" hooking her son's legs right out from under him. Her eyes dancing with amusement at his attempt to appear contrite. He couldn't remember the last time he'd skated as long or hard, or enjoyed it more.

He was probably the only NHL player who had just figured out he loved to play hockey.

Chapter Eighteen

Sunday morning came early. Savannah stifled a groan as she rolled out of bed, her body stiff from the long, grueling game the night before. She was in excellent shape—what the hell kind of trainer would she be if she wasn't?—but it had been a while since she'd played so much, so hard, and her body wasn't entirely amused.

She laughed when Rhian stopped packing to stretch his back. "Wishing we had enough Morrisons to form a second line so we had some time on the bench?"

He smiled at her as he thrust the last of his clothes back into his bag. "I think there are plenty enough Morrisons as it is," he teased. "But yeah, I'm feeling it today. I can't believe we played a full sixty minutes."

"We always do."

They lugged their bags downstairs and Rhian ran them out to the car while she helped her brothers get organized.

She had just kissed Doc goodbye when Callum caught her hand. "I'm going back to Denver just long enough to pack up some shit, then I'm headed to Moncton."

She spun to look at him. "Really? That's great."

"Yeah, I'll help out with the draft, see what I can do with the construction."

"Thank you." Relief coursed through her. "Garrick is running himself ragged."

"I'll consider myself warned, since I'm booting his ass out of Moncton as soon as I get there."

"*What?*" Savannah grabbed her brother's arm. "What's wrong?"

"With the team? Nothing. But you need Garrick in Boston." He glanced meaningfully over her shoulder as the door opened. She knew without turning around that Rhian had reentered the

133

house.

She sighed. "Yeah, I really fucking do."

Callum nodded toward Rhian, who had paused to chat with Seamus by the front door. "You know what you're getting into with all this?" he asked quietly.

Panic surged through Savannah. He couldn't know anything. No one did. Not even Garrick.

"I don't know what you're talking about. I'm not getting into anything."

Callum smirked. "Uh-huh. Keep believing it, sis."

She bit back another response, knowing she would only dig herself a deeper hole.

"You be careful," Callum said, serious now. "I'd hate to have to beat Rhian or Garrick up. I'm growing pretty fond of both of them."

You and me both.

What the hell was she going to do? The idea of passing Garrick back and forth between her and Rhian was untenable. It would drive her crazy and it would never satisfy Rhian's deep need for a family. A need she was increasingly invested in seeing fulfilled.

He deserved to be happy. They all did.

Shaking her head, she shoved those thoughts aside. There was something else she wanted to talk to Callum about before he left.

"Can I ask your advice about something?"

Callum cringed, looking from her to Rhian with wild-eyed alarm.

"I don't know what you think I'm going to ask you about, *dear brother*, but it's not *that.*"

He blew out a deep breath and she laughed. She snagged Chance's arm as he walked past. "I need you, too."

When she had their attention, she explained, "There is a young woman—a girl, really—who has been following Rhian around..."

Rhian slouched on the sofa in the family room, watching the hockey game with Chance, Angus and Bruce. Lachlan came into the room and dropped down on the cushion beside him.

"How about drinks this week?"

Lachlan lived in Cambridge, taught at Harvard, and was, apparently, counting on their friendship continuing after this weekend.

It killed Rhian that he should cut all ties to the Morrison clan as quickly as possible. This was Savannah's family, soon to be Garrick's. He had no place here.

And yet, he heard himself agreeing. Hell, he was looking forward to it. "Sure, what night is good for you?"

"Tuesday?"

"Sounds good. I'll check with Savannah to be sure she doesn't have anything going on."

Lachlan gave him a funny look but Rhian didn't bother to explain. They all knew about the lump by now, he was sure. The Morrisons were good people and he didn't doubt they could be discreet, but somehow, that didn't translate to them being good at keeping secrets.

"Even if Savannah has plans," Lachlan said with a little smile, "we can still hang out."

"Sure. Yes, of course."

Rhian was saved from having to sound any more stupid when Mary joined them and sat down on his other side. He smiled at her, then at Lachlan when he patted Rhian on the shoulder before leaving them alone. Rhian was still trying to sort out what the hell he'd gotten himself into when Mary took his hand in both of hers.

She was focused on the game, petting the back of his hand, probably without conscious thought, just as she did with any of her children. Rhian had to fight to swallow past the giant lump lodged in his throat.

He held her hand tightly. Staring at her profile, smiling when she smiled at something her husband was muttering about one of the players. He realized with a jolt that he might just love her. It wasn't the huge, frightening thing he had with Garrick, but a quieter, gentler emotion. He'd do anything for her. Anything at all she asked. He wanted to put his head down on her lap and tell her everything.

Not that he would. He couldn't. But he wanted to, so that was something, wasn't it?

God, how he wished for someone like her in his life. A weekend in her home had stripped away years of conviction that this kind of love and acceptance was something he hadn't missed. That he could happily live without it. It was a terrible, gut-wrenching pain to recognize what he'd lost. What he would never have. It hadn't hurt like this since he was a kid hoping to be placed in one of the miraculous happy, safe, welcoming foster homes the kids talked about, though none of them had ever found.

He couldn't change the past. And he doubted the future would be different. But for the ten minutes he got to sit and hold this woman's hand, he enjoyed the hell out of it.

He tried to let go of her when Savannah and Callum came into the room, but Mary didn't cooperate. He felt foolish, having been caught clinging to their mom like the orphan he was. That she clung to him all the tighter made an achy warmth bloom in his chest, rekindling hope where there hadn't been any in more years than he could count.

Callum sat on the coffee table in front of them, his expression serious. Rhian didn't know what to think when Chance sat beside him on the table, while Savannah curled up at his side and took his other hand in both of hers.

He was pinned.

Callum was the first to speak. "Savannah told us about the girl that's been following you around."

Rhian wished she hadn't, and he couldn't fathom why Callum wanted to talk about it. His confusion must have shown because Callum leaned in, his voice gentle. "Why don't you let Chance do some investigating, see if he can figure out who she is and why she might be following you?"

Rhian shook his head. "No, that's not necessary. I'm sure she's just an overzealous fan. I'll steer clear, that's all."

Callum arched one brow. "Savannah also told us how much luck you've had with that in the past."

Rhian didn't need a reminder of Deena, the crazy fan who'd tried to destroy both him and Garrick in Moncton. He looked at Savannah, tucked into his side, holding his hand tightly enough to cut off the circulation. She mouthed the word *sorry*. He wasn't pissed. Or particularly surprised. Hadn't he just thought to himself that this family was lousy at keeping secrets?

"Okay, maybe I'll report her to the police?" He didn't love that idea, but he wasn't sure why.

Callum grimaced. "Rhian, Savannah told us the young woman bears a striking resemblance to you."

Rhian had been trying awfully hard to forget about that.

"I'm sure it's just a coincidence."

Both of his hands got a firm squeeze for that piece of bullshit.

Callum sighed. "Look, man, I know it might lead to shit with your biological family, but I don't think it's a good idea to ignore it."

Rhian appreciated Callum making the distinction of biology and refrained from pointing out he didn't have any other kind of family, so it hadn't been necessary. He frowned at Savannah. Telling them about a stalker was one thing. Airing all his dirty laundry was another.

"Sav didn't tell us anything except that finding connections to your bio family might not be fun for you," Callum said, pulling Rhian's attention back to him. "But this woman knows where you live. You need to address it."

Rhian tried to think rationally about it, but he couldn't. This was like a trip to the haunted house when he was a kid.

He'd loved the anticipation when he approached a turn, knowing someone or something was going to spring out at him.

Funny how the experience wasn't nearly as pleasant now.

"I can just look into it and not tell you what I learn unless there is something you need to do," Chance offered gently.

Chance McCormick was owner and president of McCormick Associates, the largest private security firm in Boston. If anyone could manage a discreet inquiry, it would be Chance.

Rhian sighed. "Okay, do it. But tell me what you find. I might as well know."

The Morrison women squeezed his hands again, and he supposed he'd done something right. He smiled reassuringly, he hoped, at Mary, while rubbing a thumb over Savannah's hand. He wondered if he'd have the guts to do this if they weren't here beside him.

Callum and Chance were getting to their feet when Rhian blurted out the truth. "My mother's name is Diane Lynch."

Callum eased back to his seat slowly.

Chance fell onto the table with a thump. "From Boston?"

Rhian shrugged. Why did Chance sound surprised? "I'm not sure. I think maybe so. I was really young when...when I last saw her."

Kieran walked up behind Chance. "Did someone say Diane Lynch?"

Chance's hand clamped over Kieran's on his shoulder.

"Yeah, it's my mother's name. Why?"

Kieran frowned down at Chance. "Uh, just a common name in New England, I guess."

Chance eased his grip on Kieran's hand. "Was your father's name Savage?"

Rhian rubbed his thumb in double-time over Savannah's while he considered how to respond. *Shit, in for a penny...*

"No, not Savage. I don't know who my father is. If I ever

138

met him, I don't remember."

Everyone absorbed this information in silence. Rhian contemplated explaining his random last name, but he couldn't get it out. He'd said enough.

The concern on everyone's face, the encouraging looks, the tight grasps on his hands, kept him steady. For the first time in his life, he understood what it meant to be surrounded by people who cared.

It was a gift he could never repay.

Chapter Nineteen

The Bell-in-Hand Tavern was established in 1795, making it the oldest pub in America. The beautiful corner location in the heart of the city made it the perfect place for locals and tourists to stop for a drink. Tuesday night was no exception and it was packed to the rafters with people of all ages, college students rubbing elbows with bankers.

Savannah and Rhian stood in the door, searching the crowd for Lachlan. She smiled and waved when she found him defending his claim to the high-top table he'd somehow managed to score. The moment he spotted them, his expression pleaded for the reinforcements needed if they had any hope of retaining the precious real estate.

Rhian chuckled close to her ear. "You go save Lachlan. I'll get us a round. Beer okay?"

She turned toward him, their noses almost brushing. "Yes, thank you. That's great."

He smiled, his blue eyes dark in the dim light, and she shivered. His hand brushed her back and trailed along the strip of bare skin between her shirt and jeans as he turned away. Her toes curled in her boots.

Was he driving her crazy on purpose?

If Lachlan hadn't been desperate for her help, she might have followed Rhian and asked him. She wasn't sure, but she thought the little touches, the surprising but fleeting intimacies, had increased since their return from Connecticut. Or maybe she was just more aware of them.

Lachlan shooed away another group and Savannah shook off her reverie. Weaving through the dense crowd, she fastened her smile in place, aware that Lachlan was entirely too perceptive.

They chatted about work, but Savannah kept her answers vague. She was struggling with a few things at the office, but she didn't want to get into them with Lachlan. He would be happy to listen, she was sure, but she wanted to relax. A few beers, some dinner, and then shutting herself into her apartment sounded like the perfect way to end this day.

Provided Rhian would shut himself in with her.

She wasn't sure how to convince him to come to her place tonight. He'd stayed with her Sunday, after they returned from Connecticut, but last night he'd insisted on going back to his ugly little apartment. She'd tossed and turned all night.

She jumped when Rhian slid up to the table beside her. Her brother watched her curiously.

Way too perceptive.

Rhian handed out their drinks and she took the excuse to look away from Lachlan's penetrating stare. And Garrick claimed *she* could see through people?

Rhian and Lachlan fell into an easy conversation, and she listened idly. She was unaccountably aware that they had the entire table to themselves, but Rhian chose to stand next to her, their shoulders brushing.

Lachlan laughed at something Rhian said and the woman standing to his right smiled up at him. Lachlan caught her eye and the laughter died.

Uh oh.

His admirer's smile brightened. "Hi," she said loudly enough to be heard over the din of the crowd.

Lachlan was locked up tight, frozen where he stood. He swallowed hard before managing a weak, "Hello."

"I'm Sarah." She turned to face him fully, her back to the pack of girlfriends watching with wide grins.

Lachlan's eyes flickered to their shining faces and his cheeks turned a dull red.

"Lachlan."

"What's that?" Sarah asked.

"Uhh...Lachlan. My name is Lachlan. L-A-C-H-L-A-N. It's

Scottish for land of lakes." Her brother's blush deepened with every word.

Sarah's confident expression faded, replaced by mild confusion. She was a beautiful woman. She was probably used to at least a slightly warmer response from any man she chose to flirt with.

Rhian cocked his head while he watched the scene unfold. "What the hell is wrong with him?" he asked in a low voice only Savannah could hear.

She sighed. "Lachlan is really shy."

Rhian looked at her. "Really?"

"When it comes to women, morbidly so."

Lachlan stammered through a painfully long and wooden-voiced answer to Sarah's question about where he was from. By the time he was done telling her about Harvard, Connecticut, their parents, Scotland and god-only-knew what else, Sarah's eyes were glazing over and Lachlan was an alarming shade of scarlet.

"When he's nervous, he either turns into the babbling professor or goes mute," Savannah muttered.

As if to prove her point, Lachlan tried to answer another question, but no sound came out. His mouth opened and closed a few times before he coughed to clear his throat.

Rhian grimaced. "God, it's awful. I can't watch."

"She'll be gone soon," Savannah predicted morosely.

She was startled when Rhian grabbed her arm and dragged her around the table. He muttered, "We have to save him," then smiled at Sarah and raised his voice to be heard. "Hi. I'm Rhian. This is Savannah."

He threw his arm around Savannah's shoulders, and she tucked herself into his side. She prayed to god no one from the Bruins saw them, but there was no point interfering if Sarah turned her sights on Rhian instead. At least, that was what Savannah told herself as she curled an arm around his ribs and cuddled closer.

Sarah introduced herself and Rhian took subtle control of the conversation, careful to include Lachlan, prompting his response where needed. Her brother's color slowly returned to almost normal as he engaged in the conversation more and more. Rhian barely had to nudge him under the table to get him to talk.

Savannah contributed where she could, far more entertained with watching the show than the actual conversation. Lachlan's shoulders slowly dropped, and, at one point, with some help from Rhian, he actually managed to be outright charming.

Rhian was hard to resist on a normal day. Now he was being sweet. And protective. Sides of him she'd never seen.

Sarah took out her card and wrote her cell phone number on the back. Rhian's arm tightened around Savannah and she squeezed him back, a silent victory celebration. Lachlan looked positively stunned and Savannah buried her face against Rhian's shoulder to muffle her laughter.

Sarah and her friends departed, leaving Lachlan to smile sheepishly at Rhian. Any one of her brothers would have taken the opportunity to give Lachlan a ton of shit, but Rhian just clapped a hand on Lachlan's shoulder and grinned.

For that alone she loved him.

Goddamn Garrick. He hadn't warned her how fucking scary it would be. He was going to flip when she told him she loved Rhian, too, and she had no idea what he'd think of the plans she was hatching.

Goddamn Grace. And Mark. And Philip. They hadn't warned her, either.

Rhian caught her eye and her heart did a little jig in her chest. Getting Garrick on board would be a walk in the park compared to convincing Rhian to take a chance on her. On them. That was going to be a Mount Everest climb.

Rhian lifted his glass. "To Sarah."

Lachlan turned pink.

Savannah laughed. "Yes, to Sarah."

She watched Rhian over the rim of her glass, enjoying the way his eyes danced as Lachlan muttered his thanks. Her brother still had the little white card clutched in his hand.

Rhian's head snapped to the side and he took a quick step toward the windows. His glass hit the table with a loud crack.

"Fuck! There she is again!"

Rhian could hardly believe his eyes. Whoever she was, she was fucking persistent.

And he'd had enough of the mystery.

Shoving past the next table, he jammed the bar on the emergency exit door and flew out into the street.

The girl, the one that had been following him around Boston for days, froze, her eyes going wide. He was almost close enough to grab her when she spun and bolted down the street toward Haymarket. He pelted full speed after her.

"Rhian! Wait!" Savannah cried from behind him.

He didn't slow, gaining on his little stalker. He'd be damned if she got away from him. He wanted answers, and he didn't want or need Chance and the rest of the Morrison clan to get embroiled in his stupid shit. He would address the problem himself.

Right now.

She took a right onto Hanover Street. Rhian ran faster, aware Savannah and Lachlan chased him. At least, he hoped it was them and not the police.

He made the turn just as the girl reached the next intersection. An arm appeared out of nowhere and yanked her around the corner so fast her head snapped back. She screamed and disappeared.

Rhian's heart skipped a beat. It was idiocy for him to fly around the corner without any idea of what waited for him, but he did it anyway.

And stopped cold.

In the middle of the deserted Haymarket square, a big, hauntingly familiar man held the struggling girl. She clawed at his arm, demanding that he let her go, but he ignored her. All he did was stare at Rhian with absolute hatred.

Rhian was thrown back almost twenty years.

The man hadn't aged a day. He sneered at Rhian. "If you know what's good for you, you'll stay the hell away from her, *Savage.*"

The voice was the same, too.

Jimmy.

Chapter Twenty

Savannah watched with horror as a huge, ugly man dragged the girl down the street. She would have demanded he release her, but it was obvious they knew one another by their bickering. If they'd looked even a little alike, she would have been certain they were siblings.

God, *Rhian's siblings*?

He'd known Rhian's name. She turned to ask who that man was, but the questions died on her lips.

She grabbed Lachlan's wrist when he reached out to touch Rhian's shoulder.

"Rhian?" she said gently.

He spun as if she'd shouted his name, staring at her with wide, unblinking eyes. There wasn't a hint of color left in his face.

"Holy shit," Lachlan whispered.

Rhian didn't take his gaze off her. She hoped that was a good sign. Garrick had told her Rhian had flipped out once. It had shaken Garrick to the core. She supposed it hadn't been a good time for Rhian either.

"Honey, it's okay. Let's just go home."

He took a quick step away and she barely checked the urge to leap forward and grab him.

"I'm fine," Rhian said tersely.

He so obviously wasn't. She eased closer. When she was within arm's reach, she put out her hand. "Come on, let's go—" *Home.* No, he didn't have one of those. Yet. She didn't want any confusion about where they were headed. "Let's go to my apartment, okay?"

Rhian grabbed her hand in a tight grip.

Now what? She didn't dare try to walk Rhian across the

city. "Lachlan, we need a cab."

"The Millennium Hotel is around the corner." Lachlan said softly. "I'll go arrange one."

She nodded. "We'll be right behind you."

He gave them a wide berth, then broke into a run.

They followed more slowly and found Lachlan standing by a taxi, the door open. She climbed into the back seat without hesitation, towing Rhian in her wake. He sat stiffly, not even looking at Lachlan when he eased in behind them and closed the door.

As soon as the car pulled from the curb, Rhian folded his hands in his lap and stared out the windshield. He was doing his damndest to appear calm, she could tell, but tension radiated off him in waves. She looked down to see him wipe shaking hands down his pant legs.

She grabbed his hands in both of hers.

"I'm fine," he snapped, trying to pull his hands away.

Another lie. She didn't let go.

When she started to slide across the seat and into the door, she realized her brother was taking up far more of the narrow seat than needed. She braced her feet and pushed back, smashing Rhian between them.

Rhian looked at her, then Lachlan, with obvious consternation, but didn't argue. He didn't relax, either, but his hands turned to grip hers and they no longer shook.

Lachlan started speaking, his voice barely audible over the sounds of the engine and the pavement beneath their tires. She rubbed Rhian's hands, trying to warm them. Him. When they stopped at a red light, she realized Lachlan was cheerfully reciting his introduction to epistemology lecture, of all things. He'd once admitted it was more effective than Valium for putting underclassmen to sleep. And while Rhian wasn't out cold yet, he was looking at Lachlan like he was slightly mad, which was a significant improvement over the pale-faced shock from just a few minutes before.

147

They swerved to a stop in front of her building and she jumped out to pay the driver while Lachlan steered Rhian inside. She caught up with them on the first landing and together they nudged Rhian up the remaining flights of stairs and into her apartment.

Without stopping, she grabbed her iPad from the kitchen counter and towed Rhian back to her bedroom. He hesitated inside the door, her brother hovering behind him. She stripped the comforter to the foot of the bed and hailed Garrick over Skype.

"Thank you, Lach. I've got it from here."

He glanced at Rhian, still pale and little wide-eyed, and then gave her a frankly dubious look. Before she could come up with a good explanation, Garrick answered.

"Hey, Sav—"

She handed the iPad to Rhian, who took it automatically.

"Rhian?" Garrick said, immediately concerned.

Rhian opened his mouth to say something, but when no words came out, he closed it again with a sigh. The look of consternation was back.

"Rhian? Baby?" Garrick's voice rose. "Are you okay?"

Lachlan looked between her, Rhian, and the bed she'd just prepared for him. For them.

She pulled her brother out into the hall.

His face was pinched with concern, though thankfully not of the enraged, over-protective brother variety. Yet. "You sure you know what you're doing?" he asked.

She fought not to blush as she gently urging Lachlan toward the door. She mumbled something about sleeping on the couch, hating the lie but not wanting to get into explanations right now. Hell, she didn't have any explanation to give.

How the hell would she explain any of this to her brothers? Her parents?

She shoved that aside for now. She needed to get back to

Rhian and Garrick. The rest she'd figure out later.

Lachlan cast a last glance toward the bedroom before drawing her into a fierce hug.

"Be careful."

She slumped with relief. "I will. He'll be okay."

"It's you I'm worried about."

"I'm fine. Thank you for helping me get him home. I'll call you in the morning, all right?"

He kissed the top of her head and left.

She sagged against the closed door, then took a deep, steadying breath and ran down the hall.

Garrick studied Rhian's pale face and tried to guess what had happened. He hadn't a fucking clue.

"Rhian, baby, I love you. Tell me what's wrong."

Rhian blinked and looked right at him. His pupils were pinpricks in a sea of blue, but his gaze was focused.

Garrick could hear Savannah speaking softly to someone, the sound fading as they moved away. Had she left Garrick to comfort Rhian on his own? He couldn't blame her if she had, but he was at a complete fucking loss on how to go about it.

"I'm okay."

Rhian's voice brought Garrick's heart rate from a gallop to a steady trot.

"Okay," he agreed, though he knew it was bullshit. "Want to tell me what's going on?"

Rhian appeared to think about that for a moment. "No."

Garrick actually smiled. "Fair enough." He'd be damn sure to get back to it later, but for now, seeing Rhian's lips quirk was enough.

Savannah peered over the edge of the iPad and Garrick slumped with relief. Rhian looked up at her with a painfully sad smile, tinged with apology. Garrick's heart constricted.

What the hell had happened?

Savannah kept her gaze on Rhian. "Want to tell me what happened out there?"

Aware that Rhian could see his face, Garrick fought for a calm expression while his brain rioted with questions. *Out where? Savannah doesn't know either?*

"It was him," Rhian said in a dull voice. What little color that had returned to his face, fled.

"Who?" Garrick asked.

Rhian screwed his eyes closed and shook his head. Savannah looked at Garrick.

"What do I do?"

"I don't know," Garrick admitted, hating that it was true.

"What would *you* do?"

Rhian huffed. "I'm sitting right here, you know. And I'm fine."

They both ignored that patent lie. He hadn't even opened his eyes.

"*What,* Garrick?" Savannah demanded.

"I'd get us both naked and lie down on him," he admitted.

The color returned to Rhian's face, with a vengeance. "*Garrick.*"

"It's true," Garrick returned. And he wasn't going to pretend otherwise, at least not until Rhian could open his fucking eyes.

The iPad jerked, three times, before Savannah successfully pried it from Rhian's hands. The view swung around, and Garrick was looking at the ceiling, the pillows, the footboard, the floor.

"Savannah, are you guys okay?"

"Yeah, we're good," she replied. She sounded like she was trying to lift something heavy.

Something shook the iPad, but Garrick was still left with nothing but a view of the light above the bed.

"Hey," Rhian protested.

"Don't be a baby," Savannah returned.

"But..."

Garrick glared at his iPad and ground his teeth. "Everybody okay over there?"

Goddamn, this was the worst fucking method of communication ever invented.

At last the image blurred again and he was staring into Savannah's concerned gaze. His guts knotted.

"I hope you're right about this," she said.

"About what?"

She handed the iPad back to Rhian and he bobbled it.

Garrick blinked. Rhian was sitting on the edge of the bed. Buck naked.

The iPad dropped, presumably to Rhian's lap. Savannah—now upside down to Garrick—stood wearing nothing but bikini panties and a tank top.

Garrick stared, agape, as she pulled the tank top over her head, exposing full breasts and smooth skin. In spite of his gut-churning concern about Rhian, heat pooled in his belly and his cock twitched hard against his fly.

Chapter Twenty One

Rhian blinked with surprise as Savannah stripped down in front of him. In her haste, she didn't bother to turn her back. In his shock, he didn't bother to look away. He did what he'd always wanted. Stared. Long and hard. He had zero capacity for artifice at the moment. He felt scraped down to the bone, his soul naked and raw.

He was positively shocked when his dick lifted with interest. It spoke to the power of his attraction to Savannah that arousal could wrestle through the endless confusion and static in his brain since seeing Jimmy.

She grabbed an old t-shirt Rhian recognized as Garrick's and pulled it on, covering her gorgeous body to mid-thigh.

He closed his eyes and tried to gather his wits. They seemed too far away to grasp, scattered on the pavement of the Haymarket.

The iPad waivered in his hands and he barely kept it from crashing to the floor.

Garrick deep voice came from his lap. "Baby, that's one hell of a view, but I'm really not in the mood for Skype sex right now."

Rhian opened his eyes. The iPad camera was pointed right at his dick.

A huff of laughter shook him. To the core.

He snapped out of his daze.

With crystal clarity, he pictured the man. Not Jimmy, he knew, but who? And the girl, struggling in his grasp. His heart slammed against his ribs. Rushing blood roared in his ears and bright spots appeared in his vision.

"Whoa, Rhian!" Garrick's shout was distant and tinny. "What happened? Rhian!"

Rhian let the iPad fall.

Savannah caught it. *"Shit."*

Rhian looked around the room. He needed his clothes. Where the fuck did she put them?

"Savannah," Garrick called. "Can you lie down on top of him?"

Rhian stood.

Savannah jammed the iPad onto the bedside table, propped up against the lamp. Rhian saw her alarm and regretted scaring her. Regretted exposing her to any part of his fucked-up, broken life.

He should be getting dressed. Leaving.

"Oh, no," Savannah said in a dark voice. "You're not going anywhere."

Had he said he was leaving out loud? He didn't think so.

He was still trying to find his damn clothes when Savannah hurled herself against his chest and toppled them both onto the bed.

They landed with a bounce, Savannah on top of him, his legs hanging over the side of the mattress. He could easily throw her off of him. Some part of him wanted to. She wrapped her hands around his face and cupped his cheeks, her thumbs resting at the corners of his mouth.

"Will you let me help you?"

The little voice in his head screamed *yes, please*, but he managed a reasonably calm "How?"

She ran her hands through his hair, pressed their foreheads together and rubbed her nose against his.

Shit, that *did* help.

He stared at her from inches away. He could see every variation of green in her irises. They were beautiful.

"If I get off you, will you stay? I'm not strong enough to drag you into this bed, but I swear to god I'll try."

Seconds ago he'd wanted to leave. Now, lying beneath her, he wanted to stay. He didn't know why. He could only think of all the reasons why not.

He nodded.

She eased off him and crawled across the bed, grabbing pillows and piling them high against the headboard.

"Come here."

He slid cautiously to the head of the bed and, at her urging, sat up and settled into the mountain of pillows, his shoulders to the headboard.

She dragged the heavy quilt from the foot of the bed, and he recognized it from Garrick's farmhouse. He longed for it to still smell of woodstove and Garrick. She crawled over his legs and up his body, her hands sinking into his hair, their foreheads touching, their chests and bellies aligned. She thrust aside the pillows on either side of them and drew her legs up to hug his ribs, settling her full weight into his lap as she wrapped herself around him and the quilt around them both.

It wasn't the same as when Garrick smashed him to the bed, in what Rhian was coming to accept as their weird but effective ritual. She was a feather compared to Garrick's heavily muscled frame and considerable height, but she held him close. Tight. Where Garrick used brute strength and size, Savannah managed the same impact with gentle caresses and soft words.

Garrick pinned him. Savannah held him. It worked.

With a sigh, the tension began to slip away.

Savannah turned his face so they both looked at Garrick. Rhian stared into those deep brown eyes, Savannah's cheek against his, and felt whole again.

Garrick smiled tenderly, his eyes warm with humor and relief. "I love you."

Rhian tried to smile, rubbing his cheek against Savannah's. She rubbed back, nuzzling against him like a kitten.

Rhian swallowed and wet his lips. "I love you, too, Garrick."

When had those words stopped being hard to say? Let alone in front of Savannah.

He let that worry go. His brain wasn't capable of anything more taxing than sitting there and enjoying Garrick and Savannah. He stared at Garrick beloved face. Inhaled Savannah's delicate scent and absorbed her warmth.

Every muscle in his body went lax under Savannah's soothing ministrations. He was awake, but floating. He curled his arms around her and skimmed his hands under her shirt and along her spine. The long strokes were meditative, matching the rhythm of his breaths. His eyes drifted closed.

He heard Garrick ask again what happened and listened to Savannah recount the night's events. It was interesting. She'd understood more than he'd thought—that something about that man specifically had freaked him out.

He didn't dwell on the idea that Jimmy was somehow ageless and in Boston. He didn't shy from it either. It was okay to think about it now.

He was safe.

Savannah wriggled on top of him, trying to get comfortable. She wasn't as adept at this squash-your-lover thing as Garrick. But then, it was her first time. And they weren't lovers.

God, he wanted that. To be her lover. He wanted her with a depth and passion that stole his carefully controlled breath.

To touch her. Taste her. Pull her against his body as he thrust into hers.

It would be heaven.

He shifted against the mattress, the fog of calm dissipating.

Damn. How the hell was he going to disguise his growing erection when she was *sitting on it*? Increasing alarm ended his peaceful stupor. His eyes popped open and locked on Garrick's.

Garrick's eyebrows went *way* up as he studied Rhian's expression.

Oh shit. He knows.

Savannah slid against the writhing muscles beneath her.

155

Rhian had been perfectly still for the better part of fifteen minutes, but now he seemed to be having a hard time getting comfortable.

She looked at Garrick and watched one side of his mouth curl up in a slow, lopsided smile.

What the hell did that mean?

Maybe she was doing this wrong. Should she make Rhian lie down? Or press him more firmly to the bed? She tried holding him tighter, slipping one hand from his hair and curling an arm between the headboard and his shoulders.

That didn't help at all.

Rhian squirmed. Garrick grinned like a fool.

What was wrong with that man?

She jolted when Rhian slid a hand down her back and over her ass, shocked when he gripped one cheek hard and held her still. Awareness of the hand on her butt, the hard panes of his body beneath her, surged through her, but she made herself ignore it.

She needed a better way to comfort Rhian. His pale face had gone flushed and he was shooting Garrick a narrow-eyed glare.

She snuggled closer and only then did it finally strike her why Rhian couldn't get comfortable. Truth be told, it didn't so much *strike* her as dig into her thigh.

She bit her lip to prevent a hysterical and completely inappropriate laugh from erupting.

Her gaze locked with Garrick's.

Garrick wasn't surprised when Rhian sat up and lifted Savannah from his lap.

"Sorry. I have to... umm... take a break. I'll be right back."

He rolled from the bed and Garrick stared at his lover's broad, bare back and that glorious goddamn ass.

When it was out of his limited view, he turned his attention to Savannah and found she was still enjoying the sight as Rhian no doubt bolted from the room.

Garrick chuckled, then laughed out right at the sheepish look on Savannah's face at having been caught.

"Sorry," she said.

"Don't be."

She smiled, but it faded to a frown when she looked toward the door again.

"Are you worried he's going to take off?" Garrick asked.

"No." A little smile returned. "I hid his clothes."

"Clever girl."

She shrugged, still looking down the hall.

"You okay?" he asked gently, cursing that he had to ask again only because he wasn't there to see, to *know* for himself.

Savannah turned to look at him. "I'm okay. I think we both are."

Garrick was pretty sure Rhian was feeling more than okay. In fact, he'd bet his last dime that was why his boyfriend had just fled the room.

"So," he began cautiously, "was Rhian, uhh...I mean, did you notice..."

Savannah's face split in a wide grin. "Oh yeah, I definitely noticed."

"And?" Garrick tried very hard not to squirm in his seat.

She cocked her head and looked at Garrick. Right through him, as only she could. "I'm not sure."

He didn't flinch from her stare. "Whatever you decide, it's okay."

She opened her mouth to respond, but snapped it closed and looked over her shoulder before saying anything.

Rhian immediately came into view and climbed back into bed. His—thankfully not little—issue had subsided.

Savannah jumped to her feet. Garrick lamented the T-shirt and panties hiding so much beauty.

She smiled at him. "I'll be right back."

Garrick grinned, watching Rhian stare in the direction of the door, just as Savannah had done minutes before.

"How ya doin'?" Garrick asked, arching his eyebrows when Rhian looked at him with an identical sheepish look on his face.

"*Fine.*" The tone, more than the blasé answer, gave him away.

Garrick smirked. "She has that effect on me, too, you know."

"What?"

"It's okay, Rhian. Whatever you want. I mean, I wouldn't be mad if—"

"No."

"But—"

Rhian looked away. "Hi, Sav."

Garrick wiped his face clean of any expression but concern and watched Savannah climb back into the bed and right on top of Rhian.

Rhian opened his mouth to protest, but Savannah slid a hand over his mouth.

"Maybe I need some of this, too. Would you please hold me?"

Rhian's arms immediately encircled her waist.

Garrick decided it was time for him to say goodnight.

"Rhian, I have to go now. If you're okay?"

Rhian rolled his head to the side and grimaced at Garrick. "I'm fine. I'm sorry if I worried you earlier."

"Don't apologize. I'm only sorry I'm not there." Garrick swallowed back his frustration over that and smiled. "I'm going to leave you in Savannah's capable hands, all right?"

"I'll take good care of him," she promised. Hell, she almost purred it.

Garrick's lips twitched but he controlled them in time.

Rhian's eyes narrowed on him. "I love you."

Holy shit, he said it first. Garrick rubbed a hand over his chest to soothe the ache there.

"I love you, too, baby. And you, Savannah. I love and trust you both."

Rhian's brows drew together. Savannah winked.

The iPad went blank.

Chapter Twenty Two

The bedroom was suddenly very quiet, their breathing the only sound in the still, warm air around them. Savannah pressed her face into Rhian's neck, trying to collect herself. It wasn't easy when she desperately wanted to rub against the steel bar pressing ever-more firmly against her thigh.

Carefully, she drew her hands down Rhian's neck and over his shoulders. Her fingertips brushed his biceps and drew a little pattern on each.

He rippled beneath her. There was no other word for it. Every muscle in his body tensed and released in a long wave that began at his legs and worked his way up to his shoulders. She shuddered at the exquisite feeling of so much strength heaving against her. She gasped when his erection nestled into the crease where her thigh met her pelvis.

His eyes fluttered closed and a deep red stain bloomed from his cheeks to his neck and chest. His breaths deepened. His cock swelled against wonderfully sensitive skin.

"I'm sorry," he muttered. His color edged toward scarlet.

I'm not.

She burrowed closer and rubbed her face against his throat, under his chin, over his shoulder. She traced her palms down his arms.

God, he was beautiful. She didn't have to open her eyes to see. She could feel it. Everything she knew about training and the human form translated through the touch of her body against his, drawing him in her mind's eye.

She felt his jaw flex. "You're not helping," he said through clenched teeth.

"I'm not trying to," she admitted, her voice muffled against his skin.

"What *are* you doing?"

"Enjoying myself. Immensely."

She rubbed her cotton-covered mons against his belly, the elastic of her panties dragging along his cock. The most delightful little noise surged from his chest before he choked it off with a cough.

"We shouldn't." His voice had gone hoarse.

She lifted her head away from his warmth and musky scent so she could see his face. "Why not?"

"I'm with Garrick."

She smiled. "So am I."

"Exactly."

She understood his reluctance. These were unusual circumstance to be sure. But it was right. She no longer had a doubt about that.

He shook his head. "It's not a good idea. It would complicate things."

"They couldn't get any more complicated than they already are." That wasn't strictly true. He was right. They could make this whole mess a whole lot messier. The idea thrilled and terrified her. The risk was fucking *huge*.

She traced his beautiful face, generous mouth, and ridiculous cheekbones with her fingertips.

She didn't kid herself. It wasn't going to be easy. But it *would* be worth it.

Garrick had once told her that Rhian deserved to be loved, and that he made Garrick want to be the kind of person who was worthy of Rhian's love in return.

She understood that perfectly now.

Rhian stared into Savannah's brilliant green eyes. He'd wanted her months ago when they'd both been single in Moncton. Now he wished it were only that. Desire he could shut off. If it was a simple matter of sexual attraction, he could crawl out of this bed, raging hard-on be damned, and walk right out the door.

But it was so much more than sex. He wanted to hold her. To keep his arms and legs wrapped around her and just fucking *cling*. The need was different than what he had with Garrick, though just as powerful. And the result was the same.

It frightened the holy hell out of him.

Obviously being in love with Garrick had broken him of the perfectly healthy inclination to run away from what scared the pants off him. Because here he was, still in bed, clutching Savannah to him.

She shifted, trapping his cock against damp panties.

He swallowed. Hard. "I don't know what to say."

Her smile lit up her eyes. "What do you normally say to a woman you want?"

It should have sounded arrogant, but it didn't. Given the rigid evidence crushed against her pussy, he couldn't deny her assumption. He did want her. Like water. Air.

He brushed the backs of his fingers down her cheek. "You come here often?"

She gave a husky laugh. "Every chance I get."

He chuckled.

Quick wit, staggering beauty and brains to match. Had he ever stood a chance?

He threaded his fingers into her hair and cupped the back of her head. He'd longed to touch her, even while swearing it would never happen. Now the possibilities seemed limitless.

"I do want you," he said softly. The risks were real, still scaring the crap out of him, but the reward was too sweet.

Her smile sweeter still.

He urged her closer, hesitating when their lips were a hair's breadth apart. Her eyes fluttered closed and for a moment, the world stopped.

His lips brushed hers. It was not nearly enough. He captured her mouth, his fingers clenched in her long hair as desire roared through him and he shuddered in its grip. She gasped and he slipped his tongue into her mouth to twine with hers.

They kissed like old friends. Like lovers who had been together for years. Yet, only now did he learn the taste of her lips, the texture of her tongue and teeth. Her hands ran through his hair, touched his cheek, always moving. Touching him, everywhere, like she was seeking him out. These gentle caresses should have been innocent, but they were as thrilling as the hot, damp pressure against his cock.

He plunged his tongue along hers. Tilted his head. Then hers. Deepening the kiss before easing back to tease along her lips. It felt like he'd been here a thousand times before, while *finally* discovering what he'd dreamed about didn't come close to the reality.

His pulse thrummed in his ears, the rhythm matching the throb of his cock. He hummed against her lips, overwhelmed by her taste, the wriggle of her hips. *Her.*

He curled a hand over her ass and ground her down against him. Their mouths parted on a mutual gasp.

"God, Rhian." She licked her lips as she undulated against him.

He teased his mouth along her jaw, under her chin, questing to find the tender spots that made her moan louder, wriggle harder. He found a lot of them. She shared her passion so freely, his ears rang with it.

He skimmed his hands up under her shirt and dragged it over her ribs. His fingers explored the soft, warm skin beneath the old cotton, tingling with each discovery. He could spend the entire night learning every inch of her.

With an impatient grunt, Savannah sat up and whipped the shirt over her head.

Holy crap.

He watched, mesmerized, as her hands curled and lifted her high, firm breasts to his gaze. She made little circles with her hips, rubbing along his shaft. He didn't know where to look.

To touch.

He clasped her hips with his hands. He hadn't meant for her to stop—good god all-fucking-mighty he did not want her to stop—but needed an anchor against the storm of her passion.

She touched his face, and he tore his eyes from her breasts to her smoldering green gaze.

A last gasp of reason asserted itself. "Are you sure?" he asked.

"Are you?"

A hint of fear curled through his arousal-fogged brain. He had to be honest. "No. But I'll be traded away soon and—"

She cut him off with a kiss. By the time it ended, he was panting.

"Rhian, I want you. You want me," she said against his lips.

"God, yes."

"Then all I'm asking for is now. Today. The next few weeks. Then we'll see what happens next."

Nothing will happen next. He needed her to understand that.

She sat up and clasped his wrists, dragging his hands up her ribs. His brain stuttered when a slow, sultry smile curled her lips. The pads of his thumbs skimmed satiny skin up to her full, soft breasts. He cupped them in his hands.

Christ, he loved Garrick, but he had missed this. The heavy weight in his palms. The hard pucker of her nipples. He dragged his thumb over the stiff peaks.

She bit her lip, and they both stared at his hands on her, her pink nipples and silk skin pale against his fingers.

"We're friends, aren't we?" she asked.

Rhian blinked and stared at her breasts in his hands. That was a hell of a question to ask at this moment.

His lips twitched. "Yeah, we're friends."

"Then you know I'd never do anything to hurt you."

He swallowed past the knot lodged in his chest and looked up into her bright green eyes.

He believed her.

Chapter Twenty Three

Rhian hauled Savannah up over him. He rubbed his face against the soft skin between her breasts, and over one firm globe. Then the other. At last, he drew a hard peak into his mouth.

Her reaction was instantaneous and shocking. "*Yes. God, Rhian, yes!*" Her shout bounced off the walls and echoed in his head.

He sucked harder and she cried his name again, grabbing his head with her hands and clutching him close. He licked every inch of skin he could reach. Laved one breast with his tongue. Nuzzled his face into the valley before worshiping the other. She shamelessly shoved herself into his mouth and groaned her encouragement.

God, she was so like Garrick. Totally without hesitation. Asking for what she wanted. Demanding it. *Loudly.*

He wanted to give her that and more.

His cock ached, lodged against her writhing body. More than anything, he wanted to shove her down and onto him, thrusting into her ready heat.

Shit. Condom. He needed one. *Now.* To say he hadn't arrived here tonight prepared to have sex with Savannah would have been the understatement of the goddamn century.

He hated the idea of leaving the bed and hunting for one. It was too soon to let the world intrude. Time and distance would only let his brain start worrying and his heart start panicking. Because really, what the fuck was he doing here?

He released her breast as a cold tendril of anxiety curdled inside his belly.

Savannah slid down his body and kissed him senseless. She attacked his mouth. Chased the worry away and replaced it with a tidal wave of need.

He poured every ounce of his passion into the touch of her lips. His hands roamed everywhere he could reach. No sooner had his fingers traced the edge of her tiny panties that she lifted up and wrapped her long fingers around his cock.

He groaned. She tightened her hold and pulled.

"Oh shit," he growled, lost to her assault.

She kissed him again and he adored her aggression, falling under the spell she wove with tongue and fist. He raced toward completion, his hips kicking into her hand, the drag of his sensitive crown against her palm exquisite. He was on the edge *way* too quickly.

He traced the back of his finger over her panties and the swell of her mons beneath. She jerked at his touch and spread her knees wider, urging him on.

He hooked his fingers into the soft elastic and tugged the soaked fabric to the side, holding it there. His other hand traced down the same path, encountering nothing but smooth skin until he brushed the infamous "landing strip". God, how many hours had he spent wondering what it would look like, feel like, after her naughty admission in the back of the taxi that day?

He petted her there and promised himself he'd get a good long look another time.

She growled at him. "Please, Rhian."

"So eager." He chuckled, delighted by her demands.

Her relentless hand paused on his dick and she raised one eyebrow.

His laughter died and his plea caught in his throat.

Clever woman.

He slid the pad of one finger lower, into thick, hot cream and between swollen lips. She groaned and twitched against him. A needy sob caught in her throat when he bumped over her clit. He didn't stop, pushing farther until he sank his finger into her to the hilt.

"*Rhian...*"

He liked how she said his name, held his gaze. She was here. With him. There was no confusion. No one else. They both loved Garrick, but this, tonight, was purely between them.

She arched above him, impaling herself, seeking more. He flicked his thumb across her clit and she did it again, this time pumping her hand along his shaft.

To say they fell into a rhythm would be generous. Guided entirely by the thrash of her body against his hand, they were enslaved to the heaving need, hips and hands working furiously against one another.

He was rapidly losing the ability to reason out even the simplest things. He slammed his eyes shut, trying to block out at least one sense's stimulation. On the next withdrawal, he added another finger, shoving harder, higher, urging her toward the peak. His own climax was bearing down on him with embarrassing speed.

She whimpered with pleasure, gasping his name again. It didn't help. At all.

The friction from her hand turned hot, but like the search for condoms, he couldn't abide the idea of stopping to find lube. He flinched at the dry drag of skin against skin, but it wouldn't stop him from coming. And soon. His cock seeped pre-come and Savannah paused to rub her palm over his crown, nerve endings dancing, almost high with relief. Still, the next pump of her fist burned.

And then her hand was gone.

"No," he gasped.

Her grin lit up her face. She slipped her hand over his, buried between her legs. Her thumb joined his on her clit. His mouth fell open when one thin finger slid into her body, captured in her tight channel beside his.

She fisted a hand in his hair. "Kiss me."

His mouth locked onto hers. Their hands moved in counterpoint to the kick of her hips. Their thumbs battered her clit. He swallowed the sounds forced up out of her chest, his own groans, as their hands fucked her, drenched in the flood of her arousal.

His body throbbed, his cock bouncing off his belly, her thighs. He rolled his hips, trying to find some friction, some goddamn relief. He could have taken himself in hand, but he wouldn't pull his hand from her hair, holding them close as they made out like a couple of horny teenagers, all hands and mouths and rapidly diminishing finesse.

At least, *he* was losing all his finesse. Savannah didn't miss a beat when she drew her hand away from her body. He congratulated himself on some semblance of coordination when he immediately replaced her departing finger with his own, plunging deep.

He relished her groan against his lips, sure she would tumble over the edge any moment. Then her cream-drenched fingers wrapped around his cock and pumped hard and fast.

He gasped into their kiss, her name little more than a whisper as he sucked in a breath and thrust his cock into her grasp. Her hand tightened in his hair, her green gaze locked on his face.

That was it.

His orgasm exploded from him, striping his chest with come, a howl torn from his throat. She arched above him, forced her pussy down on his hand, and cried out his name. Her fingers convulsed around his cock in time with each ripple in her tight sheath, tugging another racking shudder up from his balls.

Eventually, Savannah collapsed on top of him, her face buried against his neck. She trembled, and he wrapped his arms around her back. He hadn't begun to catch his breath, but already bone-deep tranquility settled over him. His brain hazy, he enjoying the aftershocks rippling through the placid calm. How could he be this content when he was more certain than ever that he'd never find level ground again?

Savannah and Garrick had completely fucked him up.

The lull of warm skin and the long day dragged at him. His panic attack earlier had drained his reserve until only a mere thread of worry remained. Paltry against the waves of contentment crashing over him.

Savannah's fingers thread through his hair and it soothed him further. He loved her touch. Her endless gentle caresses.

His eyes closed, his breath evened out, and he slipped into sleep.

Chapter Twenty Four

Savannah woke at dawn with Rhian curled around her back, his face buried in her hair. His heavy arm and steady heartbeat told her he was still asleep. Well, at least his big brain was. His little brain was up and ready to tackle the day, judging by the pokes to her bottom.

She and Rhian had fallen asleep early the night before—and without dinner. She'd considered rousing him to eat something, to make love again, but he'd looked so peaceful sleeping. He hadn't stirred when she got out of bed to get a washcloth and cleaned them both up.

She'd emailed the office to say she was working from home today, then poked and prodded Rhian until they were under the covers. He'd rolled toward her, and she'd curled against his chest and promptly fallen back to sleep.

She hadn't gone to bed before eight o'clock since she was about seven years old. She was well-rested, but also *starving*.

And horny.

The question was, which need was more pressing? Feed them? Or cement the change to their relationship in the most obvious and intimate way?

He had no clue of her intentions for the three of them. And once he did, he was probably going to balk. She couldn't blame him. Any sane person would question whether a permanent threesome could work. She'd had doubts, even while staring at contented faces of Philip, Mark and Grace.

But then, she hadn't fallen in love with Rhian yet.

She had a strong suspicion that telling Rhian she loved him would put him in a panic. He wasn't ready. Their emotional bond was strong and growing every day, but for him it probably wasn't love—not yet—and even if it was, he might not be able to admit it.

171

Or he might never fall in love with her. She'd end up brokenhearted, and in the process, have complicated matters with Garrick irreparably.

Yeah, to hell with breakfast. She needed to touch him, to reassure herself that he was there. With her. That the risk was worth it. He'd only agreed to stay for "a while". She wouldn't waste a minute of it. If he woke with doubts, she'd erase them any way she could.

She wriggled back until they were nestled together from shoulder to knee.

His warm hand caressed her belly.

He was awake. And he hadn't leaped from the bed and run screaming. That was something, right?

"Good morning," she murmured.

"Good morning." His rough voice sent shivers down her spine.

"Sleep well?"

He hummed, burrowing his face into her hair until his lips pressed to the back of her neck. She almost burst with happiness. He was *cuddling.* And his morning wood was getting woodier by the second.

She smiled and ran her fingers over his arm, along his hip. "I was thinking last night. After you passed out on me."

His laughter stirred her hair and tickled her nape. "Sorry about that."

"Totally understandable. I tired you out."

She felt his smile against her neck. "Yeah, you did."

God, the brush of his lips and the rumble of his voice sent electric shocks all the way to her fingertips and toes.

"Anyway," she said, struggling to stay on point, "I wanted to talk to you about something. About us."

As soon she said it, she regretted her choice of words. Her warm, cuddly lover went as stiff as a board—and not in a good way. She grabbed his hand and held it to her stomach.

"What about us?" he asked in a perfect monotone.

She gave herself a stern lecture to be patient. She'd expected this. And while she'd like to talk to him about the emotional aspects of their relationship, she wasn't foolish enough to go there. Yet. This was about something far more practical.

"We don't have to use condoms."

He stopped breathing, his hand stilled. *Crap.* Now she'd freaked him out. She'd hoped the sex, at least, wasn't going to be scary him. For crying out loud, he had sex with *Garrick.* She was downright subtle compared to him.

"We don't?" he asked, his voice several notes higher than it had been a minute ago.

"Well, let me ask you something?"

"Okay," he said slowly.

"Have you been with anyone besides Garrick in the past six months?"

Rhian's hand stroked across her belly and the tight muscles along her back eased. Maybe he could deal with this after all. She was usually good at reading people, but he was a challenge. In hindsight, she realized she should have had this conversation facing the damn man.

"No. A little more than six months ago there was one woman. One time. And others before her, here and there. But I used protection. Always. And Garrick probably told you I only had limited experiences with men in high school. None since."

She nodded and refused to let her imagination wonder about the details. She could spend hours listening to those experiences, but now wasn't the time. She focused on the practicalities and tried not to squirm. "Okay, then. I'm on the pill, and I've seen your blood tests so I know you were clean in Moncton, and again when you got to Boston. Garrick and I are also tested and clean. So, you know, if you want to skip the condoms, we can."

"Uh..."

"And not just you and I, obviously. You and Garrick can go raw, too."

He liked that idea. A lot. She wriggled against his erection and he gasped.

"Okay," he managed to choke out.

She smiled. "Great."

He shifted behind her, more of a twitch, and his shaft slipped along her wet, swelling folds. She rolled her hips against him, seeking more. His grip tightened, and he bit the back of her neck.

God, he already knew how to press her buttons. "Now?" she groaned.

"What?"

"Maybe you could not use a condom *now*?"

He shoved her down onto his thighs, his cock lodged harder against her pussy. "God, yes."

She looked back and he caught her mouth in a long, drugging kiss, squirming against him, his moan humming against her lips. They escalated from sleepy arousal to blazing desire in the space of a heartbeat.

His fingers dove between her legs and circled her clit before plucking it away from her body. She danced in response, throwing her leg back over his as two fingers sank deep. Growing pleasure and mounting need forced her to cry out his name.

Of course she'd wondered what kind of lover Rhian would be. She'd pictured him with Garrick, heard the details, but she hadn't known. Would never have guessed he would be so forceful. Could so quickly and perfectly take charge.

Garrick was fearless and demanding, sometimes overwhelming. She could imagine any lover of his being swept along in the wake of his confidence and authority. Rhian, though, was a quieter, gentler man. And yet, no less overwhelming. More than capable of sweeping her along.

As if to prove her point, he rolled and smashed her face

down on the mattress.

Oh fuck, yes!

He laughed and she realized she'd shouted that out loud.

"Sorry, I'm noisy," she mumbled, her cheeks heating. She'd been spoiled by Garrick, but maybe with Rhian she should dial it back. Garrick would be furious with her for even thinking it, but he wasn't realistic about these things.

Rhian nibbled her neck and shoulder and ground his cock into the valley of her ass. "I bet Garrick doesn't mind," he growled.

His teeth tortured the perfect spot high on her neck and she bowed her head, encouraging him. "No," she said into the mattress, "he loves it."

He hummed something that sounded like agreement. "I do to. I want to *hear* you."

Joy surged. His words set her free. She canted her hips up against him and he rocked forward, his shaft running along the sensitive skin and tight muscles surrounding her anus.

"God, Rhian. I need you."

He slid against her again and sucked on her neck. She didn't hold *anything* back, yelling about the wonderful things he did to her.

And then he was gone. "No, please—"

Her voice strangled in her throat when he lifted her ass in the air like she weighed nothing. Her knees tried to plant on the bed, but he spread her thighs wide with his, leaving her suspended. Her hands scrabbled for purchase on the fitted sheet.

She was putty in his hands. A puddle of need. His strength. The way he moved her however he wished. Held her above the bed. Jesus, she'd never given any thought to what it might mean to have such a physically powerful lover.

Now she'd never *stop* thinking about it.

The plump head of his cock brushed against her clit, across the entrance to her body, and she whimpered, begging for more. He let her hover there, enthralled by anticipation and the utter loss of control. She wanted to shove herself back, impale herself on his heavy shaft, but couldn't.

"Please, Rhian."

She jerked with surprise when his lips landed on the small of her back. His tongue dipped into the divots to each side of her spine at the top of her ass. His morning beard ticked her skin.

"You're beautiful," he rumbled.

His tender words surprised and delighted her. She wanted to say so many things in return, all of which were lost when his cock slid against her opening. The head nudged forward.

She groaned, glorying in the stretch. In the beauty of the connection.

He lifted her higher, and, with a powerful thrust, slammed into her to the hilt. The dull thump of his pelvis striking her ass echoed beneath her howl of pleasure.

"Like that?" he asked, his hoarse voice laced with amusement. His hips didn't stop moving, grinding against her.

"*Like?*" she burbled. "It's fucking amazing."

He laughed. "Oh, we're going to get to the fucking amazing part next, I promise."

She tried to help, to move, but he wouldn't relinquish his control. He just kept making gentle, maddening circles with his hips. She could picture the bunch of release of all those glorious muscles and she groaned, wishing she could see.

The image of herself in bed with Rhian and Garrick at the same time popped into her head and her brain stuttered. She *could* see. Someday. God help her, she had *two* powerful, demanding lovers who would fuck each other, too.

She thought she might just die of happiness on the damn spot.

"Jesus," he groaned reverently. "I've never...this is the first time I've ever done this."

She smiled against the sheets. "Fucked a woman?"

He laughed, exacting revenge with a long, slow withdrawal followed by a fast, deep plunge. "Without a condom, yes."

She liked being his first at something. "Good?"

He folded himself around her, her legs framing his, his chest to her back. "Fucking amazing." His words tickled her ear.

"I thought that was the part that came next?"

He chuckled against her neck. "As you wish."

His body rolled over hers, his shaft running along her clinging walls. The ridge of his thick head almost slipped from her body, before pausing, then sinking back in. He moved slowly, carefully, undulating over her back and thrusting into her as if she were fragile and not shouting at him to go faster. He ignored her demands. Fucked her as he pleased.

She loved it. Shouted louder. Apparently immune to her demands, she wondered if he was hard of hearing. He might well be after this.

It didn't matter. Instead, worried he would torture her with this long, slow fuck for the rest of the day. She wanted that even as her body clamored for more. She cried out when his warm, surging weight lifted off her back and his cock lodged deeper in her channel.

Lifting her again, he settled between her thighs, his knees shoving hers farther apart. She missed his heat but held her breath in anticipation of what he might do next.

He moaned. Shifted his clasp on her hips. "Fuck, I have to…"

"Do it!" she screamed.

God, and he *did*. His strokes were fast, powerful. She shuddered with the force of each impact, the shock still working through her while he was already almost completely withdrawn. And then thrusting back in again.

He repositioned her however he pleased, his next thrust stabbing the head of his rigid cock right where she needed it.

She squeaked. There was no other word for it. Every damn time he punched forward, shaking her entire body and nailing her g-spot, she let rip another undignified squeal.

Good god almighty, how fast, how long, could he go? He relentlessly reduced her to incoherent noises and thrashing limbs.

"God, shit, I'm close, I'm close," he growled, his thrusts shortening until he shunted back and forth against her g-spot at an inhuman speed, forcing the most exquisite climax up out of her body.

She keened, head spinning, back arching as wave after wave of ecstasy tore through her. Her belly clenched, and she shook with the strength of the shudders rippling low in her body. She'd never had an orgasm like this in her life. It stole her breath. His powerful thrusts coaxed more cries, overwhelming her.

Her galloping heart tripped when he groaned and thrust deep one last time. His release pumped into her, burning her, and made her spasm again.

He trembled against her but otherwise held perfectly still until they both collapsed onto the bed. His damp face landed on her back, his nose burrowed into her spine.

She couldn't move, her nervous system zapped into paralysis, unsure what exactly had happened. She was vaguely aware of the huge wet spot beneath her belly and thighs but couldn't make sense of it.

Gasping for air like she'd sprinted a mile, she slowly uncurled her aching fists from the sheets. "What the hell was that?"

His huff of laughter cooled her damp skin. "I think they call it sex."

She chuckled. *Look who's being fresh now.* Like she'd needed another reason to love him. "I'm not sure I've ever had sex like that. What the hell am I lying in?"

The damp sheets beneath her were getting cold and uncomfortable. She loathed the idea of moving from this spot with Rhian's weight on top of her. He grunted and she whimpered when his cock slipped from her body.

"You came," he said.

She smiled. "I sure as hell did."

"No, I mean, you ejaculated."

"I *what?*"

His chuckle was decidedly smug. "You ejaculated."

"I did *not.*"

His bark of laughter shook the bed. "Yes, you did. Trust me."

"Truly?"

"Yes." He kissed her shoulder blade. The base of her neck. "I guess you haven't done that before."

"No, I, ah..."

A long slow lick warmed her spine. "Are you okay?"

She warmed at the concern in his voice. "I'm fine. Way better than fine. That was amazing."

She felt him smile against her skin. "I'm glad you liked it."

"I did. Though I think I'd like to stop lying in the evidence, if that's all right with you."

He rolled off her and she no more than lifted her torso from the bed when he slipped a hand under her stomach and hauled her on top of him.

Seriously, the guy was ridiculously strong. As his trainer, she was aware he could bench press her if he wished. How had it never occurred to her how much fun it would be if he did?

His brows drew together. "Is this okay?"

"Yes, yes, of course." She smiled and leaned down to kiss him. She meant for it to be a peck, but it ended up a long, lingering exploration.

Chapter Twenty Five

Rhian lay back on the bed, floating in a combination of post-coital lassitude and the low hum of arousal brought on by Savannah's kiss. It would be a while yet before his junk was ready to get back in the game, but he was still enjoying the hell out of this.

It also served as a terrific distraction. He'd been working on instinct—and well outside his usual comfort zone—when he'd hauled Savannah on top of him. Her surprise had burst the bubble of confidence and reminded him of the host of reasons they shouldn't be doing this.

He opened his mouth to say god-only-knew what, but she silenced him with another kiss. When she released his mouth, he stared at her tousled hair and red, bee-stung lips. He'd done that to her. And Jesus H. Christ, she looked incredible.

"Don't," she said softly.

"Don't what?"

"Freak out."

He sighed. She knew him too well. "There's a lot to freak out about."

Her warm lips brushed his eyebrows, his forehead, the corners of his eyes. Rhian tilted his head, rubbing their faces together as she moved here and there to kiss him again. It was such a foreign experience. Before Savannah, no one had ever done anything like this.

Garrick loved to cuddle, but not soothe him with such lavish attention. Garrick's affection was a living blanket wrapped around him, something he'd come to love, even if it was sometimes overwhelming. These feather-light caresses quieted him, like discovering a source of heat and light on a cold night.

Savannah folded her hands on his chest, rested her chin on

them, and stretched out on top of him. "Is there anything I can say to make you believe this is a good thing?" she asked.

Was there? He shrugged. "What do you think Garrick is going to say?"

She thought about it, then smiled. "Yee haw?"

He grinned. She was probably right.

"Rhian, I don't want you to get the wrong impression."

Amazing how he could go from mellow contentedness to gut-curdling dread in the span of a heartbeat. This would be where she snapped out of whatever starry-eyed delusions she'd had last night and explained his place in her world. In Garrick's world. And he would agree, even as a part of him died. Together, they could make Garrick see the sense of it.

Then he'd leave. Boston. Them.

"Hey. Where'd you go?" She cupped one hand over his cheek. "I just want you to know, this isn't some sexual escapade or thrill. Not for me. It's more than that."

She couldn't possibly mean—

"I care."

Rhian's brain ground to a halt.

Fear clutched at his chest, fucked with his breathing. He was a goddamn idiot. He should get up and go, but instead he lay there, trapped by her direct gaze, wanting desperately to tell her the truth.

He shouldn't give her more power to hurt him. The rational, logical side of his brain screamed at him to protect himself. But counter to every instinct he'd ever honed, he gave her a piece of himself.

"I care, too."

She searched his face. "So you'll stay?"

"For now." No point departing from brutal honesty now.

The truth was, it didn't matter if he slept with Garrick, or Savannah, or both of them together—though that last thought sent a shiver through his body that got his dick to take notice.

In the end, he'd leave, or be left. That was life.

Savannah squirmed and he realized he was squeezing her tight against him. He tried to let go.

She reached behind her to hold his hand against her back. "Please. Don't."

He traced his palm down the long curve of her back, soothing her. Instincts again. They were killing him.

She smiled at him. Either he was doing a shit job of making his expectations clear, or she was willfully ignoring them. He didn't know how to make her see the light.

His stomach filled the silence, noisily announcing an objection to skipping dinner last night.

Savannah's eyebrow quirked. "Hungry?"

"I could eat a cow."

"I don't have a cow." She said it as though this was truly regrettable. "But I can make cheesy eggs, bacon and toast."

Rhian's stomach voted for him, agreeing loudly. "How many eggs?"

Savannah laughed. "You've met my brothers. Are you questioning my ability to feed you properly?"

"Point taken."

He jumped when she pinched his side. "Now get up," she ordered, and sprang to her knees beside him. "I'll let you have dibs on the shower while I start cooking. Then after breakfast and some time to digest, we'll stop by your place so you can change, and we'll go for our run."

He groaned. He'd been hoping to spend the day in bed.

With her.

Savannah raced over the Charles River from Boston into Cambridge, Harvard's campus just ahead. To her right would be a spectacular vista of the Boston skyline, but it wouldn't hold a candle to the view right in front of her.

Rhian's ass flexed, his quads bulging as he slowed on the

downhill slope of the bridge before reaching the stairs. If she could, she'd have someone film him from all angles, just so she could watch. For hours.

She lamented the chill in the air and Rhian's T-shirt, wishing she could watch the ripple of muscles in his shoulders and haunches, too. Every single inch of the man's body was magnificent.

Rhian Savage is athletic trainer porn.

She laughed and almost lost her footing on the stairs before Rhian's arm looped around her waist and hoisted her down to level ground.

"Thanks," she said between breaths. She wasn't sucking wind, but her lungs were definitely working hard. Rhian was the same, so she'd held her own at least.

"Where to now?" he asked. "Back to the apartment?"

They usually ran the round trip in one go, but she didn't want to rush back to the apartment. She was enjoying being out with Rhian, without the tension that had ebbed between them until last night. Now they seemed to have a thousand reasons to brush up against one another. The touch of a hand, a shoulder bumped. Smiles came easier.

"How about lunch? We can call Lachlan and see if he's free."

She didn't mention that Lachlan would probably like to see for himself that she and Rhian had survived the night in one piece.

Rhian agreed and she called her brother as they walked into the buzz of Harvard Square. Lachlan needed a few minutes to get to them, so Savannah led the way to the news agent in the heart of the Square and just a few feet from Lachlan's office.

She took a couple bottles of water to the register while Rhian poked through a magazine stand nearby. Someone came into the shop, and she did a double take when she glanced out the door, hardly noticing when the cashier handed back her change.

"Rhian." She stepped up to the dirty glass door. "Come here."

He put his hand on her back. "What's wrong?"

"Look who is standing on the corner."

His gaze narrowed as he searched the milling crowds. She knew the moment he saw his look-alike stalker, his eyes widening. She grabbed his arm before he could dash out the door like last time.

"How the hell did she follow us here?" he asked.

"I don't think she did. Look. She's talking to two girlfriends. And she's wearing heels. There's no way in hell she followed us on foot."

Savannah stared at Rhian's beautiful young stalker. She hadn't imagined the resemblance, though it wasn't as pronounced today. The young woman had the same blonde curls as Rhian, but hers were long, reaching halfway down her back. Savannah wished she could see her eyes.

The young woman turned and smiled before walking into the subway station. Rhian gasped.

"You see it too, don't you?" Savannah asked. She slipped her hand into his. He appeared more stunned than panicky, but she wasn't taking any chances.

"My god, she's..."

"Gorgeous. Like you."

"I'm not gorgeous," he muttered, his cheeks turning pink as he tried to shake her hand loose.

She snorted and held on. "Yeah, right. Have you looked in the mirror recently?"

His cheeks edged toward crimson, his eyes not quite meeting hers. "Shut up."

She laughed. "Shut up? That's the best you can do? *Shut up?* Oh, my sexy, beautiful friend, you're going to have to do better than that if you want to win an argument with me. Look at you," she continued, enjoying how he cast his eyes around the little shop, desperately searching for an escape. His neck and ears glowed a dull red. "The eyes, the hair, the smile. You have these amazing crow's feet. And then, of course, there's the body. Should I tell you about your body?" She pitched her voice low, so only he could hear her. "I've dreamed about licking every square inch of your long, gorgeous—"

Rhian clapped a hand over her mouth. "Hi, Lachlan!"

"Hi, Sis."

Savannah spun at the sound of Lachlan's deep voice. He stood not three feet away, one eyebrow way up. She barely suppressed the urge to fidget.

Once again, she wondered how the hell was she going to explain two boyfriends—*two lovers*—to her family?

"Hi!" she said, a shade too brightly, and kissed Lachlan's cheek.

Rhian reached to shake Lachlan's hand, careful not to touch her. "Lach."

Lachlan looked between them, his lips pursed in thought. She couldn't get her perceptive brother out of the store and to the restaurant fast enough.

Chapter Twenty Six

It was decadent and lazy, but Rhian was grateful to take a taxi home from Harvard Square after scarfing down an enormous lunch. Tomorrow he'd hit the gym, go for a run and generally work himself into the ground. It was the best way to get through the days Savannah had to work while he waited for the biopsy results. In truth, he probably ought to indulge a little more often. He was getting thinner and eventually Savannah would notice and kick his ass.

Worse, he worried she and Garrick would find it unattractive.

Not that it was an issue right now. Only an hour ago she'd been telling him she wanted to lick his long, gorgeous...what?

He stared at her ass, at the perfect height in front of him as they climbed the stairs to her apartment. His mind blanked. His feet kept moving, one in front of the other, while he became hypnotized by the sway of muscle and bitable flesh.

He wanted to ask her about the licking she'd promised, but didn't want to appear like he was fishing for a compliment. Nothing could be further from the truth. What he would be fishing for was that licking.

He almost ran into her when she stopped at her door.

"I should do some work," she said as she stepped into the apartment.

Dreams of imitating a human popsicle went out the window. "Okay."

She waved at the living room. "Go watch TV, nap, whatever. I won't be long."

He nodded, deflated. Now might be the time to go back to his place. Some distance might help him think straight.

He'd tried not to dwell on it, but he hated how she'd been careful not to touch him in front of Lachlan. He'd done the

186

same, following her lead, but it stung. First he and Garrick couldn't be out because of their careers, now he and Savannah couldn't because...well, why the hell couldn't they?

Oh yeah, because he was the extra bonus dick, not the real thing.

He turned toward the door. "I'm going to head over to my place to shower and change. Give me a shout when you have time."

He had his hand on the doorknob, almost free, when Savannah flew around him and slammed her back against the door.

"What the hell just happened?" She searched his face with those all-seeing green eyes.

"Nothing. These clothes are a little ripe from our run and you need time to work."

There, that sounded perfectly reasonable. Nothing like *it makes me want to puke when I think about being your dirty little secret.*

She rubbed a palm over his chest. "I don't want you to go."

His stupid heart lurched. He was doing a lousy job of managing his own expectations.

"I'll be back," he heard himself promising.

"Right away?"

He sighed. "Right away."

"With a suitcase?"

His brain stuttered. "A suitcase?"

She ran both hands up over his shoulders and around his neck, drawing him closer. "So you don't have to go back as often. Bring clothes. Your razor." She paused to trail a finger along his jaw. "The contents of your freezer."

His ass clenched and his knees wobbled. He caught himself with a hand on the door above her head, their faces mere inches apart.

"Craving ice cream?" he asked.

She smiled. "We can probably find a use for that, too."

Rhian didn't make a conscious decision to kiss her. It was simply imperative. Like his next breath. His body throbbed. Fire thread through his veins. He tried to extinguish it by pinning her to the door.

Funny how that didn't help.

Shit, wasn't I about to leave? He ground his hips forward and slipped a leg between hers. Soon they were humping up against the door like a couple of horny teenagers.

He cupped her ass in his hands and hoisted her up. She wrapped her legs around his waist.

"God, I love how you manhandle me," she muttered.

Her tongue delved into his mouth, making it damn hard to respond. Not that he had anything to say. *I like manhandling you* seemed fairly self-evident.

He staggered away from the door, not because of her weight, but because Savannah was rubbing against him like a damn cat. Blood rushed from his brain to his dick so fast, he nearly dropped her.

He crashed into the kitchen table and the zing of pain cleared his head. He realized two things. First, he would probably kill them both on the way to the bedroom. Second, it was too damn long to wait.

He dumped Savannah onto the tabletop and stepped away. She tried to hold onto him with legs and hands. He stilled her protest by stripping his shorts and boxer briefs to his ankles.

That got her attention.

She laughed and immediately yanked off her running shoes and tossed them over her shoulder into the living room. It was a race to see who could get naked faster. An easy win for him, but only because she had to wrestle a sports bra over her head. The minute she had, he hauled her up against him, bent her backwards over his arm, and devoured her mouth.

He was ravenous. For her. For this. Determined to make a permanent impression. He shouldn't think that way, but hell, it was hard to hold onto anything but the most primal urges when Savannah Morrison was in his arms.

Cupping her ass, he looked down at her splayed beneath him and a shuddered. He could see she was ready for him, for this. He thrust all the way into her in one long push.

Her eyes lost focus, her mouth hanging open. "Oh god. Rhian. *Rhian.*"

God, he fucking loved how she cried his name. All the time. Eyes opened, eyes closed, facing him or away, he always knew she was perfectly aware of *him*. That it was his cock encased in her hot, clinging body. His hips that jammed against hers, grinding his way into heaven.

She moaned and planted her hands behind her, grinding back. He gripped her ass more firmly and changed the angle so his cock was forced up against the front wall of her pussy.

She whimpered as he rubbed there, oh-so gently. Her eyes raked over his chest, down to his abs, his belly, then stared at the point where her body clung to his as he slowly pulled back.

"Holy shit, that's hot," she breathed.

He snuck a peek before whipping his gaze back to her face. "Too hot. Can't look."

She laughed. "I'm not talking about that." She checked for herself, watching him slide in. "Though, wow, that *is* hot. I'm talking about you."

Her eyes focused on his chest. Abs. Belly.

Holy shit, he'd never again be able to hang with his teammates in the trainer's office if she didn't knock it off. How could he forget the look on her face as she studied him?

He withdrew, slowly, dragging his cock through clenching muscles. He gritted his teeth against the ecstasy roaring through his body.

"You're beautiful," she said.

He surged forward harder, eliciting a squeak of ecstasy. He did it again.

"Perfection. All that definition. Muscle. Strength." She

panted out the words in time with his increasingly rapid thrusts. "I could stare. At your. Hip dip. All. Damn. Day."

What the hell is a hip dip? He pulled her ass higher and pushed harder.

"God, you're pretty," she groaned.

He faltered, growing self-consciousness throwing him off.

Pretty?

Sweat trickled down his back as he lifted her to meet his next thrust. She lit up in his arms. Her embarrassing praise forgotten as each plunge made his knees wobble. His ears rang with his own name, his heart squeezing painfully in his chest.

At some point, she became incapable of articulation. Or maybe he became incapable of understanding anything but the long, low moans rumbling from his chest and the startled whimpers he punched from hers.

The fire in his veins coalesced in his balls. Tension gathered at the base of his spine. She arched above the table, her head thrown back, her moans reaching a crescendo as her body clamped down around him.

Jesus Fucking Christ.

Rhian exploded, his mind nothing but perfect, screaming pleasure as shudder after shudder tore up out of his soul.

Garrick sat in Rupert's office, staring out the window carved into the cinderblock wall above the desk. He'd been going through the motions for days, trying to focus on the mountain of work ahead and not obsess about what the hell was going on in Boston.

He was doing a damn poor job of the not-obsessing part.

He was haunted by the image of Rhian's pale face and startled eyes. He hadn't spoken to either of his lovers since that night, but had received daily good morning greetings and good night wishes by text. And they'd sent their love. Even Rhian.

He told himself to take comfort from that, if nothing else. Rhian was fine. Safe. Savannah was looking after him. If anything happened—another panic attack or news from the doctors—he would hear.

Goddamn it, he was too far away.

His stomach had turned to acid, worry eating him from the inside out. When he wasn't anxious about Rhian's mental and physical health, he was worried about Savannah's. She had taken on a lot. His gratitude was enormous, but of little help to any of them.

A loud knock on the door jolted him. He'd been so far off in space, Rupert had gone back to work with him sitting there gazing out the window like a love-sick idiot.

Rupert met Garrick's eyes and they both shrugged. They didn't have another meeting until this afternoon.

"Come in," Rupert called.

Garrick's jaw dropped as Callum Morrison stormed through the door. He pinned Garrick with a fierce scowl and narrow-eyed stare in a familiar shade of green.

"Don't you answer your fucking phone?"

Garrick and Rupert both shot out of their chairs. Garrick tried not to look guilty. He'd intended to call Callum back, but he'd also assumed the damn man was in Denver where he belonged.

"Callum," Garrick managed, extending his hand. "What are you doing here?"

"I'm saving your bacon, buddy." Callum sounded decidedly grim. He took Garrick's hand in a firm grip and kicked the door closed behind him.

Between the two of them, they filled Rupert's little space.

Rupert did a decent job of hiding his nerves, but Garrick knew him well enough to see them. For one thing, he didn't come out from behind his desk.

Garrick suppressed a sigh. "Callum, you've met Rupert over Skype a time or two, I believe."

Callum barely gave the man a nod before glaring to Garrick. "You're going to Boston."

"What?" Rupert asked before Garrick could snap his gaping mouth shut.

Callum pinned Rupert with the full weight of his stare. "I'm here to help. Garrick has to go."

Garrick steadied himself with a hand on the back of his chair. "What happened? What's wrong?"

"Garrick can't just leave," Rupert exclaimed. "He has a lot of work to do here."

Callum's grunt dismissed Rupert completely.

Garrick's patience snapped. "God damn it, Callum, what the hell is going on?"

"Nothing. I don't think. I don't know." He threw up his hands. "All I know is my sister is up to her eyeballs in her new job and taking care of Rhian, and you need to get your ass to Boston and help her."

Garrick grabbed Callum's arm. "But what—"

"Get your house in order," Callum barked, yanking his arm free. "I have no idea what the hell that will look like, and I don't give a shit. Just go!"

Rupert slammed his hand down on the desk, his pale cheeks burning with two bright red spots. "Just who the hell do you think you are, barging in here and telling him what he has to do?" Rupert's British accent became increasingly clipped, his volume soaring with his anger. "We are in the middle of draft negotiations and a major construction project. He can't just hie off to Boston because you demand it."

"Who the hell am I? Who the fuck says *hie?*" Callum's face was almost as red as Rupert's now. "I'll tell you who the fuck I am. I'm his future brother-in-law, if he doesn't fuck it up, and I'm part owner of this team. That's who!"

"Well, I don't give a rat's arse. You don't get to throw this organization into chaos because you've unilaterally decided to be a bloody-minded arsehole!"

Garrick stared at Rupert in shock. Then at Callum, who appeared wholly underwhelmed with Rupert's show of temper.

Callum sneered at Rupert. "You're going to have to get over it, Duchess, because I'm staying and he's going."

Duchess? Garrick inhaled so fast he started to cough. No one paid him any attention.

Rupert blinked, his back poker-straight as his eyes narrowed on Callum. "Listen, *Daniel Boone*, maybe you think your brash new-world style is charming, but I'm bloody well not impressed. We can call a meeting of the owners and decide this like the civilized businessmen some of us are. Until then, we need Garrick here."

Goddamn, Rupert was showing a hell of a lot more mettle than usual. Garrick couldn't have been happier. Why couldn't the guy be like this all the fucking time?

He swung his head to look at Callum—beginning to feel like he was sitting court side at a tennis match— and saw Callum's lips twitch before he arranged his expression back into a furious scowl.

"How about this? We send Garrick to Boston," Callum suggested, as if Garrick wasn't standing *right there*, "and hold off on the meeting until you've had a chance to decide if I can actually help around here, instead of assuming I'm just some dumb hockey player with a big bank account and pucks for brains."

Rupert somehow managed to look down his nose at Callum, though they were about the same height. "You couldn't possibly jump into the draft at this stage. You have no idea what's needed."

"Screw you, too, Smythe. I've read every report and I know a good hockey player when I see one, on ice or on paper. I've studied this team for months. I know the Hamilton kid will fill out our defensive line and why. I know Belov is thinking about retiring and we need to sign strong goal talent who will last past a few seasons. I know every damn thing you know, *and* I have the advantage of actually having played hockey, which I would bet my last fucking dollar you've never done in your damn *life.*"

Garrick had never seen Rupert's jaw bulge like that.

"Fine," Rupert growled through clenched teeth. "Let's see how we do. You stay, Garrick goes. And when next season you're not pleased with the results, you'll have no one to blame but yourself and your monstrous ego."

Callum took a fast step toward Rupert and in the blink of an eye Rupert's bravery deserted him. He stumbled back, barely managing to stay on his feet when his back slammed into the filing cabinets.

"Callum!" Garrick barked, not sure what to say, who to defend, or where the hell to insert himself in this mess.

Garrick couldn't say who looked more horrified by the sudden shift in the room. Rupert regrouped first, standing tall once more, though noticeably further away from Callum. He turned to Garrick. "Go."

"What?

"Go. Go to Boston. Your mind has been there for months anyway."

"But Rupert—"

"Shut up before I change my mind," Rupert snapped. "As much as it galls me to admit it, Callum is right." He eyed the man in question as if he was something stuck to the bottom of his shoe. "Savannah and Rhian need you. You can work your ass off from there. I doubt we could prevent it if we tried, which, frankly, I won't."

Garrick hesitated. "Are you sure?"

Rupert tore his eyes from Callum. "Yes. Go. Send my love to Savannah and Rhian. Tell them I'm sorry you've had to stay here as long as you have."

"What about—"

"I assure you," Rupert said with another dubious glance at Callum, "if he's not up for the task, I'll call you back. Let's hope he's capable of more than high-handed douchebaggery and can pull his weight."

Callum's eyes widened, but he held his tongue, his glare hot enough to set Rupert on fire.

"But—"

"GO!" They shouted in unison, their eyes locked on each other.

Garrick went.

Hell, he ran like the building was under attack, his feet barely touching the ground as he burst from the arena.

For the first time in days, Garrick smiled a big, huge, happy grin.

He was going home.

Chapter Twenty Seven

Savannah trudged up the stairs to her apartment, her laptop bag heavy on her shoulder. She'd spent the entire day wishing she was home with Rhian while suffering through endless meetings to plan for the coming season.

The day could be tallied as a success, but she was glad it was over.

She dropped her bag and kicked off her shoes in the front hall, then called out to Rhian.

He stepped around the corner just as both their cell phones chimed.

It was a text message from Garrick. *Truck packed and ready to go. Leaving first thing tomorrow. I'll be there soon.*

For one glorious moment, Rhian looked truly, perfectly happy. It hit her like a punch in the chest.

Then his eyes darkened, his brows drew together and he turned away.

Shit.

She leaned back against the door. "It's going to be great."

He shook his head. "I should clear out. At least until you've had a chance to talk to him. I don't want to be in the way."

He'd have to get through her first.

She choked back her desire to yell and spoke calmly. "Rhian, you're not going to be in the way. Why would you say that? I want you here. He will, too."

Of course, Garrick still had no idea what he was about to walk into. She didn't feel even the slightest need to warn him. No, the issue was going to be convincing Rhian.

She considered asking him if she should clear out. Why wouldn't she be the one in the way? She didn't bother, though. He still thought of himself as the outsider, in spite of the fact that both she and Garrick were now his lovers.

Then she considered telling him the truth. That she, too, was in love with him. It might help.

It might also send him running faster than ever.

"Come on," she said, holding out her hand. When he took it, she towed him into the living room and pushed him down on the couch, then knelt on the floor between his knees.

She smiled at his curious, slightly alarmed expression.

She took his hands in hers and rubbed her thumbs over his skin. "We're just figuring things out. Don't skip out on us now."

"But—"

"But nothing, Rhian."

The fear in his eyes dug at her. She crawled up over him, hiking her skirt until she could straddle his lap, cradling the rising bulge in his sweats between her thighs.

"Think about it." She cupped his face and kissed the worry lines between his soft blond eyebrows. "What it will be like..."

The images flashing through her mind were too hot. Too delicious. She squirmed, rubbing her rapidly swelling bits against his.

His lips parted, and the deep blue of his eyes was lost to dilated pupils and heavy eyelids. Jesus, he was beautiful.

He blinked slowly. His hips started kicking in little jerks against her.

The long day fell away. The comfort she'd tried to offer Rhian, given back to her ten-fold. She wriggled against him, her breath catching. "Think about adding Garrick to this. To have him here, too. His hands, his tongue. His cock. His *imagination.*"

Rhian's groan was pure agony and ecstasy all rolled into one.

Their hips caught a rhythm. She arched her back, grinding down on top of him. "I want to see you suck his cock. Take it into your throat and..."

Rhian's hands clenched her hips and shoved her down on

his cock. She lost the thread of her explicit ramblings.

"Tell me more," he gasped.

Someone likes dirty talk.

She threaded her fingers through his hair and held on as their gyrations became more forceful. "I want you to watch him fuck me. Want him to watch how you manhandle me. God, I love how you manhandle me." She paused to suck in a deep breath. Then the words fell from her mouth. All her desires. A litany of naughty fantasies and desperate wishes. Everything she wanted to try. Do. Watch. His grip was almost painful now, the thrust of his hips more powerful with every picture she painted. She told him how she wanted to fuck them both at once. And watch his face when Garrick's huge cock stretched him open. She told him, in exacting detail, how she knew how good that felt. "Then I want to watch you fuck Garrick. Watch *his* face as you plow into him with all that power and—"

Rhian arched beneath her, his head thrown back against the couch. "Oh god, now. *Now!*"

She rode his bucking legs, his cock grinding up against her clit. She sobbed as pleasure welled up and spilled over, her thighs quivering and pussy clenching.

He shook as hard as she did. Clung as tightly.

They collapsed back against the couch and she caught his mouth in a long, messy kiss, desperately trying to convey her love. For minutes, maybe hours. And still she hadn't said enough.

Maybe it was time she said it out loud.

His hand stroked down her back, and she lamented the fact she was still wearing her damn suit.

God, and he'd just come in his pants. She started to giggle.

"I haven't, you know," he said, his voice hoarse.

She choked back her laughter. "Huh?"

"Fucked him. I haven't fucked Garrick."

She leaned back and cocked her head. "I don't understand."

A blush rose on his cheeks. "He's fucked me, but never...the reverse."

Her brows drew down. "Really?"

He shrugged.

"But he loves it."

"He does?"

"He certainly said as much to me. I haven't had a chance to try it yet myself. But plugs and stuff, yeah."

"Wow. Thanks for those images." Rhian blinked, looking a bit dazed.

She grinned. "You're welcome. But tell me, why not?"

He shrugged again. "We haven't gotten around to it?"

She sent him an arch stare.

"Okay, I don't know. It's never come up, honestly. I was so freaked out by what was happening, and what I was feeling, that I never really...asserted myself when it came to sex."

Savannah wasn't at all surprised that Garrick had overwhelmed Rhian with his lovemaking. God knew she'd been there. "He has a way of taking control, doesn't he?" she asked with a little smile.

Rhian laughed, a wonderful sound. "Yeah, he does."

"You're pretty good at it, too."

His cheeks went from pink to red.

She laughed. She loved that he still blushed, in spite of all they'd done together. "In fact, I seem to be having the same trouble with you that you've had with him. I can't quite seem to assert myself."

"I'm sorry."

"Please," she said dryly, "do *not* apologize."

He almost smiled. "Okay."

"All I'm saying is that I see how it can happen. And just like I'm going to take control from you and do as I please someday, you can do the same with Garrick. I'll even help you wrestle him to the bed, if that's what you want."

Rhian's face went slack as he stared off into space, his cheeks flushed. "Yes, please."

Someone *really* had a thing for dirty talk. Rhian shifted beneath her and they both grimaced. Her rapidly cooling panties were a little gross. His sweats had to be as bad or worse.

She slid back on his legs and his hands tightened around her waist. She smiled and patted his hands. "How about a shower?"

His face scrunched up and he plucked at his sweats. "Yeah, I think that's a must."

With matching groans, they hauled themselves up off the couch. Savannah smiled at the easy way they moved around the apartment together. When she stripped, Rhian took her clothes and sorted them along with his clothes into the laundry hampers. She wandered down the hall to the bathroom and started the shower, pleased when he climbed in with her a few minutes later.

He belonged there. And not just in the shower.

Now how the hell she was going to get *him* to believe that?

Rhian lay in bed that night, Savannah's head on his shoulder, their heartbeats in sync and slowly returning to normal.

They'd gone slow this time, nothing fancy. As vanilla as it got. Missionary position. No toys, no unusual positions, places or orifices. Simple sex. Lovemaking.

He shoved that last thought aside and watched as Savannah crawled out of bed and got them a washcloth. He should have done it, but she always beat him to it. He might be younger, but she recovered faster. Or maybe she wasn't struggling as damn hard as he was to wrap his head around what was happening between them.

This was insane. How did a loner like him end up in this woman's bed?

He took the warm cloth from her and wiped himself down. He was still startled by the feel of waxed, smooth skin, but he definitely liked it.

While Savannah went to toss the washcloth in the sink, he automatically checked for the lump, hoping that this time it would have magically disappeared. No such luck.

Savannah stopped in the process of cuddling up to him and propped herself up on one elbow. "What's wrong?"

He grimaced. "It's nothing. I'm being stupid."

"Tell me," she said.

As usual, he wanted to and he had no idea why. "I was just checking the lump. It's still there," he said as if surprised. His attempt at humor fell miserably flat.

Savannah brushed the hair back from his forehead. "I'm sorry."

"Do you want to—" He clamped his mouth shut. Jesus Christ, why would he even ask her that?

"Can I?"

He hesitated, then nodded, frozen in place as her hand slipped beneath the covers and over his chest before settling on top of his, still clutching his sac like it might run off somewhere.

He let go and slowly guided her to cup his balls. He aligned his fingers over hers and pressed until she felt the hard knot that had no business in his junk.

Rather than yank her hand away in horror or discomfort, she prodded gently, learning the size and shape of it, the way he had countless times. When she was done, she ran her thumb over the loose skin in a comforting caress.

"Come here," she whispered, her voice husky. He closed his eyes, afraid if he saw tears he'd embarrass the hell out of himself.

He rolled toward her and rested his head on her shoulder, his arm around her ribs, their legs tangled together. She reached over to snap off the light, and in the dark, close comfort of her arms, he did the unthinkable.

He let himself cry.

Chapter Twenty Eight

Rhian sat on the edge of the bed, his leg bouncing maniacally, and tried to wrestle his nerves down from nauseating to merely heart-pounding.

It had been a long day, his anxiety steadily creeping higher with each passing hour. Savannah had gone to work at the crack of dawn so she could be home before Garrick's earliest possible arrival time. Rhian had been shocked to hear himself offering to do the grocery shopping while she was gone. Then, for some damn reason, he'd done the laundry, changed the sheets, and even cleaned the bathroom.

Now he sat fidgeting while Savannah roamed around the apartment and straightened up what he hadn't already tackled. Which wasn't much.

Savannah's idea for how to greet Garrick had sounded sane enough when she'd told him this morning. The more time that passed, though, the more doubts he had.

If Garrick had hauled ass and driven eight hours straight through from Moncton, he'd be arriving in the next hour. They were ready, just in case, but Rhian would probably be sitting here for hours.

In his underwear. And nothing else.

Savannah had bought him these boxer briefs on her lunch break today. She said she'd noticed he didn't have many pairs and thought he might like to have more, while swearing he never had to wear them on her account. She and Garrick both seemed to enjoy the fact he rarely wore any.

He'd been touched that she'd thought to buy him the damn things. Had actually had to make an excuse about putting them with his stuff so he could have a minute alone in the bedroom. Was a grown man supposed to get sentimental about underpants?

They were simple white. Not particularly sexy, as far as he

could tell. Maybe a little tight and see-through, but nothing extraordinary.

Savannah, on the other hand, had chosen to wear something that hit him like a punch to his chest every time he saw her.

His Bruins jersey.

The heavy fabric fell to the tops of her bare thighs, the sleeves rolled up to her wrists, the shoulders so wide the seam fell almost to her elbow. Why something big enough for her to use as a tent looked so fucking hot, he had no idea. All he knew was that every time he saw SAVAGE emblazoned across her shoulders, his dick twitched and he felt a little lightheaded.

The sound of a key in the front door echoed through the apartment.

Rhian shot to his feet. Savannah's footsteps echoed as she ran toward the bedroom. And him.

He leaned against the bedroom doorframe, his arms crossed over his chest, trying like hell to appear casual while staring holes in the front door. Savannah skidded to a halt beside him and sent him a smoldering look.

She eyed his mostly transparent boxers and totally obvious anticipation, and her lips quirked. Her long, bare legs just inches from his, she draped herself along the opposite side of the doorframe.

Rhian suddenly wanted to change the plan. To grab her and hold on until he was sure Garrick wasn't going to freak out.

The front door swung open and Rhian forgot how to breathe. His eyes devoured Garrick as the damn man wrestled with the key, trying to get it out of the lock. He hadn't even noticed them yet.

Rhian barely held himself together. His heart thundered in his chest and he choked back the urge to shout Garrick's name.

God, I really do love him.

Would he ever get used to it? Should he?

The front door swung shut with a bang and Garrick hiked

the two huge duffels higher on his shoulders. "Savannah, baby, are you here?"

She and Rhian exchanged a quick nervous glance.

Garrick turned and walked into the apartment before he saw them waiting.

He staggered to a halt and his mouth dropped open. Then he fell to his knees.

"Oh shit," Rhian said as he started to run. "We killed him!"

Savannah laughed as she chased Rhian down the hall. She would *never* forget the look on Garrick's face. Oh god, they had shocked the bejeesus out of him. She'd been sure he'd guessed...

She dropped to the floor the same time as Rhian. Together they hauled the straps off Garrick's shoulders, shoved the bags away, and grabbed hold of him. He knelt, staring at them wild-eyed, like he couldn't believe what he was seeing.

Then he gazed at her with such abject gratitude, she had to swallow past the lump in her throat.

He curled a big hand around the back of Rhian's neck and stared like he was trying to memorize him, here, in their house. He smiled and Rhian smiled back.

Savannah cupped Garrick's cheek and his gaze cut back to her. She cupped Rhian's cheek, too, and Garrick watched with wide eyes. His smile wobbled.

Hers did too. She tucked her lips next to his ear. "I get it now," she said softly.

Garrick nodded, his eyes growing suspiciously shiny.

Savannah looked at Rhian. "Kiss him," she said.

Rhian hesitated, countless questions in his eyes.

She ran a thumb along his jaw. "Go ahead."

His smile flickered, still uncertain, but he turned to Garrick. "I love you."

Garrick swallowed hard. "I love you, too, baby."

Rhian slammed his mouth over Garrick's.

Savannah couldn't tear her gaze from the two gorgeous, *huge* men making out in front of her. She'd never seen anything hotter. There was nothing about these men that wasn't hard, masculine. Their ready strength and gloriously fit bodies made their chemistry an aggressive thing. They were perfect together.

Rhian's bare skin glowed in the reflection of the sunlight coming through the skylights, a stark contrast to Garrick's dark clothes.

God, Garrick still had his damn coat on.

Laughing, she went to work on the buttons, her hands brushing Rhian's chest as she tugged the heavy fabric aside. Garrick tried to help her, but he was more hindrance than help, eventually giving up and sinking his hands into Rhian's curls, only releasing them when she needed him to.

She managed to get the jacket off and his shirt unbuttoned. Rhian kissed a path to Garrick's ear, his throat, all the while fumbling with the cuff of Garrick's shirt, growling when he couldn't unbutton it.

Garrick yanked the shirt over his big hands, buttons popping free and skittering across the hardwood floors. Rhian sat back and laughed until Garrick discarded his T-shirt, too, baring his chest to eager eyes.

Savannah dove in to capture a nipple with her mouth. Rhian caught the other, and together they tackled Garrick to the floor.

She'd had no intention of their first time making love as a threesome taking place in the kitchen, let alone on the floor, but damned if they were going to stop now.

She caught Rhian's eye across the broad expanse of Garrick's chest and winked, loving the sparkle of amusement lighting his gaze. He pulled off Garrick's nipple with a loud pop, ignoring Garrick's hand behind his head trying to tow him back.

"Now you kiss him," Rhian said.

She wasn't going to argue with that. She stretched up over Garrick and looked down into his beautiful, dark chocolate eyes. Her long hair hid their faces.

Thank you, he mouthed.

She smiled. *No, thank you.*

His hand brushed her shoulder and cupped the back of her head. "I love you," Garrick said out loud.

"I love you, too," she said against his lips.

Their tongues tangled, and the passion that had burned from the moment they'd first kissed, all those months ago, flared to life. Only now it was more. They had *more.*

Garrick was soon twitching and writhing beneath her. It was like trying to hold onto a ship bucking in rough seas, his arms holding her close the only thing that kept her from being tossed overboard. Rhian's hair brushed her ribs. Her hip. A hand that could not possibly belong to Garrick swept over her back and stroked across her ass, making her writhe as frantically as Garrick.

When Garrick gave a particularly hard shudder, her curiosity got the better of her.

She ended their kiss with a gasp. "I have to see."

She turned to watch Rhian's tongue dip into Garrick's belly button, his stomach jerking against Rhian's mouth. She could see from the shiny trails across Garrick's skin that Rhian had teased under the curve of his pecs, traced the lines of his abs, but never gone below his navel.

Savannah grabbed hold of Garrick's jeans and yanked his button-fly open with one hard tug. She waited for him to lift his ass off the ground so she could strip him to his ankles.

Rather than pull them all the way off, she left his feet trapped. Garrick was inclined to take charge, and she and Rhian were likely to let him. The role reversal was fun. No point making it easy for Garrick to take back the upper hand when he finally snapped out of the stupor their little surprise had created.

Garrick wriggled, trying to get his legs free, but she stopped him with a touch. Well, if you could call wrapping her hand around his rock-hard erection *a touch*.

"*Please*," he begged, his voice hoarse.

She bit her lip and slowly shook her head. "No, I want Rhian to do it."

Rhian lifted his head, ending his tongue's thorough investigation of Garrick's hip dip. "What?"

"I want to watch you suck Garrick's cock."

The words echoed in the hallway, punctuated by the sound of Garrick's head dropping back to the floor with a thunk.

"Oh my god," Garrick muttered.

She saw how Rhian's hand shook and recalled his response to her dirty talk the day before.

"He told me, Rhian. How you can take him all. Down your throat." She swallowed, her voice increasingly husky. "I want to see. He's so big. How can you possibly do that?"

Rhian stared down at Garrick's cock with dark, dilated eyes. Garrick groaned.

Savannah released her hold on Garrick's shaft and sat back on her heels, cataloging her response to watching Rhian slide down and straddle Garrick's legs.

She and Garrick had discovered she had a thing for hearing about his sexual exploits with men. Hell, her kink had led to him being with Rhian in the first place. But hearing about it and seeing it were two different things. Now she'd know for certain just how far her voyeurism went.

The fact that she couldn't tear her gaze away from Rhian's lips was a pretty good indication that all of her voyeur-kink systems were go.

She groaned as loud as Garrick when Rhian opened his mouth and took Garrick in. Her breath reduced to pants when Rhian's jaw worked and she imagined his tongue curling around Garrick's thick shaft. Rhian's cheeks hollowed out and a long suck pulled Garrick's hips up off the floor.

Garrick's eyes had gone dark. His mouth hung open. He fisted his hands in Rhian's hair, the blond curls threaded through his fingers, his knuckles white.

Rhian whimpered and closed his eyes, his nostrils flaring as color seeped into his cheeks and chest.

"God, Rhian," Garrick sighed. "What you do to me."

She laid a hand on Garrick's chest. Rhian looked for all the world as if he were as turned on as Garrick. The head of his cock strained against his boxer briefs, pre-come staining the cotton.

He worked his mouth over Garrick's cock. His hands curled around Garrick's hips and dug in.

Garrick stopped moving. Stopped breathing.

Rhian tilted his head and pressed forward until Garrick's entire length disappeared into his mouth and down his throat.

"Oh my god," Savannah whispered, her words barely audible over Garrick's harsh groan.

Garrick's heart pounded against her palm, but she couldn't look away from Rhian. Her body was on the verge of ignition with nothing but the sight before her and Garrick's skin beneath her fingertips to send her over the edge. Sweet, shy, sometimes hesitant Rhian swallowed around Garrick without a hint of inhibition. His lips stretched until they lost color and his throat convulsed before he eased back. She could hear him suck air in through his nose as his cheeks hollowed, once again lifting Garrick right up off the floor.

"*Rhian!*"

Her ears rang with Garrick's cry.

Rhian didn't so much as blink. He sucked the head of Garrick's cock, his eyes still closed, his skin flushed, and plunged again.

"My god, Garrick," she breathed. "Look at his face. It's like he's in heaven."

"I know," Garrick moaned.

Rhian pulled back and a hint of a smile curled lips before

he took Garrick into his throat again.

She ran her hand over Garrick's fingers and petted Rhian's curls before slipping her palm down his neck to his shoulders. She wanted to touch his throat, to feel him swallow around Garrick, but worried it would make his apparently non-existent gag reflex kick in.

She could see how Garrick fought the urge to writhe, his body twitching, his face a mask of concentration as he desperately tried not to do anything that could hurt Rhian.

Had Rhian claimed Garrick was in control in the bedroom? Because right then, Garrick was a slave to Rhian's every action.

Garrick released his grip on Rhian's head and scrabbled for Savannah, clamping a hand on her thigh and a fistful of Rhian's jersey. "Come here," he growled, sending a shiver down her back.

As much as she wanted to keep watching Rhian, she couldn't resist kissing Garrick. Deeply. Her mind spun as his tongue twined with hers, jerking and retreating as the breath was sucked from his body before returning with a gasp.

She could guess what Rhian was doing. Picture what she'd already seen. Her pussy ached, her belly quivering with the need to be touched. Filled.

She practically keened into their kiss, barely stopping to beg. "*Please.*"

Garrick snaked his hands down her belly and up her thigh under Rhian's big jersey. She spread her legs, her knees wide, shamelessly opening herself to him.

Garrick gasped, his fingers twitching against her. The back of his head ground into the tiles as his back arched high.

"Oh god, Rhian. I'm gonna...I'm going...I'm...*oh fuck!*"

Rhian pulled off, wrapped his hand around Garrick's balls, and gave them a firm tug. "Not yet."

"Oh *Jesus*," Garrick groaned. He stared up at Savannah in a daze. "What the hell just happened?"

Rhian peered over her shoulder.

"That's called oral sex, Garrick." The scratch of Rhian's voice sent new shivers down Savannah's spine. As did the little smirk hovering on his red, swollen lips. "I have it on good authority that you're familiar with the concept."

Chapter Twenty Nine

Garrick blinked up at his lovers, trying to regain control of his faculties while they laughed at him.

Rhian rested his chin on Savannah's shoulder. "He's cute when he's confused."

She turned to Rhian. "God, your voice sounds amazing. Is that because you took him so deep?" Garrick felt her shiver with delight. He could relate.

Rhian nodded, a full smile blooming. Garrick's heart stuttered in his chest.

Savannah reached for Rhian. "Come here."

Rhian's kiss was fierce, his arms dragging her to him as his tongue plunged into her mouth.

Garrick lay on the floor, on the verge of heart failure. His pulse pounded alarmingly and watching his lovers kiss only took it higher.

Their kiss ended softly with Savannah's hand on Rhian's cheek. Their lips meeting for a dozen more gentle nips.

Garrick watched, stunned as Rhian lifted Savannah and moved them both as if she didn't weigh a thing. She landed so that they straddled Garrick's knees, Rhian's chest to her back, both looking down at Garrick with little smiles and knowing eyes. Rhian wrapped his arms around Savannah and rubbed their cheeks together.

Garrick gulped and laid a hand over the ache in his chest. "You two are the most beautiful thing I've ever seen."

Savannah's smile grew. Rhian's eyes widened.

Savannah wriggled her ass back against Rhian. "Please," she begged.

Garrick almost made a grab for Rhian when he stood. Then Rhian shoved his briefs down his thighs and off his legs.

Savannah smiled down at Garrick, laughter in her gaze.

It should have been a simple question. "Are you and he...have you...?"

Rhian knelt behind Savannah and smiled. She fell forward. catching herself on her hands, her elbows locked, her mouth just inches from his painfully erect cock.

She licked her lips and Garrick whimpered.

"Oh yes," she murmured, "we have."

Garrick's racing heart skipped a beat, returning to its gallop when Rhian wrapped his hands around her hips, biceps bulging.

Her eyes fluttered closed. "Oh god, we *are,*" she cried.

Rhian didn't wait, didn't hesitate, plunging into Savannah fast and hard from the first stroke. Savannah arched against him, her eyes sightless, her face flushed.

Garrick hadn't thought he could be any happier than he'd been when he'd fallen in love. Twice. He'd been wrong.

He watched in awe as his lovers made love to each other. Savannah's blissful face was as fascinating as Rhian's fierce concentration. His gentle, submissive lover was mesmerizing when he took control. He pounded into Savannah, powerful, commanding their every movement.

On a particularly forceful thrust, Savannah's arms gave out and her face landed on Garrick's hip, her panting breaths teasing his aching cock. Rhian's goddamn jersey scratched over his thighs, tickling him. Savannah's nails dug into the sides of his ass where she held on for dear life. Her voice hoarse as she cried out in delight. His name. Rhian's.

Cobalt blue eyes locked on his face and he stared back. Sweat trickled down Rhian's temple and over flushed cheeks. His biceps knotted and his abs rippled as he lifted Savannah and worked his hips. Fast and hard.

Savannah pleaded for more. Garrick, captivated by Rhian's open expression and direct stare, felt each impact like a sledgehammer to his heart.

This could work. Holy fucking shit, this could work.

He threaded his fingers into Savannah's hair. "God, look what you've done, baby," Garrick said, his voice hoarse. "You should see his face. So beautiful. So fucking turned on. He loves to fuck you."

Her nails raking his skin, Rhian's movements losing rhythm as Savannah screamed through her orgasm. Garrick's achingly hard cock tapping his own belly in time to the thrusts Rhian pounded through all of them.

Garrick held Savannah's face to his hip, his joy boundless, his orgasm barely held at bay. "Please, Rhian."

He wasn't sure what he was asking for, but Rhian knew. He fell forward to land on his elbows, and Savannah cried out between them. Her knees spread across the floor and their weight landed on Garrick's legs, their bodies still joined, her arousal warming Garrick's skin.

Rhian lunged forward and captured Garrick's cock with his mouth. His lips barely nuzzled the head before he took it all the way to the back of his throat. The soft, warm muscles of Rhian's palate bumped against the hyper-sensitive head.

It was enough. Too much.

"*Oh, fuck,*" Garrick ground out, trembling.

Rhian's hips went faster than before.

Savannah screamed. "Yes, Rhian. Just like that!" She canted her ass up to meet his thrusts.

Garrick tried like hell to memorize everything he could about this moment, his heart bursting with happiness.

Then his mind went blank, his vision blurred. The only sound in the world was the thunder of his pulse as pure joy shot down his spine and tightened every muscle in his body. He cried out and shuddered violently, pouring everything he had down Rhian's throat.

Rhian swallowed furiously until he couldn't stand to be without oxygen another second.

He threw back his head. His first breath was a gasp, his next a howl. His hips slammed against Savannah, shoving deep.

"*Rhian!*" Her muscles clamped down on his pulsing cock.

He jerked against her, his nervous system doing its level best to short circuit as his orgasm tore up and out of him. *Holy Jesus.* Garrick's strong hand gripped his neck as all three of them quaked against one another.

With a final groan, his eyes popped open and he drowned in Garrick's warm, brown gaze. *Wow.* His heart kicked over in his chest at the undiluted happiness there.

Rhian collapsed on top of his lovers. Savannah sighed, not in the least bothered, it seemed, by his weight above or Garrick's legs beneath her. He buried his face against Garrick's stomach and took a deep breath.

That had been a whole hell of a lot more powerful than he'd expected. He'd known it would be hot, but *that*...that was more than just great sex and intense gratification. Way beyond making it simple for Garrick to have two lovers at once. Or being allowed to be with Savannah and have two lovers himself.

Something terrifying shifted in Rhian.

The frantic beat of his heart was no longer due to exertion. His muscles drew tight.

He tried to take a deep breath. To clear his mind. He didn't want to panic. To embarrass himself.

He couldn't fill his lungs.

He lifted his head with a jerk. Shoved himself away from them. Withdrew from Savannah too quickly.

She winced and looked over her shoulder at him.

Oh god. I'm sorry. I'm sorry. He couldn't find his voice. Wasn't even sure what part he should apologize for. His inconsiderate departure. His panic. He sprang to his feet. Had to steady himself against the wall as he stumbled away from Savannah and Garrick sprawled on the floor.

Savannah threw herself off Garrick. "Oh shit!"

Garrick sat up. "What—" His eyes landed on Rhian's face and the words died in his throat.

The blood drained from Rhian's head.

It was too much. Too huge. Too fucking wonderful.

How would he ever survive when they left him?

Savannah watched the color leech from Rhian's face and his pupils shrink to pinpricks in his wide blue eyes.

"Rhian, it's okay."

She moved aside to let Garrick sort out his still hog-tied legs. His boots hit the floor and fabric rustled behind her. She kept her gaze on Rhian and stood.

Rhian crept further away, cornering himself by the bedroom door. His breathing was uneven, rasping in his throat, but he was looking at her.

The expression on his face broke her fucking heart.

She could guess what had set him off. She'd expected that the first time the three of them were together would be phenomenal. But even she hadn't been prepared for what had just happened. She'd never been more content than she'd been while squashed between the two men she loved.

She swallowed back the lump trying to force its way up her throat.

I love you, too, Rhian.

She kept it inside, fearing it would worsen his panic.

He was terrified. Of her. Of them. Of believing in what this could be.

How the hell were they going to get past this?

Garrick came to stand behind her, his big, naked body pressed close. She was soothed by his warmth, until Rhian's eyes strayed to the door. It might have been wiser for Garrick to pull on his jeans. In this state, she wouldn't put it past Rhian to run out to the street bare-assed naked, and it wouldn't help anyone if Garrick chased him in the same condition.

"Rhian?" Garrick said gently.

Rhian peeled his eyes off the door to stare at Garrick. "I should go."

"Please, Rhian. We're here, and we want you to stay with us."

Savannah slipped her hand into Garrick's.

"It can't work," Rhian said in a harsh whisper.

"It already does," Garrick returned. Together they took one step forward. "What part of what just happened didn't work?"

Rhian looked at Savannah, then back at Garrick. He slid to the floor. "It's not that simple." He sounded resigned.

Moving carefully, Garrick dropped to his knees and crawled to Rhian's side. Rhian blinked, motionless while Garrick gathered him into his arms. He ended up between Garrick's outstretched legs, his back to Garrick's chest, Garrick's back to the wall.

Savannah wanted to tell him it could be simple. All he needed to do was believe.

She went to them, straddling their legs and settling on the floor facing them. Garrick could drag Rhian into the bedroom and lie down on top of him, but this was better. It was important that she and Garrick did this together.

She wrapped her arms and legs around Rhian *and* Garrick and held on. Garrick did the same, smashing Rhian between them.

They waited, patient and relentless while Rhian slowly relaxed. Eventually he put an arm around her while his other hand stroked down Garrick's thigh.

She looked into his beautiful face. "Are we okay?"

Rhian sighed. "Yeah. But we have to stop doing this."

Garrick hugged them tighter. "No, Rhian. You can't—"

Rhian put a hand over his shoulder to cover Garrick's mouth. His lips twitched. "I meant the human pretzel thing. My ass is going numb from this cold, hard floor."

Savannah laughed and Garrick grinned. "Mine, too," Garrick admitted, releasing them.

Rhian helped her stand and hauled Garrick up behind him. He cast one last look at the door, almost longingly. "You sure you want me to stay?"

He asked it evenly. Without emotion. She wanted to shake him.

"Yes, Rhian. We want you to stay," she said firmly, letting her exasperation show.

Garrick cupped his cheek with one hand and spoke in a sweet voice. "If you ask that again, I'm going to tie you to the bed for a week to prove it."

Rhian's lips twitched. So did his dick.

Garrick didn't miss a thing. His eyebrows went up. "That sound good to you?"

Rhian shrugged and bit his lip. "Maybe."

Savannah resisted the urge to point out his dick was giving him away, practically waving a "yes, yes, yes!" She smiled at him. "You have the most interesting ideas, my kinky friend."

She pushed him through the door and into the bedroom.

"*Me*?" he asked. "This from the woman who wanted to watch me suck off her boyfriend?"

His light tone eased the lingering tension. They'd cleared another hurdle. She looked forward to the day she didn't constantly have to be on the lookout for the next one. She swore to herself they would get there.

"He's your boyfriend, too," she reminded him. "And it was hot. Don't you have a gag reflex? At all?" She climbed up on the bed. Rhian followed her without hesitation, Garrick close behind.

Rhian grinned and the sight slammed through her. "Nope."

Savannah grinned back. "Will you teach me?"

His smile slipped and he blinked with surprise.

Garrick's eyes went from cinnamon to chocolate. His voice

dropped to a deep rumble that made her knees week. "Will you teach *me*?"

Rhian's mouth opened and shut, repeatedly, nothing but stuttering breaths passing between his lips for a good thirty seconds while he no doubt pictured Garrick swallowing his cock.

Chapter Thirty

Rhian knelt on the bed and tried to wrap his head around the idea of giving his lovers deep-throating lessons, and what the consequences of those lessons would be.

Nope. He couldn't possibly imagine having not one, but *two* lovers with such a skill.

That they wanted to be with him, to give him their time and attention, still scared the shit out of him, as evidenced by his embarrassing meltdown in the hallway. But he was steadier now. He'd decided, while sitting on the hard floor surrounded by his lovers, that he could do this. For a while. He wasn't going to let the truth—that they would never keep him for the long haul—interfere with the pleasure of having them now.

A slow smile crawled across his face and he watched, rapt, as matching grins bloomed. Panic or not, it stroked his ego that these two gorgeous people wanted *him*.

Garrick pounced and kissed him fiercely. Rhian kissed him back. Hands ran all over his skin. He loved the soft pads of Savannah's fingers as much as the rough calluses on Garrick's.

Both good. Equally exciting.

That was true about everything with these two. And not just physically. He knew what it meant, in his heart, but he kept it to himself.

A rough hand slid down his belly, rubbing, circling, until it hovered just above his rapidly recovering dick.

Garrick abruptly stopped kissing him. "Whoa-ho, what is this?" He sat back to watch his hand trace over Rhian's bare skin.

"What is what?" he asked, reaching for Savannah. If Garrick wasn't going to kiss him, then he'd find someone who would.

Garrick hand tickled beneath his navel, where there was no longer a treasure trail.

Savannah watched what Garrick was doing with a smile. "I waxed him," she confessed. "Well, not me personally."

Rhian snorted. "No, you gave that honor to some crazy Brazilian lady trained in the art of torture."

Savannah laughed.

Garrick's hand didn't stop moving, drifting over smooth skin, but never touching Rhian's cock. Rhian growled, trying to force Garrick's hand where he wanted it with a jerk of his hips. No luck.

"Shit, that's hot," Garrick whispered. His hand dipped to cup Rhian's bare balls. "It makes you look bigger."

Rhian's dick did its level best to rise to the occasion. Garrick rose onto his knees and slammed their mouths together. Savannah had warned him Garrick would like the waxing. Guess she was right.

Rhian nudged Garrick away and smiled at her. "Thanks."

She smiled, grabbed his face and kissed him just as fiercely.

God, he could get used to this.

They took turns kissing him. Sometimes soft. Sometimes ferocious. Rhian was breathless by the time Savannah and Garrick kissed each other. It was far more exciting to watch than Rhian would have guessed. He stroked their cheeks, smiling when Garrick cut him a look.

Eventually, somehow, the three of them were in one big sloppy kiss. Rhian had no idea whose tongue was on his, whose mouth his tongue was in. It didn't matter.

Lips cruised over his neck, his shoulders. He latched onto Savannah's neck and sucked up a red spot as Garrick did it to him. He was usually opposed to hickeys—god knew they'd caused him trouble in the past—but tonight he didn't care. Who would see it? He didn't have practice and it wasn't like he gave a shit if his oncologist saw it.

Fuck, his *oncologist*. Lumps, doctors, and test results had no more business in his head tonight than any other aspect of the future.

He was pressed between his lovers, Savannah's breasts in his hands. Her lips nibbled under his chin as he flicked his thumbs over her tight nipples. Garrick scraped his teeth over the nape of Rhian's neck, raising goosebumps all over. Garrick's big hands palmed his ass cheeks. When one finger slipped into the seam and over his anus, he made that goddamn noise.

Savannah lifted her head. "What was that?"

Garrick chuckled against his skin. "Have you not heard that before?"

Rhian groaned with despair. Garrick loved to tease the sound from him, and he was usually too far gone to stop him.

"It sounded so..." Savannah stopped, almost purring as she considered it.

"Stupid?" Rhian said.

Garrick tapped a finger against Rhian's tightly clenched anus, rubbing and wriggling until the tip slipped inside. He made the sound again.

"*Needy*," Savannah decided.

"Hot," Garrick agreed. His finger pressed harder. Even dry, it felt fucking fantastic easing into him. Rhian choked back the sound.

Savannah arched one eyebrow. "I want to hear it again."

Garrick's lips brushed his neck. His shoulder. "I think I have just the thing."

Rhian swore he wouldn't make it easy, even as his entire body tightened with anticipation. What the hell was Garrick going to do?

Rhian wasn't expecting Garrick to shove him forward. He wobbled, then fell to the bed with Savannah beneath him. He barely caught himself on his elbows instead of landing on top of her.

"Sorry," he murmured, trying to figure out what the fuck Garrick was doing.

Her knees caged his ribs as she settled beneath him. "I'm not."

He loved her smile. Her bright green eyes sparkling with humor. He ran his fingers through her silk hair, tangling a mass of it into his fist when Garrick's lips touched the base of his spine. Two big hands palmed his ass and spread him open.

He's not going to—

The hot tickle of Garrick's tongue slid down the electrified skin in the valley of Rhian's ass.

Oh Jesus. Oh Jesus. Rhian squirmed as new and wonderfully illicit sensations roared through him. His ass clenched, released, begging for this touch.

Garrick's tongue circled his entrance. Long slow licks that lit Rhian on fucking fire. "Oh my god, Garrick. *Garrick.*"

The tip of Garrick's tongue stabbed against his anus, wriggling into Rhian.

He made the noise. Repeatedly. The sob of pleasure tore from his chest with every attempt to breathe as Garrick fucked his ass with his tongue.

God, it was so good. The ring of muscles fluttered against Garrick's mouth, eager for more. Relaxing and opening under his skilled touch. Rhian spread his knees on the bed and thrust his ass back as Garrick speared him again.

Savannah stared at him in wonder.

The heat of a blush seared his face as he rocked his ass on Garrick's tongue. He spread his legs farther.

Savannah groaned. "God, Garrick, you should see his face."

Rhian whimpered when Garrick's tongue withdrew.

"Beautiful?" Garrick asked, his lips brushing Rhian's skin.

"Gorgeous."

Garrick slid a thick finger past totally lax muscles. Rhian sighed. His ass clenched around the invasion, then eased. A second finger slid in next to the first and worked its way deeper into his ass. His muscles quivered, immediately soothed with more long licks around the digits lodged in his ass.

He was so focused on what Garrick was doing, he didn't

notice Savannah's hand snaking out until it was wrapped around his cock.

"Oh, fuck," he moaned.

She ran her hot fingers along his length and he shuddered. She stroked again.

He shook his head. "Too much. Please, not yet."

Savannah looked sorry for him. "Poor baby," she cooed. She cupped his cheek and drew his face closer.

Their lips brushed in a series of gentle kisses. He dragged his knees up, bent in half around Savannah, his thighs forcing hers higher. With his ass tipped in the air, he pressed Savannah to the bed with his chest. Garrick pumped his fingers, spread them, testing muscles that were so fucking *ready*.

He lost himself in Savannah's kiss. His hips started to move of their own accord. Garrick moved with them. He pulled his fingers almost all the way out and scissored them, taking him to the razor's edge of pain, before he thrust deep again. Rhian felt fuller, and realized a third finger was lodged in his ass.

He panted against Savannah's lips. Her languid movements suddenly stopped, then she gasped and jerked beneath him.

"Are you all right?" Rhian asked.

Savannah laughed and moaned at once. "Garrick has two hands."

Rhian closed his eyes and tried to hold back the tidal wave of need cresting over him. "God, what is he doing to you?"

It took several tries before she could answer. "Three fingers?"

"Yes." He grunted when Garrick forcefully reminded him. "Three fingers. One tongue."

Savannah tried to smile, but it wobbled badly. "Please, Rhian. I need you. Now."

He shifted closer and his cock slid along the swollen, wet folds of her pussy. Garrick's departing fingers brushed along his cock and balls. He gritted his teeth and Savannah whimpered beneath him.

"Please," she moaned.

Shit, he might come the moment he entered her. He tried to think about something else. His game stats. Taxes. The time he found half a bug in his salad. Something other than the fingers thrust in his ass. The lick of a broad tongue against his perineum. His hips twitched, searching, and he despaired that he didn't have the coordination to find the entrance to her body, let alone fuck her properly.

He yelped when Garrick's fingers, still wet with her arousal, wrapped around his cock and guided him.

Fucking hell.

He ground his teeth and tried to keep his head on straight as he surged forward, sinking into Savannah's gloriously hot, tight sheath.

Her shout of relief rang in his ears. Garrick's goddamn fingers worked in his ass.

God, they weren't giving him an inch to think. To breathe.

Rhian slammed his eyes shut and fought back the storm brewing in his balls. He stayed still. Except for the panting. If he moved even an inch, he'd blow, and he didn't want to do that. Not yet. He wanted Garrick to fuck him.

So. Damn. Much.

Rhian took a deep breath when Garrick finally pulled his fingers free. He wrapped himself around Rhian's back and pressed his cheek against Rhian's. They both looked down at Savannah's flushed face. "You ready?"

It took Rhian a moment to realize he was supposed to answer that. "God, yes."

Savannah thrust her hand under a pillow and produced a bottle of lube.

Rhian groaned. "God, you're as bad as he is."

"I learned from the best."

Garrick chuckled. "I'm so proud. Now give me that."

She did and Garrick moved back. Rhian was acutely aware

of Garrick's every movement. Cold plastic brushed against his ass and a flood of cool liquid poured into and over him.

He grunted. "Sure you used enough?"

"There can never be too much," Garrick growled. "Once I start, I'm not stopping until you're screaming."

Savannah shuddered beneath him.

Rhian tried to smile at her. "Are you okay?"

"Are you kidding?"

He was amazed he could laugh, the sound cut off abruptly when the head of Garrick's cock pushed hard against his hole. He stared down at Savannah, unblinking. She soothed him with gentle touches to his face and hair, and another long, hot kiss.

Garrick's fingers gripped him hard enough that he'd have bruises come morning, but it didn't matter. Nothing did but the burning pressure, the searing heat of Garrick's cock against his ass.

Rhian groaned and shoved back, forcing the thick head past tight muscles that sang with relief. His cock drew along Savannah's snug sheath in the process, the walls clinging to him like a fist.

"Oh, Jesus," he cried, bucking between his lovers. He stuttered to a halt, thrust as far into Savannah as he could get, while Garrick tunneled deep into his ass.

Rhian shouted words even *he* didn't understand. He reached back, wrapped a hand around Garrick's neck, and held on for dear life. He no longer knew up from down. Where he ended and they began.

Garrick's weight pressed him down into Savannah, grinding his pelvic bone against her clit.

She cried his name. Then Garrick's. Rhian's heart leapt at the sound of both. At that moment there was no difference. There were not three people in this bed. There was one. One entity. One unit. Them.

Rhian wanted to stay there, between them, connected at the most intimate level, forever. At least, he wanted that in his head. And his heart.

His cock, though, wasn't going to be able to stand this much longer.

"God, Garrick, do it. *Move.*"

Garrick must have heard how desperate Rhian had become. He fucked Rhian hard and fast from the first thrust and Rhian gloried in every inch, each vein and ridge of Garrick's cock, moving through him.

Rhian didn't hold back either. He used what little strength and coordination he had left to fuck Savannah for all he was worth. He reveled in the unbelievable racket she made. The zing of her fingernails scoring his skin. When he thrust all the way into Savannah, Garrick was there with him, stretching him wide and forcing him farther. Then Garrick was yanking him back, dragging him from Savannah's sweet, clutching heat as Garrick's shaft sang along his screaming nerve endings.

Rhian relinquished any illusion of control. Garrick pushed them faster, harder, and Rhian loved it. His ass would not let him forget this for a week, and he wanted more. And Garrick gave it to him, all the while directing him as he fucked Savannah.

Rhian's climax gathered, and he strove for it. Needed it. Garrick's arm wrapped across Rhian's chest, his hand clamping over Rhian's shoulder. Savannah laced her fingers through Garrick's. Her other hand made a fist in Rhian's hair.

Rhian soared, a bundle of sensation and wonder.

Garrick broke first. "Oh *fuck!*" he roared, hugging Rhian tight and slamming into him. Rhian ground down on Savannah's clit and she arched beneath him, the muscles in her pussy clamping down on his cock just as the hot flood of Garrick's come filled his ass.

Rhian's orgasm hit him like he'd run straight into a wall.

God, it was perfect.

He clung to Savannah, his ass clenching, burning around Garrick's thick shaft. The ripples of Savannah's orgasm flowed over his throbbing cock, dragging his farther into the abyss.

Eventually, he collapsed on Savannah, not proud of it, but weak as a baby and unable to hold himself up. His lovers moved him gently, rolling to the side and easing them apart. They petted him, smiling at one another as he lay there, boneless. He tried to smile back. He could hardly keep his eyes open, but didn't want to look away from their faces. Someone cleaned him up. Someone else pulled the covers over them. He lay between them, humming with contentment.

He wondered when they could do it again. He might have actually said that out loud, given how Savannah and Garrick laughed when he thought it.

He didn't care. For now he had something he craved. Something he'd needed his entire life and had only found with them.

Peace.

Chapter Thirty One

Garrick sat in the kitchen, staring off into space, his bare chest warmed by the sun coming in through the windows. The last week had been amazing. His arrival. The crazy reunion on the floor not far from where his bare feet rested on the rung of the counter stool. Making love to Rhian in their bed that night. Making love almost every which way since. He slept like a baby, every night, with at least one lover in his arms, and the other within reach.

Of everything, he most cherished the moments Rhian forgot to be worried, the tension lost from his face as ecstasy or sleep conquered all. Garrick was in awe of the way Savannah teased it from Rhian. Made him laugh. How it smoothed the skin between his eyebrows and his crow's feet would pop with his smile.

Rhian was heart-stoppingly attractive when he was amused. Aroused. Content. Hell, he was beautiful even in the throes of a panic attack. But Garrick very much preferred the way Rhian looked when Garrick and Savannah coaxed him into letting go.

Happy.

Now how the hell did they keep him that way?

He and Savannah had talked about it. Several times. Her worries matched his exactly. He'd had faith from the moment he'd walked through the door and seen them together that he and Savannah were on the same page. He'd since confirmed it, just to be sure. After all, a man probably shouldn't just assume his girlfriend also wanted a permanent threesome.

Was there a better word for that?

He should look it up. Savannah probably knew. He'd ask her as soon as she woke up.

In Moncton, he'd grown accustomed to meeting Jack and the construction foreman at the arena at the crack of dawn.

Here in Boston, he was in the habit of leaving Savannah and Rhian curled up together in bed in the mornings while he came out to the kitchen to work. This morning alone he'd already sent a dozen emails and texts back and forth with Jack and Rupert.

Things in Moncton were doing just fine without him, thank Christ. Callum was proving useful, making a far greater contribution than Rupert had credited him capable of. From what Jack had said, the fireworks were still going off between those two, but increasingly less often.

Garrick considered reminding Rupert that Callum was technically his boss.

Nah. Garrick had bigger fish to fry right here in Boston. Those two could work out their own issues.

Garrick pictured Rhian huddled in the corner of their hallway the day Garrick had come home. From post-coital bliss to terror in the space of minutes. He dreaded the next time it would happen and *hated* that he and Savannah couldn't prevent it. Hell, they would probably be the cause. Garrick was determined to get Rhian to a place where that kind of fear never again lurked in his head or heart. No one should have to live with that. And certainly not this man. Whom, more than ever, Garrick loved with all his heart.

And it was the same with Savannah. Garrick had spent countless hours watching her with Rhian, coaxing those precious smiles out of him. Garrick had no doubt that she loved Rhian, too. She hadn't said it yet, but it was there. She stared at Rhian like the sun might rise over his head. And while she *was* adventurous, they wouldn't all be here, together, if her feelings didn't run deep.

He should have guessed she would come to understand who Rhian was, and be drawn to those same things that called to Garrick. How could any adult with a brain and a hint of compassion resist Rhian's strange combination of strength and vulnerability?

Certainly Garrick and Savannah couldn't. And he wasn't

going to give anyone else a chance to discover how compelling their brave and nervous lover was. Savannah and Garrick would be enough. Would give Rhian everything he needed. Wanted. They had to.

A squeak came from down the hallway and he glanced up to see Rhian slip out of the bedroom, his loose sweatpants barely clinging to his hips. Garrick's heart rolled over in his chest. Just like always. He'd never get tired of looking at Rhian.

Rhian padded barefoot to Garrick and absently dropped a kiss on Garrick's lips. Rhian probably had no idea how happy his casual affection made Garrick. In fact, he appeared to still be half asleep as he staggered to the cabinet, selected a mug and poured himself a large cup of coffee.

Rhian knew his way around this kitchen better than Garrick did. That made Garrick happy, too. He hid his smile behind his coffee cup.

"Good morning," Rhian said, his voice rough.

Garrick schooled his features before putting down his mug. "Morning. Sleep well?"

Rhian smiled softly and Garrick thought his heart might bust out his chest and land at the damn man's feet. "Slept great," he murmured.

Garrick pictured Rhian pressed between Garrick and Savannah all night, their legs tangled, their arms all around him.

Rhian took a gulp of coffee and brushed Garrick's shoulder as he walked past him. "I'm going to go stretch out in the living room. For some reason, my knees and quads are killing me this morning."

Garrick grinned, unrepentant, and watched Rhian bypass the couch and shove the coffee table to the wall. Garrick had assumed "stretch out" meant Rhian was going to go back to sleep on the couch. Garrick should have known better.

Rhian's smooth skin glowed in the sunlight pouring through the skylights and front window as he bent to touch his toes. Each flex of muscle was highlighted by warm light.

Garrick wanted to run his hands over every inch of him, but held back. They were three now. Eventually he'd be able to jump Rhian's bones whenever he felt like it, but for now the balance still seemed too precarious to risk throwing it off.

A loud knock on the door made Garrick jump. Rhian stood. They weren't expecting anyone. Garrick slipped off his stool and went to the door, decency requiring he do up at least a couple of the buttons on his fly before he opened it.

Three men stood before him, two of them looking awfully familiar. The youngest and smallest of the bunch rushed through the door and slammed Garrrick against the wall.

The stranger got right in Garrick's face—a neat trick, since their rude visitor was a good six inches shorter. "Who the fuck are you?"

Garrick gaped at the ferocious little man, momentarily speechless.

Rhian's laughter echoed in the hallway. "Let him go, Kieran. That's Garrick."

The arm against Garrick's neck immediately fell away. "Oh. Uh, sorry."

During the long awkward pause to follow, their visitors alternated looking at Rhian—shirtless, barefoot, hair wild with bed head—and Garrick—in pretty much the same condition except he also had hickeys all over his neck and chest. As discreetly as he could, Garrick buttoned the rest of his fly. It wasn't much help, but it was the best he could do. Maybe they'd think the hickeys were birth marks?

Rhian waved their visitors into the kitchen. "Hey, Chance. Lachlan. Come on in."

They each shook Garrick's hand, clarifying who was who on their way past.

"Coffee?" Rhian asked, reaching for more mugs.

Garrick stood to the side and watched Rhian act the polite host, as if he lived there. He seemed comfortable in the role. With these men. The Rhian Garrick had known back in

Moncton had never once invited anyone to his apartment. Hadn't had friends, even, until Garrick had forced his way in. This man, the one getting out cream and milk and sugar, joking with Savannah's brothers and laughing at their banter, was a goddamn revelation.

Garrick wanted to run down the hall, throw himself on Savannah and positively hug the stuffing out of her. She'd already done so much. Brought Rhian so far.

Garrick joined the conversation, listening more than adding anything, and watched the brothers. He remained on the opposite end of the kitchen from Rhian, enjoying how three heads swiveled as they looked between them. Garrick wasn't sure, but Chance, in particular, seemed to be piecing things together pretty quickly. Quicker than Savannah might like.

Fortunately, other than the occasional raised eyebrow, no one seemed upset. Definitely not mad. Possibly they *were* a little confused.

And hell, who in this house wasn't fucking confused about all this?

Christ, he needed Savannah out here. Was she ready for her brothers to have a clue about what was really going on? That was not something Garrick was willing to guess about.

He was about to retrieve her from the bedroom when she breezed into the kitchen, fully clothed, her hair neatly tied up. She looked like she'd been up for hours.

He shot her a dirty look and she winked back.

"Boys! What are you all doing here at this hour?"

Lachlan took a deliberate look at his watch. "What hour? It's nine o'clock in the morning. Why aren't you at work?"

She shrugged. "I'm working from home this week. I wanted to spend time with—at home."

Their guests might have missed the hesitation and the way her gaze darted to him in panic, but Garrick hadn't. And from Rhian's suddenly downcast eyes, he hadn't either.

Fuck.

Savannah took the mug Rhian held out. He never looked at her face. She grimaced at his profile before turning back to her brothers. "What are you doing here if you thought I'd be at work?"

Lachlan shrugged. "I didn't know where Rhian lived and I figured he might be here."

Everyone's eyes bounced back and forth between Garrick and Rhian again. Rhian stared fixedly at the coffee maker. Savannah's cheeks started to turn pink. Garrick fucking refused to squirm.

Rhian turned at last. "Did you need me for something?"

Chance circled the kitchen island and put a hand on Rhian's arm, while Lachlan eased around the other way to stand behind them.

The hairs on the back of Garrick's neck stood on end. Why the hell were they blocking him in?

Chance's grip on Rhian's arm tightened. "I have some information," Chance began. "About your biological family. And the girl who's been following you."

Chapter Thirty Two

Rhian swallowed past the bile scorching his throat. No one moved, all eyes glued to him.

Why had this ever seemed like a good idea?

Then he pictured the girl in Harvard Square and her shockingly familiar smile.

"Tell me."

"Let's sit down," Kieran suggested, leading the way to the living room.

Rhian tried like hell to appear calm as he staggered on wooden legs to the couch, practically falling into it. Chance and Kieran slid the coffee table back where it belonged and sat down in front of him. Savannah sat next to him and took his hand, then Garrick shoved them both over to take up a position on the other side.

Rhian looked up at Lachlan hovering behind Kieran. "What are you doing here, Lach?"

"I came to make sure you're all right."

Rhian's stomach heaved, barely choking out a "thank you" to Lachlan for being here in case he flipped his lid. Again.

Nothing like an entire family knowing you had issues.

Almost as bizarre was his reaction to their obvious concern—*warmth*. Drawing on their support, he focused on Chance. "Okay. Tell me."

"Your biological mother is Diane Lynch. She lives here in Boston."

Rhian sat perfectly still as he absorbed this information. He told himself to breathe. It almost worked.

"Okay, I more or less knew that," he said slowly. He braced for the other shoe to drop, but no one spoke. "And?"

Kieran put a hand on Rhian's knee. "She's from old Boston

money. Big money. And politics. Her father was good friends with some of the more notorious Kennedys."

"Notorious?"

"The president," Kieran supplied. "And his brothers."

Rhian blinked. "Holy crap." What the fuck else was he supposed to say to that?

"There's more," Chance said. "She lives a few blocks from here, grew up on Beacon Hill." He gestured, presumably to indicate the very townhouse they sat in, perched as it was near the top of said hill.

Rhian's coffee tried again to force its way back up. "What else?" he asked, desperate to get this over with.

"She disappeared about twenty five years ago. Took off to parts unknown, though we now suspect that was Chicago, at least eventually. If my calculations are right, she was already pregnant with you. She was known to be a party girl, a real wild-child, and a constant source of frustration for her father. Her mother died when she was young. Her father also lives around the corner from here, not far from Diane."

Rhian swallowed hard. *Jesus. I have a grandfather?* Of course, he'd known, biologically speaking, that it was true, but that this person was around the fucking corner was somehow...frightening.

A long silence stretched while he tried to absorb what he'd learned. He wanted to hide from it. Curl up in a ball and burrow into Garrick while wrapping Savannah in his arms.

"What about the girl?"

Chance sighed. "She's your sister, Chelsea. She just turned eighteen and is a senior in high school."

Each new truth crashed into him like a blow to his chest. He didn't know how much more he could take.

"And you have a brother, James, though everyone calls him Buddy. He's nineteen."

Jimmy. Rhian shuddered. "I've seen him, too."

"Yes, I showed Lachlan a picture and he said as much."

Lachlan's brow creased with worry. "I hope that's okay."

"Sure," Rhian said automatically. Technically, none of this way okay. He had two siblings. Or half siblings, anyway. He was fairly certain—and grateful—he and Buddy didn't share a father.

Then Rhian did the math. "Fuck," he whispered. "She was pregnant with him when...when she...maybe that's why she didn't come back."

A small sound escaped Savannah. Garrick's hand landed on his thigh and held on. Rhian didn't dare look at either of them. He felt stupid enough for saying that out loud.

Chance cleared his throat and Rhian was mortified to discover it wasn't just his lovers fighting for composure. All three men before him looked somewhere between devastated and furious.

Funny how he didn't feel either of those emotions. Mostly, he just felt small. Like he was five years old again.

He managed to choke out, "Anything else?"

"Your mother doesn't claim to have any other children. I've got people searching in Chicago for your real birth certificate, but they may not find it. She could have used any name back then. If they find a Rhian—spelled either way—on the right date, they'll let me know."

Rhian nodded. "Maybe I wasn't born in a hospital."

"Maybe not," Chance agreed.

"If the girl...Chelsea, my sister..." He could barely wrap his mouth around the word. *Sister.* "...if she knows about me, then do the rest of them?"

Chance shook his head. "I don't think so. I'm curious to know how Chelsea found you, actually. Your grandfather, Seamus Lynch, is a powerful philanthropist and heavily involved in children's charities. There's a wing in Children's Hospital Boston named for him. He's well known for being an active presence in his grandchildren's lives. My guess is that Diane never told him."

Smaller and smaller. He wished he could disappear. He wasn't supposed to care what that woman did, but here he was, hurting again. Stupid bitch.

"Do you want me to contact them?" Chance asked gently.

Rhian jerked upright. "What? No way."

"Rhian," Kieran said gently, "it's likely they don't know. They're your family."

"I have no family."

Nothing changed that.

Savannah stood alone in the kitchen and rolled her shoulders for the tenth time in two minutes. With a resigned sigh, she accepted the tension in her neck and shoulders wasn't going anywhere.

With one eye on the living room, she went about making more coffee. She wouldn't be able to tolerate a drop of the stuff at this point, but it gave her something to do while Garrick chatted with Kieran and Chance in the corner and Lachlan spoke softly with Rhian on the couch.

She watched her brother, saw how he searched Rhian's face for any reaction. Rhian still clung to the blank façade he'd been hiding behind since Chance had dropped the bomb on him.

To someone who didn't know him, Rhian appeared calm. But she saw his tells. His white-knuckled grip on the couch cushion. How his shoulders didn't move when he nodded or otherwise responded to Lachlan's quiet conversation.

She had no idea what they were talking about. Maybe Lachlan was lecturing on epistemology again.

Garrick glanced at Rhian, then caught her gaze. They were trying to give Rhian space, even if it killed them. Rhian had made it clear that was what he wanted when he'd untangled his hands from hers and twitched his knee from under Garrick's grasp.

Garrick had looked ready to pounce and force Rhian to

take their comfort. She'd stalled him with a shake of her head and stood, prattling about coffee. Garrick had frowned but taken the hint.

Maybe their love was simply more than Rhian could handle at that moment. The thought was crushing, but she tried to understand it. At least until her family was gone.

I have no family.

He'd looked haunted when he'd said it. She'd wanted to argue with him, but honestly, in the face of what Chance had told them, she hadn't the heart. Rhian's biological family sucked, and he wasn't in the right frame of mind to hear lectures on how families could be built. Chosen.

Kieran leaned around Chance and they both looked over to check on Rhian. Lachlan continued to speak, his voice calming Savannah from across the room even without being able to hear his words. Like everyone else, his complete focus was on Rhian.

Rhian had a family. He just hadn't realized it yet.

Savannah contemplated the bag of coffee grounds in her hand. She probably should do more than stand there like an idiot. She focused on scooping the right amount into the filter and tried very hard to ignore the bitter sting of guilt gnawing at her.

Her brothers had taken Rhian in as one of their own. Maybe Kieran had come to support Chance—though Savannah knew in her heart that wasn't the case—but Lachlan had no reason to be there other than to be a friend to Rhian. But what would they think when they learned the truth?

She had to find the guts to tell her family. They needed to know they were getting two new sons. Brothers. Not one.

Yeah, that was going to be fun.

She'd never before been frightened that her family would think less of her. Would question her decisions. It was nauseating.

She wasn't ready. She was absolutely secure in her love for

Rhian. But until she was as certain Rhian would love her back—and more than that, *commit* to her and Garrick and not bolt—she wasn't prepared to take the risks that came with—

"Hey, Sis."

Savannah dropped the carafe back on the hot plate with a clatter and spun to face Kieran.

He cocked his head. "What were you just thinking about?"

She laughed and could hear the hint of hysteria. "I was wondering how much my brothers love me," she admitted far too honestly.

Kieran surprised her with a fierce hug.

She took a deep breath when he released her, refusing to let her voice wobble. "What was that for?"

"You looked like you needed it."

"Thanks," she said, her eyes wandering back to the living room, "but I'm not the one who needs it most."

Kieran studied Rhian thoughtfully. "I'm pretty sure he doesn't want anyone to touch him right now, let alone hug him."

She sighed and nodded. "You're probably right."

Kieran watched her while she arranged the mugs, as if lining them up perfectly was of critical importance.

"More than life," Kieran said, out of the blue.

"What?"

"Your brothers. We love you more than life. We'd do anything for you."

That was nice to hear. It didn't change the fact that her brothers weren't known to tolerate her being with *one* man well.

"I hope that's true," she said, sneaking another glance at Rhian.

Suddenly Kieran was right in her face. "You doubt it?"

"I think there are things brothers don't want to know about their sisters."

His gaze narrowed on her face. "Coming out is always hard, baby sister, even when you have a family like ours."

"By *like ours*, do you mean *incredibly nosey*?" she asked, pleased when it didn't come out sounding nearly as alarmed as she felt.

Kieran's eyebrow arched. "So sayeth the girl who used to raid my very well-hidden Playgirl stash and leave them all out of order?"

Savannah blinked. "Wait. There was an order?"

Chapter Thirty Three

Garrick ground his teeth and barely resisted shoving the last of their visitors out the door. He smiled, shook hands and generally acted the good host until he thought he'd lose his damn mind. Finally, the door shut behind Lachlan.

He didn't give Rhian a chance to escape, hauling him into his arms right in front hall. Rhian didn't hug him back, not moving except to jolt, once, when Savannah threw herself against his back and held onto them both.

Garrick pressed his cheek to Rhian's. "You okay?"

"I'm fine."

He wasn't. They all knew it.

"Do you want to talk about it?" Garrick asked gently.

"Not even a little."

No surprise there. Garrick often had to cajole, tease, and beg information from his recalcitrant lover. This time, he left it alone.

Rhian touched Garrick's cheek, and Garrick pulled away to look at him. He wasn't sure what to expect, but it sure has hell wasn't a kiss.

If Garrick has been asked thirty seconds ago if he was in the mood, he would have said he was about the furthest thing from it, but his body lit up when Rhian's tongue traced over his lips, begging entrance.

He leaned back. "Are you sure?"

Rhian wrapped a hand around the back of Garrick's head. "Yes. Please. I need you." His other arm curled around Savannah. "I need you both. Now."

Garrick exchanged a long look with Savannah.

Their next kiss was hard. Fierce. Hands grappled at clothing. At Savannah. They took turns kissing her. Kissed her both at once. Kissed each other.

Garrick wasn't sure whose hands were doing what, but his jeans came loose and fell to the floor at the same instant he shoved Rhian's sweats to his knees. Kicking his jeans aside, Garrick knelt and took Rhian into his mouth, sucking him until his cock stood at attention, rock hard and ready.

Savannah's hands played over his hair, dancing across his face and under Rhian's balls, squeezing and rolling them while Rhian helped her out of her clothes and his hips danced in reaction to their undivided attention.

"More," Rhian gasped. "I need *more*."

Garrick stood. "Then you'll get it."

He towed Rhian to the kitchen, spun him to face the island and placed his hands on the cool marble. "Stay there."

Rhian nodded, his breath already coming in short, sharp pants. He leaned into the counter, his beautiful ass tilted out.

Garrick dragged his lips and teeth along Rhian's shoulders and ran his hands down Rhian's back and over the perfect, firm globes of his gorgeous butt. He was determined to drive Rhian out of his mind, if that's what he needed.

The sound of the freezer door opening caught his attention.

Naughty, naughty Savannah. God, how Garrick loved her.

Rhian made his little sound, the needy sob that said without words that he was as excited as Garrick by the sight of Savannah holding the ice-cold butt plug in her hand.

She put the plug back in the freezer and Garrick frowned until she fished a container of lube out of a drawer. Garrick chuckled. She'd once complained about his penchant for leaving the stuff stashed all over the place, certain that some guest would get a rude surprise upon discovering it. Now she was the master of tucking bottles in hidden drawers, behind utensils, every damn place they could possibly need it.

He took the lube from her and slicked up one finger. His lips returned to Rhian's shoulder while Savannah attacked his neck on the other side. Rhian groaned. Anticipation shook Garrick, and Rhian was in much worse condition. He trembled in their arms, his head hanging down as he took quick, deep breaths. Garrick and Savannah's mouths met over Rhian's spine and he captured her lips in a long kiss, their tongues tangling.

Savannah palmed one side of Rhian's ass open. Garrick's finger slipped in without resistance.

Rhian gasped. "God, yes. That's what I need."

The second finger brought Rhian's head up, his eyes wide and sightless while Garrick stretched him. He massaged the muscles inside, while Savannah's narrow fingers worked against the tight entrance on the outside.

Rhian cried out. "God, do it."

The third finger was Savannah's. "Better?"

"Yes," Rhian panted. "Better. *More.*"

They worked together, thrusting deep and pulling out, forcing Rhian's muscles to relax, to take them. His hips worked in tight circles, chasing their hands, fucking their fingers for all he was worth.

Savannah looked at Garrick, as shocked as he by Rhian's uninhibited need. As desperate to meet it.

She practically ran back to the freezer.

Rhian's needy moan sent chills down Garrick's spine and put a little smile on Savannah's lips. It was soon lost, though, to a long groan as the butt plug came back into view. It was a big plug. Garrick had been saving it, the tease as much or more a part of its value than actually using it.

He hadn't anticipated Rhian needing it, wanting it this much.

Garrick reached to take it from her, but she held back and pressed her lips to Rhian's ear. "I want to do it."

Rhian nodded. Fast. "God, yes. You do it. Please. I want you to do it."

Garrick's heart lurched. He'd never heard Rhian so

desperate.

He slipped his fingers from Rhian's ass and stepped to the side. His other hand ran from Rhian's collar bone to his cock and wrapped it in his fist. He palmed one globe of Rhian's ass and held it open for Savannah, watching her pour lube over the plug, slicking it thoroughly, then tap it against Rhian's tight entrance.

Rhian jumped. "Fuck, that's cold."

"That's the idea," Savannah said with a low chuckle. She pushed the plug forward ever-so gently.

Garrick watched it slowly disappear into Rhian's body, every centimeter another thrill down his spine and twitch to Rhian's cock in his hand.

"Please, Savannah," Rhian cried. "Do it. Shove it in me. *Own me.*"

Savannah's head snapped up to stare at the back of Rhian's head. Worry lined her face.

Garrick didn't know what to think, either. "What do you want, baby?" he asked.

"I want you to make me yours. I want you to make me *forget.*" He shoved back on the plug, taking another inch. He grunted with frustration, sounding almost pissed off, like his control was slipping and the bad stuff was creeping back in.

Garrick's put his hand over Savannah's and shoved, hard, forcing the widest part of the plug into Rhian, stretching him as open as he'd ever been.

"Like that?" Garrick asked, his voice a low rumble in Rhian's ear.

Rhian whimpered and Garrick was alarmed to see a single tear squeeze out from behind his eyelid.

"Yes," Rhian gritted out between clenched teeth. "Just like that." Savannah twisted the plug and Rhian stretched up on his toes. "God, please, just like that."

Savannah eased the plug back and Rhian's heels touched the floor, then she pushed it in again, opening him. This time his feet remained planted, his knuckles white against the dark green granite countertop.

His face smoothed, the lines bracketing his mouth and eyes for the past hour easing away. His eyes opened. The pain was gone. The worry. The frightening mask of impassivity Rhian had held onto since he'd been told the awful creature who'd given birth to him was just a few blocks away.

Garrick gazed into bright blue eyes and saw only one thing.

Love.

Rhian stared at Garrick's warm, dark eyes and felt truly safe for the first time since Chance had announced he had information. Had that only been an hour ago?

It no longer mattered. Garrick's ferocious kiss doused his anxiety. He was only here. Now.

Savannah's lips cruised across his back, remarkably coordinated and thorough, given how hard she worked the plug against his sphincter. The still-cold silicone surface burned against his skin, soothing muscles as it tortured them.

With a final shove, the plug slipped past the last of his barriers and locked into his body, his muscles clamping down around the neck.

He groaned, not caring if he sounded as needy and totally fucking delighted as he was. "Holy shit. It's *big*."

Savannah's warm hands rubbed over his ass, soothing him one moment, pressing his cheeks and wiggling the plug the next. "It looks amazing in you." She hesitated. "Are you sure it's okay?"

She's asking now? "Yes, god, yes. It's okay. Great. Fucking amazing."

She smiled against his shoulder blade. "Oh, we're going to get to the fucking amazing part next," she promised, using his own dark promise against him.

His knees trembled, and he might have slumped to the floor had Savannah not spun him around and kissed him. Her

246

fingers speared into his hair and held his head while she devoured him.

Garrick's hands ran over both their bodies, stopping to tap the plug, doing something to Savannah that made her squeak and jerk against him.

She ended their kiss, but left her hands where they were, forcing him to look at her. "You're ours, Rhian."

He tried to nod. "Yes." He was. Absolutely. Theirs to do with as they pleased.

He kissed her again, trying to tell her with actions what he couldn't find the words to describe.

She kissed him back and Garrick tortured them both. When Savannah squeaked for a third time, Rhian ran his hands around her body until he found Garrick's fingers in her ass, thrusting deeply.

He broke their kiss and that goddamn sound escaped. Every time he moved, the plug in his ass brushed his prostate, sending electric shocks through his entire body. His cock leaked, smoothing the thrust of the swollen head against Savannah's soft belly as she writhed on Garrick's hand.

Panting, he tried to hold on. To follow their lead. To let them take control of him so he didn't have to think. Just feel.

"God, I have to fuck you." The words burst from him, breaking through his fraying control. His finger slid in next to Garrick's, just as she had done to him, and she plastered herself to his chest, clinging to him.

"Please. God. Do it. I want you to fuck me. Own *me.*"

The words startled him and he staggered back, his ass slamming onto the stool behind him. He grunted as things shifted inside him and Savannah practically crawled up his body. He helped her, trying to keep her safe above the hard floor, he and Garrick scrabbling to balance and lift her. Suspended, she grabbed his face in both hands. "Please, Rhian. Don't make me wait."

His control was shot, so it was Garrick who slowly lowered

her onto Rhian's aching cock.

"Sweet Jesus," he muttered as he slid into her heat, his head spinning as she bore him down on the plug in his ass. He slipped his elbows under her knees and cupped her ass so she was bent in half, her full weight his to control.

Her kiss told him she approved. Mightily.

He fucked her slowly, lifting her just enough to rub along her clinging walls, then let her fall again, taking him deep, the rocking motion creating wondrous zings low in his gut, the plug a constant grind against his sweet spot. He could tell when Garrick thrust his fingers back into her ass, and not just from her shouting. Garrick's fingers bumped against his shaft through the thin wall that separated them and Rhian thought he would die.

Jesus, how much could he take?

"Garrick," Savannah pleaded, groaning as Rhian shifted his grip and the angle. The sound cut off when the pressure of Garrick's fingers disappeared.

Then Garrick was above them, all around them. He grasped the counter on either side of Rhian, his arms a frame to keep them from tumbling to the floor. Rhian stared up into his eyes and stopped moving, fascinated as Garrick's and Savannah's faces contorted with concentration. Bliss.

He was shoved back against the counter a moment before Savannah became almost unbearably tight and the thick presence of Garrick's cock in her ass pressed heavily against Rhian inside her.

"Oh my god," Savannah cried. "Rhian. *Rhian!*" He silenced her with a kiss, overwhelmed by the sound of his name on her lips while Garrick surged farther and deeper into her ass.

Garrick's thighs shoved his apart and his weight shifted back, jamming the plug hard against his prostate. His eyes slammed shut as he tried to absorb what was happening to him.

He was enveloped in their arms, in her body, by them. "It's too much," he cried, dimly aware of the tears spilling down his cheeks.

Garrick stopped moving and Savannah's fingers traced over his wet cheeks. "Baby?" Rhian could hear the alarm in Garrick's voice.

Rhian looked at them. Saw the worry in their eyes.

"Are we hurting you?" she asked.

He shook his head. God, no, that wasn't what he'd meant.

"You're both…" He looked at them again and his heart hurt. "You're both so beautiful. This is insane." He laughed in disbelief. Relief. "How the hell did I end up here?"

He meant in love with two people, but he hoped they'd think he meant on a damn stool.

Garrick eased back a little, but before Rhian could protest the loss, Garrick shoved himself forward again, rocking Savannah and making them all cry out. Then he did it again.

Rhian tried to help. He swore to god he did, but he was overwhelmed by the onslaught of emotion and sensation, barely able to do more than cling to Savannah.

It was perfect. He couldn't understand how the hell they always made it so damn perfect.

"You belong to us," Garrick said, like it was the answer to the question he hadn't asked out loud.

"And we belong to you," Savannah added, her face pressed against his.

"And…we…belong…to…*you*." Garrick chanted, each word punctuated by another hard thrust. His deep voice vibrated along Rhian's skin, his final thrust almost brutal.

Rhian came in a blinding flash, shouting words he couldn't understand and wouldn't remember. Certain he'd wish he'd kept them to himself but unable to contain them.

Garrick and Savannah slammed against him, over him, through him. Her cry of ecstasy a second before Garrick's roar of satisfaction. Their bodies quailed against his, the plug in his ass forcing his orgasm to go on until he was empty. Drained.

Completely theirs.

Owned.

Chapter Thirty Four

Garrick was trying very hard not to smile like a simpleton.

He was almost certain Rhian had no idea he'd shouted how much he loved them both while he was howling through his climax. Nor had he registered Savannah's return of that love, gasped between countless kisses to his face.

Goddamn, it had been *perfect*. And would be again. Soon. Not that Garrick was going to press the issue on either front. Not, at least, until one of them said it when it wasn't strung together with a whole lot of f-bombs, a string of *gods*, a handful of *damns* and at least one *Jesus, Mary, and Joseph*.

For now, it was more than enough. More than he'd dared to hope until a few days ago, and he'd never dreamed Rhian would say it this soon.

And technically, he hadn't. Not really. But kind of.

He rubbed his lips to get rid of the smile.

The three of them were strolling down Beacon Hill toward Boston Common in search of sunshine, Starbucks and some time in the park. Acutely aware that no one had asked Chance the exact addresses for Rhian's biological family, Garrick couldn't stop searching for familiar faces.

Oddly, Rhian didn't seem to be similarly concerned. But then, he had no reason to expect anyone would recognize him, even if they were to march right by on the narrow sidewalk.

For once Garrick was thankful for prickly New Englanders' distaste for eye contact with strangers on the street. But how could a mother not recognize her own child? Especially one as beautiful as Rhian?

Weaving around a tree planted in front of a huge old townhouse, Garrick's arm brushed Rhian's and he fought the urge to thread their fingers together, hating that it wasn't possible. He *could* hold Savannah's hand, but Rhian couldn't

251

because they worked together, so Garrick shoved both his hands in his pockets. He made a study of the uneven bricks beneath his feet while he wrestled with the frustration. They'd figure this shit out eventually. Or get used to it. They were a threesome and, goddamn it, they were going to stay that way.

They rounded the next corner and Garrick automatically scanned for people who looked like Rhian. He was stunned when he found one.

All three of them stumbled to a halt.

The beautiful blonde girl was on her phone, walking straight toward them and not paying the least bit of attention to the three people blocking the sidewalk. Like most Bostonians, she probably figured they'd move out of her way, and if they didn't, she'd just plow right through them.

"Chelsea," Rhian said, shocking Garrick.

Chelsea's head jerked up. "I have to go," she said quickly, and hung up without waiting for a response. Then she stood, frozen, and stared at her brother.

They all stared back.

Garrick understood immediately how Savannah had known this girl was related to Rhian. The resemblance wasn't just close, it was downright eerie, extinguishing the last doubts Garrick had harbored that Chance hadn't accurately identified Rhian's family.

The longer the silence stretched, the more painful it became, and not just Rhian's grip on Garrick's arm. Chelsea's face went from shocked to suspicious, her blue eyes narrowing. She took a step back.

Rhian let go of Garrick and held out his hand. "Please. Don't run." When she didn't move, he walked toward her. "Do you have time for a cup of coffee?"

Garrick and Savannah exchanged a quick look. This had to be damn hard for Rhian, but his face didn't betray a hint of anxiety. Chelsea, on the other hand, appeared decidedly alarmed.

Garrick decided then and there that if she said no to Rhian, he would throw her over his shoulder and duct tape her ass to the chair at Starbucks.

"Sure," she agreed reluctantly, gesturing over her shoulder. "There's a place right around the corner."

No one told her they knew. Or that they lived right up the street.

They followed Chelsea the block to the Starbucks on the Common and scored two tables near each other. Garrick was tempted to rearrange things so they could sit together, but Savannah stayed him with a hand on his arm. As much as he hated leaving Rhian to deal with this on his own, it was probably for the best. They would be close enough to see and hear if Rhian needed them, but far enough that they couldn't hear their conversation.

"Chelsea," Rhian said as they hovered over their table, both too nervous to sit yet, "this is Garrick. And Savannah."

Chelsea shook their hands and smiled, murmuring, "Nice to meet you." Her eyes narrowed on Garrick's hand on Savannah's back. She'd probably seen Rhian doing the same thing and thought Garrick was poaching on her brother's woman. Garrick decided he might like Chelsea just fine.

Savannah took everyone's orders and went to the counter. Watching Chelsea for her reaction, Garrick put his hand on Rhian's back, just as he had with Savannah. It wasn't an overtly sexual or even intimate gesture, but it sure as hell didn't go unnoted. Chelsea's eyebrows disappeared beneath her blonde bangs.

Savannah returned, and Rhian and Chelsea eased into their seats. Savannah handed Rhian his coffee and put her hand on his shoulder, her thumb brushing his neck. "Here you go."

"So, how do you three know each other?" Chelsea asked, innocently enough. Garrick wondered if the others could see the curiosity blazing in her eyes.

Rhian opened his mouth to answer, but before he could, Garrick said the closest thing to the truth that was fit for public consumption.

"We're Rhian's family."

Rhian watched Garrick and Savannah take their seats a couple tables away, wondering what the hell Garrick was talking about.

Rhian had no family.

He looked at the woman sitting across the table from him and realized that, for the first time in his life, he *was* awfully damn close.

He glanced at Garrick and Savannah again.

Awfully. Damn. Close.

"They care about you a lot, huh?"

Rhian brought his attention back to his sister. *His sister.* How many times would he think that, say it, before it stopped being scary?

"Uh, yeah." He glanced over at his lovers. They both watched him carefully. "I guess they do."

He could tell she wanted to ask more, but she just nodded. "I'm glad."

"Me, too."

They shared a smile and their resemblance struck him again.

"You must look like your mother," he said.

She cocked her head. "You know, right?"

"I figured it out with some help."

"Then she's your mother, too."

He shrugged. "Technically."

Chelsea sighed. "Fair enough. And yes, we both look like her. Thank god. My father was a real asshole. And ugly one, to boot. He took off when Buddy was barely a year—you know about Buddy, right?"—he nodded—"and Mom was still pregnant with me."

"I'm sorry."

"From all accounts, I'm not. Jimmy was no prize."

Rhian grimaced. "No, he wasn't."

Chelsea frowned. "You remember him?"

"Yes."

Rhian tried not to go back to that awful apartment, hiding under the table. He didn't mask his reactions, though. He felt a completely foreign connection to this woman, and for some damn reason, it put him at ease.

Which was funny, since it also scared the shit out of him.

"Does that mean..." She didn't finish her question, fiddling with her cup and staring at the table top instead.

"Go ahead. Ask me."

"Do you remember her leaving? What happened?"

She didn't know the truth. So he told her. All of it. Even how he'd ended up with his new name. He didn't spare her a detail, or soften anything about either of her parents. Her direct and weirdly familiar blue stare told him he could be honest.

By the end, her fingers were tightly knotted in her lap, her shoulders hunched.

"I'm sorry, Rhian."

Rhian waved it away. Having told Savannah, then Garrick, and bits and pieces of it to the Morrison brothers, it didn't bite at him like it had when he was the only one who knew.

"It's okay. I turned out pretty well in the end, I hope," he said lightly.

It was his stock answer when people expressed their sympathy over his craptastic childhood, though most didn't know the half of it. This time, though, for the very first time in his life, he meant it. He was doing okay. It hadn't broken him.

"So, how did you figure it out?" he asked. "I can't imagine your mother admitted it."

"What? To abandoning you? Hell no."

"Then how?"

Chelsea smiled. "I'm nosey. It's a great failing of mine, as Grandfather likes to point out. Constantly. He's always promising I'm going to regret what I discover, but since that day I found your birth certificate, I've become an expert at snooping."

One hundred questions nearly choked Rhian, but he stuck with the here and now. "How long ago was that?"

"Four years, almost. I had to go slow. It took me a few weeks just to make a copy, then even longer to withdraw enough money to pay a PI and not alert Grandfather."

Rhian choked on his coffee. "You hired a PI at age fourteen? That's pretty precocious."

Chelsea grinned. "Nosey, remember? And I wanted to know the truth. The mother's name on the certificate was Diane Williams, which intrigued me since I had to assume it was my mother—there are no other Dianes in my family—and my godfather's name is Robert Williams. He lives in Back Bay. There was no father listed, but her last name and your middle name made me wonder."

She watched him closely and he told himself not to ask. He flinched when her hand covered his.

"Do you want me to stop?"

Rhian took a long sip of his coffee and checked to see Garrick and Savannah's gazes riveted on him. He took a deep breath. "No, tell me."

"I've heard the stories about my mom's disappearance and then coming back years later, hooked on all kinds of crap and pregnant with me. Buddy in tow. But I'd never heard she'd lost a child. I figured she didn't want to talk about it, but I wanted to know. Especially because Robbie—my godfather—has been like a father to me my entire life, and I thought he might be your biological father. That he might not know."

"You seem to have understood your mother pretty well for a kid that age."

"She's good at a lot of things, but pretending to give a crap about anyone but herself—and maybe Buddy—isn't one of them."

Rhian grunted. That certainly jived with his memory, as well.

"You look a little like him. Robbie. Something about the chin and lips."

Rhian swallowed hard. "Okay."

She patted the back of his hand. Comforted by an eighteen-year-old girl.

An eighteen-year-old girl who just happened to be his sister.

"Anyway, as you can imagine, I didn't learn what I expected, which was, frankly, where you were buried." She cringed in apology. "Which, of course, I'm really glad about."

He smiled a little. "Me, too."

"Then a couple years ago I confronted her and she flipped her lid. I mean, really wigged the fuck out."

She hesitated, biting her lip.

"You're not going to get any shit from me about swearing," he said with a chuckle.

She grinned. "Right. Anyway, since then, she's been different. Not that she wasn't a pain in the ass before, but for the past two years, she's been little more to me than the roommate who pays the bills."

And here Rhian had thought it wasn't possible for him to hate his mother any more than he had already. "I'm sorry."

It was Chelsea's turn to wave it away. "Hell, it's probably a blessing. I got the worst of it to stop by threatening to tell Grandfather. Now she's afraid of me, which infuriates her, but keeps her in check."

"Does she know I'm here?"

"I don't think so. I didn't tell her jack shit, I promise, and I doubt she had someone look you up after I did."

257

Rhian hardly flinched. "Okay. Let's not tell her."

"Agreed."

"And Buddy?"

Chelsea sighed. "In a fit of absolute stupidity, I told him about you, though not your name or anything. He must have figured out who you were when he saw you that night. We do kinda look alike."

"Just a little," Rhian said with a smile.

"I don't think he has any idea who you are, or what you do, but if he comes near you, tell me."

Rhian didn't like the idea of Chelsea locking horns with that ugly bastard. "Don't put yourself at risk for me."

"There's no risk. I'll just threaten to go to Grandfather. Buddy won't do anything to hurt Mom or put his trust fund at risk."

"Would your grandfather even care?"

"*Care*? He'd flip his fucking lid. I've almost told him a hundred times, but I couldn't. He'd never forgive her, which I don't really give a shit about, but I don't think he'd ever forgive himself either. He'd be devastated that she'd left you. That he had a grandchild he didn't know about."

"Maybe he's better off not knowing then. Is he frail?"

"Grandfather?" Chelsea laughed, a big sound that shook her whole body. "God, no. He's going to outlive us all. Still plays golf, tennis, racquetball, and rows out on the Charles."

"Wow."

"Yeah, I think you probably got your athleticism from him. I love Robbie, but his idea of exercise is bringing his cell phone to his ear."

Rhian laughed, then sobered. "Please don't tell him either."

"Robbie?"

"No. Well, yes. Or your grandfather."

She nodded. "I won't."

He must have looked uncertain, because she rushed to

reassure him. "Look, if I'd found you in some hovel, destitute, I would have told him two years ago. But by the time my guy caught up with you, you were in the Juniors and being scouted by some big teams."

Rhian grinned at her detailed knowledge of the sport and his career. She and her investigator were certainly thorough.

"Since you seemed to be doing all right, I left it alone and promised that once I was free of the witch, I'd figure out a way to introduce myself."

"Which you did."

"Well, all I did was stalk you. I was so shocked when you moved to Boston, I wasn't sure what to do. I wasn't ready, you know?"

Rhian shrugged. "I hope you're ready now."

She cocked her head. "Does that mean you'll talk to me again?"

Shockingly, he was *looking forward* to it. For all they'd known each other for less than an hour, he had something with Chelsea he'd never felt for another human being on earth.

Kinship.

Her hand grasped his. "I get it. I feel it, too."

Rhian stared at her for a long time, terrified and elated. He changed the subject before he embarrassed himself. "The guy who grabbed you the other night. Buddy?"

"Yeah. Our brother the sociopath."

"So he takes after mom."

Chelsea laughed. "You do remember her."

Rhian's smirk faded. "Yeah. I do."

"God, Rhian, I'm so sorry." She wilted in her seat.

He shrugged and twirled his empty cup. Chelsea's phone buzzed in her pocket, not for the first time. She silenced it without looking.

"Do you need to get that?" he asked.

"No." It immediately buzzed again. She sighed and pulled it

out. She managed to enter a text of biblical proportions and hit send in under twenty seconds. The reply was almost instant. She sighed again. "I'm sorry. I do have to go soon. I was supposed to meet some friends a few minutes after we bumped into each other. They're getting worried after I hung up on them like that."

"I understand. I'm glad you have people looking out for you."

She glanced meaningfully at Garrick and Savannah. "I'm glad you do, too."

He smiled.

For a long time, they just looked at each other. His sister. It was weird. But not all bad. She asked for his number and he rattled it off while she entered it into her phone under the name Savannah. "Just to be safe."

He was unaccountably proud that his sister was so damn clever.

His phone vibrated. "I just sent you a text, so you have my number, too."

He had a way to reach her. It kind of freaked him out.

"Well, I should go," she said.

Rhian nodded and she stood. Garrick and Savannah immediately rose and cut through the crowd.

"Wait." *God, am I really going to ask this?*

She looked at him curiously.

"What's my name?"

Chelsea's brows knit with confusion. "What?"

He swallowed. "On my birth certificate. You mentioned a middle name. I don't even know if my first name was Rhian."

Chelsea went pale, her big blue eyes enormous in her face. "It is Ryan. Spelled the common way. Ryan Robert Williams."

Garrick clasped his shoulder. Savannah rubbed his back. They were trying to ground him. And damned if it didn't work.

He smiled at Chelsea. "Thank you."

Chapter Thirty Five

Savannah sat at the island in their kitchen and stared at the massive piles of paperwork scattered around Garrick's laptop. He was working more hours than ever, though without the signs of strain that had been evident while he'd been in Moncton. He slept like a baby—usually after a shattering orgasm—and took long runs with her and Rhian. She was relieved to see him happy and healthy, but it weighed on all their minds that at some point, he was going to have to go back. Even if only for a few days.

She needed him here. At least until they were sure Rhian wasn't going to bolt. Their threesome was coming together, but the glue was still drying and she didn't think it would work if any of them had to leave before it set.

Just when the hell that would be, she had no fucking idea.

Nor was she certain what had to happen to make it stick. She sighed into her coffee. Knowing where the hell Rhian would end up next season would be a big help. It wouldn't change how she felt or her plans for the future, but Rhian always had one foot out the door, sure that it was only a matter of time before he landed in some city far, far from here.

One bright spot on the horizon was Chelsea. She and Rhian had texted and planned to get together for another coffee. Savannah was looking forward to getting to know Chelsea. But more than that, Savannah was happy for Rhian. He seemed to be adapting to the idea of having a sibling with remarkable ease. It no doubt helped that Chelsea was another victim of her mother's incapacity to actually *mother* anyone.

And Chelsea created another connection between Rhian and Boston. Another reason to visit, to stay. To make this place his home. Because even if he was traded to Timbuktu, he'd have to spend the off-season somewhere. And come hell or high water, Savannah and Garrick were going to convince him the best place to spend it was with them.

Rhian's phone rattled against the hard granite and she fished it from the pile of devices charging on the counter. Since Garrick's arrival, they'd banished all phones and iPads from the bedroom, ensuring their attention was where it should be. On each other.

It took her a moment to recognize the three digit exchange for Dana Farber Hospital on the screen.

Ripping the cable away, she ran down the hallway, sliding her finger across the screen to answer it before it could go to voicemail. She flew across the bedroom and landed on the bed, half on top of Garrick, who fortunately was awake enough to protect his sensitive bits. She thrust the phone at Rhian.

He took it and pressed it to his ear with a curious look for her.

"Hello?"

Rhian's stomach plunged when he heard the familiar voice on the other end of the phone.

"Mr. Savage? This is Dr. Kantov."

"This is Rhian Savage," he croaked.

Savannah whispered in Garrick's ear and then they curled around him. Garrick dragged him back against the warmth of Garrick's broad chest, while Savannah tucked into his side.

"I'm calling with good news," Dr. Kantov offered.

"Good news?" Now his voice was three octaves higher than usual.

Arms tightened all around him. He tilted the phone from his ear so Savannah and Garrick could hear.

"Your lump is something called a sertoli non-germ cell tumor. It's quite rare, but, happily, also completely benign. I can refer you to a surgeon who can go over the benefits of removal, but in the meantime, you don't have anything to worry about. You do not have cancer."

Rhian laughed. And laughed. He couldn't stop. He was drunk with relief.

He managed to thank the doctor and, with Savannah's help, write down the diagnosis, the name of the surgeon, and how to contact her.

The moment he hung up the phone, it was ripped out of his hands. His breath left him in a gasping chuckle as two bodies tackled him to the bed.

Hot mouths attacked his neck, his face, capturing his mouth before showering their affection and relief all over his face, neck and chest. He lay there, stunned, hearing the laughter but hardly recognizing it as his own.

The lump was benign. He didn't have cancer.

The gentle caress of fingers over his increasingly full and tight balls jarred him out of his stupor. He was healthy. Strong.

And it was time to celebrate. He considered jumping up and down on the bed, screaming like an idiot, but that lacked a certain dignity he liked to maintain. He decided to make Garrick scream like an idiot instead.

With a twist, he flipped over and pinned Garrick onto his back on the bed.

He grinned down into Garrick's happy, smiling eyes. "I want to fuck you."

Garrick's mouth fell open, and his eyes darkened from cinnamon to chocolate. "Okay," Garrick said, his voice rough.

Was it really that simple? For the life of him, Rhian couldn't figure out why the hell he hadn't done this before.

He turned to Savannah and found her kneeling beside them, a bottle of lube in her hand.

"You must have been a Girl Scout."

She grinned. "*Be prepared* is a great motto. Don't you think so, Garrick?"

Garrick stared up at Rhian, his cheeks pink, his breathing already faster. "Huh?"

She leaned down to whisper in Garrick's ear. "Are you ready to be prepared?"

Pink cheeks turned red. Garrick swallowed, his cock a steel spike against Rhian's belly. "Yes."

Rhian jumped off Garrick and grabbed his hips. With a single heave, he flipped him over and planted him on his knees.

"Jesus fucking Christ, Rhian," Garrick gasped.

Savannah laughed and crawled around to sit facing Garrick. "Look at you." She ran the backs of her fingers down Garrick's face. "You like it when he takes control."

Garrick nodded. Rhian grinned and spread Garrick's knees wider. Garrick gasped again.

"I do, too," she confessed.

Garrick groaned and arched his back, tipping his ass up to Rhian.

Savannah's smile turned wicked. "Just wait until he's in you, Garrick. The strength. The power. You're going to love it."

A thin sheen of sweat glowed on Garrick's skin, his ribs heaving with each deeply drawn breath, and Rhian hadn't even touched him yet. God, Garrick wanted it.

Rhian grabbed the lube, all the while scolding himself for being a selfish bastard. He was now achingly aware of how little he'd instigated sex, or any kind of affection or intimacy. With Garrick *or* Savannah. Garrick's body pleaded for his touch, his hoarse words confirming what was so evident in every line of his body. His face.

He needed this.

From Rhian.

Who'd held back because he was a coward. And a jerk.

Rhian swore he would spend the rest of the day, week, *month*, making it up to both of them. He didn't believe the three of them were going to be a long-term thing—while he increasingly suspected they did—but he had agreed to stay, for now. And while he was here, he would commit fully. Be an equal partner. *Act.*

He traced his slick finger down the valley of Garrick's ass, watching shivers race over his skin. He paused over the dusky bud of Garrick's entrance and circled gently. Muscles fluttered beneath his touch. Rhian slid one finger into unbelievably tight heat.

Garrick groaned, long and loud, his head dropping to hang from his shoulders and rest in Savannah's lap. Rhian pumped his hand, thrusting easily as Garrick readily accepted him and pushed back for more. Rhian slipped a second finger in beside the first.

Garrick groaned almost continuously. God, he was going to be ready too quickly, and Rhian wanted to take his time. Savor it. He slowed, careful not to graze Garrick's prostate.

Rhian remembered how he'd hesitated a week ago when Savannah had brought out a new butt plug and waved it in Garrick's direction. Garrick had been more than willing, but even witnessing Garrick's high color and wicked smile when Savannah had thrust it home, hadn't snapped Rhian out of his selfishness.

Garrick had never asked for it. And given that Garrick was generally such a pushy bastard, Rhian had let himself go along, never questioning it. He was an idiot.

Leaning over Garrick's back, he rubbed his mouth across the nape of Garrick's neck. "I'm sorry I didn't do this months ago."

Garrick's head lifted and his eyes slowly peeled open to look at Rhian. Rhian couldn't resist scissoring his fingers, watching those eyes flare before narrowing. "I didn't think you wanted to."

"I wanted to." He put every ounce of love, trust and honesty he could into three little words.

They held still, sharing a long look while Rhian applied steady pressure to quickly loosening muscles.

Savannah's fingers trailed down Rhian's cheek, then Garrick's. She gazed at them the same way—with the same warmth and desire. Rhian realized it was the same for him. He felt for her just as he did for Garrick.

Maybe it showed on his face—the love or the terror—because Savannah leaned forward and kissed him just as Garrick turned his head to do the same. They ended up in another three-way kiss. They were getting the hang of these things, though it was still messy. And hot.

He began to pump his arm again and Garrick departed the kiss with a gasp, shoving his ass back on Rhian's fingers. Rhian grinned down at Savannah and sat up to return his focus to the task at hand.

Garrick clamped a hand around Savannah's thigh and dragged her closer. She laughed as she fell to her back on the bed, her legs spread, her knees framing Garrick's head.

He trailed kisses along her thigh.

"What are you doing?" Savannah cried.

Garrick chuckled. "It's called oral sex. I have it on good authority you're familiar with the concept."

Rhian laughed. He'd said the same thing to Garrick the night he arrived in Boston. The night Rhian had known he was in way over his head and hadn't run anyway. More remarkably, he didn't regret it. Not right then. Not even a little.

He tapped a third finger against Garrick's tight muscles, gently massaging them, before wedging past the barrier and deep into Garrick's ass.

Garrick jerked, a shudder racking his body, and looked back at Rhian. Rhian could get lost in those warm, brown eyes.

"Please."

Oh god. Garrick was begging. Garrick loved it when he or Savannah begged, but Rhian hadn't fully understood why until now.

"Soon."

He enjoyed Garrick's frustrated growl almost as much as the thrill of being in control. He wondered if Garrick realized how much trouble he was in for, now that Rhian had a taste for it.

Garrick tried to control his breathing and focus on Savannah. His throat ached from the rush of air heaving in and out of his lungs and the sounds he choked back as Rhian stretched him open.

The burn felt good. Great. But that wasn't what made him want to howl with joy. It was the determined look on Rhian's face. The way he took complete command over Garrick.

This was a different Rhian. The one Garrick had been trying to find for months. The man Garrick had known was trapped behind countless worries and a bone-deep belief that he didn't truly belong in Garrick's bed. In Garrick.

He shivered when Rhian's finger brushed his prostate. He tried to give his balls a yank but his hand was slapped away. Then Rhian's hand was there, holding tight. Forcing his orgasm back. *Fuck.*

Weak as a baby, Garrick could barely hold himself up on one elbow as he kissed a path across Savannah's belly. He teased one finger along her slit, watching how she alternately stared up at Rhian and down into Garrick's face. He could tell by her smile she saw the change in Rhian, too. And was enjoying it as much as he was.

On a particularly big stretch, Garrick grunted. Maybe she wasn't enjoying *quite* as much as he was.

Garrick drew little circles around her clit, picking up speed. He loved how her smile wobbled and she blinked, focusing on him. Her eyes narrowed and her hips bucked, begging for more, but he held back until she was keening for it.

"Garrick, please!"

He eased one finger into her tight channel. "Better?"

"No!"

He chuckled, locked his lips over her clit and sucked it into his mouth. She shivered beneath him. She was closer than he'd guessed, and he happily pushed her over the edge with a series of pulsing sucks that had her back arching from the bed, her voice echoing off the walls and ceiling as she climaxed.

He rode the waves with her, acutely aware of Rhian's fingers lodged deep in his ass, no longer moving. He hoped Rhian was watching Savannah, enjoying her uninhibited release. Rhian liked her unrestrained honesty, her ecstatic abandon, as much as he did.

When she slumped back on the bed, he eased two more fingers into her channel and fucked her with them. Hard.

Savannah moaned, long and loud, riding his hand for all she was worth.

"Shit, Garrick," Rhian muttered. His hand returned to its mind-bending ministrations.

"You should talk," he gasped, no less out of his mind than Savannah.

He pressed his face to her writhing belly, unable to concentrate on using both his mouth and hand while Rhian took him higher. He was more than ready, but damned if he wasn't even more turned on because Rhian refused to be rushed.

He was glad he hadn't pushed Rhian. Glad he'd waited, resisting the urge to add this act to all the other things, sexual and not, he'd demanded. He didn't regret making those other demands, but he was right to have waited on this. To have Rhian give this freely, enthusiastically, and without any persuasion made it ever sweeter. Gave Garrick so much hope about the future.

Rhian turned his hand, separating his fingers until the line between pleasure and pain blurred. Garrick rode it, high as a kite, his eyes wide, his open mouth pressed to Savannah's stomach.

Savannah ran her hands through his hair. "God, you look like you're in heaven."

"Am."

He canted his hips. Forced Rhian on, deeper. It was better than heaven, damn it.

Twisting his fingers, he attacked Savannah's g-spot while he still slung to the last shreds of his rapidly unraveling consciousness.

Savannah went up and over with a shriek, her fists locked in Garrick's hair. The pain was a welcome distraction from the exquisite pleasure radiating from his ass.

He didn't let up. Kept Savannah on the knife's edge for as long as she could stand it, bringing her back to earth slowly. She opened her glazed eyes and looked at him, her little smile content, her body still twitching with aftershocks.

Rhian pulled his fingers from Garrick's ass.

At last.

He hardly winced when the bottle of lubricant brushed his ass and a flood of cool lube slid into him. He hadn't done this in years. All the times in the past, he'd had to remind himself to stay relaxed. Not now.

Nothing would make him hesitate to take Rhian into his body.

His resolve faltered when the broad head of Rhian's cock pressed against him. He still wanted it, but man, how had he forgotten how goddamn *thick* Rhian was? He took a deep breath and ignored the laughter in Savannah's eyes.

The stretch grew, and his mouth gaped against her belly. His eyes just about popped out of his head. Jesus, it felt good. Fantastic. But, also, *huge.* Savannah was grinning at him, one hand fisted in his hair, keeping his eyes on her while his undivided attention was on the glorious stretch as Rhian pushed forward.

The head of Rhian's cock popped past his burning muscles and he grunted. His head spun, barely aware of Rhian's hands wrapping around his hips, holding him completely still while he adjusted to Rhian's presence in his ass.

Anticipation shivered up Garrick's spine until his entire body shook with it. "God, Rhian, *do it.*"

Rhian shifted and he gasped. Shocked. Rhian's fingers dug

into his skin, thumbs pulling his cheeks open as Rhian lifted him, arching his back further, tilting his ass higher. Then with one long, powerful thrust, Rhian seated himself to the hilt.

The world swam before Garrick's eyes. "*Rhian.*"

"Yes?" he replied as he slowly slid back out.

Savannah watched Rhian with absolute fascination.

"God, that's good," Garrick groaned as Rhian pushed forward again. Garrick swore he could feel every ridge and vein as they rushed past his hyper-sensitive ring.

"Yes, it is." Rhian sounded as if he spoke through clenched teeth.

On the next thrust, the collision of their bodies rocked through Garrick. He whimpered a noise that came dangerously close to the one he loved to tease from Rhian. He clamped his mouth shut, swearing he wouldn't make another sound.

Rhian picked up speed.

Garrick's resolve lasted less than ten seconds.

"*Fuck!*"

"God, Garrick, tell me this is okay. Tell me I'm not hurting you," Rhian said without easing his increasingly powerful thrusts.

Garrick tried to answer, but he couldn't catch his breath. Terrified Rhian would stop if he didn't say *something,* he managed to strangle out a sentence in time with the hard smack of their bodies colliding.

"Yes...Good...Fuck...Harder...Christ...You're...Strong!"

Rhian slammed home hard on the last word and Garrick gave up trying to tell him how amazing it was. How good it felt. It was too much. His brain was fried. Swamped with the chemicals that go with happy and aroused. He blissed out, floating on raging desire, higher with every thrust.

He didn't know if he was going to come. Or when.

He didn't care.

He would happily, joyfully hang suspended here, like this,

for hours. Days.

Reality snapped back into focus when Rhian dropped onto Garrick's back . He wrapped his arms around Garrick's chest and yanked them upright. Rhian sat back on his heels and Garrick's ass slammed down on Rhian's thighs, fully impaled on Rhian's thick shaft.

"Oh Jesus. Rhian, fuck, that's...please, I want—"

Rhian ground up against him, his hips gyrating over and over. Garrick lost the ability to speak.

The pressure. The burn. The endorphins. It was almost too much. Each swivel of Rhian's hips bumped his cock against Garrick's prostate. The intimacy of Rhian's arms around him, his lips tickling Garrick's shoulder, stole his breath. He teetered on the edge of bliss, frozen. It was huge. Too big.

Rhian rubbed his face against the side of Garrick's neck. "God, you're amazing."

Garrick squeezed his eyes shut against the tears springing to life at the loving, reverent tone in Rhian's voice.

"Savannah," Rhian growled.

Garrick opened his eyes to watch her crawl toward them, her eyes glued to his face. His eyes. His tears.

Rhian reached out and cupped her cheek. She kissed his palm and looked up at him over Garrick's shoulder.

Rhian clamped his hands around Garrick's waist again and used his incredible strength to lift and lower Garrick, who was too far gone to help. He just held on in the storm. Barely.

Rhian's hips punched up, thrusting his cock into Garrick's ass, his penetration deep and complete. Savannah's hot mouth closed around Garrick's cock, her hand grasping his shaft, the other cradling his balls.

Garrick cried out. Howled. His entire essence, his body and soul, honed down to the exquisite joy he would only ever find with these two incredible people.

The world went white, his mind with it. His orgasm bowed his spine and exploded from his balls, electric shocks shivering through his body. Sore muscles clamped down on Rhian's thick shaft, screaming with tension and relief.

Rhian ground up into him and shouted in his ear as the warmth of his climax filled Garrick's ass.

He was lost. Given over entirely into their hands. Their love. Savannah and Rhian didn't stop moving, sucking, fucking, coaxing another shudder, and another, from him, until he groaned, in agony. Ecstasy. He begged them to stop and to go on forever.

To take everything he had to give. It was theirs. It always had been.

Chapter Thirty Six

Savannah sat in the bright sun outside the cafe in Quincy Market and smiled about nothing in particular. It was a good day. They'd slept in, gone for a run, showered as a very cozy group, had Rhian for lunch and sandwiches for dessert.

What could possibly not be good about this day?

She couldn't take her eyes off her boys where they stood in line to order their coffees. Her mind kept drifting back to the previous night. She'd never seen Garrick so far gone. Nor Rhian so completely engaged in what they were doing. In what *he* was doing. She and Garrick had just been along for the ride, letting Rhian take them where he would. And he'd had a number of destinations in mind. But none as shattering as that first.

She would never forget the look of wonder on Garrick's face as Rhian penetrated him. Nor the long stare Rhian had locked on her when he'd lifted Garrick onto his lap and called to her. She'd never felt more connected to them.

She'd never loved them more either.

Chelsea dropped into the seat across from her. "Hi!"

"Hi there."

"Are you dating Rhian?"

Savannah's mouth fell open, trying to come up something to say while her brain scrambled for an answer.

Shit. She had to say no. Right? But she wanted to say *yes.* God knew it was a lot more complicated—and wonderful— than just that. Either way, she wasn't sure if she could trust this girl with the truth of any of it. They hardly knew her.

"It's complicated," she said at last.

Chelsea snorted. "I guessed as much when it took you two minutes to answer a simple yes-no question." She glanced through the window at her brother and Garrick, her expression serious. "I get it, though. Don't worry. I know he can't do weird shit. He's famous."

Savannah laughed, albeit nervously. Chelsea was perceptive, but they were also doing a piss-poor job of hiding how they felt about one another. Savannah hated that they might need to be more careful. "Can we leave it at that, then?"

Chelsea shrugged her acceptance with a little smile. Savannah wished she could read the girl's mind and know she would keep them safe. Keep *Rhian* safe.

"Ladies." Garrick's deep voice brought their heads around as he and Rhian sat on either side of them. Garrick handed Savannah a cup. "Latte for you."

"And decaf mocha with peppermint for you." Rhian placed Chelsea's steaming cup before her.

Chelsea smiled at Rhian like he'd invented chocolate just for her. "You remembered."

Rhian shrugged self-consciously and suddenly looked not one minute over his twenty-four years. Savannah rubbed his knee under the table and he flashed her a grateful smile before settling in to talk to Chelsea. He leaned into the table to be nearer his sister, their hand gestures mirroring each other's.

Savannah enjoyed watching the show of emotion on Rhian's face. Her heart leapt when he gave Chelsea their address at the apartment if she needed to find him. He asked about her friends. If she drove. Told her about being drafted by Moncton. Garrick asked a couple questions here and there, but he, too, was more spectator than participant, and neither Chelsea nor Rhian seemed to notice.

Savannah jumped in when Chelsea mentioned she was going to Wellesley College in the fall.

"Congratulations. You must be very proud. That's a wonderful school."

"Thanks." Chelsea made a face, adding, "All girls, though."

Savannah shrugged. "I went to Harvard and there were times I wished I'd picked Wellesley instead."

"You did?"

"Go to Harvard? Yes. Or wish I had chosen Wellesley? Because that's also a yes."

"Why didn't you?"

Savannah smiled ruefully. "No hockey team." She ignored Rhian and Garrick's laughter.

Chelsea cocked her head. "What?"

"No hockey team," Savannah repeated. "I wanted to play ice hockey, and for some silly reason, Wellesley doesn't have a team."

Rhian cleared his throat. "And you were offered a scholarship to play for a Division 1 team," he reminded her dryly.

Garrick looked at her. "You were?"

Savannah rolled her eyes. "My bothers talk too much."

"Captain at Harvard her junior year."

She shot Rhian a bland look. "You can stop now."

"Won the division championship her senior year. Named MVP."

Rhian's face lit with pride, whether over her accomplishments or his ability to shock Garrick and make her blush, Savannah couldn't tell.

Either way, she liked it. Chelsea congratulated her on her successes, of which she was proud, but right then it felt like her greatest accomplishment was bringing Rhian Savage out of his shell.

Rhian sat back and watched Chelsea talk to Savannah and Garrick. His lovers had both gone to top notch schools, like his sister would in a few months, and they had tons of advice, happily answering all her questions.

Rhian had, on occasion, regretted not going to college. Hockey had been more important, his ticket out, but he'd also been a decent student and thought one day he might like to go

275

back.

Maybe in twenty years when they finally kicked his ass off the ice.

Chelsea laughed at something Garrick said, or maybe it was at the face Savannah made at Garrick in response, and Rhian smiled. It was shocking how much it already mattered to him that Chelsea was happy. Healthy. He wanted her to be successful in whatever she chose to pursue.

He'd barely gotten used to feeling these sorts of things for Garrick. And Savannah. And here it was again.

He loved his sister. And he swore he'd do whatever he could to help her through life. If she let him, he would gladly be her brother.

How fucking scary is that?

Rhian snapped out of his musings when Savannah asked if Chelsea had a significant other.

"No, no one special. I had a boyfriend a while back, but we broke up when he left for school in California last fall."

Disappointment shaded Chelsea's voice and Rhian seriously wanted to punch that foolish boy in the face. Hell, now he understood why the Morrison brothers were such a giant pain in the ass.

His burst of laughter brought the conversation to an abrupt halt. All three of his companions looked at him like he was a nut.

He waved a hand at Chelsea to ward off her frown. "Sorry, I wasn't laughing at what you said, I swear."

Chelsea's eyes darted to something over his shoulder. With a cry, she jumped to her feet. "Buddy! No—"

Rhian spun in his chair, barely catching a glimpse of Buddy bearing down on him before a huge and powerful fist slammed into his temple. The world went black. The next thing he knew, his head was hitting the paving stones beneath their table.

Stunned, he blinked to try to clear his head. He heard Garrick shout and chairs screeching across brick all around him.

I need to get up, damn it.

Years of practice let him do it. He spun to face Buddy on unsteady legs, shivering at the cold rage in his beady eyes.

He'd felt an instant kinship with Chelsea, but there was nothing like that with his brother.

No. *Not my brother.* Just as he had at age four, he would damn well choose who he called family. And this fucker wasn't it.

Buddy struggled to hold onto Chelsea as he dragged her toward the sidewalk. She clawed and kicked at him, almost succeeding in breaking free. Her brother wrapped a meaty arm around her neck.

Rhian's head throbbed—the bastard packed a wallop—but his feet felt connected to the earth again. He plowed through the tables toward Buddy. "What the fuck do you want?"

Buddy snarled at him. "I told you to stay away from her!"

His arm tightened and Chelsea's eyes bulged. Rhian could hear her breath scraping past the constriction. Barely. Rhian stopped moving.

His eyes never left Buddy's as Garrick sidled to the right. Savannah's hand clenched the back of Rhian's shirt, a reassuring presence in a world gone haywire.

Buddy's gaze swung to Garrick. "Stop or I'll punch her in the head like she deserves."

"Stay there. Please." Chelsea looked at Garrick, her gaze pleading. "I don't want anyone to get hurt. I'm okay. I'll go home with him."

Garrick put his hands up and froze. Buddy backed away.

Rhian couldn't tear his eyes off his sister. "Chelsea. Are you sure?"

"Yes, it's okay. I'll contact you later."

Buddy shook her by her neck. "You'll never speak to any of them again."

Rhian and Garrick both took another step.

"No! It's okay," Chelsea cried. She tried to look over her shoulder at Buddy. "It's okay, Buddy. I agree. I'll never talk to them again."

Rhian thought his heart would crack in two. He clenched his teeth to force back the shout of denial. He almost didn't see Chelsea wink at him as her brother dragged her away.

They stood where they were, arrayed across the café, until Chelsea disappeared around the corner. Then Garrick ran to them, clamping his hands on Rhian's arms and holding him steady as Savannah immediately began a thorough examination of his injuries. She turned his face to the sun and he winced against the flare of pain.

"Eyes are reacting to light," she murmured, pressing her fingers against the growing welt on his temple.

"*Ouch.*"

She grimaced. "I think he just stunned you. Do you feel nauseous?"

"I'm fine." His need to take deep breaths belied his assertion entirely. "Or I will be. Maybe a concussion, but I don't think so."

He let Savannah move his head and check his eyes again while Garrick waved off members of the café staff, promising everything was all right.

Rhian wished like hell that was true.

Savannah ran her fingers down his cheek. "What do you want to do?"

"Can I call Chance?"

Savannah didn't question him. She pulled out her phone and speed-dialed her brother-in-law. Rhian took the phone and led them to a quiet corner of the patio.

Chance answered immediately. "What can I do for you, sister of my heart?"

Rhian blinked. "Hey, it's Rhian. Do you seriously answer the phone that way every time Savannah calls you?"

Chance's big laugh boomed in his ear and he winced against the pounding in his skull. "What can I do for you Rhian?"

"I need your advice." He explained what had happened. When he was done, there was a long silence on the other end of the line. "I'm going to put you on speaker. Garrick and Savannah are here."

He thought he heard Chance mutter, "Of course they are," as he pulled the phone from his ear.

"Rhian, how do you feel about going to the cops with this?" Chance asked once they could all hear him.

"Not great. Why?"

"If Chelsea is in danger at home, the best way to protect her is to make sure the cops know she lives with a psycho."

"Even if it means risking setting off that psycho? And giving him, and probably my mother, my name?"

"According to Chelsea, she and Buddy haven't told your mother anything. There's always a chance she won't figure out who you really are."

Rhian laughed bitterly. "God, you're probably right. Even if she saw me, she probably wouldn't have a fucking clue."

Savannah's arm slid around his waist and Garrick leaned into his side.

Chance's sigh was clear through the speaker. "I'm sorry, man. It's not right. But I do think pressing charges is the best way to go."

Rhian had known Chance was a law-and-order kind of guy before he called, so he wasn't surprised. Not really. Rhian recalled his promise to himself to be Chelsea's brother in truth.

"I fucking hate it," he admitted, "but I'm going to do it."

Chance got down to business, directing them to the police station in city hall right across the street. "Ask for Patrick Brown when you get there. And keep an eye out for me. I'm on my way."

The line went dead. Rhian handed the phone back to

Savannah.

Her forehead was lined with worry. "Are you sure?"

He wasn't sure about any of this. He smiled sadly. "What would your brothers do if it was you in trouble?"

Savannah sighed and nodded.

Together, all three of them turned and walked toward the police station.

Garrick, Savannah and Chance stood a few feet away while Rhian sat in the chair by Detective Patrick Brown's desk and told him everything, including how he knew Chelsea. Garrick tried not to flinch. The proverbial fan was spinning on high and the shit was flying toward it at full speed.

Garrick twitched with the need to protect Rhian from his mother. He wanted to haul Rhian out of that damn chair and drag him home right now. But he couldn't. Wouldn't. This was Rhian's choice and damned if he wasn't making a good one, in spite of the risks.

When Rhian was finished, Detective Brown—Patrick, as Chance had introduced his friend—called Savannah over, and Rhian came to stand near him and Chance. But not near enough. He was stiff as a board, never touching Garrick. Garrick swayed toward him, hoping to bump shoulders, but Rhian edged away. There was a clear boundary around Rhian now, and Garrick didn't think he could penetrate it without tackling him to the ground.

Fuck.

By the time it was his turn, he was sweating bullets, certain Rhian would bolt as soon as he turned his back. He ran through the events for Patrick with as little emotion as possible, repeatedly glancing over at Rhian. He stood a good three feet apart from Savannah and Chance. Garrick's stomach churned.

As soon as he was done, the others came over.

Patrick looked up at Rhian. "You have more than enough cause and witnesses. I'll stop by the café today to speak with the staff to get corroboration, then I'll bring him in."

"Fine," Rhian said from much farther away than was necessary.

They waited while Patrick filled out the last of the paperwork. Garrick forced himself not to stare at Rhian, let alone glare until he burned a hole through that thick skull. When it was his turn to sign, he noticed a framed picture of Patrick with his arms around a man in a tuxedo and a beautiful woman wearing white.

He stared at the picture for a long time until Patrick cleared his throat.

"Sorry," Garrick said lamely. He noticed Patrick wore a wedding ring. "Is that your ah—" Shit, husband? Wife? He couldn't tell which of the two people in the picture Patrick was married to. "—wedding?"

Patrick grinned, his entire face lighting up. "It is."

Chance seemed to find Garrick's question hilarious.

"That's my husband, Brandon." Patrick said.

Garrick smiled. "Congratulations."

"And my wife, Destiny."

"Oh...ah..."

For the life of him, Garrick didn't know what the hell to say. A surprised but nervous laugh burst from Savannah.

Chance chuckled and slapped Patrick on the back. "Best wedding we've been to in years. That was a hell of a party."

"Thanks."

While the two men reminisced, Garrick looked over at Rhian and barely resisted the urge to leap from the chair. He'd moved even farther away. Savannah reached for him, but he darted back another step, leaving her hand suspended in air.

Chance's eyebrows rose as he took it all in.

Savannah's hand fell to her side. Garrick stayed seated. Rhian fell into the chair at the next desk over as if his legs wouldn't support him any longer.

Garrick had always wondered what it sounded like when the shit hit the fan. Turned out, it was deathly quiet.

Chapter Thirty Seven

Savannah tried to get some work done, but it was a waste of time. Every time she saw Rhian, she was shocked he was still there in the apartment, and hadn't run out the door. He sure as hell had left the building in every other way.

She'd examined his eyes and bruises a dozen times since they'd returned to the apartment from the police station. She was certain he was physically fine. Emotionally, all bets were off.

Her phone rang and she answered the call without looking at her phone. "Hello?"

"When will you get here tomorrow?"

"Uh…whaa?"

Her mother sighed. "Did you forget you and Garrick are supposed to come out here tomorrow, so we can finally meet him?"

She sure as shit had. Damn. "Uh, no. I'm sorry. I'm just distracted." She paused to collect her thoughts. "It's been a strange day."

Garrick muttered, "You can say that again," from the other side of the kitchen island. He was staring at Rhian, too.

"Well, I hope you can still make it. We want to meet this man. You said he was *the one*, after all, and Dad and I need to check the man who managed to turn your head so thoroughly."

You already met one of the two, *Mom. Surprise!*

Savannah rubbed her temple. "Yeah, sure, Mom. We'll come out tomorrow morning." Rhian looked over at her from the couch. "And if it's all right with you, we'll stay at the inn."

"Oh sure. I don't expect the two of you to sleep in one twin bed."

If only it were that simple. "Great. Also, Rhian will be with us," she said as casually as humanly possible.

She could feel Rhian burning holes in her back with his eyes. She probably should have asked both men if they minded, let alone wanted to go, but she wasn't going to give Rhian a chance to say no.

"Oh, okay," he mother said blithely. "Tell him he can stay here at the house if he'd like."

"I'll let him know," she said, lying through her teeth.

"Wonderful!"

Savannah tried to brush off the guilt. She'd figure out how to tell her mother. Maybe this weekend. But not now. And not on the phone.

They chatted for a while and Savannah told her mother about Rhian's test results. She held the phone away from her ear and felt a surge of victory when Rhian smiled at her mother's loud shouts of congratulations.

As soon as her mother was finished, though, Rhian went back to the compulsive channel surfing that had captured his attention for the better part of the afternoon.

Rhian stared at the phone in his hand and wondered how the hell this day could go any more sideways. A text had just come in from his agent, Sergio.

Got a line on Boston and Pittsburgh. Any preference?

Damned if Rhian knew.

Two months ago, it would have been Pittsburgh without hesitation. A couple hundred miles separation from Garrick, Savannah, and Boston was just what he'd had in mind.

Now? What the hell *did* he want?

He glanced over at his lovers, who were both trying very hard not to be obvious that they were watching him like a pair of hawks.

Can I get back to you?

He was pretty sure he knew what Sergio was going to think of that request.

Dude. Not much time. If I don't hear from you, I will go with better deal.

Rhian's heart squeezed painfully in his chest. *Understood.*

How cowardly would it be to let Sergio make the decision for him? Pretty fucking pathetic, he decided.

He jumped up when someone knocked on their door.

"I'll get it," Rhian called before either Savannah or Garrick could get up from their work. After sitting and staring at nothing for an hour, he was suddenly restless.

Hand on the doorknob, he paused. Maybe he should march right back into the kitchen and tell Savannah he was in love with her. Their reactions would certainly help him decide what the hell he was going to do next.

The knocking started up again. Declarations of love would have to wait a few minutes.

He opened the door and all thoughts of the future, of love, disappeared.

Rhian backed away, his heart turned to stone, his legs numb.

He'd wondered if he'd recognize her. He did. Instantly.

"Mother."

A stool crashed to the floor in the kitchen.

"Shut up. Don't call me that," she snapped as she blew into the apartment on a waft of expensive floral perfume and slammed the door behind her. "What if someone heard you?"

He realized he was backing away from her when he walked into Savannah and Garrick behind him. They each put a hand on his back and stood at his shoulders, aligning themselves with him. Against her.

It didn't help.

"What do you want?"

"What do you think I want? How *dare* you accuse Buddy of assaulting you? He was protecting his sister."

Memories, long lost, resurfaced. Her anger. Rage. She'd

said he'd ruined her life.

He swallowed. "*What do you want?*"

"Buddy is loyal to me." She said it as if Rhian hadn't been. *At age four?* "He's my best friend. I will not let you sully his reputation with these charges. He's my *son*."

Clearly, she chose to believe she only had one of those. How nice for her. And she was lecturing *him* on loyalty?

He stood a little straighter. He had a good six inches and at least a hundred pounds on her. Rather than react like a child in the face of his mother's rage, he locked gazes with her. "Buddy is a goddamn—"

The door burst open and Chelsea flew into the apartment. She shoved past her mother and flung herself at Rhian.

He caught her and held on.

Their mother rolled her eyes. "Aren't you two a match made in heaven?" she said, her contempt obvious.

"I'm sorry," Chelsea mumbled into his chest. "She looked up your address in my address book online. I didn't know she had the password."

Rhian ran a hand down her hair. "It's okay. It was bound to happen eventually." It struck him, as he held onto his sister and stared at his mother, that this was the first time he could remember hugging a member of his family. Or being hugged by one.

Chelsea lifted her head. "Can I live with you for the summer? Until I go to school?"

Rhian blinked. *Shit.* A hug was one thing. Living with his sister? His mother rolled her eyes again. Suddenly, the answer was easy.

"Yes."

"Over my dead body!" their mother shouted.

Chelsea threw her backpack to the floor and spun on her mother. "What do you care? I'm eighteen. You can't stop me."

"Oh yes, I can. I can make sure you don't get access to your tuition fund. It might be your grandfather's money, but I *am* the trustee."

Chelsea paled and lunged at her mother. Rhian caught her and shoved her back into Garrick and Savannah's hold.

"What will it take?" he demanded.

His mother eyed him, considering. "Drop the charges."

"Done."

"And none of you can ever tell my father that you even exist."

Rhian nodded. "Fine with me. Going forward, Chelsea can stay with me any time she chooses, for as long as she'd like. No threats to her tuition or I go back to the cops."

"Done."

"And Buddy stays away. He comes near her, or any of us, and we go straight to Grandpa's house, right around the corner."

His mother looked ready to spit nails. "Fine," she ground out.

And just like that, he'd run out of things he wanted to say to his mother.

No wait. There *was* one more thing.

"Now get the fuck out."

He slammed the door behind her.

Garrick paced their apartment like a caged animal. His skin prickled with sweat and anger. His muscles twitched with the need to do something. Things like holding, kissing, loving, cajoling, *forcing* Rhian to stop ignoring him and Savannah.

It had been an hour since Rhian's monster of a mother had been there, and Rhian hadn't left Chelsea's side on the couch since. Savannah sat next to him, trying to hold his hand, but he kept pulling free to do something or other with his phone, Chelsea's phone or the remote. Garrick was ready to pick Rhian up by the scruff of his neck and march him into the bedroom for a little reminder of all the reasons why he shouldn't be shutting them out.

But he couldn't. He didn't know what Chelsea knew. What she should know. What Rhian wanted anyone to know. And while Garrick was perfectly happy to push the envelope when it was just the three of them, he wouldn't steal Rhian's right to decide who knew what, particularly when it came to his sister.

Garrick did another lap around the kitchen, his fingers yanking at his hair. The clock tick was a constant reminder that at any moment, Rhian was going to announce he had to go. He'd already called the hotel to move them to a two bedroom unit, flatly refusing Garrick and Savannah's offer that they stay here.

Totally unacceptable.

A knock on the door brought Garrick back to the hallway, bearing down on the damn thing before anyone could rise off the couch.

He flung the door open, hoping it was Rhian's mother again. He was seriously considering breaking every rule he'd ever been taught and punching the damn woman in the face.

It wasn't Diane. It was Chance, Kieran and Lachlan—the three fucking musketeers—none of whom Garrick had any desire to see.

Chance frowned at him. "Patrick called when Rhian dropped the charges. We wanted to check to see if everything is okay."

It wasn't. Not by a long shot. And why the hell couldn't they have called?

He left the door open and returned to his pacing. They could let themselves in.

As soon as her brothers filed into the living room, Savannah dropped Rhian's hand, stood up, and offered to make everyone coffee.

Lachlan stared at her, long and hard, and she turned pinker with every passing second. What the hell was up with that?

Garrick forgot all about Lachlan, though, when he saw the look on Rhian's face.

Oh shit. *Here we go again.*

Rhian also stood, his posture wooden, and introduced his sister.

Once they'd all shaken hands, he smiled grimly. "We were just leaving."

"No," Garrick barked, bringing all eyes to him. *Smooth, LeBlanc.* "I mean, Rhian, can I have a word with you in the office?"

Rhian hesitated and Garrick narrowed his gaze. He'd fucking wrestle him into that goddamn room if he had to.

He must have been projecting his intentions loud and clear, because Rhian scowled and stomped off down the hall. Garrick followed, scrambling for what he would say. He knew, without a doubt, that Rhian shouldn't leave. Not yet. Not after his mother's visit. And not after the heartbroken acceptance all over his face as he'd stared up at Savannah a moment ago.

They had shit they needed to work out, goddamn it.

Savannah followed them into the tiny bedroom they'd set up as a work space but rarely used. Garrick had to shove the old door to get it to close, but this conversation needed to happen out of earshot of the rest of the household, and the overly cheerful conversation from the living room wouldn't be enough to mask it.

"I'm leaving," Rhian stated before Garrick could say a word. It didn't sound like he meant for the day. Or a week.

Savannah reached for him. "No, please."

Rhian stepped back and her arms fell to her side.

Garrick's heart plummeted. "Please, Rhian. Don't leave. You and Chelsea can stay here. With us."

Rhian shook his head. "You two go to Connecticut. I'll be fine."

Savannah stepped closer. "You can come with us. Bring Chelsea."

"And what? Pretend to be your pal while you introduce Garrick to your parents?" Garrick had never heard Rhian use such a cutting tone before.

Worse, Garrick had never seen Savannah so uncertain and confused. His panic ratcheted higher. He had to stop Rhian. They needed him. So damn much. And he needed them, too, damn it.

Though, more than anything, Rhian needed *Savannah*. He needed her humor, the way she brought out his confidence. He connected with her. Her family. Better than anyone Garrick had ever seen him with.

Suddenly, Garrick was about to do the one thing he swore he'd never do. If it fucking killed him, he was going to be the man Rhian deserved.

"Wait," Garrick said when Rhian turned toward the door. "You go. I'll stay here."

"What?" Savannah cried.

"You're better for him," he said, his voice thick. "You both have that thing. The strength I love so much in both of you. He needs that from you. I want..." He swallowed past the lump choking off his increasingly unsteady voice, "I want you both to be happy. That's the most important thing. Take Rhian to Connecticut. Tell your parents—"

"No!" Rhian grabbed Garrick's arm and shook him. "Damn you. No! You don't get to decide for me." He turned to Savannah. "You don't want to make a family with me. Even if you felt about me the way you do about Garrick, it can't work."

"But Rhian, I—"

He grabbed his hair in two fists. "No! You know I'm right. You two can be happy. Whole. I'd never forgive myself for ruining that. What could I possible know about building a happy family? Look at my mother. *She's a monster.*"

He wrenched open the door and stormed out into the hallway. "Chelsea!"

Garrick furiously wiped the tears from his face before

charging out after Rhian, Savannah on his heels.

Chelsea met them in the hallway. They must have looked a fucking mess, but she kindly kept her mouth shut.

Rhian urged Chelsea toward the door. "We have to go. I don't want to be moving into the new place in the middle of the night," he said. He didn't say a word to the men standing agape in the living room, just charged into the front hall and yanked the door open. "I'll be in touch," he said without so much as a glance in their direction.

The note of finality damn near stole Garrick's breath.

He considered tackling Rhian to the hallway floor, but with Chelsea next to him, Garrick couldn't do it. It wouldn't make a difference anyway. All he'd make was a scene and possibly add to the panic he could see crawling over Rhian's face.

"Rhian, please," he begged, without a care for his audience.

Rhian's answer was to shut the door in his face.

Chapter Thirty Eight

Savannah and Garrick arrived in Connecticut early in the morning on Friday, hollow-eyed and quiet. Her parents greeted them on the porch and Savannah clung to her mother, barely choking out that Rhian hadn't been able to make it without bursting into tears.

Garrick tried to rally and be his usual charming self for her parent's benefit. She was grateful for his efforts, but knew it was killing him. She couldn't have managed it if their positions had been reversed. As it was, she was trying as hard as she could to keep her expression neutral, and still she caught her mother and father looking at her with concern all the time.

Her mother asked what was wrong, but Savannah brushed her off, saying they were both working too hard and super tired. Then the damn woman started asking about Rhian and Savannah had very nearly burst into tears again. She pretended a burning need for the bathroom to escape before the first sobs did.

By noon, she was a zombie. She held onto Garrick—his hand, a hug, anything—but it was a small comfort, his grief like hers, rolling off him in waves.

At some point they were going to have to discuss what they would do next, but she wasn't ready. She was too hurt. Too sad.

The crunch of tires in the driveway through the open front window interrupted their lunch and her heart leaped in her chest. For one hideously foolish moment, she hoped it would be Rhian.

She tried not to be disappointed to see Lachlan.

He barely paused long enough to kiss their mother and shake their father's hand before he grabbed her by the arm and dragged her into their father's office, slamming the door behind them.

"What the fuck is the matter with you?"

Savannah stared out the window, her back to Lachlan, and tried to remember the last time she'd heard him swear. "What do you want, Lach?"

"You were holding Rhian's hand!"

Savannah didn't bother to check her tears. Could her brother have chosen a worse time to jump on her about being too friendly with Rhian?

"Leave me alone," she said quietly.

"How could you do that? How could you do that to him?" Lachlan demanded.

Her breath hitched when she tried to gather enough air to speak. "Garrick isn't upset, Lachlan. We have no secrets. Just leave it alone. Please."

"Not Garrick," Lachlan roared. "*Rhian!*"

Savannah turned. "What?"

Lachlan blinked when he saw her, no doubt struck by how horrific she looked after crying. Again. His shoulders slumped and he dug at his eyes with his thumb and forefinger. "God, I don't think I've ever been this mad at you. You broke his fucking heart."

Savannah blinked. "What the hell are you talking about?"

Lachlan pinned her with another glare. "Why won't you acknowledge him? Why do you push him away when we're around?"

"I-I-I don't understand. You know?"

Lachlan slammed his hands on his hips and looked at the ceiling for a moment, as if someone upstairs might grant him patience. "Of course I know, you idiot. So does Chance. And Kieran. How the fuck could we not notice how he stares at you like the sun and moon rise and set on your ass? And you're no better. Neither is Garrick, the poor bastard." Lachlan's laugh conveyed his pity. "He looks like he wants to fall to his knees and thank god every time he sees either one of you."

For the first time in twenty-four hours, Savannah smiled.

Garrick did tend to fall to his knees around them.

But Rhian was gone. Her smile was lost. "You're not wrong, Lach. But I'm not sure what difference it makes. And what the fuck do you want me to do? Tell mom I'm in love with two men?"

"Yes. For starters."

Savannah tried to begin at least three responses, but no sounds would come out.

"Oh, get over yourself," Lachlan snapped.

Savannah stared in shock at her brother. Man, he was a *bitch* when he was riled.

"She'd never turn her back on you." Lachlan bobbed his head side-to-side, as if conceding a point. "You might have to give her some time. And Dad. But they'll get there. You know they will. Hell, two more boys, and both hockey players? They'll be delighted once the shock wears off."

Savannah laughed. God, he was right. "*Mom!*"

Lachlan smiled. He waited for their mother to open the door before he kissed Savannah's cheek and left, closing it behind him.

"Everything all right, dear? I thought I heard Lachlan shouting."

"You did."

"Really?" her mother asked. "What on earth for?"

Savannah tried to smile, but nerves and the persistent ache of grief made it hard. "I screwed up. Big time."

Her mom took her hand. "What is it, honey?"

Immediately supportive. That was her mom. "I have something to tell you that you might have a hard time understanding."

Her mom nodded, not saying anything. Just waiting for it.

God, she should have asked Kieran how the hell he'd outed himself. Then she pictured her brother and his complete inability to hide anything, and knew the answer—he'd told the truth.

So she did, too. "I'm in love with Rhian. And Garrick. And they love each other."

Her mother's benign, encouraging smile didn't slip an inch. "What?"

"We're together. The three of us. In one relationship. And it's wonderful, Mom. Really amazing. But Rhian left. In part because I couldn't figure out how to tell you about it. About *him*. I was scared and a coward and now I don't know how we'll get him back." The tears started again.

For the first time in her life, her mother didn't try to wipe them away.

She slowly lowered herself into one of the big chairs. The same one Savannah and Rhian had cuddled in all those weeks ago. The chair she'd been in when she'd fallen in love. Again.

"Oh." The sound of her mother's voice, calm but confused, did nothing to settle Savannah's rioting anxiety.

"Mom?"

Her mother stared at her hands, clenched in her lap. She didn't answer.

Savannah died a little.

"I guess we better go check into the inn," she said, trying not to believe the worse and failing miserably. "We'll be there when you're ready to talk or want us to come back."

She could barely get her legs to work, staggered by grief.

Her hand was on the knob when her mother called out. "Wait!"

Rhian sat on the uncomfortable couch in his new, equally ugly apartment, in the same hotel he'd come to loathe sometime over the past few weeks. That he'd lived like this for months, years even, made him feel a little sick. Like he'd wasted so much valuable time in his effort to be as unattached as humanly possible.

Chelsea's presence made it a hundred times worse. For her, it was an adventure, though she was used to far grander surroundings. To him, it was a horrible reminder of what his life *hadn't* been.

He shook out the Boston Globe he'd bought that morning on his lonely run and spread it out across the table. He was on the hunt for a decent place to live for the summer, then he'd figure out what came next.

He found some options. A few sublets, at least, though the idea of living with someone else's stuff freaked him out.

Funny how that had never bothered him at Garrick and Savannah's place.

Shaking his head, he shoved the paper aside. "Come on, let's go get your stuff."

Chelsea appeared in her bedroom doorway. "What if they're home?"

"We'll get some coffee and try again in an hour."

She shrugged. "Okay, let's do it."

The townhouse, perched near the very top of Beacon Hill, was deserted when they arrived. Rhian stood on the street and stared at the huge house he'd walked past more than once. It was the same age and design as Garrick and Savannah's building, but where theirs had been cut into six apartments, this place was a single four-story residence. It reeked of money.

Chelsea finally lost patience and shook him out of his stupor. "Come on. It's just a house."

He laughed at himself and the countless Little Orphan Annie fantasies he and all the rest of the foster kids had hoped could come true. This place wasn't anyone's salvation. He took a moment to thank god his mother hadn't raised him.

Once they went inside, they didn't linger, running straight to Chelsea's room and stuffing her clothes and other belongings into any bag they could find. She had some luggage, which was quickly filled and stacked in the front hall. They'd just finished bundling together shopping bags full of the last of her things when the front door slammed shut.

"Oh, shit," Chelsea muttered.

Footsteps thundered up the stairs, then Buddy came barreling through the bedroom door, charging straight toward his sister. Rhian had to hand it to him. The idiot was fucking consistent.

The difference this time was that Rhian was ready for him. He dropped his bags and slammed into Buddy with all his weight and strength. The entire house shuddered when they hit the wall.

Buddy's head cracked against the plaster and Rhian jumped away before Buddy could recover—which he did with remarkable speed.

Maybe it was genetic.

Didn't matter. Rhian dodged a punch and swung hard, connecting with Buddy's face. Buddy came right back at him. Rhian ducked again. He could do this all day. Hockey had trained him well.

"Stop!"

The shrill demand came from the door as his mother rushed past him to check Buddy's injuries.

No, not his mother. *Diane.*

The damn woman cooed over Buddy's bloody nose.

Rhian caught himself before he rolled his eyes. Shit, *she* did that all the time. He hoped to hell that wasn't genetic, too.

Chelsea gathered up her bags. "We're just getting my stuff. We were about to leave."

Diane turned on her, the familiar mask of rage falling into place in a blink of the eye. "You're not going anywhere, young lady!"

Rhian sighed. He'd feared this exact thing would happen. He'd already dropped the charges, after all. They should have come get her stuff first. *Damn.*

The crestfallen look on Chelsea's face made Rhian furious. Rhian got right in Diane's face. "Shove it, *Mom*. We made a deal and you're going to stick to it."

"I'm not your mother," she hissed venomously. "I left you behind. I never even looked for you. Did you know that? Never a regret. I was pregnant with Buddy and I knew from the moment he was conceived that he was special. He understands what family means. You never will."

Rhian laughed. Not the maniacal laugh so often employed in the presence of fucking crazy people, but a genuine chortle of delight. "I've got a family."

And he hoped to hell they would forgive him.

Because holy shit, it was true. He understood what family was better than this crazy bitch. Leaving him was the best thing she'd ever done for him, and giving him Chelsea was a damn close second.

He looked at his sister and they shared a smile of perfect understanding.

Diane sneered at her daughter. "You're an ungrateful bitch! You think I'm going to pay for your fancy school now?"

Chelsea crossed her arms and stared her mother down.

Rhian smiled at Chelsea, then at the monster who had given birth to them. "Keep your money, bitch. I'll pay."

He was fucking delighted to finally have something to do with the money he'd saved over the past couple years. He wasn't a complete rube—he knew Wellesley College would be expensive. But he'd make it work. Take out loans if he had to.

The grin of pure, unadulterated love and gratitude Chelsea sent him made him feel ten feet tall.

They grabbed everything they'd packed and ran like hell out of that awful house, leaving the rest of their putrid gene pool behind.

Chapter Thirty Nine

Their escape would have gone more smoothly if they'd had the foresight to order a taxi. Instead they stood like a couple dorks on the corner, waiting for their ride, piles of crap all around them.

Chelsea was still smiling. "Thanks for offering to put me through school."

"You're welcome. It wasn't an empty promise. We'll make it work."

She threw her arms around him and gave him a loud, smacking kiss on his cheek. "You're the best brother in the world."

He imagined he was a fascinating shade of red now. "Uh, thanks."

"And very generous."

He nodded, not sure what to say.

"But I'm going to talk to Grandfather about Mom's behavior long before I drain your bank accounts."

"But—"

"I won't tell him about you if you still don't want me to. But I think you should reconsider." She eyes him speculatively. "He makes pretty good family. Seems like yours is still pretty small."

Until he begged a certain two people's forgiveness, his family was one, and she was standing right in front of him.

"I'll think about it," he allowed. "I might consider expanding, once I get my current relations sorted out."

She grinned. "Does that mean you're going to stop being a dumb-ass about your...errr...friends?"

"What?" He choked on an embarrassing nervous laugh.

"I don't know what happened, and if you've got cause to

kick their asses to the curb, you know I'll support you, but I kind of got the impression you eighty-sixed Garrick and Savannah because I was around. And you don't need to. I get that you love them."

Rhian stared long and hard at his overly perceptive sister. "That's not the reason I did it." He stood firm against her dubious look for all of ten seconds. "Okay, not the *only* reason. I pushed them away because I never figured it could be for real. Permanent. I figured someday..."

"They'd just up and leave you with Mrs. Rosenberg?"

Shit, when she put it like that...

"Yeah," he admitted.

"So, you were going to let her win, huh?"

"Who?"

"Dear old mom, of course. You were going to walk away from two incredibly sexy, brilliant, kind people because she fucked with your head that badly?"

When he just stared at her, she threw up her hands.

"Look, not that I blame you. I don't. What do I know? I was stuck with her and I'm sure there will be more than one boyfriend in my future who will point out that it wasn't for the best. But come *on.* You smiled all the time. And the way your eyes would track them everywhere? How they were always finding reasons to touch you? Brush up against you? Hell, you three should come with a warning label and a bucket of ice water."

His face felt like it was going to catch fire. How the hell could he talk about this shit with his sister? She was a mostly grown woman, with an obviously active and accurate imagination, but still—she was his *sister*.

Oh shit.

Hindsight was a bitch.

He'd been certain Savannah was rejecting him. That she was ashamed for her brothers to know about him. But what if it was just this? The basic discomfort of revealing the details of her sex life to her brothers? He'd only known his sister for a week and it was already awkward. Christ, with six nosey, intelligent, and ruthless brothers, he'd never tell anyone anything.

At least until he was sure.

Rhian wanted to sit his ass down on the brick sidewalk and howl at his own stupidity. Goddamn, why didn't he tell Savannah he was in love with her?

Chelsea put a gentle hand on his shoulder. "You just figured out how fucking stupid you are, didn't you?"

Rhian grimaced. "How can you tell? You barely know me."

"Dude! We have the same face!"

Rhian smiled. He looked at his sister and all her worldly possessions around their feet. He felt bad causing her more upheaval, but it couldn't wait.

"How do you feel about a trip to Connecticut?"

She laughed. "I thought you'd never ask."

The taxi pulled up to the curve and they spent the next few minutes packing an unbelievable amount of crap into the trunk before climbing into the back seat.

"I hope it's okay, but we're moving."

"As long as I get that nice little office room and a bed, I'm good. I love this neighborhood."

Rhian laughed and gave the driver the address to Savannah and Garrick's apartment—*his* apartment— and checked his pocket for the key.

He pulled it and his phone out, quickly firing off a text to Sergio.

Boston. I definitely want to stay in Boston. Take any deal they offer.

Three hours later, Rhian and Chelsea parked in the Morrison's driveway in Connecticut. Rhian was dismayed to find Lachlan sitting on the porch.

Lachlan stood and crossed his arms over his chest. "Took you goddamn long enough," he said with what Rhian hoped was a hint of a smile. "Chelsea, why don't you hang out here with me for a while? This porch is about the only place in this house where a cell phone works, anyway."

They sat together on the swing and Lachlan set them to swaying. They both looked at Rhian expectantly.

"Go on in," Lachlan said. "Savannah and Garrick aren't in there, but Mom is worried sick about you."

Rhian nodded, wondering where they were. He needed to see them. Now.

He barely made it through the door and closed it behind him before Mary came out of the kitchen and headed straight for him. She yanked him into a tight hug. "Are you okay?"

He sagged against her. "I don't know."

She rubbed his back and held him for a while without speaking. Then she towed him into the living room and pushed him down onto the couch. He could hear the game was on in the family room and figured that was where he could find Bruce.

She took his hand. "I don't know the details, but I know you saw your biological mother. And I'm assuming that's Chelsea on the porch with Lach."

He nodded, not surprised she already knew some of it. Just remembering his confrontation with his mother made him cling to her tighter, his back straight as he tried to find the right words to tell her everything that had happened without actually breaking down like a baby.

In the end, he failed.

He managed to hold it together until he told her about his mother telling him in no uncertain terms that she'd never once looked for him. Had no regrets.

He couldn't remember when his head ended up on her shoulder, all he knew was that her hand felt good on his back, her steady silence its own comfort. When her hand stopped moving, he opened his eyes to find Bruce standing in the door, looking at his wife and the man weeping like an idiot all over her.

Rhian sat up and used a sleeve to dry his face while Bruce came over and sat on the fancy coffee table in front of the couch.

Rhian smiled. Now he knew where Savannah and her brothers got the idea coffee tables were for sitting on.

"What's got you worried, son?" Bruce asked.

Rhian loved that Bruce called him that. He hoped today wasn't the last time he'd hear it.

"I don't know what I'm doing. I don't know how to be in a family. How to be a good brother. A good husband."

"You're a good person, Rhian," Mary said, as if that answered all his questions.

"That's all that anyone here expects of you," Bruce added.

"But, you don't understand," he began, hesitating. It wasn't his place to tell Savannah parents, no matter how much they meant to him.

"We do understand." Bruce said, then grimaced. "Okay, maybe I don't understand it entirely, but Savannah told us what's going on." He glanced at Mary, who nodded encouragingly, then turned his attention back to Rhian. "We only want what's best for her. For all of you."

Rhian stared at Bruce. He couldn't possibly mean...

"Now, you better go get them," Bruce said, standing to make room for them to rise. "I took them down to the rink. Thought it might ease their minds for a while."

Mary patted Rhian's hand, then disappeared down the hallway. She returned with a Morrison hockey jersey.

"Here," she said, passing it to him. "They're wearing the green tonight."

He took it from her and turned it over.

SAVAGE.

The material bunched in his fists as he swallowed past the boulder lodged in his chest.

Mary smiled. "I just finished it a few minutes ago. I'm probably the only one who's glad you're late."

Rhian pulled the shirt over his head and put his hand over the Morrison crest on his chest. "Thank you, Mary."

Bruce smiled. "Honestly, son, you might as well call her Mom. And around here, I'm Dad."

Rhian smiled. "Okay."

Chapter Forty

Garrick and Savannah had been holding hands and skating in mindless circles for an hour. Savannah's father had snuck them into the rink earlier, with the promise they could stay as long as they liked. Garrick wanted to keep going around in circles until the pain went away. Until they both stopped hurting. He'd become detached from reality sometime yesterday when Rhian's eyes had gone dead, and he needed to fight his way back. Skating was familiar. Safe. Maybe, eventually, it would help.

He was pretty sure he hadn't made the best impression on the Morrisons. Not that he'd embarrassed himself or anything, but he wasn't himself. They seemed to know it, too. He worried that they'd forever remember the dud Savannah dragged home one weekend and he'd have to overcome that.

He and Savannah had hardly said a word since coming on the ice, except for Savannah's quiet admission that she'd told her mom everything. He had figured as much once they'd come out of the office. She also said her mom was telling her father, probably now.

Garrick was *not* looking forward to going back to the house. He wondered if anyone at Berkshire Academy would care of the two of them just went in circles like this all night.

He looked down at Savannah again, the skater in him enjoying how she glided over the ice. He was a great lummox by comparison. Her green jersey was well worn, with many rips repaired and the Morrison emblem obviously having been sewn on more than once.

He loved that he had his own jersey. He'd been touched when Mary had given it to him, then almost made a complete fool of himself when she told him Rhian had already worn it once.

Rhian had told him about the Morrison hockey games. He

couldn't wait to be a part of it someday, but damned if he hadn't also looked forward to it as a way to skate with Rhian again.

He squeezed Savannah's hand. "We're not giving up, are we?" His voice echoed in the empty arena.

Savannah almost smiled, still looking at the ice ahead. "Nope."

The sound of skates skimming across ice came from behind them. "I sure as hell hope not."

Garrick's heart lodged somewhere in his throat and he spun to see Rhian gliding toward them. Savannah gripped his arm so hard, he thought she might tear the sleeve off his jersey.

Rhian was also wearing a Morrison jersey. Garrick had never seen a more beautiful sight in his life. His heart ached when he saw Rhian's eyes were swollen and red, his eyelashes spiked with moisture.

Rhian stopped twenty feet away and Garrick jerked forward, desperate to touch him. Hold him. Savannah's hand held him still.

"Are you okay?" Garrick asked.

Rhian bit his lip and looked at Savannah. "I cried all over your mom."

Savannah let out a little breath. Almost a laugh. "She's used to it."

"From grown men?" Rhian asked with a self-deprecating laugh.

"Don't tell my brothers I told you."

Rhian smiled again and this time it made it all the way up to his beautiful eyes. Garrick heart started beating properly for the first time since Rhian had left them.

"We missed you, Rhian," Garrick said.

Rhian's eyes searched their faces. His smile faded. "I missed you, too."

Garrick put his hand over Savannah's on his arm but

couldn't tear his eyes off Rhian. "I love you. You get that, don't you?"

Rhian's blue eyes locked onto his. "I love you, too." Then he looked at Savannah. "And you. I love you, Savannah Morrison."

Garrick grinned, and for the first time in thirty years, nearly fell off his skates while standing perfectly still.

Savannah grabbed Garrick when he wobbled. She laughed as tears rolled down her cheeks.

"I love you, too, Rhian. I'm sorry I didn't tell you before. I've known for a while, but I thought it might spook you."

Rhian lifted one shoulder. "You're probably right." He glided five feet closer. Not close enough. Still out of reach. "I'm sorry I walked away."

It had been more like a run, but she kept that to herself. "Why did you?"

Rhian stared down at his skates and licked his lips nervously. "I was scared. Witless, to be honest. I thought...I thought you couldn't possibly want to keep me. Not really. And you didn't want your brothers to know about me and—"

"No, Rhian—"

He looked up at her. "It's okay, Savannah. I get it now. You can thank Chelsea for that. But it was easier for me to believe you were ashamed of me. Of us. It validated what I had always believed in my heart."

Savannah swallowed back her tears enough to whisper, "And what was that?"

"That I'm not someone people want to keep around. I'm not family. And that you'd abandon me, too. Like she did. Then my stupid biological family turned up and I..."

He paused, struggling for breath.

"You what, Rhian?" Garrick asked quietly.

"I remembered how much it hurt. To be left. I thought I remembered it all before, but when I saw her, it really came back. How I sat on Mrs. Rosenberg's couch for hours, staring at the door, waiting for my mother to come get me. The terror. I was so confused. And even then I knew she was awful. So what would it be like if...well, I couldn't bare the idea that it would hurt that much more when *you* left me. I didn't think I could survive that again, only worse, you know?"

Garrick's grip on her hand was painful, but they both held still.

"And now?" she asked quietly.

"And now I know it doesn't hurt any less to carve out your own heart than it does to have someone else do it for you."

Garrick made a low painful sound in his throat.

Rhian looked lost, standing alone on the ice with naked longing in his eyes. "You two are everything I ever wanted. Every goddamn dream I ever kept hidden in my heart. Right in front of me. I don't want to be the stupid, scared bastard who runs away. That's not who I am anymore."

Savannah smiled through her tears. "Then who are you?"

Garrick wobbled on his skates again when Rhian fell to his knee on the ice.

"I'm the man asking you to keep me. Forever."

Rhian's breath left him in a great whoosh when Garrick crashed into his chest. A big hand curled protectively around the back of his head to prevent it from slamming into the ice as Garrick and Savannah fell on top of him.

Arms clung, legs twined. He was still trying to replace the air in his lungs when their mouths met and they were in one big, happy kiss. It was messy and ridiculous and absolutely fucking perfect.

Rhian touched them everywhere he could reach. He sank his fingers into their hair, brushed their cheeks, wrapped his arms around their waists and held on for dear life. His ass and back were numb from the ice, his cock as hard as a rock anyway, before they climbed to their feet. They couldn't seem to go a foot closer to the bench without touching. Kissing. Saying, "I love you."

They practically fell off the ice, barely sitting long enough to tear off skates and yank on street shoes. They ran along the path back to the house at full speed and burst through the kitchen door.

Mary yelped with surprise, then laughed and turned to Chelsea. "I told you it was going to work out."

Chelsea threw her arms around Rhian's neck and planted a loud, smacking kiss on his cheek. "I'm staying here. I already got my bags from the car and Mary is promising to let me bake her some cookies." She stepped back and eyed his disheveled appearance. "For god's sake, go away before I have to get that ice bucket. Sheesh."

He grinned, unrepentant. "Come on," he said, grabbing his lovers' hands. "I hear we have a room at the inn."

Savannah and Garrick both turned pink, murmuring apologies to parents and siblings alike as Rhian unceremoniously dragged them through the house and shoved them into his rental car.

"We'll see you in the morning," Savannah called out the window as he backed out of the driveway.

"Yeah, right!" Chelsea shot back from the porch.

Savannah's mother grinned and flung her arm around Chelsea's shoulders. His sister looked like another Morrison already. Rhian laughed as he tore down the street toward the inn.

He broke a minimum of seven traffic laws in the quarter-mile drive. At least he could blame the crappy parking job on Garrick. It wasn't nice to grope a man's junk when he was trying to concentrate on driving.

If anyone at the inn thought it was strange that they bolted up the stairs in a knot of clutched hands and laughter, he was too happy and too focused on his lovers to notice or care.

He fell onto the bed and pulled Garrick and Savannah

down on top of him. Clothes flew in all directions, laughter liberally sprinkled between squeals and grunts as they rolled across the bed.

Savannah fell onto her back and dragged him over her with two fists in his hair. Her legs came up, and he sighed as he slid into her to the hilt. He had barely settled there, his control tenuous at best, when Garrick's big hands spread his knees, bent him in half above her, and thrust a thick, heavily lubricated finger deep into his ass.

Rhian writhed and shouted his encouragement. Garrick stretched him open with a second finger. Then the heavy press of his thick shaft as he sank as deep as he could get into Rhian's ass.

Rhian laughed, kissing Savannah's cheeks. Her eyebrows. Her swollen, red lips.

He'd done the unimaginable.

He'd found his home.

Epilogue

Rhian sat at their kitchen island, trying to keep calm while he listened to the clock tick. Garrick and Savannah sat across from him, keeping a close eye on him as he fidgeted with his phone. His leg bounced maniacally on the rung of the stool.

Savannah smiled. "It will be fine, Rhian."

"I know."

Garrick's dubious look confirmed he wasn't fooling anyone.

For the life of him, he couldn't remember why he'd agreed to let Chelsea to tell her grandfather about him. It was true that it was better he heard it from her, so that she could lay it all out for him and let him absorb the shock in private. It couldn't be easy for anyone to learn his daughter had abandoned his grandson twenty years before. From the way Chelsea spoke of the man, it was obvious he loved his grandchildren fiercely.

But why did he have to be told at all?

Rhian sighed. He knew why. It had been eating Chelsea up to have to lie to him about where she was living, let alone keeping something so important as Rhian's existence from the man who had stood by her throughout her life. Protected her, knowingly and not, from their hell-beast of a mother. If it had just been a matter of leaving the man ignorant, Rhian could have withstood the pressure. But Chelsea was miserable worrying that one day he would learn the truth and be furious with her for keeping it a secret.

Rhian hated it when Chelsea was miserable. He smiled ruefully. His sister had him wrapped around her little finger.

Rhian checked the clock again. Where the hell was she? She'd left a couple hours ago and they'd not heard a word since.

As if on cue, Rhian's cell phone chimed.

We're coming over.

Rhian jumped up from his stool. "Oh shit. She's bringing him here."

Garrick came around the island and pulled him into his arms. "It's going to be fine."

Rhian rested his chin on Garrick's shoulder and took a deep breath. "I know."

Garrick's chest shook with a chuckle.

Savannah came up behind him and wrapped her arms around them both. "We're here."

Rhian sighed and relaxed in their arms. "I know."

And it made a huge fucking difference.

They stayed like that, rocking gently. Rhian closed his eyes and held on. Goddamn, he was the luckiest son of a bitch on earth.

Savannah brushed her face against the back of his neck. "We don't have to leave for the first open house for a couple hours."

Rhian nodded. They were on the hunt for a bigger apartment. They loved this one, particularly for the memories it held, but it didn't work anymore.

For one thing, Chelsea's room was far too small and dark. She would leave for school in a few weeks, but Wellesley was only fifteen miles outside the city, and they all expected—wanted—her to stay with them on holidays and over the summers. Savannah was already working on getting her an internship with the Bruin's front office.

Chelsea, amusingly, had developed a passion for professional hockey. *Go figure.*

Rhian really hoped she got the job. Just last week he'd signed a five-year deal with the B's, and he wanted to show off his brilliant sister to his friends and colleagues.

That they had decided to portray themselves as "roommates", as far as most of those friends and colleagues were concerned, was another key reason they needed to find a place with more than two bedrooms for four people.

Also, Savannah had been giving Garrick a ton of shit about how he'd unleashed her inner screamer, and now she struggled like hell to keep quiet during sex. They all did, having more than once resorted to clapping their hands over each other's mouths. Rhian liked to joke that they'd have to put Chelsea in a separate wing to be sure she wouldn't hear Savannah in full passion.

Truth be told, he missed the noise. A lot. And he knew Garrick did too.

Rhian made a note on his mental list of things to do to ask about sound-proofing at today's open house. More and more, he thought they should buy, not rent. It wasn't like they were going anywhere.

Everyone jumped at the sound of a key in the front door lock. They moved to the hallway and stood waiting when the door swung open, his lovers aligned behind him. Rhian stared at a handsome older gentleman standing in the hallway, Chelsea at his side. She chewed on her lips and wrung her hands, looking between her grandfather and Rhian.

Shit, one of us should keep their shit together. He'd kind of been counting on it being Chelsea.

Turned out, it would be their grandfather. He walked into the apartment with his gaze pinned on Rhian's face. His movements were remarkably graceful and athletic, particularly given his age. He stood tall, his clothes tailored perfectly to his lean frame, his silver hair neatly trimmed.

Rhian couldn't think of what to say. His grandfather stopped right in front of him, silent, and Rhian figured he was having the same problem.

The old man yanked him into a ferocious hug.

Rhian blinked, his arms waving uselessly at his sides before he hesitantly wrapped them around his grandfather.

"I'm sorry. I didn't know. I swear by all that's holy, I did not know," his grandfather said.

Rhian had no idea if his grandfather's voice was always so hoarse, but he could feel the despair in the strength of his hold.

Rhian gulped. This was more than a little awkward, but he felt a terrible sympathy for the man. Rhian had known his mother for who she really was his entire life. This poor man had learned the truth about his daughter today.

Rhian looked at his lovers, their arms around his sister, all three of them crying.

Goddamn, how am I supposed to not get misty if even Garrick *is crying?*

He sniffed, trying hard not to wipe his face on the old man's blazer. He patted his grandfather's back, trying to ease him. He would do anything to get him to stop apologizing for that woman. "It's not your fault. You didn't know."

He didn't hear Rhian until the third or fourth time he said it. He pulled away abruptly. "I'm terribly sorry. I'm not usually...well, I'm a stranger to you. I shouldn't have assaulted you like that." He turned away and wiped his face dry.

Rhian took pity. "There's no need to apologize. For anything. I imagine this is quite a shock."

"Yes. Yes, it is." His grandfather looked his way and seemed immediately transfixed by what he saw.

Rhian was back to not knowing what to say.

His grandfather stuck out a hand. "I'm very happy to meet you," he said formally, his dignity restored. Then he laughed. "In case it wasn't obvious from my blubbering all over you."

Rhian smiled and shook his hand. "I'm happy to meet you, too."

"Congratulations on your deal with the Bruins. I'm a big fan. I'm still trying to absorb the fact that I sat rinkside all season and didn't know it was my own grandson skating past me. You're a gifted player."

"Thank you," Rhian said. How many times had he seen this man and not had any idea?

"Tell me, are you happy with your agent? He's got a good

reputation, but if he's not taking good care of you, we can find a better one. Also, I understand you got a big signing bonus. Let me introduce you to my money manager."

Rhian laughed.

Chelsea rolled her eyes. "Grandfather, leave him be." She smiled at Rhian. "I warned you he can't resist interfering in his grandchildren's lives."

"Young lady, I'm only looking out for you. I should have recognized long ago that your mother shouldn't be trusted." His mouth settled into a thin, pale line. "Ever."

No one argued.

"In any case," his grandfather said, "I should apologize. Again. I've been terribly rude." He turned to Garrick and Savannah. "Please introduce me to your visitors."

Rhian, Savannah, and Garrick all looked at Chelsea, who shrugged. "Sorry, I thought it should be up to you to decide."

Rhian nodded. "Mr. Lynch—"

"Please, call me Grandfather."

Rhian faltered. When his grandfather looked like he was about to apologize again, Rhian rushed on with the introductions. "These are my partners, Savannah Morrison and Garrick LeBlanc."

His grandfather's brow wrinkled as his gaze shifted between the three of them.

Chelsea laughed. "Now he thinks you're in business together. You're going to have to spell it out."

Rhian didn't hesitate. If the man couldn't accept it, then he was out. It was that simple. "Grandfather, Garrick and Savannah are my best friends and partners. For life."

Not one iota of confusion cleared from the old man's face.

Rhian silently pleaded for his sister's help.

Chelsea took pity. "Grandfather, there are only two beds in this apartment and I sleep alone in one of them. Therefore, these three sleep…"

Rhian sent his sister an exasperated look. Did she have to explain it in terms of their sleeping arrangements? *Subtle as a brick.*

Comprehension dawned with a rush of pink on the old man's cheeks. "Oh, right. I didn't...I never..."

Silence fell while everyone waited to learn one man's verdict on their unusual relationship.

His grandfather turned to Garrick and thrust out his hand. "Thank you for taking care of my grandson." They shook, then he smiled at Savannah. "And you, dear. Thank you."

Savannah took both his hands in hers. "Thank *you*, Mr. Lynch."

"I'd be honored if you'd both consider calling me Grandfather, too," he added with a nod.

She and Garrick grinned.

Rhian smiled, slung his arm around Chelsea and winked at his lovers. "Well then, Grandfather, welcome to the family."

About the Author

Samantha Wayland has always dreamed of being a novelist. She wrote her first book as an escape from the pressures of her day job. That fascinating piece of contemporary erotic mystery/suspense with elements of paranormal, international intrigue, and god only knows what else, is safely tucked under her bed, where it will remain until hell freezes over. Since then, she's learned a lot about the craft and turned her attention to writing contemporary MM and MMF ménage erotic romance.

Sam lives with her family—of both the two and four-legged variety—outside of Boston. She used to spend her days toiling away in corporate nerdville but was recently sprung from that hell. Now when she's not locked away in her home office, she can generally be found tucked in the corner of the local Thai place with a few beloved friends (and fellow authors).

Her favorite things include mango martinis, tiny Chihuahuas with big attitude problems, and the Oxford comma.

Sam loves to hear from readers.

Email her at samantha@samanthawayland.com, or find her on Facebook as Samantha Wayland and on Twitter as @SamWayland.

Also by Samantha Wayland

With Grace

A man yearning to explore his sexual tastes but afraid to turn up the heat, the woman who loves him but is hungry for more spice...and the chef who craves them both.

When Grace, Philip and Mark find a mobster's flash drive full of incriminating information, they are quickly embroiled in a dangerous situation. They stay together for safety, but proximity ignites the sparks they've long been fighting to ignore.

When three friends dare to succumb to their appetites, they find the perfect recipe for love.

Destiny Calls

Patrick didn't think it would be a big deal to kiss Brandon, his best friend and fellow police officer. Hell, they'd done crazier things to escape a bar fight. But then he had no way of knowing just how hot it would be.

Destiny Matthews is not a woman who is afraid to ask for what she wants, and when she sees her two best friends kissing, she knows just what she's going to ask for. Before she can convince Patrick that he's not as straight as he likes to protest, Brandon is attacked by an unknown enemy.

While they fight to protect each other's lives, they prove time and again that they're even better at protecting their own hearts.

Fair Play

Hat Trick Book One

Savannah Morrison is the new athletic trainer for the Moncton Ice Cats, a professional hockey team in the wilds of New Brunswick. It's a good thing she's got plenty of knowledge and grit, because as the only woman trainer in the league, she has to work twice as hard to win the players' respect. The last thing on earth she would do is date one of them.

Twelve year hockey veteran Garrick LeBlanc isn't ready to hang up his skates, particularly since he hasn't figured out what the hell he's planning to do next. He needs the new trainer to keep him fit to play, and she's got the skills to do it. Too bad he lost his mind and hit on her the day they met. Now she hates his guts and he's made an art of ignoring her.

When the team is put up for sale, Garrick and Savannah have to work together to save their jobs and their team. Somewhere along the way, they discover Garrick isn't just a hockey player, Savannah isn't only passionate about her work, and just maybe they've got more in common than they thought.

Two Man Advantage
Hat Trick Book Two

Rhian is working his way up the ranks of professional hockey, with the dream of making it to the NHL getting closer every day. He's doing it alone—no family, no friends—and that's the way he likes it. Then he arrives in New Brunswick, and meets the Moncton Ice Cats. Suddenly, he's got friends—and even something that might be an honest-to-god crush.

Garrick is lonely and counting the days until his last season with the Ice Cats is over and he can move to Boston. When his girlfriend suggests he take a lover—as long that lover is a man and Garrick tells her all about it—he laughs it off. But damned if his buddy Rhian doesn't take on the starring role in his fantasies. Good thing Rhian is way too young—and straight—for what Garrick has in mind.

Rhian takes a chance when Garrick's increasingly confusing signals start making sense, and soon discovers he's bitten off more than he can chew. Sex with strangers is simple. Sex with his best friend? Complicated.